LINDA STEVENS

Kindly
Welcome

D1500652

*A novel of the Shakers
in the Civil War*

First published in 2017 by
Nakasero Hill Press

ISBN: 978-1-9997517-0-8 (Hardcover)

ISBN: 978-1-9997517-1-5 (e-book)

ISBN:978-1-9997517-2-2 (Paperback)

Library of Congress Control Number: 2017950535

Cover image: Arthur Hughes, Jr, 12th October 1863, by
Lewis Carroll. Bridgeman Images

Author photograph by David Rigby

Typeset in 11½pt Fairfield by
www.chandlerbookdesign.co.uk

Printed in the United States of America

The peculiar grace of a Shaker chair is
due to the fact that it was built by
someone capable of believing an angel
might come and sit on it.

Thomas Merton

For

EVAN RICHARD DAVIS
(June 17, 1950 – August 6, 2009)
Without whom...

And for

JANE ANN RIGGIN
... at last.

SOUTH UNION, KENTUCKY · 1860-65 ·

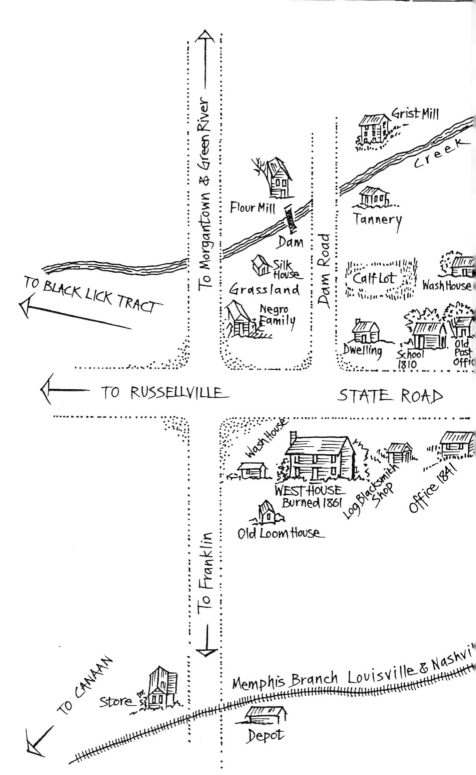

To Morgantown & Green River

Grist Mill

Creek

Flour Mill

Dam

Tannery

Silk House

Grassland

Calf Lot

Wash House

Negro Family

Dam Road

Dwelling

School 1810

Old Post Office

TO BLACK LICK TRACT

TO RUSSELLVILLE

STATE ROAD

Wash House

WEST HOUSE Burned 1861

Log Blacksmith Shop

Office 1841

Old Loom House

To Franklin

TO CANAAN

Store

Memphis Branch Louisville & Nashvi[...]

Depot

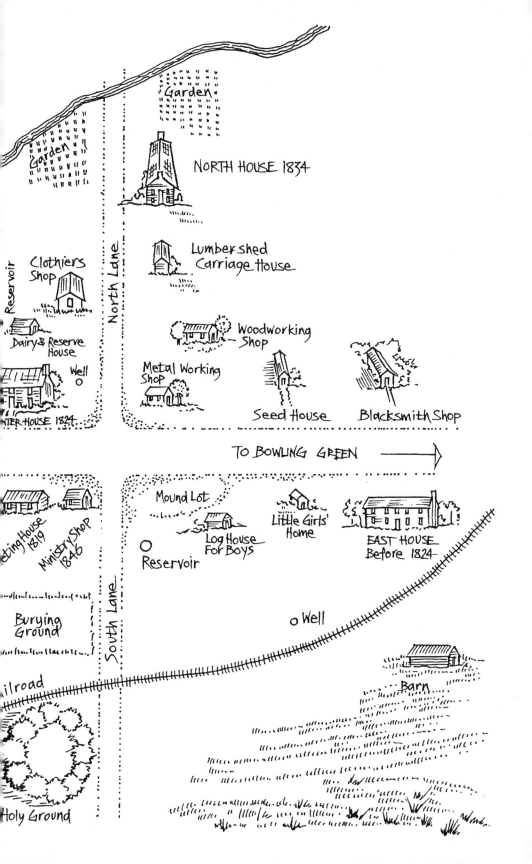

CONTENTS

Foreword

E ven those who have written books about the Shakers find it difficult to explain the organization of Shaker communities and families. Thus, as the story opens, some references will be obscure. Trust me: all will eventually be revealed.

Thinking it unfair, however, to throw the reader into the waters of the Gasper without water-wings, the following explanation is offered.

A Shaker Society – each community is a Society, the group of which Societies forms the United Society of Believers in Christ's Second Appearing – was, in the days of the large communities, divided into families, seldom made up of more than a hundred men and women, usually far less. There were generally two to eight families in a community, and each family had its own dwelling house, as well as a life separate from the rest of the community. The families normally gathered together only for church meeting on the Sabbath, and not always then.

In the simplest terms, a prospective Believer was "gathered in," or made his or her first move toward joining the Society, by confessing his sins and intentions to a full member of sufficient seniority, at which time the fledgling Believer was sent to live in the Junior or Gathering Order. In the Kentucky community at South Union, this was the East family. If the individual decided to continue and become a member, relocation to the Second Order, at South Union the North family, followed. The final step in this sometimes lengthy procedure was the signing of the covenant, a dry legal document which among other things placed into community holding on a theoretically irrevocable basis all of an individual's personal possessions. At South Union most such members lived in the First Order, or Church family, at the Center. The dwelling house of a fourth family, the West, was destroyed by fire early in 1861.

Each family's dwelling was surrounded by the out-buildings and shops necessary to maintain its own industries and general lifestyle.

In the normal course of events a Shaker family could be known within the Society by no fewer than three different names. Remembering the mind-bending process of keeping track of Russian patronymics while reading *The Brothers Karamazov*, however, I have tried to use just two of the usual referents.

The Shaker hierarchy, if it can be called such, consisted of a system of elders and eldresses – two of each sex for each family. This makes sense, given Shaker doctrine, which is based around the worship of a deity both male and female: the Eternal Father and Mother Wisdom. In addition, two men and two women served as elders and eldresses assigned to the ministry. These four lived over the ministry shop or the meeting house itself; all other elders lived in the dwellings of the families they served. Each family also had deacons and deaconesses to oversee its various work groups – laundry, mill, tanyard, farm etc. – one each, male or female, depending on the sex of the laborers who carried out the tasks in question. The United Society, as a community of communities, was under the spiritual supervision of the ministry at Mount Lebanon, also called "the Holy Mount," in Columbia County, New York.

Even the property of Shakertown at South Union was slightly

complicated: a patchwork of farms brought into the Society by its earliest members, as well as others carefully acquired over the years – reaching at its largest a total acreage of about six thousand – so that such parcels of land as Canaan, the Knob, Black Lick sugar camp, the Grassland or South America would be referred to in farm matters.

And. The Shakers continue to be what they have always been, great keepers of records. Living in a community where incursion of debt is forbidden and all property is held in common, the Believers have always felt obliged to keep meticulous account of everything, including the day's weather, lest anyone ever ask where the money was spent or how the crops came to be sold. Records during the Civil War were kept no less carefully than they have been at times of less stress, which is a credit to the Believers themselves – although for obvious reasons those who kept the journals during the Rebellion often seemed more preoccupied with the number of troops who called for supper than in the number of seed papers prepared on any given day.

The events of this volume, for the most part, follow the chronology of extraordinary journals kept by two Shakers: Eldress Nancy E. Moore and Elder Harvey L. Eades, who fashioned a permanent record from the sundry journals written by those who were at South Union in the days before his return from apparent exile in the Shaker community at North Union, Ohio. He then assumed responsibility for the journal himself and continued to maintain the Society record until seventeen days before his death in 1892. Most of what occurs on the pages that follow, therefore, is based on fact, and a majority of the characters are likewise based on actual persons. Exceptions to this are the Anger, Burke, Innes, Littlebourne and Hannon households, the farmer's wife Keziah and her fieldhands, Elizabeth Barrie, Jedediah Haller, Jimmy Sweet, Meese Gillies and Hetta Sutter, and Michael Bird's flatboat party – all of whom are fictitious. Any other character identified by a full name (and a majority of those identified by first or last name only) appears in Shaker records or other documents of the period. Those named in full either actually participated in the events chronicled in the manner described, or – from all historical evidence – could have been expected to behave in the manner depicted, had they been called upon to do so. All letters, book extracts, newspaper articles and military communications are authentic (with the understandable exception of those generated by fictional characters) and are reproduced verbatim. It was not always easy to determine from which newspaper a cutting came, and – because educated guesses sometimes had to be made – correction is invited where error is found. Several fictional incidents have obviously been embroidered against the fabric of historical fact.

Only one of the major sequences of events herein did not actually take place. That nothing similar ever occurred is a miracle in itself.

1922

How different this house had been, in the days when this hat was made. Amos Anger sat alone in his retiring room, turning the small, flat-brimmed straw hat in his hands. The deep green of its silk band had faded considerably since the summer afternoon he had stood quietly by the loom, watching Sister Polly Rankin's slim, sure fingers as she wove it for him. The straw itself was now choked with dust that came away in sheets as he ran his hands over it. But unlike the man who held it, and the village where it was made, the hat had changed little in the years that had passed.

In years gone he had shared this room with three other brethren; now it was his alone. Once upon a time, from the windows at the south end of the passage, it had been possible to stand and watch the brethren and sisters of all South Union's families on their way to and from the meeting house of a Sunday. Now a neighbor was long settled in the house that had been built where the meeting house once stood, and the few Believers who remained at Shakertown met instead for worship here in the Center house – where now they all lived. There had been four families here, and hundreds of Believers but, unlike this straw hat, that had all changed.

Even those who remained would be gone soon, Elder Logan Johns back East and the last South Union brethren and sisters to homes of their own. This in itself was too much for Amos to imagine: never in his life had he been completely alone.

When he knew South Union would be sold, its green and giving land divided up and its belongings put to auction, Brother Amos remembered his secret treasure, hidden in the stable eaves. Brittle of bone, he could no longer climb so high himself, but in losing so much of what was dear to him he could not bear to leave it behind. Thus he enlisted the help of a neighbor boy and stood watching the rafters from the ground below, using the unerring memory of childhood grief to guide the boy's hand across the beams and abandoned bird's nests. Such nimble legs as the child possessed Amos had once had himself, and only a minute or two ticked by before the boy climbed back down from the haymow with the little hat in his hand. It would just about fit him, Amos thought as the child wiped the August heat from his forehead before bolting for the barn door – and the end of an old man's peculiar errand.

Amos glanced up from his knees and the hat which lay across them, out the window and east where the Great Road rolled back up toward Bowling Green. In his youth the road had clattered with carriages like those in the stable, carrying travellers making the distance between Bowling Green and Russellville for reasons of their own. Seldom had he seen either of those places, despite their proximity. Once he had wanted to see as much of the world as the world would see, but – like many other urges – that one had quieted and finally passed altogether. The carriages on that road, many of them, nowadays moved without benefit of horseflesh. The Shakers themselves possessed a motorcar. Amos had ridden in it and understood the wisdom of its acquisition, but in his heart he preferred to sit behind a horse. It was what he knew.

At the bottom of the still, near-empty house Amos could hear the sisters packing. An empty case stood by the skirting board near his feet, but how he might fill it was a puzzle to him. A few clothes, brushes, a razor, his Bible – James Littlebourne's Bible; on the final morning he could easily pack them in the few minutes after morning prayers and before breakfast. Putting his things away now would be a waste of time. Surely everything he owned would see some use in the days that remained to him here, and time wasted showed disrespect to Him Who had provided it in the first place. And so he sat rocking, tracing the brim of the straw hat with his forefinger. When he thought of it, in his life only two things had ever truly belonged to him.

Of those two, this was the only one left.

1844

The shutters were still closed tight on Silver Street, where he had been drinking the night before, as the haggard and hungover sailor ran down the hill toward the landing. The hour was early but he was late.

Damp patches were spreading across his back and under the arms of his blue jacket by the time he reached the wharf, and he was out of breath. Legs aching, gasping for air, he leaned over, put his hands on his knees, and shook the damp from his wild, red hair. Still huffing, hat in hand, he straightened up again and looked with desperation around the crowded port of Natchez. Turning his head downriver he stared hard, as though mere stubbornness and strength of will would bring back the *Johanna R*. The broad beams of the southbound transport were all strangers to him, and where his own sternwheeler had stood last night now was tied *Kate Fleming*. He threw his hat to the ground, cursing loudly in the terms that come easily to those who blaspheme with fluency. In Natchez-Under-the-Hill such language was commonplace and his outburst drew no notice.

He collected his hat from the dusty planks beneath his feet, brushed it with the heel of his hand, and took a seat on one of a stack of firkins behind him. He had to laugh, and he spun his hat on his finger as he did so. It wasn't as though he hadn't been warned, and a thousand times if only one. Captain Haller liked him well enough, and he the captain, but the captain was a married man respectful of that commitment. Austin Innes, on the other hand, prided himself that he never slept alone when he went ashore, never slept twice in the same bed, and was never asked to pay. All this the captain – and most if not all of the crew – knew full well, and it had happened many times that the amorous sailor left his lady's lodgings just in time to jump aboard *Johanna R* as her cables were being taken up. There was no reason to believe his luck could last forever, and here in Natchez it had come to a crashing halt.

The supreme irony, of course, was that for the life of him he could not recall the lady's name, despite the fix she'd left him in. Roll him to exhaustion she might have, dragged him back to the ticking even when the sun came through the window and time was come and gone for him to be about his business, but whatever of the rest of her he might recall – what legs she had! like vises! – her name now completely escaped him. He smiled at his predicament as he realized that if the captain would not have him back aboard he would still not recall the name by which he'd known the reason why. By tomorrow he would likely not remember any of her at all.

He couldn't remember any of them, come to that. Although he was sure more than a few had reason to remember him. He could not say with any certainty, but he knew in his mind's eye that from Thunder Bay to the Balize of the Delta there were women raising redheaded, blue-eyed babies – all of them boys, he hoped – and cursing the day they met Austin Innes. If he had given his name, which he might not have. Such were rivermen.

Where he would go from here was a worry, and he rubbed at the strawberry stubble rising on his cheeks as he considered it His own *Johanna R* would put in at Baton Rouge before sailing on to New Orleans, there to lie a day or two before putting back north to Saint Louis, loaded full with coffee and iron and cotton. She had on him only an hour or two at most and he could easily catch her in any vessel that would have him on its way south. Catch her in Baton Rouge with luck; find her for sure in New Orleans.

He took his pipe from his pocket and chewed the stem end. The day was already powerfully warm, and the hour not yet eight. He looked overhead for the sun, then glanced back over his shoulder toward Silver Street. It looked remarkably different in this early light, lacking as it did amongst other things (including the sound of intermittent gunfire) the sound and sight and scent of half-naked girls giggling and waving from the open windows. Oddly, he knew most of them by name.

Truth to tell, Austin knew Under-the-Hill almost to its last brick and harlot. He had been up above the bluffs now and again, walked the streets amongst the nabobs and had his look at their fine homes. A fair hand at faro, he had that way made the acquaintance of the barber William Johnson, and – seeing no obstruction to passing time in the company of a free Negro (or indeed one who was not free, although such encounters could get a white man shot) – he often went along to Johnson's barbershop on Main Street, just across from McAlister & Watson, to have himself cleaned up a bit. But the air up from Under-the-Hill was not so fine to Austin's lungs as that below.

None of this, of course, was bringing him closer to Baton Rouge, and thus he returned his calculations to the cipher at hand. He shifted himself on the firkin and walked his eyes up the landing to Andrew Brown's timber mill, taking notice as he did so of the presence of likely steamers between this point and that.

A touch at his shoulder started him, and he turned.

"Without liking to disturb thee, friend, we have loading to do here," said a soft voice from the other side of the goods stacked around him.

Innes leaned sideways, the better to see the small band of clean-shaven souls in wide-brimmed straw hats at work moving the boxes and barrels. While he'd sat festering and daydreaming amongst their possessions they'd begun loading them out from under him, stowing them aboard a neat little green-timbered flatboat, one of the solid mass of those arklike Mississippi mainstays that daily took wharfage at Natchez landing. He stood up, still absent-mindedly chewing at his pipe, and watched the peculiar little group – each man dressed identically to the last – with some fascination.

Noticing the sailor's obvious curiosity, the man who had first addressed Austin paused awhile to mop his face and neck with a handkerchief.

"Surely, friend," he said jovially, "it cannot be that thee has never seen men at work."

Austin was caught tight as a tick by his embarrassment and unsure what to do about it. "Oh, no," he said stupidly, and could think no farther. Embarrassment came seldom to him and he stuttered while he sought a verbal escape.

The odd-spoken gentleman, realizing his small joke had performed the unlikely task of rendering its recipient uncomfortable, sought to put the situation right.

"However young the day," he said, checking the sun's position and thereby tricking Austin into looking up, "it would seem it has not gone quite as thee would have hoped."

Austin smiled at the big man's near-clairvoyance. "Getting out of bed this morning was more a problem than it would have been if I'd had the good sense to spend the night alone," he said with a wink. "She was a bit more than I took her for, and she missed me my boat. You know how it sometimes goes."

The man settled his straw hat on the back of his head and seemed to have run short of conversation. "In truth, friend, I would have to say I don't," he said, then put his handkerchief in his pocket and went back to work.

Innes felt himself falling into a great hole he'd dug on his own behalf. His only means of climbing out now he'd hit bottom was by closing his mouth, and this he did, finding a graceful exit from the conversation by shouldering the landbound end of a hefty box that was halfway airborne at the hands of another of the four men. Silently, occasionally bumping into each other, the matched quartet and the errant sailor pursued their employment until the full load was aboard, evenly stacked around the goods already laid up in the broadhorn's generous hold. His usefulness exhausted then, Austin Innes squeezed up through the hatchway and onto the arched roof, where his sometime partner in conversation stood surveying the speed of the river.

"Well, good luck gettin' where you're goin'," he said brightly, extending his hand.

The big man dried his sweaty palm on the front of his linen shirt and took Austin's hand energetically. "And thee's headed which way?"

"Oh. Well." In the time spent helping to load these strangers' flatboat he'd quite happily forgotten the trouble he was in. "I'll be chasing down to New Orleans when I find a boat," he said.

"The brethren and I are on our way down there ourselves," the apparent leader of this curious little group told him, sliding his thumbs along the backs of his suspenders. He squinted up into the strong Mississippi sun. "Thee's welcome to come along with us. Say yea or nay, just as thee likes."

It was perhaps the most peculiar invitation he had ever received. Perhaps even more peculiar was Austin Innes' swift acceptance of it. He nodded without hesitation and leapt back onto the landing to see to the ropes that held the flatboat fast. His host stood where he was on the roof of the hold, admiring the limber grace and familiarity with which this little stranger went about his business, and nodded to the one of his fellows who had gone astern to catch the last line as Austin threw it.

Innes stood with his hands in his pockets, watching as his prospective shipmates stood to the sweeps in anticipation of moving the flatboat into the river. The heads of all four men turned to him with confusion as the landing and the gunnels parted company, and a voice called, "Aren't thee coming?"

Raising his arms in the air, shifting forward and launching himself from the wharf, Austin Innes seemed to fly like some rare redfeathered waterbird toward the lazy little broadhorn, and landed with a flat-footed thud on the narrow deck – just an instant before it was too late.

If he had hoped to catch *Johanna R* at the wharf in Baton Rouge, or even New Orleans, Austin Innes had been a riverman long enough to know this was not the boat on which to travel.

A flatboat with experts at the sweeps could make, say, thirty or more miles on a good day, but these were no experts. Perforce every hour aboard this undeniably agreeable little broadhorn left him farther behind *Johanna R*, and what was more than passing strange was that every minute as it ticked by left the prodigal sailor less interested in the success of the pursuit.

The four men, he learned in good time from his talkative host, were coasters from Kentucky. Hearing this Austin took a further look for what he had already not seen: the Wabash Coat of Arms, that whimsical pennant flown by peddlers of virtually any stripe to indicate their willingness to trade, and the jovial jug that usually adorned it. He had lived long enough to know all things had their reasons, and here was no exception; these gentlemen were followers of a religion that saddled them with the cumbersome name of Believers in Christ's Second Appearing. By this meandering monicker they drew not the slightest flicker of recognition in Innes' blue eyes. In time he would learn they did not take spirits, hence the absence of a whisky jug pennant to peg them as tradesmen.

His host identified himself as Brother Michael Bird, and the estimable brother shrugged as he confessed the world had taken to calling his people Shakers, saying with good grace that they were willing to take the world at its word. This news Austin took with some alarm, for he had heard in Zanesville of these "Shaking Quakers". He eyed Bird and tried to square the image before him with the vision of weird Ohio fanatics who danced and sang by way of worship and chose to live man and woman together without deriving the traditional enjoyment from that arrangement. And if memory served, he had read in one of the author's works Mr. Dickens' opinion of the Shakermen, and it was likewise unsettling. Nonetheless he looked for madness in Brother Michael's eyes and found none there.

That aside, he could not entirely rule out the possibility that he might be the lone sane man on a broadhorn crewed by lunatics, a quartet of Christian cannibals for all he knew, but something held him where he was.

Brother Michael's three fellows – Timothy, Eli and George – had less to say to Austin than did their obvious captain. But if his only real companion aboard this dawdling craft was a talker it soon seemed he was also a listener of great energy and patience. Never before in his life had Austin Innes felt he had much of importance to tell, but to Michael Bird he seemed driven to confide it all, as if the conversations of a lifetime had been storing up in his mind to be drawn out at long last by the lone soul capable of retrieving them.

The flatboat drifted south, calling now and again at this or that settlement along the river. Trailing along behind them the Shakermen had a little skiff, and this they would use to crisscross the river or for minor excursions when the boat itself was tied to the shore. On board they carried goods grown or made at Pleasant Hill, the town from which they'd travelled. Built on Shawnee Run off the waters of the Kentucky, the fertile lands and agile hands of Pleasant Hill produced more than its inhabitants could use. The garden seeds, brooms, jeans, tinware, hats and other oddments stowed below would thus be peddled to the world from which these industrious Shakers kept themselves aloof and the proceeds used to buy that which they could not make at home. In New Orleans Brother Michael Bird would scout for tea and copperas, spermaceti and anything else of which his people had need. At the end of this journey the brethren would sell their flatboat for timber, then book themselves and their goods aboard a likely northbound packet and return home upriver by steam.

Brother Michael was something of a sorcerer, it seemed to Austin Innes, able to coax from him things he had held close and quiet all the days of his life. He alternated between prodding and listening while the young man – younger than his audience, at least – spun the tale of his childhood in the Indian Territory not far up the Arkansas, whence his parents had come from Pennsylvania after a miserable passage out of Glasgow.

His father was a farmer, his mother a farmer's wife who raised up four boys in comparative peace before providing her husband with a fifth over whom it seemed no control could be exercised at all. Austin had come into the world an angry screamer, and while he ceased his screaming in his own time the anger never subsided. Willful and destructive, fearless and impulsive, he played with fire and twice in his boyhood burned this or that of his father's outbuildings to the ground. He tormented the livestock, had no apparent aptitude for farming, and showed a complete lack of interest in cultivating any. The elder Innes had no need to fear attack by Indians; he had Austin to beware of.

To his mother's amazement the boy taught himself to read from her Bible, but if he harvested any of the Good Book's philosophy as he slowly deciphered its words she was unable to detect it. Finally literate, he was driven to read as if by demons and books that could not be borrowed were stolen.

And while nature had also blessed him with good looks – extraordinary cornflower-blue eyes and a head of red hair that was the envy of most womenfolk – his sturdy body was shorter than that of any of his brothers and considerable advantage was thereby taken in the interests of punishing him for his frequent transgressions. The older Innes boys teased their youngest brother to distraction, denounced him as a runt (or worse, depending on their individual vocabularies), and not infrequently blows were exchanged. More often than might have been imagined, Austin came up the winner in these altercations – making up for his size and weight with an agility and grace for which his brothers were at a loss to account – and in time they simply gave up and excluded him entirely from their society.

Shunned thus by his brothers, the despair of his parents, Austin began to disappear into the wilderness for days at a time, and finally his father had had as much as he could take. Handing his youngest boy five dollars (most of what there was at the time, Austin now supposed), Richard Innes said the back of him was what they wanted most to see. At the age of fifteen he left the farm willingly and never looked over his shoulder, never wrote home, never wondered how his kinfolk were faring. Austin Innes left home at a run and spent the next dozen years running ever faster – but somehow never quite fast enough to overtake his own heart.

He drifted north and east for awhile, living rough and lucky in the hills, preferring his own company to that of anyone he could reasonably expect to meet. Finally, and quite by chance, he came through a deep woods to the western shore of the Big River, and seeing it for the first time decided there could be no greater ambition in life than to know it end to end. A passing keelboat took him on in place of a poleman the captain had had to shoot: the boy was small but as a substitute for a dead man he showed promise.

In New Orleans he ran away and was taken in by a prostitute who put a little French on his tongue and taught him the more delicate arts connected with deriving from life on the river its fullest measure. When she tired of him – or needed money, more likely, for the boy took a good deal of her working energy – she gave him to one Weatherall, a flatboatman, who took him by horseback up the Natchez Trace to Nashville.

His life thereafter was awash in river water, aboard flatboats and keelboats and steamboats, until he one day found himself in a position to go aboard a vessel under sail and the temptation was too great. He had done a bit of sailmaking aboard the Durhams, and thus saw no harm in exaggerating his expertise sufficient to get hired up for a proper ship under canvas: he said he was a sailmaker, then became an able one by watching his betters and practicing on his trouser hems by moonlight.

Except for experience, Austin Innes had not changed much over time. Explosive, unpredictable, he was a young rooster of a man who as easily earned the dislike of his shipmates as their affection. Once on the Great Lakes he changed ships as often as his captains changed their minds about the value of his capable work when balanced against the volatility of his nature. A shameless womanizer, a scrapper as happy to fight as merely disagree, the little redhead was a puzzler, a hellion whose depths could nonetheless be plumbed and great tenderness found. It was to Innes that illiterate sailors brought their infrequent letters from home, and it was he to whom the same dictated their replies; their confidences would not be betrayed, and this they knew. Away from port, when mates lost track of him they looked aloft, knowing he bought books ashore and then read them in the rigging. This peculiar practice it was that earned him the title of Professor from his bemused shipmates. When his captains didn't hanker after killing him they quite liked him.

This and more Austin told Michael Bird, or the Shakerman guessed, as they sat across from each other on the roof of the hold.

Quiet then on this Shaker flatboat, pulling on his pipe, Austin Innes was more frightened than he had ever been in a life that was remarkable for the fact that he had never been afraid of anything.

His thoughts ran away from him as Brother Michael went forward to speak to Brother George at the gouger. What had kept him in bed so long this morning, as *Johanna R* steamed out of Natchez without him? It was easy to blame the sweet skin of the lady whose name he could not remember, who took hold of his arm as he rose and pulled him back into the rumpled linen. But might there not have been more to it than merely that? Might not it have been that there was someone tied up at the landing better suited to the task of carrying him from where he was to where he ought to be than was Jedediah Haller? He ran his fingers through his long red hair, a desperate man terrified of believing he might be at peace for the first time in his life. He buried his face in his hands.

Returning from the gouger, Brother Michael saw the young sailor sunk on himself and let him be, presuming him to be asleep. He couldn't have got much rest the night before.

He had never known any group of people love to sing the way these Shakermen seemed to. For no apparent reason, as the day went by, one or the other of them would cause a hymn to rise and then the other three would join in. As hymns went theirs seemed no better or worse than any others Austin had heard, but the singers showed signs of deriving from the singing a satisfaction out of all proportion to the material at hand. After they had tied up to shore and had their supper that first night they had sung for fully an hour, then one of their number read aloud from the Bible, and then they commenced to sing again. Austin remained aloof from this performance, content to be a spectator from his vantage point on the roof hatch. The final round of song apparently put them in mind to take their rest from the day's labors, and the brethren rolled out their bedding on the broadhorn's modest afterdeck and fell to their sleep without further word to their passenger. Thus left to his own devices he took his boots and jacket off and leaned back on his hands, looking up at the starlight. Too early yet to turn in.

In fact, even when finally he stretched himself out on the roof, he found he could not sleep at all. There was nothing unusual in this; sleep had a way of being his most reluctant mistress. He lay instead on his back, listening to the Mississippi lap against the flatboat, frustrated in its attempts to reach the shore.

It was Austin, weary of his own inactivity, who jumped to shore to loose the cable that morning, and when he took it in his teeth and leapt back aboard he simply dropped it and moved quickly forward to man the gouger.

Brother Timothy turned quickly to Michael Bird, a question in his eyes, but Bird shook his head and put a finger to his lips.

"This he knows," Bird said. "Let him be."

Standing at the lead oar, steering the little broadhorn downriver, taking his directions from the big man at the starboard sweep, Austin began to see that this was not really prosperous aimlessness: there was considerable method to the Shakermen's meanderings. They knew the names of all the villages and settlements they passed along the shoreline, at which to tie up, which isolated cabins expected a visit, where to take the skiff for an excursion crossriver. At most stops they met people with money in their hands, local folk who knew them from the exchange of a few picayunes on previous occasions and thus greeted them with something akin to affection.

Austin hung back, leaning on his oar while he lit his pipe, and watched as these gentle brethren were pressed for news from upriver by interrogators who most surely knew by now that they were unlikely to get much by way of gossiping reply. The Shakers seemed to harbor no small disinterest in the doings of the world. Still, here on the river there was an etiquette to be observed, and it seemed clear that the people of these shore hamlets and outposts feared they might give offense if they did not ask.

Austin Innes had a natural curiosity about people that seemed at odds with his nature. His books, now loose on the river without him aboard *Johanna R*, were full of the accumulated wisdom of men who had pushed their own vision farther than he feared he ever would. He had a considerable need to know what made of men the men they were, and he was happiest when leaning against life's great oar, watching the affairs of mankind and trying to make sense of how it worked. There was a sense to these Shakermen, and while at certain moments he might feel he had caught the tail of its coat in his hand the moment would soon pass, the whole unravel, and finally he would be left with just a thread.

*   *   *

The afternoon was passing into evening and three of the brethren had gone ashore in the skiff on some mission or other, leaving Austin alone with Brother Michael on the flatboat, tied up to a tree on the western shore. Perhaps Bird had not gone with the others because they feared leaving him alone with the cargo. The thought shamed him.

Bird, a large man with a barrel chest and admirable arms that would have offered good service to a blacksmith, found a kind of entertainment in watching Austin mend his own tattered jacket, pulling his sailmaker's needle through cloth that, while resistant, would have been happy with considerably less. Austin was balanced on the edge of the roof, facing into the setting sun to make the most of the light, and Bird settled next to him, hands playing a rhythm on his knees, saying nothing.

Curiosity, which had been plaguing Austin all day long, suddenly bubbled up out of him, and before he could temper it the question was there, blunt as a butterknife.

"Of womenfolk, do you ever wonder – ?"

"Never."

"But for God's sake, that's impossible," Austin insisted. "A man's a man, whatever he may believe."

Seconds passed. "A question for thee, then, brother," the Shaker said, and his familiarity caused his companion to flinch. "These nights, these hours thee passes in carnal pursuits by thy own admission. Do they bring thee joy?"

Austin's face felt suddenly full, hot. This was a question he had not looked for and was not anxious to answer, requiring as it did a confession not only to him who asked it but to him who would answer it as well. Dark came over his blue eyes like a summer squall over a fallow field, like dark-of-the-moon in some distant and heathenish place.

"No," he said simply.

"My joy comes elsewhere, as perhaps it does with thee," Brother Michael said. "Among my people we do not serve the Lord by bringing forth a new generation of the flesh. Our joy is in the bringing of a new-made spirit to the hearts of men and women. Believe me, friend Innes, there is as much to be gained from making new life in the soul of a child of God as there is in the making of the child itself. For certain this does not hold for everyone, and it is well that that is so, but for us it is a revelation."

By habit in moments of concentration Austin's hand sank down his pocket in search of his pipe, and withdrawing it he packed the bowl and lit it. The first curl of smoke rose high above his head and he flicked the spill into the river. With the hiss of drowned flame he and his companion heard the dip of oars as the brethren returned in the skiff.

Michael Bird went to hear their news and left Austin Innes to his pipe.

After supper Austin retreated to his end of the roof as the brethren took to their evening hymns and prayers. What seemed an uncommonly short time had passed, compared to other endeavors of this kind, when he saw Brother Michael's large frame edging along the leeside walkway.

Bird eyed him carefully, as if unsure how to begin, and Austin was instantly on his guard.

"Thy voice," he said at last, "has a very pleasing quality."

Austin laughed aloud and then quickly looked out over the Mississippi in an attempt to disguise the depth and nature of his amusement.

"Thy gift of musical speech is a certain sign of God's affection," the big man said with obvious discomfort, confused as he was by the effect of what he had considered a compliment and the logical foundation of a request.

"Forgive me, Brother Michael, if I say I never heard it put quite that way," Austin said, his voice still ragged with subsiding laughter. "And to put it plain I never heard it from any but a woman."

Bird's ruddy face reddened. "Well," he said as he recovered his composure, "the voice can be used for all manner of things. The brethren and I thus wondered if thee would perhaps consent to gift us with a reading from the Bible."

A chill blew through Austin on this warm summer night. He could not refuse these good men so small a request. But was not a Bible read aloud by a man of pure voice and no conviction a Bible somehow sullied in the reading, and did not this course of action therefore defeat the purpose intended? By now Michael Bird knew the impressive depths of Austin's imperfections, but he seemed unperturbed by them. It was thus not Austin's place to say no, especially as to say yes caused him no injury, and by this reasoning he resolved to act accordingly.

"If you like," he said, sliding from the roof and following Bird aft to the waiting prayer circle. Brother George, sitting cross-legged on the deck with Eli and Timothy, opened his Bible – its cover grown limp and fuzzy with use – and handed it up to Austin.

He uttered a single word, "There," and pointed to the spot where they had left off the night before.

Austin Innes settled himself on the aft roof ledge as Bird joined his fellows on the deck adjacent, and glanced at the top of the page. They had been reading Deuteronomy and were well into the second discourse of Moses. The memory rushed up into him and he closed his eyes as he recalled reading it as a child, slowly and deliberately as he taught himself to make words of the letters.

He began from the spot indicated and read along, conscious of the intent and godly eyes that focused on this godless reader at his labors. The words of Moses flowed out of him, some familiar and some less so.

Then came these:

And now, Israel, what doth the Lord thy God require of thee, but to
fear the Lord thy God, to walk in all his ways, and to love him, and
to serve the Lord thy God with all thy heart and with all thy soul,
to keep the commandments of the Lord thy God, and his statutes,
which I command thee this day for thy good? Behold, the heaven
and the Heaven of Heavens is the Lord's thy God, the earth also,
with all that therein is. Only the Lord had a delight in thy fathers
to love them, and he chose their seed after them, even you above
all people, as it is this day. He doth execute the judgement of the
fatherless and widow, and loveth the stranger, in giving him food
and raiment. Love ye therefore the stranger: for ye were strangers
in the land of Egypt. Thou shalt fear the Lord thy God; him shalt
thou serve, and to him shalt thou cleave, and swear by his name.
He is thy praise, and he is thy God, that hath done for thee these
great and terrible things, which thine eyes have seen. Thy fathers
went down into Egypt with threescore and ten persons; and now the
Lord thy God hath made thee as the stars of Heaven for multitude.

Austin Innes looked up through the strands of his own red hair and saw the four deep-listening faces lit only by the Mississsippi moonlight and the stars that hung low over the river. His eyes met theirs. They were no longer strangers to each other.

They did not ask him to stay for the hymn-singing, and he did not ask. Instead Innes bid the brethren goodnight and sought his spot forward on the roof, behind the gouger. He had none of his books, nor even a newspaper, and he missed his reading sorely. He sat with his legs dangling as the Shakermen wound up the evening's devotions and began to settle himself down, giving thought to his future for what was very likely the first time in this particular decade of his haphazard existence.

He had been, he thought, too long on the river. Years had gone by since he last sailed the Lakes, and he thought perhaps he might now make his last steamboat journey for awhile when he found *Johanna R* in New Orleans. Something about the weather that blew across Lake Erie had always appealed to him and he thought to join up with the St. Lawrence, on his way to trying that life again. Or he might let the Ohio carry him east to Pittsburgh, and from that grey city work his way to the northern coast of the Atlantic. He had never ridden in the white wake cut by the fleeing leviathan – of which he had heard tell, or read, or perhaps even dreamt, he could not say which for sure – and to do so would make of him an ocean sailor, an occupation for which he believed he had the spit.

Nothing personal against the sternwheelers, make no mistake, for he was prone to make even his most considerable decisions by the fly of a copper. But Austin Innes on this calm evening examined his desires and discovered he was wishful of sail. If there was indeed a Heaven, then in sail was found the drum to call believers – the wind's low rumble of perdition against beholden canvas – and it was the rhythm, not the destination, that moved him.

Damp with the heat, Austin took off his blouse and rolled over on the roof. The cool of the green wood stung briefly at his chest and he pushed himself up, holding his weight on his arms, until skin and wood had reached some friendlier accord. He touched his cheek to the timber and watched the moonlight glance off the river and onto the shoreline. There was little to see beyond the cane that lined the bank and the first stand of trees, especially in this light. The Spanish moss hung thick from the branches, like a French petticoat against the legs of a pretty girl, but in this instance he could only guess what lay beyond. The planks were a sounding board to the ear, and Austin smiled as he listened to the river singing, first raising his head, then laying it down again. How many nights had he camped with his fellows off the Durham boats (there was safety in such numbers, and a keelboat crew need little fear the bloodletting Indians and larcenous marauders of whom the few inmates of this broadhorn were rightly wary), felt the muscles of his arms wild with soreness from hauling the great cordelles that moved such craft upriver, and tried to sleep along these very same riverbanks? How was it that he had never heard until this night the lullabye that began with twilight and lasted til daybreak, the better to catch all shifts of sleepers out? Here was not the calliope and coonjine of the city wharf, punctuated by the steady thud of cotton bales on the cargo floor; here instead was the sound of a million mud-happy varmints making their presence known, males and females engaged in a duet that multiplied exponentially below the treefrogs like employed in song until the harmony was fit for Heaven. He had never noticed it before – not for what it was.

Austin rolled on his back, put one arm under his head and lay the other across his belly, and wondered if the singers read their music off the stars, just as sailors found their way by them.

He fell asleep.

Four days south of Natchez, still plodding along the river shore, the flatboat had reached only the distance of Bayou Sara, some seventy-odd miles below Natchez with at least another twenty to go before they tied up at Baton Rouge. And while well they might make that port by tomorrow, depending on the pressures of Shaker trade, it by now made little difference to Austin's course of action whether he saw Baton Rouge in this life or the next. His outlook on his predicament had become something akin to philosophical.

He had taken it upon himself to go over all the Shakermen's clothes, shoring up here and completely restitching there. And as the heat of the day rose over him he was rethreading his needle when he cast a lazy eye downriver and was caught up short. The bow of the boat steaming upriver had a familiar squint to it, a look of home, and he realized in an instant that, if he had not been wily enough to catch *Johanna R*, she at least had been resolute enough to come back for her wandering boy.

He looked around for Michael Bird, near panic in his eyes as if anyone could stray far or hide long on a broadhorn. He spotted the big man at the starboard sweep and turned noisily to him.

"That's my boat!" he yelled, and pointed downriver as his faithful *Johanna R* drew closer. "She's been to New Orleans and back! Made good time, too!"

Brother Michael looked back over his shoulder, watching with his hand firm on the oar as the younger man came toward him. "That's fine," he said. "I'm happy for thee."

As the steamer approached, sailors on her deck spotted the excited figure on the flatboat roof and recognized at once by his red hair their lost Professor. Waving at him, shouting, they called his name over and over, not realizing their very presence was the cause of his activity.

Shifting his weight from foot to foot, knowing time was not now on his side, Austin ran his hands over his pockets. He had almost forgotten, in the four days since Natchez, that he had a purse, let alone could he remember where it was.

"I don't know what I owe you," he said, locating the leather bag in his jacket pocket and drawing it out. One eye was on Bird, the other tracked the progress of the steamer.

Bird raised a hand to slow him down. "Patience, friend," he said quietly. "Has thee memory of payment being asked?"

Austin checked the whereabouts of his feet, and remembered he had no time for embarrassment. "Board and passage..."

"...were more than paid by thy ministration to our clothes, and thy help at the oars and lines, and thy services as huntsman," Bird told him firmly. "And thy companionship was more than kind."

"Then I'm grateful," Austin said hastily, taking the man's hand for an instant. Wanting to say more but stitched for time, he ran forward and dove into the river, making with strong strokes toward the channel path of *Johanna R.*

"Thee's kindly welcome," Bird said, leaning over the gunnel to watch the young man's progress. "God bless thee on thy way," he called after, words Austin could not hear over the sound of water rushing past his ears.

With those seconds he ceased to be a flatboatman and was once again a stoker of steam, intent as his hands cut the water on being back where he belonged.

Out of his blue downriver eye he saw the lanky Davis hanging over the guards with a length of line as the boat closed the distance, and over the churning roar of the pitman arm he heard someone shout, "Look sharp, Professor! Steer for the rope!"

The heavy line was heaved over the side and trailed starboard downriver like a willful child tugging against its mother's hand. Austin made his way through the muddy water, found the rope, and hand-over-handed himself up the side a respectful distance from the churning wheel til a deckhand's arm reached over to pull *Johanna R*'s prodigal son back aboard.

The boat was swift about her business, and as Austin shook the damp from his hair and squeezed at his sleeves he knew the time for greetings and explanations was a few minutes yet to come.

Leaving his shipmates standing at the bow he ran astern along the rail. There he stood silent as a puddle widened around his boots, watching across the wheel and down the wake as the little broadhorn grew still smaller in the distance. He saw Michael Bird's fine figure watching him watch, and just before *Johanna R* lost sight of him Austin saw the Shakerman reach up and lift his straw hat high in the air, by way of farewell.

December

E xcept for the odd few he could not bring himself to part with, Austin Innes had sold every book he owned in St. Louis, and what few notions he had chosen to keep were now stowed in a haversack he could carry across his back.

He knew what he knew, and now he wanted to know the rest. He was not exactly jumping ship, for no injury had been done to him; he had suffered no dissatisfaction at the hands of captain or crew, and in truth he had no cause to take his leave in other than amicable fashion. Captain Haller had been puzzled by the news of his stoker's imminent departure when it was delivered to him; the man had in recent months taken on a generally more agreeable attitude and in all Austin Innes was a fellow whose absence his captain would regret. Austin left *Johanna R* under advice that he would be taken back aboard with pleasure whenever he succeeded at working the termites out of his system, and he was glad of the invitation. But for the moment, Austin was going inland.

His plan seemed reasonable enough: he would work his way upriver east along the southern shore of the Ohio, and somewhere along that body of water he would find folk who knew of Brother Michael Bird and his people. He had been once or twice to

Louisville, but in twelve years he had seldom strayed far from the Mississippi shore or the banks of the Lakes, and what he knew about Kentucky would fill precious few teacups. Of this, at least, he seemed sure: Shaker coasters coming down from Kentucky would of necessity use the Ohio on their way to the Big River, and well he remembered the estimable esteem in which the habitues of the river shores held the goods purveyed by the gentle Shakermen who plied such waters. Thus, however long it might take (and it occurred to him that of recent he might have learned a thing or two of patience), in time he would meet up with the Kentucky River and along its distance find Shawnee Run. A man who understood the workings of stars did not need a map, not as long as he could avail himself of the river folk's good offices, and therefore he did not put about for one.

He had reckoned without the considerable breadth of the state of Kentucky. Following the meandering trail of the river Austin found many who knew of the Shakers, if not the name of Michael Bird, but knowing this passing stranger knew of them and was that way bound many were moved to feed and shelter him and give him messages to deliver, letters to carry upriver, even orders to be filled or seed papers to be changed for new when next a Shaker flatboat passed this way. He was amazed to find himself being passed like a dearly-won parcel from hand to hand, told at this settlement where best to stop at the next, a friend by association who by degrees began to feel he might be on his way to where he was meant to be going.

A week passed, and the thick end of another, and more and more Austin found that – once he had conveyed what little he knew about the geography of the village he hoped to locate – he was likely to be told: "Ah, no. You mean South Union."

"It was said to me as Pleasant Hill," he would reply.

"The onlyest Shakers as I know is the ones down the Gasper to South Union," would come the rest. "It was me, I'd go along there and tell *them* my troubles."

This seemed sensible enough advice to Austin, so he did as he was bid. And by such directions (following the Green River to the Barren, finally finding the Gasper River shore and trying to take the deviation from plan with an open mind), some weeks after taking his leave of *Johanna R* in St. Louis, he found himself walking into a neat little village hemmed round-and-about with neat split-rail fences. An island of humanity set amid a vast sea of wintering grassland and leafless sugar maples, the frost-covered grounds within those fences gave safe haven from the cold and slippery road to citizens intent about their business. As Austin came close enough to see, there was something to be recognized about these islanders.

He hunched his back under the haversack and craned his neck to see it all as he closed in on the obvious center of the village. At the crossroads he stood looking up at the smoke rising from the magnificent twin-stacked chimneys of an imposing brick building, fully three storeys high. Whatever else might lie within these fences, this must surely mark the middle of it. Considering that house (if house it was) from the road, he determined that he had at long last arrived where he had meant to be. Flatness of the land notwithstanding, this could only be Pleasant Hill. And as the green side door of the big house opened and three men emerged, any doubt he might have harbored flew. Identical they were, in wide-brimmed hats – winter-weight, not straw, and grey, but Austin was unfazed – with clean-shaved faces and hair cropped straight at the shoulder. Watching them adjust to the chill as they shut the door behind them Austin had a sense that he knew these men, not these men but he knew *of* them, and taking hold of the fence post he called out.

"I'm looking for Brother Michael Bird," he said.

The hats turned to him in unison, and one of those he had addressed crunched across the hardened ground to the fence. "You're looking for someone?" he asked with careful interest. "Are you kin to someone here?"

"No, just a friend," Austin said, feeling the cold a bit now he'd stopped moving and blowing into his closed fist. "I came downriver with Brother Bird last summer, on his way to New Orleans, and I thought I'd come along and visit."

The man slid his hat off and scratched his head. "Well, I don't know the name and that's a fact, but it don't necessarily follow that he ain't here." He turned to his fellows, still standing by the steps and clearly anxious to reach warmer ground. "You know a Brother Bird here?" The two men looked at each other, then returned blank glances.

"Not at the Center, leastways," said the man who eyed Austin across the fence. "But here's what you do. You just carry along that way," he said, pointing over Austin's shoulder to the road that led west from the crossing, "and it'll take you to the trustees' office. They'll know of your friend there, if he's here." He touched the front of his hat with his forefinger and turned back toward his companions.

"I thank you for your trouble," Austin said.

"Then you're kindly welcome," the man replied, and was gone.

Austin wandered down the road and carried on another fifty yards or so to the smaller building his guide had indicated. He knocked at the door and, receiving no reply, opened it far enough to put his head inside.

A bespectacled face looked up at him from the opposite side of a chest-high partition. "Well, come in, friend," he said. "There's nothing for you out there but to freeze yourself."

Austin shut the door behind him and as he took his hat off saw two men at work – the trustees, he supposed. The sparse-furnished room was warm and he was glad to be inside it. "I'm looking to find a Shakerman called Michael Bird," he said, and spun his tale of acquaintanceship again.

"You'll find Shaker men here," said the second man from a desk by the far window, "and plenty of 'em, but none called Bird.

Seems to me, though, I recollect a Michael Bird at Pleasant Hill."

"That's the man, a big fellow, Michael Bird of Pleasant Hill," Austin said brightly, then caught his enthusiasm by the tail as he realized it was about to dosed full of buckshot. All was clearly not as it should be. "Is he not here?"

The first man settled himself on one elbow and looked Austin square over the rims of his spectacles. "He would be, friend, if this were Pleasant Hill, but it isn't," he said. "This is South Union. Where did you imagine you were?"

Austin slid his haversack to the floor by his boot, and the melting frost that had gathered on it crept to the floorboards. "Pleasant Hill," he said, a sense of some hopelessness rising.

"I'm afraid you've still some ways to go, east northeast a hundred and fifty miles, maybe."

Hands sunk in his pockets, moisture from his hair dripping on his nose, Austin Innes explained his journey up from St. Louis, telling of the messages and letters and orders he'd accumulated on the way down – all of it imagining he was on his way to Pleasant Hill – in an unbroken stream of words that dazzled his listeners into silence. The trustees, by stream's end obviously full of sympathy for this bedraggled young man and his predicament, offered him a chair and a cup of tea and one of the partnership came to Austin's side of the ledgers to help sort the muddle out.

His benefactor identified himself as Brother Jess Rankin, and drew a chair up close by the one in which Austin sat poking through the contents of his haversack for the many things that were not his. The Shaker man sat quietly with his hands on his knees, eyeing the spines of the books that intermittently emerged and the respect with which their owner placed them one by one out of harm's way on the floor.

Rankin regarded each bundle without much attention as it was offered, pondering as he did so the young man's difficulty. "It was a true kindness," Rankin said, "bringing all this so far. By way of thanks I think we could surely find you a place to stay here, and when next a wagon goes to Pleasant Hill you'd be kindly welcome to go along with it."

Austin's gloom lifted a bit. He wished his jacket were dry. "How long would that be?" he asked, fearing to sound ungrateful but nonetheless wishful to know.

"A few weeks," Rankin said with a shrug, "a month, longer perhaps. Until there is reason to go, there is no reason to go."

Austin let his shoulders fall with his smile that was as tired as he'd begun to notice he was. "It would be difficult for me to tarry long with nothing to keep me busy," he said. "I'm useful with my hands, and would wish to be."

The second trustee looked up from his ledger, amused.

"There is always work for willing hands," Rankin said. Then, looking at his workmate still intent at his labors, he asked: "Ought he to stay upstairs, Brother Urban?"

"No sense heating the place up, just for one," came the answer, after some deliberation. Then for Austin's benefit he added: "Wood's dear, you see. And if he'll stay here awhile, Jesse, he might as well spend his days amongst them at the East."

Rankin nodded and touched Austin's arm lightly, as if to reassure the discombobulated young man that the decision reflected no poor estimation of his character. "They'll be glad of your company over at the East house," he said.

"That one?" Austin said, pointing vaguely out the window. "The big one there?"

"That, my boy, is the Center," said the other man, and the name made sense now Austin came to think of it. "Brother Jess will take you up the East. The people there are new from the world, like yourself, although unlike yourself they've a mind to see how they get on here and are looking to stay. When they find their feet as Believers – should say, *if* they do – and they're comfortable with the way we do a thing in this place, and when the elders have a gift that the time is right, they move closer to the Center. But most of 'em in that house have been at South Union a good few years. These things happen slowly. You'll see. If you're just waiting for the wagon, you're better with the folks at the Gathering Order."

Rising from his chair, Rankin hoisted Austin's lightened haversack to his shoulder and led him back out to the road. Side by side they went east past the big Center building, and as they walked the Shaker brother did the talking, pointing out the meeting house where the membership worshipped of a Sunday, the workshops, the garden house set back from the road.

At the East house Rankin was greeted with deference, a place by the stove, and a cup of tea, his guest likewise. The women here wore linen caps, and Austin was immediately sorry not to be able to determine the color of their hair. Their dresses were long and simple, and without being able to see so much as an ankle Austin found himself looking at the kitchen implements while Brother Rankin talked with the sisters about the status of plans to rebuild the village gristmill.

A fledgling brother was fetched to show the stranger to a sunny, uncluttered room on the building's eastern side, and a bed by the window. On each wall were rails set with pegs from which hung the brethren's spare coats, a lampstand the fashion of which Austin had never seen, empty hangers – a small variety of things not in immediate use. His jacket would be out of place in this company.

"Brethren's retiring rooms are all this side of the house," he was told. "Sisters use the other side. Stairs the same, in all the dwellings." The young man considered him gravely. "Are you a Christian, friend?" he asked. "God-fearin' at all?"

"Never saw much point to it," Austin replied.

"Well," the fellow told him, "if you're just passin' through, it won't be much of a bother."

Austin smiled. "Not much," he said with shyness.

By January's end Austin had been put to work with the brethren, killing the beef cattle and hogs, salting up, and thereafter he was sent out to the fields with a planting party as February came and with it time to get the first potatoes in.

On the fifteenth day of that second month, a dry and mild one given the season, it came to Austin's notice that South Union had company of the kind it most particularly enjoyed. Brother Micajah Burnett had come down from the Shaker village at Pleasant Hill, for the purpose of firming up plans to rebuild the gristmill. Brother Burnett was something of an architect, and his advice was rightly sought in matters of this kind.

Two Saturdays later, on the first of March, Brother Burnett had made complete his calculations at South Union and was on his way to Louisville, where the gristmill castings would be laid in, and from there home to Pleasant Hill. South Union's own Brother Robert Johns would be travelling with him, to help with the business arrangements and look in on the fellowship there, but there was need and room for one more on the wagon and a boy was thus sent to find Austin in the fields. He was, the boy said, kindly welcome to go along with Brother Burnett if he'd like to gather his things together.

A few hours later the wagon pulled away, but Austin Innes was not on it. He was content to stay where he was.

Years later he would say, given the chance again, he would do no differently.

1849

A chill settled on James Littlebourne's chest that winter and wouldn't go, but when finally it went it took him with it. The long-legged son of the dead man buried his father under the spreading trees, beneath which they had sat silent together so many Sunday mornings. It was a habit his father had, although in fact he was silent always, or almost. Harry Littlebourne looked up at the afternoon sky over Ohio – a blue field wanting to oversee spring and about to get its wish – and saw in the clouds no shapes he recognized. Looking down again he put his foot to the mound that rose over the fresh grave, flattening the dark earth. He was not exactly sure how his life had changed.

There was not much Harry Littlebourne could tell about himself, even when he could be engaged in conversation, even when there was anyone around to be engaged in conversation by. There was precious little he knew that did not come from experience. His father had taught his boy to read and write, and to manipulate numbers, and how to speak with courtesy, but they were skills Harry had had little chance to practice. Beside the bed in which his father slept were a Bible and a few other books, but when Harry had read them through there were no more and no money or inclination on his father's part to buy more, no neighbors Harry knew of from whom they might be able to borrow. His father did not believe in borrowing, or in neighbors either for that matter. But the boy liked the stories in the Bible and thus read through it again and again, thereby suiting his father and eliminating the problem to an extent, given the length of the Good Book.

Harry's father was generally partial to the solitary life. What they could not raise on the farm, buy from peddlers, or barter for when the elder Littlebourne took their surplus into town, they did without. By this premise the two resided quietly together until Harry was not quite his full height.

James Littlebourne, newly stretched out and lying beneath the foot of his only child, had while he lived been a severe Quaker, working his farm in the Ohio wilderness with studious intensity and raising a boy alone. His methods were his own, tutored by no seasoned hand and riddled with eccentricities that defied any known rules of child-rearing. As soon as he was field-size the boy began to help the man work the land and tend the few animals the Littlebournes kept, but the two had never spoken of much of consequence and now they never would. In his young life Harry had seldom seen another child, or a woman, and it took years for him to piece together the vision of a home with a woman in it, despite the presence of such domestic arrangements in the only book he read with regularity. There was no woman on his father's farm, nor even a likeness of a woman, and there had never been in Harry's memory. His father never spoke of one. By the time it occurred to Harry that most homes with a child in them also had a woman – and that it was logical to assume he had had a mother when he started out, but that something had become of her or she would still be in evidence – he sensed that the time to pose questions about such matters had passed and thus he never asked. Likewise, living in such isolation, he was never moved to question why he and his father were of different colors. In a world where itinerant peddlers were the only living souls he was likely to see, where the animals and birds around him came in apparently infinite variety, there seemed no reason to believe the color of the human hide should be always the same, from man to man. Neither did he know his own age. James Littlebourne was not a talker and he did not raise up one.

The burying of his father finished, Harry went back to his cabin and – knowing what the seasons expected of him and old enough to comply – he carried on alone as spring followed winter, and summer began to make itself known. The farm was, as it had always been, able to give up far more than its now lone tenant could use and, while he briefly considered packing up the rest and taking it into town, he hesitated and finally rejected the idea altogether. There was plenty of food for him and the animals and he had his father's clothes. He wanted for nothing and he had never been to town. His father had always said business was not for children and neither was town, and perforce Harry had always stayed behind, looking after himself during the day or two his father was away. He could not say with any certainty where the nearest town was. He did not know with whom his father traded when he went away. In his youngest years his father had simply bartered with the peddlers who occasionally happened by for salt and sugar or whatever else they might need, and this Harry could certainly do although he did not much care for sugar. When necessity put a match to his boot heels the boy would move, but until then he saw no rush to be other than where he was.

The match took the form of a westbound wagon.

That sunny afternoon Harry was settled at the table with a hand of Beleaguered Castles nearly set out, as often he did when his morning chores were finished. His father had not much approved of card-playing, and it was a minor curiosity to Harry that these cards should be here at all. The deck itself was handmade by his father and by now well worn, its colors almost gone, but Harry could tell as if by feel which card he was handling at any given time. The game in his hand at the moment was the only solitaire his father knew, and while James Littlebourne had often told him it was wicked to play at cards, he gave his limited approval to the playing of a solitaire, saying that while playing at cards alone a man could only cheat himself. That being true, he would quickly learn not to do so, and there was thus a moral benefit to the activity. Harry was setting the cards down beside the aces, preparing the foundations of his castles – the door of the cabin standing open, the better to catch the day's benevolent weather through the windows – and his ears went up as he thought he heard a sound he had not heard since long before his father died. His few geese were pursuing their own interests beyond the stoop and when, suddenly, they honked noisily and wheeled themselves into the air, he knew.

The Littlebourne place was the only landfall for miles in any direction at which a prairie schooner was likely to sight a human face, and thus the wagon had as likely stopped for the benefit of a little company as for directions. Harry sat quite still until he heard the sound of a man's footsteps on the porch, followed by a knock on the side of the house. He was hard put to recall a stranger ever coming so close to the cabin. He set the cards down and went to the door to find a man shorter than himself – as most men were – and when he met the man's eyes with his own he saw his visitor recoil and step back. The fellow's hand went to his side and his jaw fell slightly.

"You speak English, boy?" the stranger asked, his voice stern but reinforced more by fear than courage.

"Speak English?" Harry said, confused, and looked over the visitor's shoulder at the wagon to see a woman and three children rapidly retreat inside it. He had not spoken to anyone since he bid his father goodbye, and the words came thickly off his tongue. So accustomed had he become to speaking only to his animals that he could not now say with confidence whether he still did so aloud, or if the words were uttered only in his mind. He stepped out his door, ducking his head as he passed beneath the lintel to avoid bumping it, and raised his hand to the wagon while there was still a soul visible to see him do so. The protective father's arm went out to hold him back as the boy called out a hello.

"I said, you an Indian, boy?" he asked.

"I live here by myself," Harry told him, thinking it more mannerly to answer a different question than to offer no response at all.

His visitor peered into the cabin, neat and spartan and eloquent enough a witness to the boy's veracity.

Harry gave no sign that he would overwhelm the man's restraint. "Thee's welcome to come in and set for a bit if thee's a mind to. And the woman, and the children," he said. He felt he was running off at the mouth, so many and so rapid did the words seem to him. "Please."

A look of total puzzlement creased the stranger's face. "Thee's welcome?" he repeated, dropping his hand from Harry's arm. "Who in hell are you, boy?"

"My name is Harry Littlebourne," came the disinterested reply. The dumbfounded man watched motionless as Harry stepped down off the shaded porch and into the sunlight, headed toward the wagon. There was the creak of leather and the sound of a pistol being cocked behind him, and a voice said:

"Don't touch my family..."

Harry peered into the wagon, where the frightened woman huddled against the crush of her possessions, her arms around her wide-eyed children. What could possibly alarm them so?

"Hello," he said to her youngest, a little girl crouched in her brother's lap. Then, looking back to the woman, he said, "If thee has use for milk for thy young'ns, there's more here than I can use and thee's welcome to it."

Looking at the brownskinned boy's dark, sloe eyes, the woman saw much that she could trust. Her fear evaporated and her hold on the children eased. "Yes, please," she whispered as she relocated her voice.

Back on the porch her husband saw the boy reach into his wagon and with a trembling hand he trained the barrel of his pistol just above his target's ear. "Marcy!" he called out.

The woman appeared in the wagon opening and helped one of her small boys into Harry's arms.

"I'm sure it's allright, Noah," she called back. "Look at him. He's not much older than your brother."

Her husband relaxed his shooting hand and was relieved to do so. He had never in his life killed a man.

A second boy jumped down under his own steam and lit out for the trees the instant he touched solid ground. Gently the woman passed her daughter out to Harry, who held her with one arm as with the other he helped her mother down over the wheel. He had never touched a child before, and the lightness astonished him. The little girl, curious but unafraid in the way some children have, leaned back and looked him long in the eye. All the straw and string that went into the maintenance of a real person was present even now in this little scrap, Harry thought to himself with some delight. The whole idea made him smile. He examined her tiny white hand with his large brown one, fascinated. Her tangled yellow hair blew across his face.

With graceful, long-legged strides he walked them to his cabin, anxious but hopeful. The girl wriggled to get down, and as he set her on her feet she went straight for her gamboling brothers. Instinctively he brushed the soles of his boots on the cornhusk mat outside the door, then took down a jug and filled it with milk for the little ones, watching with curious eyes as their mother took it out to them. Cooped up for so long on the wagon they were as grateful for a time and place to stretch their legs as for the milk. The afternoon still had a hospitable look to it – the days were getting longer – and at least one of the trees was, as Harry knew from long experience, a suitable climber. He watched them as they rolled in the cool grass beneath the branches. Which one of the boys had he looked like, when he was that size?

His guests were Noah and Marcelline Burke, and Harry leaned himself against the wall as they settled themselves. They were headed to Indiana, it seemed, come out from Massachusetts and looking to settle where the land and water were good, the threat of attack by Indians slight. Harry listened to this with divided interest as the big pot of water from the well came to a boil, and straw tea to follow. Still accustoming himself to the sound of spoken words, he had not yet reached a stage of comfort therewith sufficient to take in much meaning. His progress was impeded by the peculiarity of the Burkes' speech; the words were English but the sound was different to what he knew, and some words defied identification.

"Nice place this is," Burke told him, looking around. A double crib it was, he could see, neatly constructed.

"Needs a woman to see to it," his wife added.

"It's good land," Harry said, watching the pot. "My father and I worked it. We were never short for anything..."

"Your father an Indian, too?" Burke asked, and brushed aside his wife's objections as she sought to quiet the intrusion. "It's a question, Marce. He can answer it or not."

The pot had boiled and Harry was tending to it. "My father was a Quaker," he replied over his shoulder.

"He's not here?"

Harry shook his head. "He's out there," he said as he set down cups in front of his guests, then pointed out through the door to the trees under which the children played.

He did not at first catch the alarm as it returned to Burke's face. Tensed, suddenly fearful for his children, the man looked out past his young host's outstretched hand.

"Oh, no," Harry said quickly, now sensing the cause of his guest's confusion. "He's dead."

"I'm sorry," Marcy Burke said, suddenly understanding to

some extent the depth of the boy's isolation and genuinely touched by his attempt to appear at his ease amongst people.

"It was nobody's fault," the boy said, as if reading aloud from *The Farmer's Almanac*. "It was a chill, last winter. I couldn't keep him."

"So now you're working this place alone?"

Harry nodded and his coarse, black hair fell into his eyes. "Not all of it this year, just some," he said. "I don't need much, so I let some of it go back. I can't leave it, though, can I? I got two horses, and the cows, and some Ossabaws, and they'd die with nobody."

Sudden shrieks from the children outside drew a distracted glance from their mother. Harry could not help watching her.

"Well, we're anxious after finding our own place," Burke said. "We come all the way out from Lowell and it's a powerful long distance. Marce, here, I think she's good and ready to come off the road. My youngest boy's been sick, and the wagon's gettin' roady. We thought to make for Indiana, heard good things about it, but Ohio seems like a nice place to be."

"I never been anywhere else," Harry said flatly.

"My brother's still back East and he wanted to come out with us, but I told him to wait a bit," said Burke. He was still trying to find a way back to his original question. This redskinned boy's presence here, living as he did in the fashion of a white man in a white man's cabin, made no sense that he could devise. "Soon as we settle on a place I'll send for him. He's nineteen. That'd be about your age, am I right?"

"I couldn't say," Harry replied.

"You don't know how old you are?" Marcy Burke asked, leaning forward and putting a hand on his arm. It was warm on his skin, but not damp, despite the heat. Still, Harry pulled away; he had never in his memory been touched by a woman. Instantly he was sorry. "Your father didn't tell you? You didn't ask him?"

"We didn't talk much," he said shyly. This which had all his life seemed so normal a state of being now took on aspects of the bizarre, even in Harry's own mind. Surely any of those children playing outside near his father's grave could tell him its age.

"And your mother?" she asked.

"Honey, these things just don't matter so much to his kind," Burke interrupted, his tone knowledgeable.

"Shush, Noah, for the Lord's sake," his wife said sharply, then turned back to Harry. "What about your mother?"

"I never saw her," he said. Harry folded his arms over his chest, extended his long legs out full on the cool floorboards, and knocked the toes of his boots together with a lazy rhythm. If this was how it went when folks had company, he would as soon stay on his own. The quiet hung heavy, broken now and again by the children's noise as the Burkes sipped at their tea.

Then Noah Burke stood and looked out the door, surveying the layout of the place – the corncrib, the shed, the well – as if to save the wisdom of its arrangement for future reference. A family could have a good life on a spread like this. He turned back toward his wife. " 'Bout time we took the littl'ns up," he said to his wife. Then, to the boy: "Seems like we'd best be on the road."

Harry's thoughts were lazy. He did not object to the idea of their departure, but there was more to it than that. He looked at the woman sitting in his father's chair. She did not look out of place. Her husband, now standing with his shoulder to the doorjamb, looked as if he had always been there. Drowsing a little on the floor, sleepy from the tea and the serious chore of offering hospitality, he felt for all the world as if he'd overstayed his welcome and the Burkes were about to tell him it was time for him to be on his way home.

"I'll just be another minute," he said to no one in particular.

"What?" said Marcy Burke, looking down at him.

Harry's eyes suddenly opened wide. It was all so obvious to him, so simple. This place which meant nothing to him anymore could mean everything to this kind woman, to her family. How could he stay and let them go?

"Thee's welcome to stay here, Noah Burke," he said abruptly.

"It's a kind offer, son, but we'll never get anywhere if we don't make a start," said Burke.

"Thee's already here," the boy said, his face and eyes so surely in earnest that the man scarcely knew how to take him. "It's cleared, the water's good, the land bears fine, the fallows can be started up again if thee likes. Thee won't find better if thee goes on to Indiana, I promise thee."

"I was never looking to be a tenant," Burke said, bristling a little and at once ashamed at having done so, sensing as he did that something extraordinary was about to happen here. "Or, do you mean stay on here with you?"

"No, no, on thy own." Harry looked up and spoke quickly, as if without speed he could not hope to finish at all. "With those two boys thee surely has no need of my hand. Even when I was small this place was no great trouble to my father and me."

Burke looked at his wife who sat thunderstruck with her cup still raised in her hand, wondering how her husband would react to this poor boy's bizarre proposition and awaiting his move. He had never heard anything so outlandish in all his life. It defied logic. Had he thought the offer sound he would happily have considered it, but no one in his right mind would walk away from so fine a parcel of ground, after so long, without exacting a considerable price.

"How much?" he asked warily.

"I don't know," Harry said.

"You'd have to decide."

"All of it, then."

"All of what?"

"As much as there is."

"Boy, are you out of your mind? Do you think I'm out of mine?"

Harry considered this. He regained his feet and joined Burke at the door, then pointed to a spot on the horizon. "Well," he said, "I think one year we took the corn up as far as there..."

"You're talking boundaries," Burke said. "I'm talking money."

"What about money?"

"How much?"

This Harry had not considered. Talking and thinking at the same time presented a challenge he could not meet on his first attempt. "There's some gold, I think. Thee can have it, if thee thinks it will help."

Burke shook his head, now just this side of exasperated. "No, boy. Now listen to me. How much, to take this place? How much money do you want from me?"

Harry was astonished by this turn of the conversation. "I don't want anything from thee, except thee look kindly after my animals."

Burke felt his knees about to go, and he sat himself down again. "Did this land belong to your father?" he asked.

"None ever came to say it didn't."

"Did you ever see the papers?"

Harry shook his head, not truly sure what he was being asked.

Burke sensed this but went on. "Was there ever a man, say, who came a few times a year and took some of your crops away?"

Harry shook his head again. "No one came here, ever, not to come inside."

Burke seemed to have run clean out of avenues of approach. What does a man do when a miracle threatens to befall him? He looked at his wife, clearly as confused as her husband.

"This farm used to be my father's," Harry said, "but since he died I guess it's who wants it. I've just stayed on to look after the animals. But if thee has a use for it, as seems likely, thee can have it."

"Sit down, Harry, please," Burke said. "You don't understand." He scratched his forehead. The boy might be slow-witted – perhaps this was at the heart of the difficulty – and the man could not in fairness take advantage. If this young fellow, no more than a child in his mind by all appearances, was about to give away his birthright no decent man could allow himself to be the beneficiary of the act without making sure his benefactor knew the consequences of his actions. Clearly Harry Littlebourne did not. Without his farm,

Noah Burke thought, what would this willowy boy be but one more half-tame Indian?

"Now, try to listen to me, son. This is important to you. You're sitting on a piece of land that's worth good money. If it belonged to your father before, it belongs to you now," he explained slowly, gently, watching his wife from the corner of his eye. "You can't just give it away."

"Why?"

"Why? Well, I don't know why, exactly." In actual fact, Burke didn't know why, it just seemed logical, the way of the world. He was flummoxed by this whole conversation and had begun to sound it.

Marcelline Burke reached over the table-top – on which still sat unplayed Harry's hand of Beleaguered Castles – and took hold of her husband's fingers. "Seems like we could stay, Noah, and look after the boy's animals if he's of a mind to go."

Burke looked over at his wife. Tired, anxious for a good soaking in hot water in a home of her own. Good God, he thought, how she does want to get off that wagon. Through the door he saw his children exploring the surroundings of the cabin, chasing the geese. It was as if the decision had already been made and all that was left now was for him to accept it.

"We can talk about it," he said. Then: "I suppose it would be allright."

He saw tears rise in his wife's eyes and looked to the boy, the engine of this turn of events, who regarded this verdict as if it could have happened no other way.

"It would be good to have my horse," Harry said with a trace of apology. "He's only young and not good for much, but I brought him myself. His mother's a good worker, she'll do thee proud, and with the horses thee has with the wagon, one less won't be much missed."

"Your horse and anything else you want, son, anything," Burke said, and felt his wife's hand tighten around his own. This good woman had come with him so far on trust, but she was looking to settle and happy to stay here now that happenstance had offered them the option. How could he say no to her?

"Only my father's Bible," Harry said.

The Burkes stayed put, and so did Harry, for a day or two. He and Noah Burke took their horses out and Noah saw what the boy understood to be the boundaries of the land. Burke assumed that one day, if there were papers hidden somewhere in the cabin, he would find them, and between now and the possible future objection of some phantom lien-holder perhaps the simple transfer Burke had concocted, to which Harry had affixed his name, would suffice. In the absence of a reader of law, it would have to.

As the few hours they spent in each other's company passed, Marcelline Burke noticed the boy spent more and more of his time with the children, and spoke less and less. By the time he got to his horse and took his leave – with no idea where he was going but with Noah Burke's maps and a few of their Treasury notes rolled with James Littlebourne's gold in his blanket – he spoke almost not at all.

For all he knew, he had been born in the little house which was disappearing behind a grove of trees, trees that had always marked the outermost reaches of his orbit, and already it seemed likely that he was farther away from it than he had ever been. It was peculiar to be alone on the road, far from his father's grave and getting farther. Last night he had lain awake in the loft, knowing there were strangers in his bed and strangers' children in his father's. He was not bothered, and the fact that he was not bothered did not bother him.

He had liked the woman straight off, liked the way she looked at him. He wondered if his mother had ever looked at him that way. Just before he left the house that last time she had done the most extraordinary thing: she had put her arms around him, stood up on her toes, and pressed her lips against his chin. This had never happened to him before, and Harry Littlebourne knew he would remember the feeling, for whatever it was, for the rest of his life.

August

He would not stay anywhere and let folks beat his horse, no matter the wages nor the agreeableness of his bed. If the animal would work for no man save that he knew best it was the decision of the animal, very likely even a fair decision, and Harry Littlebourne saw no cause to take a stick to the horse in aid of changing its mind. But when Harry raised his hand to stay the course of the stick, his boss was persuaded to believe the tall young man would turn its attentions elsewhere and swung hard and wide with the rough bridle he held fast in his free hand. A buckle fetched Harry a ringing clout to his ear that set him spinning crazy-legged to the ground, and while he shook the buzzing fog from his head he heard the voice: "You're out, son. *That quick.*"

He rolled what little remained to him in his blanket. His gold had gone the first week, most likely travelling now in the pockets of a tramp who offered the use of his campfire and in the morning was gone with anything Harry might have used for money. The boy thought little of this turn in his financial affairs until he sought to buy a loaf of bread and learned to his cost that provisioners were partial to payment for such things in cash. With nothing to trade, nothing but his horse to sell, Harry boiled grasses and leaves for tea, and foraged for berries and Jerusalem artichokes for his supper, and that way kept himself in victuals until he chanced upon a farmer who offered him harvesting work. For a few weeks his employer admired the boy's strong back and disinclination to conversation, but theirs was not a relationship destined to endure. It was the farmer's wife who discovered the seven mongrel puppies last seen when her husband abandoned them as newborns, wrapped in a burlap sack and submerged in the river, bound for the heavenly reward reserved for unwanted puppies. Harry saw him at his task and fished the sack from the river, then concealed its contents in a feed box under his bunk until the squeak and yip and the sight of the gangly boy with his head beneath the bedrails brought the wrath of the missus down. That night, without even his last week's pay to buoy him, Harry was set adrift. Other than his, it seemed, there were no tender hearts on the place. As he rode out he saw the farmer's wife tending to the chickens, and at the sight of her he put his open palm to his chin.

This was not the same farewell.

Since then his fortunes had run similarly: one fellow had taken his silence for insolence; another turned him out when he declined to name the culprit in a poaching incident. That he did not know the name seemed of little moment in the circumstances: he could not find the words to say he did not know.

Thus, with the grime coming so thick at his collar he could not rub it out in cold stream water, and his linsey-woolsey trousers in an increasingly sad state of affairs, he began to wonder how the Burkes were faring. He pulled at the hair at the back of his neck and thought for the first time of his geese; he dug at a tree root with the square toe of his boot and wondered if his father could see from his lodgings in Heaven that his boy had no home of his own. James Littlebourne had always forbidden his son the luxury of tears, else Harry might have thus indulged himself. As it was he clutched at the reins of his horse, which dangled free to the ground beside him, wound them tight around his hand, and squeezed. There was no propriety in this: the animal would not wander away of its own accord, and if led away it would come back to him. They were a family.

He was aware of how thin he had become. With August in wane what work to be had was mostly gone, either finished entirely or taken up by those who had come earlier in search of it, and living in the woods on what little they could offer him had resculpted Harry Littlebourne's already slender frame with grim economy. The horse, too, had begun to suffer, and it was this last that concerned him. Not that he was clear on the errors of his ways, Harry was increasingly aware that, for the good of the animal, he must put them right. And thus when, one afternoon, he emerged from a grove of trees to find in the distance a serviceable farm with considerable surrounding land, he resolved to appeal for horsefeed – on whatever terms might be agreeable – to whatever souls might be willing to discuss the matter with him.

Approaching closer he saw the figure of a woman at the pump, her arms working at the handle, and for a moment thought he might be dreaming. Slight and gentle-boned, with dark yellow hair, in her blue-checked apron she might have been Marcelline Burke, and Harry turned this way and that as he walked, looking for Noah, looking for the children. In truth he knew he could not now find his way back to his father's farm, even if he wished to, but he knew this was not it. There was no reason for them to be in this place, but no matter: as he came nearer still he saw that this was a different woman.

She, too, in the clear and empty air of summer, had noticed the stranger, heard him coming, and she reached for the pistol that lay ready and loaded on the ledge of the pump. Harry reached up to brush dust from his eyes, and when he lowered his hand again he saw the business end of the woman's gun aimed at him and raised his hands to shoulder height. He wore no belt, and the horse carried no more than a rolled blanket, and the woman knew with a single appraising look that there was nothing to fear in Harry Littlebourne.

"Y'all just can't come from nowhere like that," she said with clear annoyance.

Harry's look was apologetic.

She looked to the gun she had gripped in both hands, loosed it and swung it behind to hold it fast at her back. Bearing down hard with her eyes on Harry she considered him boot to crown and said, "Can't be too careful now."

He nodded at this, and raised his hand to scratch between the ears of his horse. With the other he pointed to the pump.

"Just got washing to see to," the woman said. She was younger than Marcy Burke, Harry could see now he stood so close by to her, and taller. He bent to pick up her two buckets of water, and indicated the open door of the house with his chin.

"Well, that would be kind," she said – surprised at her willingness to let this long, unknown boy walk uninvited and uninspected out of the woods and into her sitting room – and followed behind him as he walked.

Inside Harry found a house grander than any of the admittedly few he had seen, with rich, dark carpets and store-bought furniture and pictures on the walls. The kitchen was a room apart, with a great iron stove. What there was not inside this house was sound, neither chick nor child, and he thought that she must surely live here alone. But even this seemed a notion out of place: her wedding ring told him this house must have one other occupant at least, and Harry looked for fresh sign of him but saw none.

He set the buckets down by the tub. He must ask her, but his voice had descended to his pockets. Plunging his hands deep down he fetched up a thread of sound, and spoke.

"For my horse," he whispered, looking at a point high over her shoulder. "Some food. I work."

The woman blushed, and looked at him again. "You're a right smart size," she said, "but pure scrawny for it. Seems like you'd ask for yourself."

"Work," he said again, and showed his arm, as if it would speak volumes to support his claims to fitness. "For feed."

"There's feed if you want it," she said, "and work plenty if you want that, too."

Opening a small door beside her she drew out a plate of cornbread. "But you eat something first. For you." She had taken in the curiosity of his speechlessness, but made no mention of it. "Understand that?"

She pulled a chair away from the kitchen table, saw him into it, and set the cornbread in front of him. Then there was coffee next to it, and so swept away was he by the woman's kindness that Harry could not bear to say he didn't care for coffee. Instead he ladled in sugar – which he cared for no better – from a small, fragile bowl (dappled with blue and surely too precious to see daily use), and tried not to take notice of the way she stared at him.

"Much of a one for sweet things, I suppose," she said.

Through the window, framed with pale lace curtains that whipped gently in the August breeze, Harry saw his horse pawing at the ground, nosing the grass and wishing for more substantial fodder. Guilt overtook him, and he pushed back his chair.

The hirelings' house was full with the last of the summer hands, and Harry took his blanket to the barn to make his bed in the haymow. In the night he rolled over and whispered to his horse in its box below, and in the morning he found the woman had left him soap and flannel and a bucket of water. His mentor in this place, it seemed, would be a man who – for reasons not vouchsafed to Harry – was known as Coot, and it was Coot who fetched him in to breakfast.

Because it was the woman's decision that Harry should stay close to the house to do hauling, painting and shifting chores,

Coot brought Harry's plate and his own to the porch of the hirelings' house in order to make clear the nature of things insofar as anyone was privy to them. The boy had learned, even in so short a time, that his style of conversation was a prized commodity amongst the talkers of the world, reliable as it was in its reluctance to interrupt, and Coot was quick to revel in the sound of his own unchallenged voice.

"Her man's got hisself to Boston," said Coot, gesturing with his spoon in the direction Harry supposed Boston must lie from this spot in the morning sunlight. "That 'uz nigh two month ago, and whatever she's heerd off him she ain't see'd fit to let the foreman have word. Could be dead, for all we know." He considered this possibility. "Ain't, I reckon, 'cause a young woman like that'n 'd cry and carry on fit to beat Jesus, sure. She can be a termagant when she's a mind, that missus." This theory, likewise, was not destined to survive its own verbalization unaltered. " 'Cept he's so damned much older'n this'n, she might not take notice, for all the good he must be to her." Coot slipped Harry a wink, and poked him with his elbow, and laughed, none of which signals alerted the boy to its meaning. Sensing the extent of his charge's youth the man assumed a sombre tone. "Could be her grandaddy, that man of hers. What he's doin' leavin' a fine young woman like that alone in Kentucky I wouldn't much keer to speculate. Got so much money he can afford another'n, he loses this'n, maybe."

At this last Harry blinked. So entranced had he been by the breadth of the great river he had crossed that the import of its crossing had escaped him entirely. Now he realized how very far south he had come. Kentucky! Men had made mention of it to him, and now he looked around him with keener eyes, anxious to see how this foreign soil differed from Ohio. At first glance the evidence did not reveal itself.

"You keep your nose open, boy," said Coot, scraping at his plate for the last of his gravy. To such a man dinner must already seem far distant in the future. "She mentions her man, you'll let us hear."

Harry nodded, and turned his attention to the breakfast that had now congealed on his plate. He looked toward the barn and saw the nose of his horse protruding, anxious to keep track of his master but unsure whether to come full out in the open air. The boy left his cold plate on the porch and walked back to the barn to draw the animal's oats and see it watered well.

The woman liked to have him close by, in case she had need of him, and Harry found that he did not so much mind being away from the land and helping her. She set him the task of painting the sitting room walls, and he directly busied himself moving her fine furniture out of the way, the better to reach those patches that wanted scraping and fining down. Often he looked up to find her standing in the doorway, idly wiping her hands on her apron, just watching him, and when he looked at her he wondered that he could ever have mistaken her for Marcelline Burke. Her smile was different, requiring of him rather than prepared to give, and yet there was no meanness there. He had never seen the look before, but then he had not met many women. The look made him anxious to please her, to take the rough patches of her walls so close and level she would have to admire them.

It was hot in the haymow, and Harry was perspiring on top of his blanket. His nightshirt was damp and clung to his chest, and sleep came only for minutes at a time. Starlight was visible through the chinks in the roof, and he began to count the ones he could see, drowsing every now and again. Below him the animals moved, stirring their own heat, but he didn't mind: he was reassured when he heard the familiar sounds of his horse.

Lying on his back with one hand by either ear he recognized the soft, skittering sounds of a rat, and lay very still. The starshine through the roofboards was eclipsed, and then reappeared, and when another hand came down by his own he realized it was not a rat but the woman, and he turned his eyes to her.

She had come up the ladder barefoot and in her nightdress. Her hair hung loose, and as she knelt down by Harry's side it brushed against his face as Burke's child's hair had done that day by the wagon. The muscles in his chest tightened, and even in such dim light he saw her smile had not changed since last he had seen her.

"I think you know," she said softly, and slid her thumb gently toward him in the hay until it caressed his ear.

Harry was frightened but dared not move. Her touch on his ear was not unpleasant, but the nature of its warmth alarmed him. She tucked her feet up under her, bending low as she leaned over him, and put her other hand on his chest. He could feel her fingertips moving against his ribs and was ashamed to realize now how thin he was.

"Too hot to sleep up here, isn't it?" she asked him, knowing full well he would not answer, and squeezed with her fingers at the damp cloth of his nightshirt. She moved her hand in small circles toward the placket's end, until the feel of her fingers on his midsection made him gasp and hold his breath as if to save his own life. She leaned closer and put her lips to his own, and he could feel a peculiar pressure between them. With one more movement of her hand his fear overcame him, and he pulled his knees to his chest, turned on his side and took hold of her hand.

Until she could see the look in his eyes the woman thought he was playing, and betrayed herself with a laugh and a teasing attempt to return her hand to its former employment, but Harry was stronger than she and she understood from the insistence of his hand that there was no game in him. He rolled onto his knees, his breath as fast and labored as a man expecting the imminent arrival of buckshot.

That quickly, it was over, and she jerked with nervous fingers at the ribbons that brought high the neckband of her nightgown. They sat together in the hay, and she found it difficult to look at him at all.

"I thought you knew," she said, and her voice spoke to him of a desperation he would have known as loneliness had he not in his own life spent so much time alone. "You didn't know?"

What she had expected him to know was more than he could imagine.

"It's why I kept you so near the house," she said.

He returned her hand to her, like a borrowed book. The air between them, which had been hot, almost charged, was now cooler, and he could trust her to hold her own hands. He slid away from her in the hay, and tugged at the hem of his nightshirt.

He could see tears winking at the corners of her eyes and was sorry if he had hurt her. She said nothing more, but eased back toward the ladder and in an instant he was alone again.

In the morning Harry did not have to be told he was best advised to leave. He had lain awake the rest of the night, with his hand on his chest where the woman's hand had been, inexplicably sorry that whatever this last service she had required of him he could not provide. The feel of her mouth on his bore no resemblance to Marcy Burke's gesture of parting, and while the end might be the same the means were disturbingly different.

Thus, when daylight began to show through the chinks, giving some proof to the racket of the roosters, Harry Littlebourne had already rolled his world away into the woollen ties that bound it, and had saddled his horse. He would not leave in darkness, for he had taken nothing that did not belong to him and had nothing to hide, but he could not work for his breakfast and perforce would not partake of it. When he saw smoke rise from the hirelings' kitchen he took leave of the barn, with his horse following behind, and made for the trees that had led him to this place those few days ago.

He could feel her presence behind him, sensed that same breath of the night before, heard her calling to him, and Harry Littlebourne had no choice. He turned, and she was running after him with her apron flying and her arms full.

"Please," she was calling, "just wait a little."

He stopped, and behind him the horse stopped, and shyly he eyed the ground rather than look the woman in the eye.

She found safe ground just a few feet distant, and held out to him a bundle of cloth. "These are my husband's," she said. "He won't wear them, and they might do you."

He hesitated, but she leaned forward to bring the bundle closer, and he could not find it in himself to decline her kindness to him. Whatever she had meant in the dark of the haymow she had not meant harm, and he would bear her no ill will.

"I wish..." she said, and blushed, and clasped her hands behind her back.

He peered at her from beneath the curtain of his dark hair, and the look gave her courage.

"What I wish," she said, "is that I could hear your voice again."

So small a wish he could not deny her, but he had no talent for conversation and none would appear as if by magic just to please her.

"What would thee have me say?" he asked, and at the unfamiliar sound of his own voice he gripped the bundle tighter.

She put out her hand to touch his arm, then thought better and brought it back again. "My name," she said.

"Thy name is not a thing I know."

"Keziah," she told him.

"Keziah, then," he said. "I thank thee."

She seemed to know that he was going because he must, but there was no bitterness in her. She looked at him, took note of his discomfort, but she was concerned for him, and every second she could detain him was precious to her.

"I met a man like you, once," she said. "My husband brought him here. He came to buy a horse, and I remember he was like you. He talked like you." Knowing she must let him go, and soon, she still hoped to send him where he might be cared for. "South of here, he came from. South Union, nearby the Barren River. Are there kin to you there?"

She need not know he had no kin anywhere; she need only take leave of him, otherwise he would remain tethered as if by strong chain to the ground where he stood.

He shook his head.

"You might just look in, if you pass that way."

Harry nodded, wishing only to be agreeable but agreeable elsewhere, and finally she understood she must leave first if he were to leave at all.

"South Union," she said, as she turned and walked back toward her grand and empty house.

"South Union," he repeated after her. At first he thought he might say her name again, *Keziah*, but in the end he thought better of it. If she heard it, she might turn and look at him again, and he could not bear to see the look in her eyes.

September

J esse Rankin felt he knew even before it began where this would end. They were called "Winter Shakers," and it was the season for them. Summer was all but finished and the corn had long ago been laid by, the oats were drawn and stacked, the wheat had been threshed and the fodder pulled. Soon farmers hereabouts would be breaking ground for the winter wheat, getting it sown, but in all jobs were coming on for thin if a strong back was what you had to offer in exchange for wages. Winter for some had a bleakness to it. It was at times like these that folks with nowhere else to go, no prospects of a steady meal and a warm bed between now and the work that came with springtime, presented themselves as prospective converts on Shaker doorsteps. They would abide quite happily through the cold weather, sustained by Shaker bounty and doing what small housebound chores might be asked of them – generally making an effort if the Believers were blessed with such good fortune – and when the weather broke most if not all of these winter arrivals would move on. The Believers shared what they had, as was their way and their commitment, but these Winter Shakers did test the patience and here was another one.

On this particular morning Rankin was alone in the office. Every available hand, young or old, was turned to and busy with chores of the season – filling seed papers, digging sweet potatoes, working on the new brick steam-house – and thus there was an unfamiliar empty feel about the place, a stillness to the road outside the office door which stood open to the dry, dusty breezes that blew by.

In actual fact, Urban Johns had given Brother Jess fair warning that this particular chore would be presenting itself before the morning was out. The young man had appeared at South Union a few days ago, and it was Brother Urban who had been looking after him. Urban had a gift for people such as this, and Jesse left him to it, content to wait for the outcome of their interviews. Urban had said last night that the young man was "quiet-spoken but sound," apparently having received an adequate confession, but was swift to add with confidence that in future, if he stayed, this new convert would bend no Believer's ear.

The long-legged fellow, who could not even say how old he was, had meandered his way down from Ohio somewhere, with not much more to his name than a horse – a handsome one, to be sure. Farmwork had kept him solvent through the summer months, along with a bit of money of which he had none left. But there was no work for him in the world hereabouts now, although Urban Johns had from their time together reckoned Harry to be a useful farmer with a touch for animals: talents for which South Union life had constant need. Johns had further said it was his belief that the boy had come here for purpose rather than lodging, and suggested Jesse find him a place amongst the newcomers. And while Rankin was happy to trust Johns' judgement and comply with his request Brother Jesse's hopes for the future, where this fellow was concerned, were not high.

Indians had tried their luck at the Shaker life before, seldom with noticeable success. The number who had tarried long enough among the Believers to sign the covenant could be counted on the fingers of one hand. Squinting at the young man who faced him over the ledgers, Brother Jess saw about this Harry Littlebourne the look of the Mingo, and since there were significant numbers of that tribe in Ohio it was certainly possible. There was no saying for sure, and where Littlebourne had come by his white-man's name being likewise a wonder the spectre of mystery was made complete.

Surely no one living at South Union was as tall as this fellow, but as remarkable as his size was his claim to creed. Rankin could not recall to mind an Indian who considered himself a follower of the doctrine of the Society of Friends, but this one not only did so, he could say what it was. There was certainly evidence here that the individual before him was a Christian: in taking stock of Harry's belongings – precious few of them though there were and each one to be catalogued and valued, the better to avoid misunderstandings later – Rankin found a well-thumbed Bible with the name of James Littlebourne written on the flyleaf in a fine, strong hand.

"Do you read and write, brother?" he asked the gangly Harry, who stood gazing at the empty road outside the office door as if totally enraptured – although nothing was moving thereon or thereabout.

"I heard of this place up by Cynthiana," Harry said, offering as was his habit what had not been asked. "I cut some wood for a lady there last month. Fine lady she was, gave me some of her husband's shirts. Seemed right kind."

"And true enough she must have been," Rankin said brightly, trying to follow the young man's train of thought and filled with admiration for Urban Johns, who must have spent hours trying to weave sensible cloth from such painful threads of conversation.

"She said how she recollected a man reminded her of me, and we ought to find each other. Maybe she thought we were some kin to each other." He was still looking out the window and had the bizarre manner of one who spoke without imagining anyone to be listening.

"Is that a fact?" Rankin said, taking note of the small knife among Littlebourne's chattels. "Perhaps I know this man. The village is very small, and it's always possible you have a kinsman here. How did this very kind woman say you two took after each other?"

"She said we spoke the same."

Jesse Rankin took considerable pains to control his amusement. For a grown man – most nearly grown, at any rate – this Littlebourne, however many years he might have, was nigh unto overwhelmingly childlike. It was almost tempting to send him along to Samuel McGowan, who had charge of the West family's boys, just for jest, but Rankin thought better of it.

"I think you'll find," he said as gently as he could, "that the manner of your speech is one that comes naturally off the tongues of many of the brethren and sisters here. Some do, some don't, others speak as they are spoken to. But many, especially those of us here who come, as you do, from the Society of Friends, are more comfortable in the plainness of speech."

Harry nodded, disappointed perhaps but undismayed.

"What's to become of my horse?" he asked.

October

"**I**sn't anybody I can think of straight off would make a better job of seeing to that boy than you," said Urban Johns. "Give it time."

Tall Thomas Jefferson Shannon set his fingers a course through his hair, not exasperated but pestered and in need of the kind of commiseration for which one habitually looked to Brother Urban. "I'm not saying he's unwilling," he said, and leaned his weight on the back of the nearest untenanted chair. "Man nor boy, I never saw the like of him for willing. Got to take the hook out there to bring him in of an evening; he won't hear the bell." He itched at his nose. "Nor much else, either, I can tell you."

"He's a good boy, Jefferson," said Urban, his voice as full of resolve as sympathy. Perhaps Jess Rankin had been right from the first; perhaps despite his age Harry ought to have been lodged in the Children's Order until they had some notion of what to make of him. "I was never so sure. You think he isn't hearing you, but it's just a different sort of hearing from most folks."

Jefferson raised himself up straight again, shifted his shoulders under his jacket, and set his jaw. He had not meant to stay so long.

"I like a man to speak to me," he said. "I like to know what a man's got to say."

Urban set his hand to his desk. "You won't get that," he said. "Near as I can tell Harry Littlebourne came into this world believing the words of a Christian should be few and seasoned with grace. Leastways it would seem so." Riffling aimlessly through the papers on his desk he was somehow inspired to pursue a less direct path. "Where you got him now? Still over with Jethro Macy?"

Brother Shannon shook his head. "He's no carpenter, nor tinsmith neither, Urban. Jethro stood to the task as best he could, but it was never very likely. There's apples yet, though, and the sweet potatoes got to go in soon, so Cyrus Blakey's got good use for him. He's got the heart of a farmer; we might as well oblige it."

Johns nodded. "He's a farmer's son."

"I mean always to encourage him in obedience, lest he fail," Jefferson said, concerned by his own peculiar and uncustomary lack of confidence, "but I don't know him to know what that means."

"A man never knows," said Urban, "but this I'll tell you: that boy moves through the world 'thout the smallest notion that it's there. There are lessons in him for all of us."

"Sure you're right," Jefferson replied, but his problem seemed still to be just where it had been when he brought it in and set it down.

"Let me ask you this," Urban began, suddenly seized by inspiration. "You see any objection to letting Brother Austin take Harry in hand?"

"What for?" asked Jefferson. "You'll never get a tanner out of that boy."

"That's not where the road goes," said Urban, leaning forward in his chair. "What I mean is, there doesn't seem to be a man alive Austin Innes can't strike up a conversation with. A man who doesn't talk at all would at least make up a challenge."

"Austin's only still up the North hisself," said Jefferson with slow gravity. Innes had not yet signed the covenant that made of him a Believer true and proper, all of which Urban Johns knew as well as his companion. "You figuring to move him to the Center 'fore long?"

Urban shook his head. "There's perdition yet aplenty to be burned out of that young man's soul," he said, "and we're both of us content enough to leave him where he is. But I trust him. One thing you got to keep after you give it to someone else is your word, and that's the breath of life to Austin. So you ask him. See what he says."

It was unfair even to say Harry Littlebourne was unaccustomed to life as he found it at South Union. Never in his life had he come upon so many people living in one house; never in his life had he imagined he would abide in such proximity to anyone, much less the several men and women he was set amongst at the Gathering Order. So rich was the diversity of the Bible stories on which he had cut the teeth of his earthly aspirations that he supposed he might have expected the stories of those who followed it to be as compelling. Still, in those first days, he could make neither head nor tail of the lives with which his own meager experience was meant to reside in the harmony common amongst angels.

Harry shared his retiring room with a young man from nearby Bowling Green, a towhead who gave his name as Meese Gillies and whose reasons for being in this place Harry might have questioned in brotherly fashion had he been more worldly in his understanding.

Not being thus, however, he listened with great patience of an evening to Meese, who poured out his battered heart and its tale of love denied by the beautiful Hetta Sutter. Pious Hetta had been gathered in to South Union just months ago, carried to such extreme behavior by her enthusiasm for Shaker preachers she had chanced to hear. Invited finally to come one Sabbath morning to watch the brethren and sisters "laboring to get good," as they called it – dancing and marching to trample underfoot the sin of worldly life – Hetta looked her fill, took careful notice, and soon enough believed.

"Was Jesus," Meese told Harry earnestly, "said He knew wasn't just everybody could live like He done, but them as could was welcome to try, and my angel she reckoned the Lamb had her in mind particular."

With her mind made up, and having taken to serious heart the opinion of Saint Paul that "Those who marry do well, but those who abstain do better," the fickle Hetta paused not an instant to inform her intended of her intentions but allowed herself to be gathered in unbeknownst to him. Her mother, too distraught at this scandalous turn of events (the Shakers then being the objects of considerable scorn and hilarity in Bowling Green) to tell Meese outright where her wandering girl had gone, simply pointed in the direction of the Great Road and left the rest to his imagination. Once he had run the thief of his heart to ground, however, young Gillies declined to leave her, and thus convinced South Union's elders his mind was set on the life of a Believer – although in fact no one much doubted that what he believed more than anything else was that his Hetta would come away with him again if he could only have a chance to wear her down. By this diversion he was able to lay his head under the same roof as the girl of his dreams, although in this New Jerusalem their pillows would ever be in separate rooms.

Sadly Meese Gillies was learning later rather than sooner to what a resolute young woman he had plied his suit, but he was slow to daunt. His daily efforts to see Hetta alone were tireless, and each evening before the candles were doused he delivered a report of his progress to Harry with the fervency Harry supposed he might better have devoted to prayer.

"Stayed by just a minute or two this morning, and seen her for a word," he said with pride on his brightest evenings. Each day, after the brethren vacated their retiring rooms on their way to the work of the morning, the sisters came through and peeled back the bedding, stretching it over the backs of chairs to give it airing. It was Meese's frequent contrivance to hang back on such occasions, hoping it might be Hetta who came to see to the chore. Often enough to keep him happy he succeeded, but just as often Hetta sent him away with a flea in his ear.

"Good spirits will not live where there is dirt," she told him, brandishing a broom and Mother Ann Lee's own true words to let him know her mind was made up.

The thwarted lover was unfazed by Harry's lack of response to his nightly discourse, but chose instead always to see his silent cellmate as a confederate in this attempt to win the rebellious Hetta back to him. He could not have understood that, however long or passionately he described his need for Hetta and her attentions, he would not make his companion understand the true nature of his predicament. Harry's isolation was deeper than his silence, and less scrutable.

Having never had a sister, and unable as he was to summon the slightest memory of his mother, Harry saw the sisters of South Union moving around him, happy in their busy orbit, and could imagine nothing more purposeful than the lives they led. Through their efforts the log house around them smelled of clean air, scrubbed linen, fresh bread and peaceful assurance. The sisters were not unfamiliar with the brethren, but – the orders of Shaker life being such – neither did they accord them any undue familiarity. Not for no reason did Believers refer to each other as Brother and Sister; it was the lesson of their very existence. With their retiring rooms separate and inviolate across the passage from one another, seldom did the brethren see the sisters at their ease or even at their labors, but there was evidence aplenty that what they did they did with cheerful industry: clothes were mended and tidy and in season, floors were swept, windows were opened and closed to the sweet air, soap and candles were made and put to clever use. One hand was not necessarily aware of the actions of the other, but the two hands working in concert built an untroubled life for them all. This, he had been told by the patient Brother Jefferson, reflected the fraternal life of the angels – to which they at South Union aspired. Certainly Hetta Sutter was within her rights to give in to the relentless pursuit of Meese Gillies and go away from this place to live a life with him, but if there was a sensible reason for this course of action Harry could not, from the proof of his own life, imagine what it was.

Austin Innes saw Harry Littlebourne in his travels round and about; indeed it was difficult to miss Harry, with his great height and his black hair and his skin the color of best brown brick. Cyrus Blakey had put him to work in the gardens by the North family, Austin's own dwelling house, and often the tanner passed the gardener at his industry on his way to his own work. Once or twice he made mention of the kindness of the morning, but the boy made him no reply, and he was reluctant to urge him on so small a matter. Mother Ann Lee had asked those who followed her to do their work as if they had a thousand years to live and as if they might die tomorrow, and Austin would not meddle in the boy's resolve to obey. But Brother Urban had asked him to keep an eye on Harry Littlebourne, to take notice of his deliberations sound or unsound, and he would do so. When time came to speak he would do that, too.

There was a scream and Harry knew as the sound reached his ears that it was Hetta. He had left the house only a minute or two before, with a belly full of breakfast and his feet now in the road on his way up to the gardens. He turned his head but knew his purpose was not to look but to be where he looked, and he ran back to the log house, holding his hat fast to his head lest the breeze catch its wide brim and send it on an adventure of its own.

He followed the trail of voices and recognized the way back to his own retiring room, at whose open door a cluster of the sisterhood stood, sheltering Hetta amongst them, as if unable to go that single step that would take them inside. Knowing he must

Harry waded gently through, and his breath caught in his throat like sawdust as he saw the source of their reluctance. From a log beam in the low rafters Meese Gillies dangled by a short length of rope. His feet drifted to and fro, close by them the chair across which Hetta might have pulled his bedlinen for airing had he not chosen to usurp its use for his own melancholy purpose. Harry turned to the sisters and saw Hetta fall limp in the arms nearest her, and from beyond them all, in the passage, he heard a low voice call, "Let's us get him down, Brother Harry. You help me get him down."

Jefferson Shannon's head and shoulders came through the pale little thicket of linen caps that stood by the door, and Harry saw the man's resolute eyes and felt the presence of a strength he had not known since his father was alive. Brother Jefferson tipped the chair back down on its four legs with the toe of his boot and as he did so stepped up on its seat. His hand went to his pocket in pursuit of a knife, and Harry saw Meese Gillies' lifeless legs rise as for a moment Jefferson took the body in his arms.

"You take his legs, brother, and I'll cut the rope," came the instruction from above his head, and Harry wrapped his arms around Gillies' knees, hoping with all the child that remained in him that Meese would twist suddenly as if to free himself. With an abrupt jerk Harry felt the weight fall to his responsibility, just for an instant, while Jefferson stepped down from the chair.

Together they carried the earthly remains of Meese Gillies down the hall, and laid him gently on a worktable ready for the ministrations of the sisters. Harry Littlebourne looked into the startled eyes of the young man he had waked up nearby not much more than an hour ago, eyes that had shaken the sleep away after a dream that must at last have convinced him the dreams of his youth would not see daylight. Down the passage he heard Hetta crying, heard the sisters as they tried to calm her. Was it for this? he asked himself.

He did not notice how Jefferson Shannon studied on him, but when the hand came to his shoulder he knew it was there. "Best not to be brooding," he said quietly. "Comes the time you might know the sadness was all for nothing." He reached over with his free hand and a touch of his thumb and forefinger closed Meese Gillies' green and staring eyes. "He knows that now." With a slight tug at Harry's shoulder he added: "And you know it now. Do him credit if you remember it."

When her mind had cleared, Hetta told the elders Meese's people would want him home for grieving, and in the evening Brother Eli McLean took him in the Shakers' best wagon back from whence he came. Next morning Hetta Sutter too was gone without word. What Meese Gillies had not won fairly through persuasion he had stolen with a short length of rope, and it was the irony that had changed her mind, rather than his feelings for her. Whatever her reasons, she could not tarry longer amongst them, and in the morning her place at the sisters' dining table was empty. In the kitchen the usual singing and girlish gabble was hushed, for they were none of them so long gone from the world that they did not know the truth of what had happened. Meese could not live with Hetta and at the same time live without her. Without him, Hetta could not live alone.

If it was not easy to pursue the life of an angel, Harry Littlebourne thought long years after, and when he thought of Meese Gillies and his Hetta, how much more difficult must it be to elect the other path? To live in the world the way world's folk must do – it was beyond him.

Sitting by the steps of the dwelling house that Sabbath afternoon Harry watched the children at play and tried to pick out a child whose voice was all he knew. Whether boy or girl, he couldn't say, nor even if it was one of these children at all, there being others in dwellings elsewhere in the village. These young ones – the children of men and women not yet decided to remain amongst the Believers – were jacketed against the autumn afternoon, one of them with a handkerchief tied snug around his eyes. The Burke children were keen players of blind man's bluff, had begged Harry to play with them until he gave in, and on a few occasions he had been It. He saw now the helpless, flailing arms of the boy who this day was It, and willed him toward the child nearest, then winced when the nimble quarry escaped. He could not say, just looking, which child had spoken, or whether.

It was at meeting for worship that morning that he had set himself to this peculiar task. The children's benches sat behind those of the grown brethren and sisters, and most often the children did not speak during meeting at all. Whether the light passed them by, to settle on the older folks and move them to speak at meeting, or whether the littlest ones were shy to share the gifts given them, Harry wasn't prepared to say. But the children's voices were seldom heard.

This Sabbath though – just after Sister Jane Wing made mention of the importance of owing nothing to anyone save love and good will – there was a clatter of small boots on the bright floorboards, and the nervous flutter of childish hands and voices that came always before one of their number ventured to speak.

Then a small voice said: "I think about stars, at night mostly."

The speaker seemed to pause to recollect the sight of far-off specks of night light seen from the open window, and gathered inspiration. "I wonder sometimes what stars could be, really, and maybe I think I know."

Another pause, then this:

"I reckon stars is gimlet holes, to let the glory through."

Harry turned quickly to see what child had spoken, and saw no small head standing high above the rest, saw no other brother or sister betray by eye or hand that the child's words had reached the ear. All remained Sabbath-still, and it was as if nothing had happened, and he turned back to look at his hands folded in his lap. Perhaps no earthly child had spoken at all. Perhaps the voice was his own. Perhaps he had been talking to himself.

*   *   *

Austin Innes found him there, still sitting, watching the children. There was peril in the tanner venturing too close to children at play, for already the young ones had found in him a clever storyteller, and if he tarried too long in their proximity he was prone to accumulate a lapful of hopeful listeners. Still, Austin considered the events of recent days made the gamble worthy of the game: this quiet boy, troubled by the death of one who might after all have been his friend (if it had been possible to tell), might have as great a need to listen as another might have to speak.

He tucked his feet under him and crouched next to Harry in the grass.

"There's serious talk now about the East folks gettin' a brick dwelling house," he said. " 'Bout time, too: been just the log'n long enough, I'd say."

Harry looked up, but his face said he was happy enough with things as they were.

"Heaven never intended we should be permanently content with things we have the power to improve," Austin said in a manner most unlike his own and, having made his point, abandoned the subject. It was his nature to try again. "They do say of young'ns here," he began, casting his hand in the general direction of the wriggling game of blind man's bluff, "that it's best to keep their minds filled with good thoughts, so's bad ones have no room to enter." He gathered a few long grasses in his fingers and pulled at them. "Hard to believe, to look at 'em like that, that there's a bad thought to find amongst 'em."

Harry looked at him, then back to the swirling, shrieking children.

"I remember once – maybe it was at meeting, maybe not – there was one of the boys piped up, 'I do wish the Lord would make us all gooder and gooder, til there is no bad left.' I've wondered since, is that boy still amongst us? And I wish I could recall him, but I can't. I suppose he's done well in life if I recollect his words. We do each other great kindness in the lessons we teach, however we teach them."

He knew that Harry was listening; the look was in his eyes. But he was watching, too, now distracted slightly by a vision that had suddenly revealed itself amid the tangle of bluffers. Harry had not noticed her before: she was smaller than most of them – not yet three years old, perhaps – and dressed in magnificent woollens the like of which these Shaker little ones would never wear. But more than that about her was her face, round and sweet and guileless as that of no child he had ever seen, touched with a rosy color that nodded around the dimples in her cheeks, and surrounded by hair the color of sunlight. She seemed not of this earth, and surely was not of this place, and he wondered at her.

"She'll break a man's heart someday, you watch her," said Austin, and sat himself and fumbled for his pipe as a once-whole man feels for his amputated leg. Years had passed since he last had had a smoke, but the memory remained fresh and dear.

Harry looked at him, surprised.

Austin smiled. They did not know how old Harry was, nor yet how young. "Child like that knows what she is," he said. "She's cut her teeth on her papa's heart, but more than one young buck will feel the bite before she chooses proper."

Another look at the tiny child – now raising her arms to catch at the fading rays of light that came through the leaves of the sugar maple trees, having abandoned hope of joining the big ones' game – and he looked to Austin again.

The older man laughed, and took off his hat to shake clear the red hair from his eyes. "Don't mistake me, boy. I'm not saying she's a bad child, or bad will come of her. She can't help being a beauty, any more than a man can help how he feels about the figure of a woman that'll come of her. A man can only decide what he'll make of how he feels."

Harry's eyes were full of a question, and Austin knew what it was.

"And that I know because I've known women in the world, known often," he said without pride, "and in the knowing I'd guess I got me ones of those – maybe not so fair as her, or maybe boys, ginger-headed ones – who're lucky not to know me. Lucky for me, I reckon, that it's the sin and not the sinner we despise." With the brim of his hat he pointed to the breathless, giggling little girl. "A child like that, nor any child, should know no bad men, nor thoughts, nor days."

Harry found now that he was drawn to this little man, who clearly knew so much more of the world than he, and had left it outside the gates of this earthly Heaven – without regret?

"What you don't overcome in this world just gets more powerful in the next," Austin Innes told him, as if he could see down the corridors of Harry's mind. "When I was a young man," he said, "I think I thought I'd go to my grave someday and leave the world behind. Now," and there was a fresh passion to his voice, "I reckon if I don't shake the world off while I'm breathing yet, I'll have more of it to deal with then than I do now."

It was then that they noticed the child had stopped in her small tracks, had abandoned her pursuit of elusive sunbeams, and was looking at them – looking at Harry, as if she could see no one else in the world and never would.

"That's Shaw Mason Hannon's youngest, May Howard," Austin said. "Shaw Hannon? His place is just yonder..." He indicated a spot north of that where they sat, but Harry shrugged. "Her mama comes by now and again to see to medicines with the sisters." He peered deep into the circle of children and found one missing. "Teddy must be gone to school, else he'd be here. Their mama brings 'em when she comes, so they see another white child."

The little girl still stood, staring with her uncommonly blue eyes, and Brother Austin held out his hand. "May Howard," he called to her, beckoning, "it's allright. Come here and be sociable."

She staggered toward them, and put a hand in her mouth, and stood close to Harry, close enough to touch him if she dared.

"You don't know Brother Harry, Miss May," he said. "He's just new here. Can't you make him kindly welcome?"

She put her hand, still dewy from her mouth, on Harry's knee, but did not speak. On top of that small hand she placed the other, and Austin heard Harry gasp.

He saw the peculiar look in Harry Littlebourne's eyes, a kind of nameless warning, and his own hands tensed. "What is it, son?" he asked. "Looks like you've seen your own ghost."

The child tottered, took fright, and fled.

They did not see Joanna Hannon come to collect little May to take her home. But when the sisters came to take the children in, to clean them up and ready them for supper, she was not among them. It was as if she had vanished with the sun. The calling in of the children reminded Harry that he had not in recent hours visited the barn to check on the welfare of his horse, and wordlessly he gathered himself on his long legs to a standing position, and with polite but distant notice took his leave of Austin Innes.

Innes sat awhile longer, enjoying the approach of evening. He did not often come this way, and to sit by the East dwelling was something akin to visiting a foreign nation. He smiled at the thought: how far he had come, and how many places he had been in his life, to sit a quarter-mile from his home and think himself a nomad. But in the quiet he could feel himself alone, and in this community of souls which he had grown in his fashion to love he nonetheless knew solitude as a precious commodity.

The sisters would be ringing the supper bell at all the dwelling houses before long, and he must get on or be late; thus he stood and breathed deep the smell of autumn and turned back in the direction from which he had lately come. Finding himself at the crossroads, however, Brother Austin made not for the North but for the ministry, and called in to talk to Urban Johns. He had not much to say, but might as well take the first opportunity to say it, and he was pleased to find Urban alone.

"Evening, brother," said Johns, busy with his Bible yet happy enough to be distracted. Bound to all Believers by faith and doctrine and Christian brotherhood, he knew his affection for this sometimes brash young man to be a bond of simple friendship. He could not remember being less than glad of his company. "Hasn't it just been the Lord's own day?"

Austin smiled, and took his hat off, and knew that whatever Urban Johns knew about the weather he almost certainly knew only by happenstance of looking out the window. "Haven't had much chance to talk to the Littlebourne boy til now," Innes said apologetically, "but he was out back the East after dinner and I happened by."

"Sad about young Gillies," said Urban, his delight in the temperature fading in the face of this reminder. "Harry took it hard, I reckon, them being so close put."

Austin shrugged. "Hard to say," he replied. "You know how little you'll hear from Harry Littlebourne in an afternoon." He slid into a chair, and stretched his legs out, and put his hat on his knee. "But you were wondering does he know his own mind, or maybe it was Brother Jefferson."

"Probably it's a bit of both," Urban replied. "He's no more than a boy, and some decisions take more than a boy to make."

Austin's smile now was for himself, and he suspected Urban was smiling with him. But it was Harry's heart, not his own, that was the subject of scrutiny here. "Leave him be, Urban," Austin said. "Move him to the Center, let him farm, and leave him be."

"Now, Austin," said the even-handed Urban, "can't anyone say..."

"I'll tell you this, because I believe it," Austin said with all the firmness that was in him. "There's no need for Harry Littlebourne to leave the world. He was never in it."

*   *   *

It was as Harry came away from the barn between the West and Center that he saw the door of the ministry open and Brother Innes emerge, twirling his hat on his forefinger and heading back to the North. Harry stopped where he was and looked long, as if he could look hard enough to understand the heart of this odd, endearing fellow. He did not know much about South Union, but he knew the little man with his bright red hair and his walk that spoke of miles travelled in a world unknown to most men was out-of-place in this company. He did not know it would be years before they spoke again, and he wondered by what route Austin Innes had come, that he had found South Union at the end of it.

1855

A ustin Innes came into wakefulness. These were troubled times, and his years on the river had served him well, teaching him as they had to keep his ears open asleep as awake. It was only January that eight world's men – Dr. Boanarges Rhea and John McCutcheon and with them a nest of others who bore the Believers no good will – came and took Brother James Richards from his bed, then had Sheriff Clark lock him up in the Logan County Jail over at Russellville and charge him with poking his nose in the affairs of their Negroes. At South Union of recent there was a gift that the careful life they pursued together could not be preserved without considerable care, and perforce Austin Innes was careful, as were they all – or tried to be.

Austin rolled from his bed, lit the candle and loped down the brethren's staircase to the Center's front door, his brilliant red hair lit by the flickering candle and the memory of summer fire.

Tossing up the crossbar, he opened the door wide and lifted his candle high. There was nothing there to see. He stood still, his linen nightshirt whipping gently around his knees as the air through the door was drawn by the windows. The little schoolmaster looked west down the Russellville road – was that a sound, just there? –

and thought first to ask whether anyone was about. But with the village so peacefully in sleep and no obvious intruder in sight he held his tongue. Instead he stood for a long moment in the night air, listening, and savored the unfamiliar solitude until he had it in mind that he could hear no movement not easily credited to the leaves moving in the trees around him.

Barefoot he stepped out onto the cold stone of the south porch, dancing slightly as he moved off the smooth white oak panels of the floor, and raised his light still higher. With the help of the moonlight he could see to the ministry shop across the road. The candle fluttered and Austin Innes brought it back to him, shielding the little flame with his free hand. His fingers glowed golden in the dark.

He shook the hair from his face and gave the night sky and the village of South Union a last look. Satisfied, the schoolmaster stepped backwards into the house, closed the door, lowered the bar, and went back to bed.

1859

Amos lay on the floor, on his back, dancing a wooden horse and cow across his breastbone. The paint on both had chipped and faded since some brother or other had carved them from scraps in the carpenters' shops, but the Shaker children who had played with them in the intervening years had not objected. The two in Amos' hands were only the tenth part of a menagerie that numbered a score and more, a collection of barnyard critters that sheltered overnight in a little wooden barn – most likely the work of the same craftsman. Elsewhere in the same room the young shepherd Andrew Bailey was guiding wooden sheep through the barn's open doors; Amos, lolling on the patchwork rug, was more interested in his mismatched team of yoke stock.

The smell of soap, fresh linen and scrubbed child hung in the air above the small bodies reaching the end of their day. Their chores, such as they were, were finished, and the littlest ones were free to amuse themselves while the boys of school age were puzzling over whatever tasks Brother Austin had set them to finish by morning. Three floors below, the dining room had been tidied, the shortbacked chairs stored in orderly fashion beneath the long wooden tables, the bare floors broomed clear of rogue crumbs and the day's dust. The kitchen sisters had seen to the cooking things and dishes with the help of the older girls, and whatever remained of the evening meal had been put by for soup tomorrow, or soap perhaps – nothing was wasted. Elsewhere in the house the brethren and sisters had dispatched themselves to union meetings from which they would drift back presently. On the second floor, in the retiring room by the brethren's staircase, Brother Austin was looking to tomorrow's lessons, his ear open to disaster in the young ones' rooms up the next flight of stairs from him. He had little fear that his work would be disturbed: in the hour or so before bedtime the littlest children contented themselves with quiet pursuits encouraged by the sisters, the better to wind them down and ready them for sleep. Thus engaged they could come to little grief. All the same he bent one ear in their direction.

Amos rolled over on his stomach and slid his beasts of burden back and forth across the patch of floor beneath his chin. He met cow and horse nose-to-nose with an almighty thump, then up-ended them and walked them in circles on their tails. Dogs could do it, and he supposed farm stock to be no less talented.

Footsteps sounded on the stairs below, the brethren on their way back, perhaps – but so soon? Amos glanced back over his shoulder and saw Brother Austin standing in the doorway, his shirtsleeves rolled to the elbow.

He stamped his boot heel lightly and addressed the company assembled on the floor. "I don't suppose there's anyone here wants to hear a story," he said flatly. The several small faces turned to him with some surprise. "Nay, I didn't suppose you would," he said, and turned towards the little girls' room.

Amos, closest to the door, was up like a rabbit and after him. Sliding into a dive on the hardwood floor he caught the schoolmaster by the ankles of his boots while Andrew took the little man by the knees. Thus hobbled, Austin Innes reached down and took Amos – still small enough to carry – in his arms.

"Well, then, I expect we'll just have to have a story..." he said with a shrug as he settled into the big rocker by the little window under the eaves. The youngest girls had come spilling out of their room and he swung Amos into his lap, so that the boy's bare legs dangled below his nightshirt over Austin's knees.

His offer of a story had taken the children by surprise because it so seldom came in wintertime. Austin Innes spent his warm-weather days in the tannery or the brethren's shop, making shoes and mending harness, and it was during those days that the girls had their schooling under the care of one of the sisters. But when the weather turned cold, come December or so, Brother Austin was called away from the tannery and took his cold-weather turn at the blackboard, charged as he was with the task of looking after the lessons of the boys – who would not be needed for planting, field-tending or harvest until the season began again come spring.

Austin in warm weather was a soft touch for stories. But in winter the children found he turned a deaf ear to most requests. "I get enough of hearing myself talk in the schoolhouse," he would tell them. And while this seemed a fair enough excuse for his silence through the winter months, when dark fell so early and the evenings felt so long, his absence from the story-telling rocker was nonetheless akin to punishment for sins the children had yet to commit.

Now, cross-legged on the floor or leaning against his knees, Brother Austin's listeners sat wide-eyed and wide-eared. Seldom in the classroom did a schoolmaster, even this one, have so grand an opportunity.

"So, what shall we have?" he asked his audience, white-clad and quiet like so many fresh little ghosts. He prodded five-year-old Nancy McClung with the square toe of his boot. "Nannie, you say and I'll tell it."

The mantle of responsibility fell hard upon the little girl. She ducked her head and pondered the question in silence, biting her lip before putting one finger in her mouth. Who knew when, or if,

Brother Austin would offer again before spring came? And if she squandered the opportunity on the wrong tale she knew the other children would be quick to say so.

Austin leaned down to her and peered out from beneath his long, red lashes. "Quickly, Nannie, quickly," he urged. "Candle's burnin'."

The blonde head suddenly bobbed up and he saw the face brightened by a flash of inspiration. "Mother Ann comes to America!" she said triumphantly.

"Mother Ann comes to America?" Austin asked after her, putting the choice to the vote of his constituency – as he always did when the request was not for the story of Jonah and the whale, his own personal favorite and cause enough to suspend the democratic process. They had had that last time; he was always amazed at how well they remembered. A thicket of hands rose to confirm Nancy's choice and the child sitting at his knee blushed with relief.

The faces turned up to him settled into attention and Brother Austin leaned forward slightly to meet their eyes.

"Don't you ever hear voices?" he asked them, his own voice quiet but lustrous in its intensity. "Isn't there ever that little voice comes up from way down inside to let you know what you ought to do and what you maybe oughtn't? Maybe you hear voices in your dreams, or when there's not much else to hear..."

Some of the children nodded. A few of the bigger boys, with their schoolwork done and attracted by the absence of hubbub, came away from their retiring room and stood leaning against the passage walls, arms folded across their chests and boots crossed at the ankles. They had all been raised on Brother Austin's stories, and their fascination with him and them remained fresh.

"Well, Mother Ann heard voices," Austin continued. "Voices come down from Heaven spoke to her heart and told her to preach what you and I believe, that we should come away from the world and live as brothers and sisters in peace and in the fear of God. There was some as believed her, but more that couldn't understand.

So. What do you think happened?"

"They whupped her terrible and put her in the jailhouse," said the shepherd Andrew, now absent of his wooden sheep.

"That they did," said Austin. "Her countryfolk in the English land just didn't know what to make of her and her Believers, what with dancing like David before the ark and singing the way they did. So whenever folks caught her and her Believers at their laboring or marching it went hard for them, and there came a time when Mother Ann reckoned they'd done what they could do in their own land and it was time to move on. So what would you say happened?"

"She heard a voice!" cried Naomi Carey from somewhere to Austin's left.

The schoolmaster touched a finger to the side of his nose and slapped his knee – which made Amos jump – and nodded.

"A voice, sure enough, and just as plain as you hear me now, Naomi," he said. "And what did that voice tell Mother Ann?"

"It told her to take the Believers to America!"

"That's just what it told her, and so she did," said Brother Austin. "And, John Perryman – " he pointed to one of the bigger boys " – what day would you sat they set sail, and whereaway?"

"From Liverpool on the tenth of May, 1774," the young man replied with some satisfaction.

"Right you are," said Austin, having arrived at the shoreline of his tale and being now in full baritone sail. "They left Liverpool aboard the ship *Mariah*, no lion of a craft but seaworthy, with her good captain Smith at the helm to see them safe bound for the port of New York. So went Mother Ann and her Believers to bring the vision to America, but it wasn't to be so easy..."

Amos' mind wandered close to the edge of sleep, lured there by the warmth of Brother Austin's voice. It was unlike anyone's voice he had ever heard, deep and rich and rumblesome and more like the sound of singing than talking. Sister Elizabeth

Barrie said it was because Brother Austin was "not from around here," but there was more magic than geography in the schoolmaster's voice, which brought the skeptical to trust and the wicked to obedience. This gift not of his own making embarrassed Austin considerably, and his fair cheeks reddened at the mention of it. He was always quick to point out that he could not sing.

With his head just beneath Brother Austin's chin, his body settled against the little man's chest, Amos felt the unfolding saga ring through his bones like a genial hand tickling his back. Ever closer to sleep, he braided his dreaming fingers in the long, broad waves of red hair that fell behind the schoolmaster's ear. Austin's warm, even breathing, the rocking of the chair, worked on Amos like a potion. He struggled to stay awake, but with each nod of his chin his eyes dimmed until finally his lashes closed the light out altogether. Brother Austin felt the difference in the boy's weight and shifted him slightly in his arms, never breaking the rhythm of his story.

"...And then the storm came, a monstrous raging gale fit for great Saint Elmo's flickering fire, full of wind and thunder and crashing rain," he said. "The ship pitched from side to side on that cruel Atlantic Ocean, tossing Mother Ann and all aboard like goosefeathers in a pillow fight. A plank broke loose, and in came the salty seawater like a battering ram, until the deck swam like the dreadful sea itself and the captain feared the very worst. He called every man jack and woman to the pumps, and pump they did as if their lives depended on it, and true enough they did depend on it. Even so, the captain of the good *Mariah* despaired of getting her whole to New York, so badly did it go on that angry sea. 'We shall founder,' he told them, and sure he believed they would do just that with the lightning cracking above them and the seas beating them from every side and the deck swimming under their feet."

He let the little ones ponder the danger – how close they had come to losing dear Mother Ann, and where would they be if so awful a thing as that had happened? – and then sailed on.

"Then there was a voice, and whose do you think it was? It was Mother Ann Lee's, raised up to quiet the fears of the captain and crew and all aboard that ship *Mariah*."

"What did she say?" came the tiny voice of Nancy McClung, now sitting with her chin on Austin's knee.

"Hush awhile and I'll tell you," the schoolmaster said, laying his hand on the little blonde head and dropping his voice to just above a whisper. "She looked out over that sodden deck, flooded and awash with seawater as it was, and told them not a hair on their heads would be lost..."

"Not a hair," one spellbound child murmured after him.

"...and every last one of them who'd set sail from Liverpool would walk safely on the other shore. She told them how she'd stood at the foot of the great mast, and how she'd seen before her two of God's bright angels, just as if I was looking at you. Those angels had promised them all safe passage, and – just as she spoke – a great wave came and crashed like thunder against the leaking plank and knocked it back where it was meant to be, true and tight and dry as the day it was made. Then all those tired, fearful people, who'd been pumping those many hours to save their own lives, they knew they could draw a breath in peace."

Tension eased in the little bodies at his feet as they felt the danger pass, and Nancy smiled. "Then what did Mother Ann say?" she asked.

Austin Innes let go his enormous, talking laugh and said, "Time for bed! Mother Ann says it's time for you young'ns to be in your beds, so prayers first and then to sleep with ye!"

The children wheeled and scattered like geese, even the big ones, to their retiring rooms either side of the broad passage, and Brother Austin – still holding the sleeping Amos – settled back in the rocker.

Sister Elizabeth Barrie appeared at the top of the sisters' staircase, with some abandoned plaything in her hand, to see the youngest safely to their beds.

"Shall I take him from thee, Brother Austin?" she asked quietly.

"Nay, nay, I've got him," Austin said. Rising and stretching his groggy legs, even at his full height he was no taller than Sister Elizabeth. "But I thank thee kindly for the offer."

"Thee's kindly welcome," she said, leaning a bit to peer into the little girls' room, the better to measure their progress. "I'll say goodnight then."

"And to thee, sister. God bless thee."

"And thee, brother."

Austin carried Amos back down the hall to the little boys' room, where next to their small, low beds the children knelt earnest at their retiring prayers. Smoothing the boy's blanket over him, brushing the brown hair back from his forehead, Austin marvelled at the ease with which children found sleep, and how deeply they slept. It was a gift he had never shared, and he was dismayed to identify his feelings as envy.

The little horse and cow lay by his feet, still near the patchwork rug where Amos in his careless haste had left them. As the children finished their prayers and climbed into bed Austin stooped and took them in his hand. Next to Andrew's bed the barn – now full of wooden sheep and chickens ready for whatever rest wooden animals take – stood open, and Austin set Amos' forgotten charges close by.

The boys softly called out their goodnights to him, and as he squeezed out the candle flame between his thumb and forefinger he heard the last few stirrings that preceded sleep.

"God bless thee, young'ns," he said, but still he lingered, his shoulder pressed against the doorjamb. He stood watching his boys settle for the night and wondered if he'd done wrong by not waking Amos for prayers before putting him to bed.

Not so, he thought to himself.

"Thy life is thy prayer tonight, Amos," he whispered to the darkness, then walked back down the stairs to his own room.

1860

The image of the long, slender man walking up the Great Road, followed at a respectful distance by the big piebald, was not one that any longer attracted much attention at South Union, so much a part of life there had it become. The name of the man was Harry Littlebourne; he lived among the brethren at the Center. The piebald was Old Sorrow, a resident of the stables just north of the turning to the fulling mill. They had known each other for years and were great companions. An able farmer, for whom Robert Johns among others of the brethren joked that a broomstick stuck in the ground was likely to grow, Brother Harry spent sufficient of his time with the big plough horse, one way and another, to render such a relationship understandable. On the other hand Old Sorrow's affection for and loyalty to Harry Littlebourne were like none anyone could recall in any animal, even a dog, let alone a horse. At times the two seemed almost to be engaged in serious conversation.

Although Old Sorrow most often followed Harry, without benefit of halter or similar compulsion, at a distance of a few feet, his great head swinging as he did so, the pair of them were also known of occasion to walk astride. The brethren would see them, horse and man keeping a similar and easy pace, making their way from one place to another in the course of their employment, and it was easy to wonder as one watched them whether the topic under discussion was religion or politics – although most everyone knew Harry Littlebourne took scant notice of politics. Of the horse it was not possible to say for sure. Either way, it was common knowledge in the village that Brother Harry was no talker, and perforce the brethren assumed that whatever he might have to say to anyone he was most likely to take up with Old Sorrow first, just to test the waters.

If the little schoolmaster Innes had established himself over time as the shortest of South Union's male population – as other than the children he most often was – then Harry Littlebourne was surely the tallest, and as dark as Brother Austin was fair. Well over six and a half feet tall when finally he stopped growing, Brother Harry stood an easy head and more higher than Innes, who at his very straightest scarcely came up to the farmer's shoulder. Harry's wiry frame, which belied his considerable strength, made him seem even taller, as if in his youth he had made his mind up to walk always on stilts.

When Harry and Austin happened upon each other in the village, as was sometimes sensible – particularly during the summer months, when it was quite natural for those who tended the harness to consult with those who walked behind the plough – the two men made something of a comical picture.

Years among the brethren had taught Austin Innes to adopt what might have seemed to some to be the vanity of standing with his head cocked to one side, looking up out of the corners of his eyes at whomever happened to be addressing him. The same had developed in Harry Littlebourne a tendency to stand with his shoulder bent, one ear down, the better to hear voices that emanated from closer to the earth (Brother Urban Johns would sometimes say that Brother Harry was perhaps in a better position than many to hear the word of God, being after all that much closer to Him, but if this was so, Harry kept God's confidence and never said). The effect of these two singular stances, prompted by physical necessity, was that either man could be recognized easily from any point in the village, if he could be seen clearly, by his height and his posture or by his coloring. Or if, in Brother Harry's case, he was being followed at a discreet distance by a piebald plough horse.

It was not so bad this year as that winter of '57, but the January just gone had been plenty cold enough for anyone who warmed to the idea of freezing. It was a good time to cut ice for the ice house, and this the brethren – among them Harry, and with him Old Sorrow – had spent the best part of a week doing. Some score and ten loads had been stacked onto wagons and hauled over to the Center to be strawed up and stored away for summer, not quite so many to the North but still a good few, all of it fine solid ice that measured some three inches thick.

On the first day of February the snow had fallen four inches deep around South Union and the mercury had risen to just four degrees of temperature above the freezing mark. Thereabouts it hovered stubbornly over the few days that followed. Brother Harry did not take this unkindly for he had a fondness for snow, and for the general quiet it encouraged around the place. Out in one of the south meadowlands burning brush all day he'd looked at the rolling white landscape and wondered whether the last two people on the earth would take the same view of the property as had the first two. Certainly out there on his own, holding his hands over his fire, he had an idea of what it must be like to be all there was to humanity. But the feeling was deceptive and he knew it: Adam in the same situation had not had the luxury of knowing most everyone else was up at Black Lick sugar camp, out tapping trees or getting set up for making molasses.

The day was lowering, and Harry was on his way back in, crunching down the road past the East toward the stables, keeping his head low to save his watering eyes from the freezing wind. He heard the hot breath of the horse behind him change rhythm and looked up. It did not much surprise him to see, farther along the road, some brother or other – at this distance he could not tell which – motioning to him, a beckoning wave that led him away from his path to the river. He altered his line of progress and quickened his pace a bit, the better not to keep his brother waiting, and saw as he neared the crossroads that it was Brother Cyrus Blakey who stood shivering in the sharp air this early February evening.

"Brother Urban asked if I'd keep an eye out for you," Brother Cyrus said, having not waited for Harry's greeting because he knew there would not be one. "He figured you'd be on your way back in from out and he'd like to see you 'fore you get there."

Harry smiled amiably and nodded, then put a salutory finger to his hatbrim before he and Old Sorrow walked on, leaving Cyrus to draw his coat about him and scurry on back to the Center and its warm stoves.

Past the crossroads, before the meeting house, he pulled left to the ministry shop and took the few steps in one. At the door he turned back over his shoulder and exchanged a look with the horse. Old Sorrow seemed to take with understanding whatever message had been given him, and with that in mind he planted his hooves and lowered his head to browse amongst the snowfall's remains for whatever of interest might lie beneath.

Inside the office Brother Urban heard the activity at the door, but he waited to hear it open before raising his gaze from the books spread before him. "Ah, Brother Harry," he said genially. "Cyrus found you. That's fine." He glanced out the window and saw the horse waiting, patient and untethered, by the steps. "Sometimes I wonder he doesn't just come in with you."

Harry grinned and regarded his large feet, one ear down.

Urban had known Harry Littlebourne since the day he arrived at South Union, that dozen years ago, a confused and quiet boy who grew into a shy and quiet man, a fine Believer, an enigma the brethren pondered with gratitude and affection. Over the years the young man had devised in his face a kind of sign language, a winking of the eyes, a wriggling of the eyebrows, a looking up and looking down, that the Believers had learned to perceive as spoken language in much the same way those who hear understand the deaf who use their hands to speak. Such were the accommodations people here made for one another. And as Urban watched Brother Harry survey his legs and the floorboards, as if they might soon give way and send him crashing to the ground beneath, he heard – almost as if the man himself had spoken – a question asked. Harry went about his life at South Union with cheerful obedience and admirable ability, and as Urban had never before asked to see him in his ministerial capacity it was only sensible that Harry should have questions.

"Well," Urban said, leaning back in his chair, "Brother Austin came by to see me yesterday." He waved Harry into a chair by the stove and Harry eased into it, peering before he did so through the frosted window to check the well-being of the big horse. "The boys are in school. Always seems so very quiet around here when Austin has 'em, doesn't it? Always does to me, leastways. When Brother John has them all out and about they make a lovely noise, and I do truly miss it come wintertime."

Harry had folded his hands in his lap and was smiling at them politely, regarding his thumbs with some care.

"So, as I say, Brother Austin's got all the boys in the schoolhouse and he says it's been on him for quite a long week or so to come have a talk to me about little Amos."

The child lived upstairs at the Center and there was no reason to suppose Harry did not know of him, so Urban plunged on. "You remember when Nathaniel and Evangeline left. Powerful sad that was. I was among them that thought Nathaniel Anger could come good of himself here; surprised me like thunder when he took himself back to the world. Then Evangeline was gone without a word like that – you know, Austin thought he heard somebody

creeping around that night, it's a funny thing, must've been her –
and we didn't quite know what to do about Amos. Somehow I always
thought, well, she'll come back for the boy. She was always right
particular about him, not that she said but the sisters don't miss
out much, so I always looked for Evangeline to come back even if
we never saw Nathaniel again. But she didn't. We just never heard."

He crossed his arms and drummed his fingers on his elbow.
Urban Johns might have been talking to an empty room, but he had
no sense of being alone. "That's not a situation I like very much,"
he said, shaking his head and pursing his lips. "It's much better
when we have clear title to a child, something with his parents'
signatures on it so we're not so open to grief if there's trouble, and
you know there has been now and again. Now you could say we
shouldn't have let it tarry the way we have, and you'd be right: we
should have looked after the matter soon as we knew Evangeline
was gone. Maybe we ought to have turned him over to the sheriff
that very same day." He smiled and seemed to be examining an
image held up to the inward eye of his memory. "But the sisters
were so fond of him, and his mama had seemed so happy here,
and we all of us just kept on thinking she'd be back if we gave her
a day or two. And then it was another day, and another, and now
he's such a splendid little fellow, and – well, truth to tell I haven't
the heart to part with him myself after all this time. It would break
Eldress Nancy's heart. You can see, can't you?"

Brother Harry, who had been spinning his thumbs one over the
other in Brother Urban's direction, reversed them toward himself.

"Now, Brother John Perryman's a fine young man, and I think
he gives a good accounting of himself with the little boys, but
he's not much more than a boy when you come to look at it and
there's some things that come with age and experience," Urban
said. "What Austin had to say, and giving it a night's consideration
I'm inclined to agree with him, is that Amos could benefit from
someone who'd take a special interest in him."

Harry raised a curious eyebrow.

"True enough, and it's not something I'd suggest as a rule," Brother Urban said, moving quickly to take advantage of this burst of communication emanating from the chair by the stove. "Normally I think it's fit and right that we leave the care of the children to the caretakers, and as I say young John acquits himself admirably. But it's something we've seen here before, hard to put your finger on just so, but there's a look of abandonment that sometimes comes to a child that's just been skedaddled on the way that little man has, and Austin reckons Amos has it. Some of the boys have brothers and sisters or parents about, and the apprenticed boys get visits now and again, and it must seem a puzzlement to a child. The sisters see it, too, and when Austin brought it up to me I mentioned it in passing to Eldress Nancy and it made a deal of sense to both of us. He's smaller than he ought to be, for his years, and inclined to inwardness a little, and between you and me and the fencepost I think the good sisters hold him just a bit closer to the apron than is good for him."

Harry had begun drawing ever-widening circles on his thigh with his forefinger. His eye wandered to the window.

"So Brother Austin suggested we might just ask someone to keep a particular eye on Amos, and he thought you'd be the exact right man," Urban said.

Harry sat bolt upright, a look of pure alarm on his brown face, and Urban held up a steadying hand.

"Now, none of us menfolk knows any too much about children, Harry," Brother Johns said, his voice assuming a no-nonsense tone. "But the young'ns are our responsibility, just as much as they are the sisters'. We were all little boys once, and we all remember what it was like, and it seems to me if you let yourself you might just enjoy spending some time with Amos. Let him come out to the fields with you, if John Perryman doesn't need him, or have a talk with him on the Sabbath. He's a lovely little mite, bright as a new button. Just wants a little extra time with the brethren, I reckon."

Brother Harry's fears were not being calmed by any of this. So great did his agitation appear that Urban perceived him to be on the verge of actual speech.

"The Lord requires of us certain things, Brother Harry, and it seems to me not a great deal is being asked here that you can't with good cheer and considerable success provide," Brother Urban said, catching the man's eye and holding it fast with his own. "It's for us to remember always, always, what our Mother Ann told us, that the little ones are nearer the Kingdom of Heaven than are we who have more by way of years. She told us this, that 'Little children are simple and innocent; they should be brought up so; and they never ought to be brought out of it. If they were brought up in simplicity they would receive good, as easily as they would evil.' Doubtless, doubtless that is so."

A peculiar melancholy seemed to take him over quickly, and he appeared to be looking at Harry without seeing him. This Harry sensed, but by this understanding he felt constrained to pay more mind rather than less.

"Every child is good in his heart," Urban Johns said. "Every child is worth as much time and love as we can give. But the preciousness of every little one who may in time grow to a Believer is something we must understand, now as we have never done before." He sat forward in his chair, taking his weight on his elbows, aware of every minute of his fifty-eight years. He was not talking to Harry Littlebourne, and Harry was not sure who had taken his place at the receiving end of the estimable brother's conversation. "So many of us are getting old, so many of us are leaving," he said. "It's difficult to know from where new Believers will come in the years ahead." He was looking out the window now, through the gathering darkness that sat like a ghostly rider on Old Sorrow's back, past the animal's listening ears, past the calf lot to the tannery and the Gasper, all of it blue in this light from the snowfall. "And if friend Lincoln is elected, then what? Then what?" he asked. "Would that prayer would give us some look into that future. The world and all that's in it may seem very different to us then."

Harry's attention had turned inward, and when Urban returned his gaze to his silent companion he sensed his brother's absence but did not feel alone. Neither Johns nor anyone else knew where Harry went at these times, but whatever the location of his private spiritual oasis a visit there always left the traveller more sure of himself. Urban was thus content to await his return.

Suddenly Harry Littlebourne looked up and put his hands firmly on his knees, as if signalling that it was time for him to go.

"You'll help with this boy, Brother Harry, of that I'm sure," Urban said, agreeing with his companion's assessment that their present business was concluded. "It will mean a great deal to us all. And to the boy."

Harry stood and took his hat from the peg on which he'd dropped it when he arrived. Then, nodding again, and smiling a little, he took his leave.

Urban Johns watched through the window as the almost absurdly tall young man settled his hat over his coarse black hair and breathed deep the freezing air. Old Sorrow's head rose and tossed, wagging from side to side. Harry took the steps to ground in a single stride and resumed his course to the stables by the river, his long legs silhouetted against the white of the Great Road. The horse waited for a second or two, then followed.

Brother Urban was always delighted by this peculiar relationship between man and beast, an incalculable gift, and he watched them until they were out of sight. The interview had gone well, he thought. Towards the end Brother Littlebourne had seemed receptive to the idea. Still, Urban Johns wondered whether this would work in any way, shape or form. First and last it had been Brother Austin's idea, but he had seemed quite sure of his choice. No harm could come of trying the arrangement.

The ledger which he had closed at some point he now flipped open. He would stay a few more minutes – after his time in the trustees' office, from which he was on extended loan in Harvey Eades' absence, the habit of keeping a watchful eye on such matters was hard broken – then go back across the road to the Center. By the look of things, the mills were doing very well. This was no surprise to him, but it was gratifying to look in the mill deacon's books and see it all written out so plainly.

It was not an arrangement that implemented itself with noticeable speed. Urban and Austin looked for Harry to make himself known to the boy, but there was no sign, and Urban wondered how many days should pass before he reminded his quiet brother of the matter. He was reluctant to do so: Harry Littlebourne was a man of his word, however silently he had given it.

But things left undone too long tend to protest that neglect. On Sabbath Eve nearly two weeks later Austin was settled over a book in his retiring room, as was his habit on a winter's evening. He heard the light sound of bare feet but did not look up: the boys often came to his room at night for a spell of quiet away from the late raucity of their fellows. They were more greatly in need of his acceptance than his attention, and thus he most often took no notice of their arrivals and departures.

On this occasion it was Amos Anger, in his nightshirt and ready for sleep, who hoisted himself onto the nearest bed and twisted his hands in his lap. He looked for awhile with considerable interest at the fixtures around him, as if there might be something he had never seen before.

"Granderson Carey's mama was by this afternoon," he said in a sudden rush. Granderson had been absent from the schoolroom for several days, down with the croup. Only this morning had he been deemed fit for human companionship and released from the sickroom. "She wanted to see how he looked after being so poorly." Having drawn no response from his host he tried again. "They have the same name. Her name is Carey, too."

Austin quietly closed his book and turned on his elbow, resting his cheek on his fist and facing Amos square. "There's a reason for that," he said.

"There is?" The boy's face was brighter now that Innes had taken notice of him.

"It's a little complicated, but leave it at this: without Granderson Carey's mama there'd be no Granderson Carey to speak of, and that would be a sorrow to us all."

Amos reflected on this in silence. Then: "Granderson said she comes to see him because she loves him."

"That's very likely true," Austin replied.

"Doesn't anybody ever come to see me," Amos said.

Austin's smile was whimsical. "You don't give folks much of a chance," he said. "You usually come calling."

Amos shook his head. "Granderson says it's because nobody wants me. Zecheriah Miles says I don't belong to nobody and never will."

This was of concern to Austin and his eyes narrowed slightly. "Granderson and Zecheriah sometimes talk more than is good for them," he said, leaning forward now and resting his elbows on his knees. "Sometimes best to know what you're talking about before you say anything."

Hearing the schoolmaster's tone the boy felt a rebuke and declared his innocence. "I didn't say anything."

"I know you didn't," Austin said. "Granderson and Zecheriah told you something that isn't true, and now you know it isn't you might as well learn twice from their mistake." He turned to reopen his book, but Amos was still in full fidget. "You belong to all of us here, and without you we wouldn't be nearly as happy as we are. Understand me?" he said over his shoulder.

"I reckon I do," the boy said without conviction.

Austin put the book down again and shifted on his chair. Amos seemed suddenly small and fragile to him, and he realized a rare opportunity had been afforded them.

"And I reckon you might feel a tad better about things in general if you went down and talked this out with Brother Harry."

Amos sat straight up on the bed.

"Go on, now," Austin said.

"He never takes notice of me," the boy protested.

"Bet he will tonight," Austin said, and winked. "Now go on." He took up his book again and Amos knew there would be no reprieve.

Sliding down the side of the bed he made slowly for the door, hoping to be recalled.

"*Shoo*," came the stern voice behind him, and with a quick slip on the polished floorboards Amos skittered through the door and down the hall to the room where Brother Harry sat quietly, alone with his Bible in the rocking chair. So hushed was the air inside, despite the pre-Sabbath hubbub elsewhere, that even the rustle of the boy's nightshirt was audible, and Brother Harry looked up. His dark skin looked suddenly pale, but he put his Bible on his lap and beckoned to the child with his eyes.

"Brother Austin sent me, else I wouldn't pester you," Amos said, visibly uncomfortable and unsure how he had come to be where he was.

Harry looked to his lap, then back to the boy.

"I was talking to him, how Granderson Carey said I wasn't anyone to care for, and Brother sent me to you."

Rigid in his rocker, Harry Littlebourne knew the time was now if ever to speak, but words failed him.

Amos ventured slightly closer, still out of arm's reach. He had never stood so close to Brother Harry, whose considerable height and inexplicable silence confused and frightened him, and he dared not venture too near. A minute passed, and then another, and the two simply stared at each other, waiting for the floor to open up and swallow them together and whole.

Finally the boy had exhausted his resolve. "Best now maybe I go," he said in a near-whisper. "You got scriptures to read, so I could just go on up."

Harry nodded, his disappointment in himself clear in his eyes as Amos made back to the door. He knew this moment so well, and knew that it had always ended badly – first for him, now for this child. Harry Littlebourne could not remember exactly when he had stopped asking his father questions, or indeed when he had ceased to speak altogether, but he supposed he had been younger at the time than Amos Anger was now. Was it the self-same question Amos was asking him that had driven him into his silence? Was it a deeper one still? The circumstances were long-gone from his memory. But if his father could not answer that question for him, Harry knew in his heart that he must answer this boy. The damage would not thus be made good, but that possibility had not been offered. This one had. James Littlebourne had withheld the comfort of his own voice from his son, but – if it was truly what was wanted – James Littlebourne's son could offer what had been kept from him to someone else, to this boy if to no other soul. Harry put his hand to his face and made his decision just as Amos reached the door.

"Thy mother," he said, "she loved thee best of all."

Amos stopped as if struck by lightning and was almost afraid to see what was behind him. He looked carefully over his shoulder and saw a different man, a different Harry Littlebourne. He ran back and leaned himself against the arm of the rocker, and when it came time to douse the littlest ones' lamps Brother Harry's room was the last place Sister Elizabeth expected Amos to be.

1861

The southern exposure of the House Divided had some fifteen apartments, and by late winter half of them had been vacated by tenants who no longer found the accommodation acceptable. Left among the paying guests were the people of the Commonwealth of Kentucky, and for them the question of whether to seek alternative shelter or remain *in situ* was, to say the least, a matter of some complication.

For many of the Deep South states, the so-called Cotton Kings, the future of slavery in the rapidly expanding United States was of major consequence. But in Kentucky – ninth in the nation's census, seventh in property value, and thus not altogether disinterested in the subject – the immediate consideration of human beings as property was, perhaps strangely, growing less ponderous by the year. The population of slaves in the state had been decreasing steadily through the 1850s until, by the beginning of the new decade, only a fifth of Kentucky's number belonged to the balance.

Kentucky was wise enough, however, to understand the importance of slaveholding to its neighbors, on whom if for nothing else it depended for trade, and thus it had long sought to find some parcel of political ground on which all could stand peaceably.

Within its borders such eminent families as the Breckinridges and Clays had down the years devoted considerable breath and paper to the seemingly endless struggle over the future of the Peculiar Institution. But in fact the fine minds of Kentucky had already made their most fateful contribution, having provided the fire-eaters the rope with which to hang the Union: the Kentucky Resolutions of 1798 and 1799, which in exploring the rights of states under the Constitution gave any state reason to believe it might abandon the joint enterprise with impunity.

Of the fifteen slave states eight stayed put in the early days before Lincoln's inauguration. And although – because of the man's scandalously abolitionist policies – the commonwealth was not one of those states whose support had contributed to his election, Kentucky was willing to adopt a wait-and-see attitude. It assumed the peacemaker's role, as it had done before in an attempt to keep the Union in one piece. Kentucky's Senator John J. Crittenden attempted compromise, and two days before South Carolina's unanimous secession vote he presented to his fellows in the Senate a detailed plan to resolve the crisis. Kentucky waited with its tail in a crack, hoping for the positive outcome that would not come.

The Democrat Beriah Magoffin, governor since 1859, was a states' rights man who saw no evil in slavery and – convinced that Lincoln's election dealt the rights of Southerners a grievously serious and convincing blow – wanted something done, *now*, but secession wasn't what he had in mind. He contacted the governors of the sister slave states, sending them a menu of demands he believed they could ask for and get if they held a conference of their own and followed it up with a conference of all the states of the Union.

Alabama, however, was calling for Kentucky to get off the fence. It was too late for conferences. If Kentucky was so all-fired interested in conferences it should hold one of its own to decide what to do with itself and then get a delegation to the border states' convention already laid on for February. The Kentucky legislature said no to Magoffin's proposal for a conference, fearing his nonetheless clear tendency toward secessionism and where it might lead, plumping instead for attendance at the futile Peace Convention held in Washington on February 4 and a request that Congress call a national convention to consider such plans as Crittenden had concocted.

As the Peace Convention began the Kentucky legislature went home, having adjourned until March 11. Meanwhile, in Montgomery, the Alabama convention was busy patching together a Southern confederacy, identifying its potential leaders and fashioning a new government from such fabrics as seemed appropriate given the tastes of the times.

Back in Kentucky, interested parties patronized the news butchers and watched with considerable nervousness, and South Union's Brother Austin Innes was one of these.

One evening, as often happened, he wandered down to the depot to read the news-sheets, and when a train came through most people round and about the platform began to throw their hats in the air and shout "Hurrah for Jeff Davis!" – and kept up this racket until the train was out of sight.

Brother Austin turned his attention back to the Louisville *Journal* when the noise had died down, but he was listening when the men who devoted their lives to sitting around the depot pontificating on matters large and small turned their attention to this display of partisanism.

"The Union people got to have more rowdies," said one man, finally and with grim determination. "Union people can't succeed 'thout they get more rowdies."

"Now what in hell is that supposed to mean?" asked another.

"Well, can't you see?" came the reply. "Every man on that train's gonna get back where he came from thinking Bowling Green's rebel when she's Union. Can't we get us a pack of rowdies to yell 'Union!' at the trains?"

Around him the denizens agreed Union sentiment was all but drowned out by the blow of Confederate noise, but under the circumstances there wasn't much to be done about it.

There was a reason for this. Certainly it was true that, while the state might be neutral, its people were not, and in Bowling Green folks who were generally more solidly behind the Union cause than that of the South nonetheless rankled when referred to as Abolitionist or Black Republican. The Confederacy had the advantage of its people's great fondness for Jefferson Davis, but there was no similar love lost between Kentucky Unionists and Abraham Lincoln – president of the nation they loved but champion of policies they feared.

When the legislature returned to session it called for a border state convention to be held in Frankfort on the twenty-seventh of May. Their session ended in early April, and a week later Confederate guns fired on the Union fort in Charleston Harbor.

In the dining rooms of Bowling Green Kentucky men of both views had for weeks previous tarried over their cigars and port, anxious "that the Ball should be opened," not for an instant realizing what a dance of death it would bring between North and South. Now as they rejoined the ladies they wondered aloud what would happen next, and their womenfolk suggested there must be pleasanter things to talk about.

Five days after the taking of Fort Sumter the new president issued a call for troops to the remaining states of the rapidly disintegrating Union. Four more slave states, pushed beyond their endurance, joined the seven already in the Confederacy. Curiously, Lincoln greeted this news with patience. Secession was the game of plantation owners up to mischief, and he could hope that if he gave them time the non-slaveholders of the South, with nothing to gain, would subdue the fractious few.

At the back of Kentucky's slow-burning stove, then, on the burner next to the soup stirred by a brown-skinned hand, still stood the question of secession, and it was soon bubbling fit to boil.

* * *

The tenterhooks on which the Shakers at South Union sat
while this confused drama was taking place were perhaps sharper
and more uncomfortable than those that pricked anyone else in
the wide state of Kentucky. Pacifists who took in the slaves brought
by new members on the proviso that they be freed in the process
– although, wisely, they gave them separate accommodation down
at the Grassland by the Morgantown road, the better not to upset
unduly their slaveholding neighbors – they elected neutrality
although their sympathies were clearly with the Northern cause.
This they did because to do so was central to their faith; there was
little hope that it would save them and they harbored none.

As Davis and Lincoln were en route to their respective
inaugurals, the elders at South Union received a letter from Brother
Harvey Eades, then living at the Shaker village in Ohio. The arrival
of a letter from Brother Harvey was always a considerable joy to the
community, for Harvey Lauderdale Eades was one of their own,
a child of seven months when his family joined the South Union
community – indeed his parents had been two of the original
twenty-six souls who had formed the core of the society there
back in 1807. The very nature of Shaker doctrine did not allow
for celebrity amongst its adherents, but had there been room for
such distinction the Eades name would have figured prominently.
And Harvey wore the name well, becoming at just 29 years of age
a member of the ministry at South Union, a man well-loved by all
who knew him.

It was thus with some surprise that in 1844, while Elder
Harvey was away in Ohio on a visit to the Shaker settlement at
Union Village, his brethren and sisters at South Union were advised
that he was not to return to them. No reason was given for the
change in his living arrangements, and the people of the village
never precisely understood his absence, although in obedience
they were disinclined to question it. Some said it was the Mount

Lebanon ministry's way of teaching him humility, but this no one could say for sure. Whatever the reasons for his banishment – for as such it came to be seen – his occasional visits to the place he must consider his home were precious to all concerned, and the wise letters which arrived from him with regularity were savored and shared.

From the abolitionist state of Ohio, then, Eades wrote thus to his friends on the disputed border:

> *It seems that Brother Urban thinks that Kentucky will go out of the Union. I entertain no such fears – Simply because I think Kentuckians have entirely too much good Sense to commit an act so insane. I have long believed the present state of things would come to pass—It has come a little sooner than I anticipated. Yet, I think that if the Cotton or Gulf States do not fire the first gun Civil War may be averted with ... all its untold horrors – But, if they shall burn powder against the government forces; Then ... the result, it seems to me, can hardly fail to be the freedom of every African that may be left alive in these now dis-United States.*

At South Union they could hope that Brother Harvey was correct in his assumptions, but they could not imagine at what cost that confirmation would come.

August

Working on a new pair of shoes for Sister Mary Mallory, Austin Innes heard a sound in the summer-sharp air and stopped for an instant to listen to it. When he had identified it he smiled to himself and went back to work as it grew louder, came closer to his door, and provided a rhythm for his hammer.

Dearly beloved brethren,
Is it not a sin,
That when you peel potatoes
You throw away the skin?
The skins feed the pigs
And the pigs feed you –
Dearly beloved brethren,
Is that not true?

Leaning forward with the last and leather in his lap Brother Austin looked out the open window and saw Brother Harry with Amos bouncing on his shoulders, on their way back from wherever they had been. Above Harry's deep-toned chant echoed the pure, tinny voice of the child, punctuated by occasional giggles as his mount intermittently skipped and hopped at the end of a line or on the emphasis of a word. More than likely they had been up at the garden the other side of North Lane; it was one of Brother Harry's favorite places and he was often up there weeding and persuading the jimson or pennyroyal when his presence was not required elsewhere. The wheat threshing had begun a few weeks ago, and Brother George Rankin had just gone down with Sisters Caroline Adams and Hortency Bedell to look after the Caanan land during the fruit season, but other than that he knew of no major projects around the village. Every peaceful day was a blessing now, and he listened to the quiet Tuesday afternoon fade – the silence broken, now that he had stilled his hammer, only by the occasional shriek of the child and the sing-song rhyme – and was grateful. No one could know how long this would remain a place where child or man could feel free to sing.

Austin passed his hand over the half-finished shoe. To look at it, one would not have imagined it was made to fit a colored foot. Certainly Austin could not tell, and it was he who had made it. His shoulders were tight from hunching over the last, and he worked his bones a bit, then stood and walked to the open door.

Amos and Brother Harry were sitting under the nearby sweet gum trees, talking. It was a constant wonder to him, seeing the strapping young man (well, younger than he) talking to this child, this man who for years had seemed to have nothing to say to anyone but his horse. Innes braced himself against the doorjamb with one hand and raised the other.

"You, Amos!" he shouted. "Amos Anger! Come here!"

The child looked up, glanced to Brother Harry for permission to do as he was bid, then gathered his feet under him and scooted to the shop.

Brother Austin stepped down to the ground as the boy approached. He had grown an inch or two in recent months, and was perhaps a bit heavier, hardier and generally more substantial to Austin's eye.

He touched his hand to his knee. "Put your foot up here, son," he said.

Amos leaned slightly backwards to bring his foot to Brother Austin's knee, watching with curiosity as the schoolmaster bent his red head and with his thumb and forefinger squeezed at the sides and toes of the boot pressed against his leg. The child's foot was sticky and tight inside the leather, and Austin had suspected as much.

"Thought so," he said without looking up. "New boots for you. Tell Sister Elizabeth, hear?"

But the boy was not listening. He had lost interest. Out of the corner of his eye he could see strangers coming up the Dam Road, past the calf lot, strangers on horseback.

"Brother Austin..." he said, touching the top of the man's head with his finger.

"Yea?"

"Who's that?"

Austin Innes straightened up as Amos resettled his foot on solid ground. "Who's who?" he said, looking at the boy. He followed the path of the indicating finger with his eyes, saw the horsemen, and stiffened. The sound of them was rising.

"Brother Harry will take you back to the house," he said.

"Why?"

"Brother Harry will take you. Just do as I say," he said firmly, turning the child by the shoulder and raising his eyes to the man still waiting against the tree. "Brother Harry! Best take Amos on back now!"

Amos knew Austin Innes' tone brooked no denial and, as the boy was fast on his feet back to Harry, Austin started on a trot toward the party riding up the Dam Road, headed for the fulling mill. Soldiers they were, scores of them, the first he had seen, with Bonnie Blues fluttering at the ears of some of their horses.

He came up alongside the mounted column, its numbers mostly un-uniformed and unidentifiable.

"Who is that?" he asked of one rider as he ran alongside, indicating with his eyes the wire-haired man just visible at the head of the contingent.

"That's Lieutenant Colonel Forrest," he was told. "Nathan Bedford Forrest."

"What army are you?"

"The army of the Confederacy," came the answer.

Austin stopped in his tracks, the breath gone from him as if the Devil himself had struck him a blow to the gut.

Back in April, as the brethren were getting the corn in, news of the firing on Fort Sumter had reached the village. Friend Lincoln thereafter lost no time asking every remaining loyal state to supply troops to redress immediately the outrage committed in Charleston Harbor: 75,000 men, of which the commonwealth's share would be four regiments. But, while Kentucky still met the general description, Governor Beriah Magoffin would have none of the use of Kentucky men against their Southern brothers. Four more states took their leave of the Union by secession, but the commonwealth still could not decide, a passionate indecision that finally earned the right to be called neutrality. Magoffin (despite his own enthusiasm for the secessionist cause) harbored the notion, probably justified, that if Kentucky seceded the North would have an invasion of the state mounted before the legislature could get its hands down from the vote. Lincoln realized the delicacy of Kentucky's position and passed the word that her neutrality would be respected – it was better than losing the state to the Confederacy, and it bought him time – and the decision became official on the 20th of May.

There were located, thus, between the borders of Canada and Mexico, three distinct nations of sorts: the United States, the Confederate States, and the State of Kentucky.

Neutrality, however long it could be expected to hold, might be the status chosen by the government on behalf of its constituency, but Kentucky men were not without minds of their own. Talk of secession, like Banquo's ghost, would not down. Those whose sympathies lay with the South could cross into Tennessee and join up at Fort Boone, just south of Guthrie. In the other direction recruiting camps had been established on the northern banks of the Ohio River, and Union-minded Kentucky men who harbored no patience for indecision flocked to them. Come summer the Navy Lieutenant Bull Nelson established Camp Dick Robinson for the training of Union troops right in Garrard County, thereby offending the sensibilities of anyone who still believed the state's best course was a neutral one.

As infighting continued at the highest government levels a variety of local defense forces was raised by the engines of the internal dispute's several contending sides, each with its own unique outlook on which way to lean should the moment to act finally arise. The scramble for Springfield and Enfield rifles was on in earnest by summer, and the gravest immediate danger as weapons were procured was less a possible clash between Confederate and Union troops on Kentucky soil, more a sparking of gunfire between the state's own bickering militias. Those who read the news-sheets – as Austin Innes did, perhaps more often than might be seemly for a man who had long ago turned his back on the world – felt in the marrow of their bones that when neutrality became an even more impossible reality than it had been a dream Kentucky would have no choice but to side with the states of the Union. There was no other way.

Austin had seen a bit of the world and knew the contentiousness of men. He was wise enough to know that when, as it must eventually, Kentucky embraced the Union cause, the full weight of that decision's collective fist would impact mightily on the little orbit of his people at Shakertown: in a neutral state the neutrality of Believers would be understandable after a fashion; in a state that had gone for the North those in the Shaker community would be seen either as collaborators or cowards depending on the attitude of the observer. Either way it would be compelled for its own safety to explain its position to neighbors too consumed by partisan passions to devote energy to understanding those who did not share them.

*   *   *

The kitchen at the Center was like a beehive. Amos was under the bottom stairs, hidden by the bridgeboard and watching until such time as he should be found and shooed away. He had never seen so many people crammed into the often busy dining hall, never seen so many of the elders there for reasons other than appetite.

"There's plenty of room for 'em up the mill pond," said Jess Rankin, come over from East, where he was Elder now. "They'll stay the night, right where we can see 'em, and then they'll go, and meantime there's nothing much there they can muss. As long as they behave themselves, we'll be allright."

Thomas Smith was in conversation with Urban Johns, and Jackson McGowan had the ear of Solomon Rankin. Eldress Betsy Smith and Eldress Nancy Moore were in and out of the kitchen, chasing after a flock of the sisterhood. Then Eldress Nancy was dispatching Sister Harriet Breedlove back to the East with instructions for the kitchen sisters there, and as Sister Harriet took to the west staircase Amos – fearing discovery – shrank back under the east staircase until she was gone.

"It's a matter of welcome, of kindly welcome," Brother Urban said with a cheerful officiousness that did little to mask his concern. He was propped on his knuckles, leaning against one of the long tables. Eating irons and plates had been laid out as usual after dinner for the Center's supper, and Urban's hands were planted either side of a plate on which lay crossed the customary bone-handled knife and fork. "The officer seems a reasonable man. If we treat them with kindness and hospitality, as we must as Christians try to do, they'll leave us in peace. Pray God they'll find the same wherever they're headed."

"They're on their way down to Guthrie," Elder Solomon said from the arched doorway that led to the kitchen. Amos could see behind him the sisters working at the big brick ovens. Suppertime had never seemed so harried. "That officer, that man Forrest, he recruited them..."

"How many?" asked Brother Thomas, now moving about inside the kitchen. This reply the sisters paused to hear.

"He wants victuals for eighty-six – is that the officers too, I wonder? Better plan for a few more, Betsy. They're calling at Bluitt's for corn, and they'll try the tavern to see if Yost can spare some oats," Solomon replied over his shoulder. Then he turned back to the brethren grouped around the table. "Found 'em mostly between here and Owensboro, he told me, and now he's takin' 'em back down to Fort Boone to train up for the Confederacy. But he was right polite, make no mistake: Memphis boys know their manners, and I have no complaint."

Eldress Nancy rushed past and he put out a hand to stop her. "Nancy, Nancy," he said, "if we offer to give them supper, and a little breakfast before they go, can you do both?"

"As long as you menfolk stay out of our way," she said crisply, and went on about her business.

Amos squeezed himself small under the stairs as the elders, underfoot and now with notice to vacate, trooped up to continue their conversation in one of the upper rooms. When their footsteps faded over his head he ventured out to the kitchen and tugged at Sister Elizabeth's elbow, anxious to help.

"Bless thee, child, thee can keep after the wood, make sure the box is full up," she said, bending down and giving him a swift kiss on the cheek for his trouble. "The ovens will be busy with bread all night."

With customary industry and frequent singing to chase away the nervousness that came of having Confederate cavalry camped within sight of the Center, the sisters rose to the challenge of feeding eighty-six and more unexpected guests. The abundant results were sent out to the mill pond encampment on wagons driven by the brethren, and the returning provisioners passed to the weary sisters – already at work on what might be found by way of tomorrow's breakfast – the message that the soldiers had been well pleased.

"Don't know what we'd have done if they'd said it wasn't enough, and that's a fact," said Eldress Nancy, laughing as she pushed back the locks of hair that crept down her forehead from beneath her linen cap.

"It's only – " said young Logan Johns, stopping short to catch at a sagging flour sack in grave danger of toppling.

"Only what?"

"Only the colonel, Forrest, they said he might like to have a little butter."

"Butter! Well, if that's all, he's kindly welcome," she said, taking down a slab of fresh-made and cutting a generous hunk onto a plate. "Where's the boy? Amos!"

The child came scudding around the worktable.

"Amos, take this over to the soldier camp," she said. "It's for our friend Forrest. He asked for butter." She settled the plate in the boy's upraised hands. "Now don't drop it. And be sure to say we'd be grateful for the return of the plate."

Amos kited out the side door, past the well and the wash house and up toward the mill, the plate bouncing in his hands. Supper for the other children – those who had not been called in to help with the kitchen effort – had proceeded without him, and while he had reached for the stray pieces of bread or bits of peach that beckoned from the worktable in the past few hours he was still hungry.

Nearing the camp, where he could see smoke rising from fires and the outlines of broad shoulders – men he did not know – he slowed his run. The adventure to which he had been assigned suddenly assumed an ominous shape of which he was frightened, and for an instant he felt the urge to leave the butter in its dish in the grass, shout the news of its arrival to anyone who might be able to hear him, and run back to the safety of the Center.

"Eldress Nancy wants the butter dish," he said resolutely to the evening air, and – having by the invocation of those magic words strengthened his resolve to carry out the task entrusted to him in satisfactory fashion – he walked on toward the camp, albeit on less hurried legs.

Within earshot of the soldiers he was spotted by a picket, a man with hair on his face, which unaccustomed sight rooted Amos where he stood.

"Well, hey there, sonny," the man said. "What's that you got there?"

"Eldress Nancy sent me," the boy said in a wispy voice, staring at the dark and crowded space between the man's upper lip and his nose. "What's that?" he asked in his turn, pointing.

"Why, boy, that's m' tickler, ain't you never see'd one?" the man replied, and laughed. The little courier was not enlightened by this explanation, but the picket hurtled on without allowing him time to ask for clarification. "Now you tell me who this is for and we'll see about you."

"Friend Forrest, is what she said," Amos told him, "and she wants the plate back."

"Well, now," the picket said with playful gravity, "ain't no colonel wants a wrangle with no Nancy, that's for sure, so we'll just tell him how it is."

Amos trotted behind his guide, still with his butter offering in his hands and a wondering eye for the long piece of equipment that lay cradled across the man's arm. Some distance inside the circle of fires was pitched the camp's only tent, and outside it stood two men dressed in peculiar suits of clothes such as Amos had never seen – decorated with yellow ribbons they were, like feast-day packages. Amos wondered if it was a holiday.

"Delivery, lieutenant," said the picket, raising his hand in a self-conscious salute.

"That'll be all. Get back to your post."

Amos watched this exchange from below, aware that the relationship between these two men was totally alien to him.

"It's butter," he told the lieutenant without being asked. "For friend Forrest, from Eldress Nancy. And please can she have the plate."

The lieutenant began to laugh, a roaring gale of sound that caused heads to raise up at fires from one end of the camp to the other.

"Well, little man, at least you know what you're up to, which is more than most men in this world can say," he told the boy.

There was a rustling sound from inside the tent, and the flap opened. Amos now saw emerge a tall, thin man – not as tall as Brother Harry, nobody was, but tall all the same – with strange grey hair that lay first flat and then curly on his head. Yet more hair, this black as pitch, sprouted below his fine, straight nose and grew down beyond his chin. His blouse was white as moonlight, and the fringed ends of a heavy yellow sash tied at his waist dangled loosely over the grey of his trousers. Amos' jaw fell at the very sight of all this, and there were no words left to him except those he had been given.

"It's butter," he said, wide-eyed, raising the plate high. "From Eldress Nancy, for friend Forrest. Can she have the plate back?"

The long figure sank to its knees and Amos looked level into the extraordinary man's eyes, colored grey to match the jacket slung across the back of a chair behind him.

"Why, so it is butter, so it is," the man said softly, taking the plate on the tips of one hand's fingers. "And weren't you good to bring it, and wasn't Eldress Nancy good to send it? But you have the better of me, young man. How shall I address you?"

The lieutenant was looking up in the air, somehow discomfited by this womanish side of his commanding officer's nature.

The boy looked down at his boots, confused. "I'm already dressed."

"And very nicely, too," said Nathan Bedford Forrest, smiling. This was not a man to take amusement from the humiliation of a child. "What's your name?"

"Amos," he replied.

"Well, then, Amos," Forrest said, rising to his full height again, "why don't you come inside and give me the benefit of your company?"

It was late, nearly dark, and surely the other children would be readying for bed. But Elder Solomon had said welcome must be made; thus it seemed to Amos that responsibility had been given him and it was up to him to shoulder it or risk disappointing those who had trusted him not do so. Forrest held the tent-flap back for his little guest and Amos went inside.

Supper had been laid out for him on a small table, and the long man sat at it, motioning the boy to a chair by the cot.

"Do you know what's going on here, Amos?" he asked, cutting into the loaf before him now the butter was to hand.

"Supper, friend Forrest."

"Now, see here," he said with mock seriousness as he buttered his bread, "if I call you Amos you can call me Bedford. That's fair, isn't it?"

Amos nodded.

"These are my men, here, every man jack of them," Forrest said. "I'm a rich man, Amos – you know what that means? – and I've put this company together myself, paid for all of it with my own money, and do you know why?"

Amos shook his head.

"Because the cause of the South is fair and true," Forrest said, talking to himself more than the boy, who had lost track of the conversation some time ago. "A man who knows what needs doing and doesn't do it is no man. You understand me?" Seeing Amos eye the bread in his hand, Forrest cut away another chunk, buttered it, and handed it across. Amos accepted the offering with gratitude.

"I do mostly what I'm told," he said, considering it was time to make some contribution to the proceedings.

"And that's a good thing, son, a fine thing. Always do what you're told, if the man who gives the order is a good and honorable one. And when you grow up, remember that your men will always follow a good and honorable man, then you'll act accordingly. A good man gives no order he would not be prepared to obey himself." Forrest picked at the quartered chicken before him and, stretching his arm across the table, put a piece of white meat in Amos' mouth.

"Tell me about your father."

"He's in Heaven," Amos replied. That was what the prayer said. No other answer presented itself.

"That's a sadness," Forrest said. "My father's dead, too. He was a blacksmith." Amos leaned forward, opened his mouth, and Forrest gave him another piece of chicken. "I was fifteen years old, and we'd just all of us moved ourselves to Mississippi. I had six brothers and three sisters."

This seemed to Amos a pitiful small family. "There's lots more than that here."

"Well, it was a worry for me, you know, to keep the farm going and look after them all. It fell to me, being the oldest, to take care. But you might just as well do a thing right if you're going to bother at all," he said.

The lieutenant put his head through the flap. "Some coffee for you, sir?"

"Leave it and get out," Forrest said sharply without looking at the man. Amos' head came up, alert.

The lieutenant pushed through the flap, set the pot down, and seemed ready to speak, but Forrest was on his feet and wild-eyed in a shot. "I said, get out!" he shouted, and as the lieutenant retreated Amos blinked in alarm and leaned back in his chair, frightened. The brethren never acted so.

Forrest quietly resumed his seat and carried on with his

supper as if the interruption had not occurred. Amos relaxed, just. "Tomorrow, Amos, I'll take my troops on down to Tennessee. And when they're ready we'll come back to Bowling Green and hold it and squeeze it til Kentucky can do no else than join with us."

"I got chores tomorrow," Amos said, his plans being to his mind every bit as important as his companion's. "Most every day Brother John takes us off for chores." Forrest's eyes unsettled him. They found him and held him, almost against his will. There was nothing to look at in this bleak, sparse tent, but Amos could not look away from the man's strange grey eyes. The oil in the lamp that hung from a nail on the tent-pole made a low spitting sound as it burned, and the small space was filled by its heat.

"Do them, then, do them well always," Forrest said. "Or... you could come with me. Would you like that? You and my boy Willie would have a high old time, you know. I'll buy you a drum, and a little gun, and you can fight like a man for your country, for President Davis."

The meaning of all this escaped the boy, but he was not tempted by the invitation in any case. "Brother Harry would miss me," he said.

"I'm sure he would," Forrest said. "A brother is a good thing to have; I know. But if you don't come with me you'll be here when I come back, and I'll look for you."

"When are you coming?"

"These things you never know, Amos, but trust me. You'll see me again."

Amos could not contain the yawn that strained his jaws. He clapped his hands over his mouth and blushed.

"You'd better go on home, now," Forrest said, and with his knife scraped the last of the butter off the Shaker plate and onto his own. "But you don't want to forget this."

Amos slid off his chair, and the big man rose from the table, took his hand, and walked him through the tent, past the campfires where men without blankets sat on bare ground. I wouldn't like to sleep here tonight, he thought.

Forrest's legs were long, like Brother Harry's, and Amos felt something familiar walking next to him, holding his hand.

"Bedford?" he asked.

"Hmmm?"

"Why do you need to have all these men?"

"It may be that we'll have to kill a great many people, Amos," he replied. "To win a war you sometimes need to kill a great many people, and for that you need a great many men. These are mine."

Amos kicked out at a stone in his path. "Thou shalt not kill," he said, remembering his Sabbath lessons. The words to him were only that.

"God makes His rules and the rest of us do what we can with them, son," Forrest said.

They reached the picket's post, and the soldier Amos had met on his arrival jumped up with alarm and saluted mightily when he saw the boy's return escort.

Forrest gave Amos the plate and put his hand on the boy's shoulder. "Will you thank Miss Nancy for me?" he asked.

"I will," Amos replied solemnly.

"And thank you for your company," he said.

"You're kindly welcome," Amos replied, as he had been taught. He walked out past the picket, letting go of Forrest's hand.

Forrest called to his little guest, and Amos turned. "Look at me, Amos," he said. "Remember my face. When I come back, I'll look for you."

Amos looked into the grey eyes that winked with light from the picket's fire, looked until he could stand it no longer. He backed into the darkness until at last he felt he could not be seen, then he turned and ran back to the Center, as fast as his legs would carry him.

*   *   *

Morning came earlier than usual for Amos, and he was still sleepy at half-past-six when the bell bid him be about the day. In the kitchen he found the sisters as he had left them: still busy, sending out to the soldiers light loaf bread, warm hoe cakes, fried ham pork, cold fresh mutton, fried Irish potatoes, fruit and coffee and tea.

The other little boys had been asleep when Amos came up to bed, and this morning they were full of questions about the soldier camp, about what he had seen there, but he was not anxious to say. As yet he was not sure. And so he told them the strangest thing: that the men there had hair that grew on their faces, and by way of illustration he put his finger under his nose – as if he felt a sneeze coming – then covered his cheeks with his hands. At breakfast the younger boys eyed the brethren with new interest. All Shaker men were smooth-faced, having perhaps shaved themselves yesterday or intending to do so tomorrow. The boys were now all cat-curious to know what the brethren would look like with this peculiar hair on their faces; they had never seen it, or if they had they did not remember. And yet Amos had said it was so, and he had been there. Still it made him uncomfortable, to know something the other boys did not.

Brother John Perryman shepherded his boys from breakfast to the dairy and preserve house, and set them to cutting and paring apples. It was simple work, well suited to small hands, and it was there for them to do this time every year. But with the chore there inevitably came occasional cut fingers and thus the kind-hearted Brother John, not long out of the Children's Order himself, kept a careful eye: the blood bothered him less than the tears.

Filling the baskets with apples and listening to the chatter of his fellows Amos gave little thought to the soldiers out by the mill pond. They were a greater curiosity to the other boys, who had not seen them, than to him.

But in fact, as the boys were intent over the apples – and with John Perryman safely out of sight for a moment – their attention turned from the excitement of soldiers to the matter of the new dentures now being sported by a few of the sisters. Last month the elders had decided to admit this improvement in the dental art for the benefit of the Society, and a dentist had come from up north to fit those of the brethren and sisters who were needful of new. Eldress Jency Dillon and Sister Prudence Houston had been the first to receive these miracles fashioned of Vulcanite rubber and porcelain – dear but practical, the trustees considered, at thirty dollars the set – and while the children had since then been wishful of first-hand examination they had thus far been denied the opportunity.

Directly after the rising bell, George Joiner now claimed as he turned an apple in his hand, he had sneaked down the back staircase and crawled along the sisters' side of the second-floor passage. Sister Pru slept in the retiring room just this side of the chamber used to store infirmary goods, and there was less to-and-fro there than at other points along the hall at this early hour. He held the boys spellbound, embroidering his tale with heart-stopping fears of imminent discovery by passing brethren and sisters until finally he revealed how through patience and sheer nerve he had divined the overnight whereabouts of Sister Pru's new teeth.

"She keeps 'em in the top of the cupboard, in a cup," he announced. "Takes 'em out first thing and chomps 'em right in."

"Did you see?" asked the bedazzled Zecheriah Miles.

"Nay," said George, revealing with a sudden, sullen look his own disappointment. "She had her back to me, but when she got up her jaw was all sunk and peculiar and when she come back from the cupboard her face looked coming on for normal so that must be where she's got 'em."

The boys went quiet as Brother John came back to check their progress, then whispered and punched each other as they agreed that must be where the dentures were.

"Ain't quite the same as goin' over to the soldier camp," said Andrew Bailey, anxious to diminish the importance of George's accomplishment since it was unlikely he could match such daring and ingenuity. "Now that took a heap of something, a little'n like Amos just goin' on over there like that. Bet you couldn't."

George Joiner bristled. A twelve-year-old derived no joy from comparison with a child not yet seven. "Well, you tell me Amos could go on in there and get Sister Pru's teeth and I'll tell you another one," he said, making sure the little boy at the end of the bench could hear.

Amos said nothing, but Zecheriah told George and Andrew to hush themselves up and that seemed to settle things.

The cavalry men were preparing to be on their way. But before they took to the road the sergeant called them to attention, and Lieutenant Colonel Forrest addressed them.

"Today, men," he told them, "we'll make for Tennessee, and be there by nightfall. And when you cross that border you leave the United States for the Confederacy. The time is now to decide whether you've got the courage to be among your country's soldiers, to do what needs doing, or whether you want to go back home and live amongst the abolitionist trash of Kentucky. But it's for you to say, to stay or to go. If you want to go with me, you'll all be better men for it, but if you want to skedaddle on home, if you can live with that, then git. But git now, because Tennessee will be too late."

The men stood dumbstruck, looking at each other and then looking at Forrest, waiting for something to happen. At first nothing stirred and there was only the sound of the impatient horses. Then, slowly, six men moved way from the rest, their belongings in their arms. They stood alone to one side, with the watch of their fellows hard on them.

Forrest's eyes narrowed and his hands went to his gunbelt. He began to speak, then to shout, and the brethren nearby heard him even over the sound of the mill – language they had never heard before and hoped they'd never hear again. The objects of his tirade stood gazing intently at the ground, their shoulders moving as if the words had pikes attached, but they stayed where they were, motionless. And when the company mounted and rode off south they were still standing there, six men who had given serious thought to soldiering with Nathan Bedford Forrest and decided against it.

That evening Amos heard Eldress Betsy tell Sister Elizabeth how the soldiers had made off with a few cabbages and melons they had not been invited to remove from the garden premises, but other than that the village seemed to have survived the night. The relief was great among the elders that this first test of the trying times had been passed with only the expenditure of a little food and patience, and prayerful thanks were raised.

Amos had knicked his thumb with his apple knife, and it smarted sore. Before he went to bed he took his injury to Sister Elizabeth, who bound it with a bit of salt pork and said it would be better in the morning, but that left him with the night still to get through. Each time he turned in his bed in search of cooler linen his thumb throbbed. He rolled on his back and put his complaining hand on his chest, the sniff of pork now strong to his nose.

George Joiner was unfair, he thought as he drowsed in the heat.

The hue and cry was raised in the morning, and Sister Pru allowed as how some soldier or other must have crept back in the night and robbed them all.

"Now, now, Prudence," said Eldress Nancy when news of the theft reached her in the kitchen, "don't fret so. We'll find 'em. They can't have gone far."

"Best tell the brethren, Nancy," said Sister Pru, still breathless with alarm. "Let's see what else them varmints have got theirselves away with. Can't just have been my teeth."

Sister Prudence's memory was not the best in the village, this

Eldress Nancy and just about everyone else knew, and suggestion was made that she might have put them down somewhere and forgotten to take notice of where.

"I put them in the same place every night," Sister Prudence insisted, exasperated to be robbed and then wronged. "They were in that cupboard, same as they are every night, and that's that."

When the Center assembled downstairs for breakfast Brother Jefferson Shannon was taken aside and informed of the night-time raid on Sister Prudence Houston's dentures, and the good brother was at some pains to contain his amusement.

"They're not where they're supposed to be, brother, and they're nowhere else, so they're gone," Eldress Nancy told him.

The brethren and sisters stood to their prayers, but before they sat Brother Jefferson tacked onto the family's heavenly petitions a purely practical request: "...and if anybody knows the whereabouts of Sister Prudence Houston's new teeth, could they just say."

Hearing this, the boys at their table struggled not to laugh and eyed each other with conspiratorial mirth, knowing the mystery's solution surely lay somewhere in their number.

Amos looked to the table opposite, where he saw Brother Harry Littlebourne looking his way, and the boy dipped his eyes back to his plate. It was difficult that morning for the little boys to keep the silence that was traditional at Shaker tables, and they worked at passing messages to one another with their eyes, or muffled behind raised hands. The elder brethren noticed and put a quick stop to their shenanigans.

After breakfast Amos saw Brother Harry exchange a word with Brother John Perryman, and when the boys flocked to Brother John to be taken for their day's work Harry cut his single sheep away.

"Thought thee and me would do some weeding today," he said.

This to Amos seemed an unexpected pleasure, and he happily followed Harry out onto the path and up to the garden by the North.

"Did thee see thy friend at the soldier camp before they took their leave yesterday?" Brother Harry asked as they walked.

"Nay," Amos said. "I was cutting apples with the boys."

"Did it grieve thee, not to see them?"

"We were cutting apples and I didn't think."

"Seems to me it would take a brave boy, to tarry so long amongst the soldiers. Was thee frighted to be there?"

What was it Brother Harry knew? Amos closed his hands in his pockets. The bundle he gripped in his left fist suddenly burned him like hell-fire. He said nothing.

"Well," said Harry with uncommon seriousness, "I was proud of thee. A bigger boy might not have gone at all."

They stopped off at the garden house for tools, then carried on up the road and passed a quiet hour working between the rows of herbs that grew there. Brother Harry seemed to be waiting for Amos to speak. Amos knew what he was expected to say, but he was lost for words. He had meant no harm by it. George Joiner had been unfair, and Amos had meant no harm.

Seeking to make Brother Harry laugh, hoping to find in humor his escape from disgrace, Amos disappeared within the sheltering stakes and rows and stayed crouched there long enough for Harry to call him out.

"What's thee up to back there?" Harry asked finally. "If thee's trampling my good plants thee'll hear it from me and regret thy feet, I warn thee!"

The boy came bounding down through the pennyroyal, his arms in the air, and smiled broadly – showing Sister Prudence Houston's false teeth.

Brother Harry straightened up, unsmiling, and leaned on the long helve of his hoe.

"Thee shames me, Amos," he said, without the slightest sign of amusement – although in truth the boy looked uncommon funny with the old woman's teeth in his mouth. "Give them here."

Amos spat the dentures into his own hand and fished his handkerchief from his pocket. Slowly wrapping them in the white cloth he bought time, avoiding until the very last second the need to look Brother Harry in the eye.

"Give them here," Harry said again, and Amos dutifully gave the parcel up. Out of the corner of his eye the child stole a look at the man's face, and the tears came down his cheeks. "Does thee know what trouble thee's brought to Sister Prudence, who loves thee, and to the rest of the family? What ailed thee, to misbehave so?"

"It was only a little minute to be bad," Amos said. "I didn't mean it."

Brother Harry sat himself down at the edge of the garden and brought the tearful child down in his lap. Having used his handkerchief to bind Sister's teeth Amos now had none, and Brother Harry – not without pity – offered his own, then waited as the boy mopped his streaming nose.

"Amos," he said with quiet firmness, "thy life is only minutes, stacked one on one to make the days and years that make thee. That bad minute, whether thee meant it to happen or not, takes its place with all the others. Thee can't escape the evil minute, once it's done. Thee can only repent the error of thy ways, and live according."

"But such a small thing, just this small…" the boy protested.

"Was it a small thing to Sister Pru? Just think of that," Harry said. "And evil can squeeze through the smallest space, I promise thee." He held his thumb and forefinger in front of Amos' green eyes, and narrowed the distance between them to a hair's breadth. "Open a space just this wide for the smallest bit of evil, boy, and all the evil in the world may work its way through, unless thee takes care. Evil makes of thee ever less than God's intention." He held up his forefinger. "This is only one finger, but without it what is my hand? Without it my work would suffer, and that would grieve God, and to grieve God would grieve me."

"Do I grieve God?"

"When thee does such things, thee disappoints Him." The tears, briefly stopped, began to run down again. "Amos," Harry said, "God has given thee thy body and thy life. Never think that this part of thy self, that minute of thy life, can be spared, that it means less than the others. It was all given thee to worship God, to be a good man in fear of Him, and whatever thee wastes is that much thee has denied Him."

He raised himself up, and the boy with him. "Take thyself off and give a good think to what I said. Wait til I come for thee." Harry went back to his weeding, and Amos knew the subject was closed.

No greater punishment existed for a Shaker child than to be sent off to contemplate his crime. Each child had his thinking spot, and for Amos it was the steps of the brick shed, to which he repaired with the heat of his transgression still tingling on his face.

To be a disappointment to God was one thing, and in his mind Amos knew that therein should lie his greatest regret. But chief among the torments of his heart as he sat on the cool steps in the morning heat was the knowledge that he was a disappointment to Brother Harry. He twisted the damp handkerchief in his small hands, shamefaced, knowing that every brother, every sister, every child who might see him now would know that he was in disgrace, know that he had committed some wrong so towering that it required temporary banishment from the family. He took his hat off and placed it flat on the ground by his feet. It seemed to him that he had been there half his life already, but he had only just sat down.

Harry had been working steadily, and when he checked the sun he knew the bell would shortly bring them in for dinner. He had returned Sister Prudence's property to her and left the boy to his misery for a few hours, and to his mind it was long enough. He stacked his implements against a tree, intending to come back after dinner and finish, then headed down toward the brick shed. Drawing closer he saw the wretched little barefoot figure, sitting on the steps with his arms crossed over his knees, his head resting on his elbow. The half-hidden face was smudged with garden grime, now streaked by the wandering trails of his tears, and Brother Harry's handkerchief dangled moist and knotted from his hand.

Approaching Indian-quiet, Harry crouched down without disturbing his stricken charge. He picked the boy's forgotten straw hat up from the ground and nudged Amos with its brim.

"The grass has no need of a hat," he said softly, so as not to frighten.

December

Whatever battles might be in progress between the gentlemen of the North and South, Austin Innes daily engaged in skirmishes of his own – and suspected he was losing. School for the boys had begun on Monday, but the attention of his erstwhile scholars was daily less on their monitors and more on the doings of the Great Road, which passed just outside the schoolhouse window.

Shakertown's location, ideal in peacetime, was increasingly impracticable with the state tottering on the edge of war. On the road to Bowling Green from Russellville, and beyond to Fort Donelson and Fort Henry, the earthen works stood sentry over the Tennessee and Cumberland Rivers. West of the village, the lane that ran north past the house of the Shaker Negroes crossed the Gasper and carried on beyond the gristmill to Morgantown and the Green River, then to the Ohio. In these early days of the turmoil, few roads in the state saw the movement of so many troops as these.

Add to this attraction last year's completion of the Memphis branch of the Louisville & Nashville Railroad, which ran just south of the village. Its path wound close behind the East house and dipped slightly as it flowed southwest toward Russellville, cutting a jitty between the Holy Ground and the graveyard. A handsome brick depot built by the Shakers stood north of the line, less than a mile from the Center. Gangs of Irishmen had been brought in to do the heavy work, and the result had been an easier means of transporting Shaker goods to the river. The cars would carry dearer cargo still.

Yesterday afternoon, with the spectacle of so much traffic on the road to sap the wandering mind, Austin was compelled to acknowledge the fact that, for all its undoubted wisdom, the Lancastrian method of education did not allow for boys to be so completely distracted from their sums and reading, geography and spelling. The schoolmaster examined his own priorities, there being none else so conveniently close to hand, and determined that as long as the boys could be persuaded to think about something their time would not be entirely wasted. He decided to be content with what he could get.

Thus, with the boys wriggling sideways in their seats, he sat on the edge of his desk, raised his hands in the air and asked:

"Which would you imagine came first, the egg or the owl?"

So bizarre a question as this left the young men in his care slackjawed, and Brother Austin felt the reins were back between his fingers. The afternoon thereafter passed in good-natured argument that occasionally heated up to a point where their teacher felt the need to open the door and let the cold air in. But that was Monday.

With today's movement out on the road no less compelling than yesterday's, and a certain amount of conventional wisdom having been successfully imparted before dinner, Austin went after his fish again.

"Let's read from the newspaper, shall we?"

The boys turned to each other in stunned disbelief. The brethren and sisters were now and then permitted to read the newspapers, if the elders gave their approval, and news of merit or purpose was sometimes passed along to the Believers if improvement could be derived from such dispersal. Everybody

knew Brother Austin read the news-sheets as much as anyone
and probably more, but the elders knew he mostly went down to
the depot to do it and they turned a blind eye: all things being
considered they reckoned he was entitled. But when the little
schoolmaster unfolded a copy of the Bowling Green *Gazette* from
his waistcoat pocket and began to rattle through its pages his
students could scarcely believe their eyes.

" 'We have heard tell,' " he began to read, " 'of a black woman
at Cairo...' " His hand darted out from behind the flimsy barrier,
pointing at Zecheriah Miles, and the disembodied voice asked,
"Where?"

"Illinois," said Zecheriah, more by way of reaction than reply.

" '... a black woman at Cairo, married to a carpenter, who turned
white. Over two years her black skin peeled off by degrees, leaving
behind new skin the color of eggshells, without any inconvenience
to herself. Five European medical men in Cairo certified the facts
of the case... "

The boys stared at him, not sure whether he was entirely
serious but willing to give him the fullness of their attention if he
should tell them it was true.

"Well, by sugar," Brother Austin said as he emerged from
behind the *Gazette*, twiddling his fingers on the paper, his eyes
merry. "That's news, isn't it?"

In September, just as the brethren began to dig the sweet
potatoes, the rebel General Gideon Pillow – having with some
difficulty kept at bay since spring his yen to do so – moved his
troops into the Hickman County port town of Columbus. He had
received his leave to proceed from the Confederate commander
of forces in west Tennessee, General Leonidas Polk now being
convinced that Federal forces were on the verge of tenanting the
self-same property in a drive to control the rivers that fed the South.
Not to be outdone, Union forces under the command of Brigadier
General Ulysses S. Grant occupied Paducah and Smithland.

Kentucky's neutrality thus slipped out of reach, beyond the grasp of those who scrambled hardest to recapture it. Governor Beriah Magoffin, incensed, waved his fists and demanded the immediate absence of all forces from his state, but the legislature met him only halfway and singled out the Confederate troops as uninvited guests. No more substantial than a spider's web to begin with, the state's position was now beyond repair. Union headquarters were established at Louisville and, as far as Frankfort was concerned, Kentucky had gone with the North.

Rebel forces, however, were not so easily turned out, and many of the commonwealth's citizenry were likewise less than convinced that they wanted them gone. Some thirteen hundred troops under the command of Brigadier General Simon Bolivar Buckner seized control of Bowling Green, pitching their camps on the hospitable shores of the Barren River less than fifteen miles northeast of Shakertown.

With upwards of three thousand inhabitants Bowling Green was no one-mule town. It offered its locals eight churches, three high schools, two weekly papers, more than two dozen clothing-fancy-drug-or-dry-goods stores, four first-class groceries, two hotels, several boarding houses, two restaurants, a billiard saloon, five livery stables, a new jailhouse, a carriage manufactory, a handsome railroad depot, several pork and tobacco establishments, a courthouse and clerk's office, seventeen lawyers, fourteen doctors, and loafers *ad libitum*.

A man could live well in Bowling Green and the Confederate occupying troops looked forward to exactly that.

But however much comfort it might offer the troops, they arrived to find Bowling Green a town divided; an impressive number of the populace had already closed up and left, being Unionists in fear for their lives. The invaders had not needed to advertise their intentions: every man, woman and child in town knew without needing to ask that when the rebels flowed up from Camp Boone and the Union troops came down from Louisville the meeting point would be Bowling Green. Folks had simply made their plans accordingly.

Some said Union troops had come down as far as Muldraugh's Hill to stop the rebels' northward drive to Louisville, engaging the Confederates there and forcing them back to Bowling Green. Others dismissed this as wishful thinking: the town had been taken without the firing of a single shot.

Part and parcel of the rebel occupation was fortification of the town and possession of the rolling stock at Bowling Green station, as well as the Memphis line of the Louisville & Nashville – on which they had arrived – as far down as Clarksville. When this last was achieved the Shakers, whose depot sat on that line, found themselves cut off from uncensored communication with their sister communities (or anyone else, for that matter) in the north. They had heard the last they would know for sure for a long time to come.

And by the end of the following month the Shakers were given cause to understand that the many chickens and biscuits they'd given up to Nathan Bedford Forrest's men – and presumably the forty-eight yards of blanket cloth that had turned up missing at the fulling mill after they departed – that night back in August were only the topmost skin of the onion the war effort would require from the community.

In this the Shakers certainly were not alone. There were thousands of soldiers drilling in the roadways, and no perceptible effort was devoted to ensuring they kept their hands to themselves. Missouri troops who pitched camp on the lawns of Warner Louis Underwood's house cut down his trees and razed some of the slave cabins in the adjacent quarters, which obscured the view of the fort to be built back of his barn. Plantation darkies from one end of the occupied area to the other found the cows drained dry in the mornings, with no milk left for the children of the houses they served. Fieldhands daily rebuilt the fences torn down by the soldiers for use as firewood and worked to salvage crops trodden down for no reason better than that the troops were too lazy to go the long way around.

The Negroes, naturally, found their work more difficult even than before, and not only because of the soldiers' light-fingered and light-footed ways. They, perhaps more than anyone, had reason to be anxious for news.

On October's final Tuesday a meeting was convened in nearby Russellville, aimed at opening up communications with the government of the Confederate States with an eye to establishing by some means a constitutional relationship. The present state legislature now being Unionist past rescue, such secessionist stalwarts as the planter George W. Johnson and General John C. Breckinridge determined to concoct their own government. The Russellville meeting lasted two days and accused the legislature in Frankfort of depriving Kentuckians of their right to do with their government as they saw fit, and – having decided there was too much Federal pressure in the state capital for them to get a fair hearing for their opposition views – delegates from thirty-two counties with Southern loyalties set in motion the machinery that resulted in the holding of a sovereignty convention in Russellville on the eighteenth of November.

That very morning of the eighteenth, Breckinridge with his brigade passed westbound on the Great Road through South Union, assigned the task of providing protection for the convention. With him were five regiments – one cavalry, four infantry, some 5,000 foot troops, and a thousand more on horseback. The Shaker children ran to the fences and watched as they might have a circus parade the procession of men, and the hundred and ten wagons loaded with tents and commissary provisions and such it had in tow. The Believers saw on the wagons some several Negroes brought along by their masters to serve as body slaves and waiters, and further counted amongst the infantry more than a dozen others, armed as were the whites.

"Someday their masters will rue the day they taught those boys to fire a gun," said Brother Urban Johns to no one in particular as he stood watching from the steps of the ministry shop.

While Breckinridge's men stood guard in Russellville the renegade legislature refined the argument that the state of Kentucky deserved better than whatever it was being offered in Frankfort, declared the commonwealth free of the United States government, named Bowling Green the new state capital, and patched together a little group of councillors that would support the new governor, George Johnson, until there was time to come up with a full-fledged legislature. A delegation was dispatched to Montgomery in hopes of obtaining for the new Kentucky equal membership in the Confederate States, and while Brother Austin Innes was teasing his boys with an article from the Bowling Green *Gazette* President Jefferson Davis was recommending Kentucky's admission to the final session of the Confederate Provisional Congress – now considered to be less temporary than permanent.

The window was a temptation, Brother Austin could only admit it: the boys had a point. He didn't actually realize he was standing there, mesmerized as he was with his hands in his pockets, until behind him the shrill adolescent voices of George Jenkins and William Snyder as they debated the veracity of the *Gazette* story retrieved him from his reverie. At fourteen and thirteen the two boys were all but hobbled by the weight of the accumulated wisdom of their years.

Across the road Austin could see a horse tied to the post in front of the trustees' office. While the schoolmaster watched, Brother Reuben Wise came out the door, swaddled in his heaviest winter coat and followed close behind by Jefferson Shannon. He hoisted himself into the saddle and reached down to shake hands with Brother Jefferson, then pulled the animal's reins and started up the Morgantown road. Jefferson watched him until he was out of sight before he went back inside.

Austin knew where Reuben was going.

*   *   *

By November's end the Believers could only accept that Western Kentucky had, for all intents and purposes, joined with the Confederate States of America, whatever opinion the legislature east in Frankfort might have to the contrary. The signs they could see as they looked out their doors were unmistakeable. Strangely (or so it seemed to Confederate enrollment officers), even the illusion of statehood did not bring with it a wave of Kentucky men hell-bent on enlistment, and with news of this drought of volunteers arose the rumor of a draft into the Confederate army. Before long the spectre of conscription stalked South Union like a thief of souls. Men of an age to fight, men whose sympathies lay with the Union, were faced with the prospect of being pressed into military service by a government whose collective eye was on the destruction of all the Northern heart held dear. Such men fled their homes and hearths when their apprehension reached fever pitch and made their way north to the Ohio River, east to Louisville, anywhere the Union still held.

Fears inside the fences of Shakertown were no less real. Conscription could reach just as easily into Shaker dwellings as others, and thereby seek to set Shaker men of peace at odds with the pacifism that was the breath of their existence. One by one the brethren with most reason to dread the Confederate enrollment officer arrived at the door of the ministry shop for guidance. Their druthers lay with the North but they would not kill or even march on its behalf. If the Confederacy laid claim to them, then what?

Reuben Wise was just three weeks shy of his forty-third birthday, a few months Austin's junior by the calendar but by feel perhaps years younger. The two men shared a retiring room at the Center, and living in such proximity Austin was aware of his brother's apprehensions about conscription even without him saying as much. Reuben's face had been dark with concern since the rumor of a draft began to circulate among the brethren, and he confided his fears to Austin – a more educated man than he but in many ways similar to himself and by reputation not given to ridicule. Long evening hours when they might have been asleep they had spent in the dark, talking about the fissure that lay between pacifism and cowardice. Something of a hot-head, Brother Reuben was certainly no coward – but he had lived the life of a Believer long enough to know he could not take up arms in a good cause, let alone a bad one. As easy to shoot the Lord as a stranger, it seemed to him, if both were not in fact the same.

"Probably best you go north," Austin told him that last night. "Get to Union Village, stay there til it blows over. This fool mess can't last long. Talk to Brother Urban."

The notion of leaving home, after so long in one place, was uncomfortable. Reuben looked at Austin as if he had something else to say, but on reflection he could not say it after all. "Probably best I go," he agreed finally, without enthusiasm. "But what about you? It's as likely they'll take you as me. What'll you do? Will you go?"

Austin blushed, flattered as much as anything by Reuben's suggestion. His smile, not visible in the absence of a candle, could be heard in the sound of his voice.

"Shoot," he said, "who'd take me as a soldier? Use me for target practice, maybe, feed me to the horses." He did not often refer to his height, which would have been a vanity, but even so it seemed to him a small fellow such as he would make a poor fighting man. The army, of whichever persuasion, would hit a sad patch before it came after Austin Innes.

"I can't leave my boys anyway," he said, scratching behind his ear. "You see 'em, Reuben. All eyes they are, like rabbits in torchlight. You think they don't know? When they have trouble they look to me. I couldn't go if friend Davis came for me himself."

"Maybe," Reuben said. "But it seems to me anybody's desperate enough to fight this war is desperate enough to take a man like you."

In the darkness the two men laughed, sharing the last joke of their peacetime. The following day, with fifty dollars in his pocket, a borrowed horse between his knees, and the blessing of the ministry on his departure, Reuben Wise left South Union. It was too much to expect a Shakerman to point a rifle at another child of God and pull the trigger.

1862

A
mos did not come down with measles, one of the few
boys who escaped unspotted. There had been a carrier
amongst the rebel soldiers who flowed through but tarried
on his way, and one of the boys had thereby been infected. Within
days the measles were epidemic throughout the population of
South Union's smaller boys.

"Next comes the plague of locusts," said Brother Jess Rankin
when Charley Spencer, one of the East boys, came out with the
scourge. "The soldiers have brought everything else."

Sister Lucy Shannon and her blood sister Olive had their
hands full with their rambunctious little patients, who overran
the beds of the Center's infirmary and soon caused the children's
rooms upstairs to be cleared of the uninfected and a quarantine
area established. The girls seemed unaffected for the moment,
but no chances were taken: the Center's smaller sisters were
moved temporarily to the frame house at the East and joined
up with the girls there. Boys who had already come through the
affliction were relocated to the retiring rooms of the brethren,
an event of considerable rarity and an indication of trust – which
put the boys on their best behavior and prompted the elders

to joke that measles was a guest that ought to come calling more often.

It was decided that Amos and two other boys who showed no signs of infection would be sent to live at the North for the duration of the crisis, a development that brought from Amos one of the only serious tantrums the sisters had ever seen him throw. He did not know the East boys, he shrieked, and he would be lonely without Brother Harry. Tender-hearted John Perryman suggested Brother Littlebourne move with him to the North, which sentimental suggestion caused Eldress Betsy to laugh aloud.

"My stars, Brother John," she said, "if you ever want a spoiled child you'll certainly know the best way to get one. You let him scream awhile; when his throat gets sore, he'll stop."

Having followed Eldress Betsy to the kitchen in an attempt to wear her down, Amos found himself a place on the dining hall floor to kick and wail. William Rice, at the age of seventy-six too frail for strenuous tasks, was asked to keep an eye on the boy and take care he did not choke during his crying jag.

Brother William sat silently, sipping the cup of sassafras tea left for him by Sister Luana Slover, and drummed his fingers on the table as he watched the boy thrash. He had not thought it wise to put a caretaker to so small a child to begin with, and here was proof of his pudding.

"Scream, Amos," he said patiently, with near-deafness as his ally. "It's lovely. Don't stop."

Eventually, convinced his display of noisy despair would get him nowhere, Amos sat up on the floor. He had not realized there was nobody left to hear him but old Brother William, who couldn't.

Rice was prepared to offer the exhausted, damp child his handkerchief but would have nothing to do with consoling him. "Bet your head smarts, don't it, boy?" he asked when Amos arrived snuffling and puffy-eyed at his knee. "Now, blow."

Three flights up from the kitchen Lucy and Olive Shannon had deputized a handful of the sisters to help in the darkened

sickroom, where the boys were like so many eels in a bucket. If
not brought to blossom outside the spots might come out inside,
this the nurses knew for trouble, and heat was the key. A count
of the small patients was taken, and enough good blankets were
taken from safe-keeping to bundle the afflicted. Clean flannel
nightshirts were brought in, and each boy was rolled and cocooned
in cloth and wool to aid the warming process. Boys whose spots
had already come out were dunked in long baking soda baths to
ease the maddening itch.

The epidemic in their midst served the peculiar function of
taking the Shakers' minds off the lunacy that was blowing along
the road at their doors. And when, as the retiring hour passed one
mid-January evening, and the sound of cavalry stopping outside
disrupted the quiet of the house, the brethren were slow to send
Austin Innes to the door.

A mounted Confederate officer too impolite to identify himself
or even dismount told Brother Austin his two hundred and fifty
men required supper and lodging – quickly, they were tired. His
presence, in itself, was no surprise. The Confederacy's lack of
virtually everything was from the outset like a bill presented daily
to the Shakers at South Union. Known for their generosity, the
Shakers were bound together by a doctrine that, among other things,
counted as sinful the turning away of anyone in need. This giving
habit of Believers was the basis for a reputation that spread like
warm butter over cornbread through the Confederacy thereabouts,
and the Shaker village at the well-travelled crossroads was already
known for the hospitality it offered to those who asked. But with
the children ailing the house had been in confusion and, as he took
note of the captain's needs, Austin was nonetheless loathe to see
the Believers' ovens fired up again on behalf of so many.

"There's a tavern just west of here, friend, a mile on the south
side," he said helpfully, stepping out onto the porch and pointing
along the Great Road. Summoned from his room to the door he

was in his shirtsleeves and waistcoat, and the night was cold on the linen. "Jacob Yost's it is, and right on your way. We've got a houseful of sick children here, and the sisters have been up and down with them day and night."

The captain came down off his horse and even from beneath the bottom step looked the schoolmaster level, eye to eye.

"Now, see here," he said, "your problems with your children are your own. I've told you what I want, and it seems to me the choice is yours: give it up of your own volition or I'll have my men break your doors down and take whatever we need." He turned his attention to the straightening of his hands in his riding gloves, aiming to give the little upstart at the door time to realize he meant no more or less than exactly what he said. "Well?"

Austin found Eldress Nancy down in the kitchen, still fussing with baking soda poultices for the boys' spots, and put the rebel captain's threat to her.

"He'll do it, brother?" she asked, exhausted.

"He'll do it, sister, of that I'm sure."

Taking her dish of poultices with her, Eldress Nancy wearily went upstairs to wake the kitchen sisters. Austin fetched the brethren and went back down to the front door.

The captain had been joined by his colonel, who asked when his men could expect to be fed.

"Two hours, earliest," Austin replied, his eyes full of apology but unwilling to give more ground than Eldress Nancy had already conceded.

The two officers exchanged looks. The terms offered were unlikely to be improved upon, and they nodded their surrender.

"My men can't just wait here in the road," the captain said.

"Then lend me a horse and I'll take you up to a place you can quarter the night," Austin said, and vaulted himself into the saddle of the mount whose reins a sergeant offered him.

Still without his jacket, but unheedful of the cold, he led the column down to the surviving buildings of the fire-damaged

West, indicating which were most hospitable to the needs of his men, which to the horses. He seldom had occasion to ride these days, and the sensation of sitting a horse in the dead of night pleased him.

The captain turned to his sergeant. "Pass the word to the men. Let them rest themselves until three o'clock, then there'll be provisions ready."

The sergeant moved off with his message, but the troops hardly needed to be told. Many were already asleep on the floors and in the haymows.

A number of the men had after all gone off with the colonel to Yost's tavern, and with matters well in hand the captain shifted in his saddle and looked Austin up and down.

"You look like a man who's ridden a horse," he said.

"Now and then," Austin said.

"It's a skill with which a man can do his country service."

"I'm sure it is," Austin agreed, as anxious now to be dismissed as the soldiers had been.

"Do you think of joining up?"

Austin turned his head to one side. The ice here was brittle and he had already wandered far from shore. "Now and again," he said, seeking safety in ambiguity. "But not so far to much effect."

The captain folded his hands over the withers of his mount. "Then if you can be of use to your womenfolk, you'd best go on."

An escort was detailed to see Brother Austin back to the house and return to the West with the horse. He had been insulted and knew it. Years had come and gone since he had felt so close to calling another man out.

Earlier that day five Texas Rangers had come through the village, desirous of commerce (or so they said), anxious to buy jeans or fine silk kerchiefs such as the Shakerwomen were known to make. The brethren had learned anything shown might as likely be stolen as paid for, however, and thus they said there was nothing to see.

Instead, Brother Lorenzo Pearcifield took the riders to the post office, got them something to eat, and later he and Elder Solomon sat with them out on the steps, hoping to persuade them to move on.

The attention of one of the men was drawn to the Center, and he seemed to be memorizing every brick visible to him from where he sat. His attentions put the brethren on their guard.

"That's a right big house, that one there," he said finally. "How many you got living there?"

"Just now, maybe ninety, give or take a few," Elder Solomon replied.

"Shoot," the Ranger said, "you put that many of us in a house and we'd kill each other off 'fore Sunday."

Elder Solomon regarded this observation, weighed his response, and decided to go ahead. "Well, the Good Man taught us not to swear or fight or kill or take whisky, and by those rules we manage to live quite well together."

"Don't know no Goodman," the Ranger replied, having searched his memory for such an acquaintance and found none. "Guess he don't live in Texas."

"Oh, He may not live there," Solomon said, amused, "but I'll warrant He's been there once or twice."

"Maybe," the young fellow said, twisting his moustache, still drawn by the idea of ninety people living in that one house. "But if y'all don't swear or fight or kill or take whisky, what makes the time go?"

"We find ways to fill our days," Elder Solomon told him. "We have work to do, work for our own living and for something to give to the poor."

"And what do you do of a Sunday?"

"Well, now," Solomon replied brightly, happy to come to the point, "that's the one thing that's 'most always the same. We read and write, and have a think, and go to meeting."

"Then, sir, I reckon y'all must be very good people," said the soldier. "I reckon this must be Heaven on earth."

February

T hat first Wednesday they could hear the cannon-fire, even at such distance. In the winter-clear air, a hundred miles due west, the troops of the North were trying to wrest control of Fort Henry, or perhaps Fort Donelson, maybe even both, from the Confederacy. This the Shakers counted as peculiar: had the sound come from the north, and more loudly, they would have understood. They had after all been given to understand that General Pierre Gustave Toutant Beauregard, rebel hero of Sumter, had given the order to evacuate the troops from Bowling Green. Had the sound come from that direction, then, the Shakers would have been less apprehensive. As it was each cannon shot that sounded put a colder edge to weather already right for its season, and the rumor of war was confirmed. The following night, when Brother Austin came back from one of his increasingly frequent news-sheet expeditions to the depot, he was full of the word that came up by the cars from Memphis: Fort Henry had fallen to the Federals, the rebel forces there having been evacuated across to Fort Donelson. Coming from Tennessee, the defeat echoed hollow, like a tragedy. To the Believers it had not quite the same sound.

*   *   *

Soon before the fall of Fort Henry Elder Solomon Rankin – whose conversation with the fractious Texas Rangers on the post office steps had strengthened his faith in the Confederate troops – was lured into an exchange with a group of fidgety rebels curious about the Shakers' unwillingness to fight. Solomon and Brother Austin had nearly finished unloading a wagonload of hot supper got up for the soldiers, and the long day was not yet over, but he was always willing to make time for a word if the subject was to his liking. Such a time was this.

"We remember what the Savior taught us," Solomon told the inquiring rebel while he lifted down the last of the cornbread. "If your enemy smite you on one cheek, turn to him the other." He set the box down and rose up again, and as he did so the soldier backhanded him an earnest slap against his right cheek. Old Solomon reeled backward into Brother Austin's shoulder, straightened himself in time to turn his face, and received the equivalent blow to his left cheek from the soldier's other hand.

Austin tensed, but Solomon made no protest.

"Get up there, boy," he said instead to his red-haired younger brother, motioning him back to the wagon as the derisive laughter of the soldiers rose around them. "Best we see what else Eldress Betsy's got needs conveying from the kitchen."

The schoolmaster hoisted himself up over the wheel and out of the corner of his eye saw the soldier, unrepentant, having learned nothing from the old man's dignity in the face of such cruel and absurd humiliation. Elder Solomon had not even raised his hand to ease the sting to his jaw, but the soldier saw none of what lay behind the Shaker's courage.

Austin Innes unwound the reins and snapped them against the horse's rump. At that instant he wanted nothing so much as to kill that jeering soldier, and his heart hollowed as he realized he had learned even less from Solomon's lesson than the man who had precipitated it.

The soldiers were fleeing Bowling Green, making for Nashville. Back in town fire was being put to the first of many buildings the Confederacy could not afford to leave standing in its wake.

The children were fearful without knowing why, and school for the boys was abandoned until some sense of normalcy could be restored. With fewer than forty brethren to look after some two hundred women, children and old men, Brother Austin could not in any case be spared to the schoolroom. Brother Harry Littlebourne took Amos up to Black Lick, and they were tapping trees at the sugar camp when they saw the first wisps go up. Then the skies northeast of them went dark as evening.

The boy looked up at what he thought were gathering clouds.

"Will it rain?"

"Nay," said Brother Harry, "that's smoke."

"All that?"

"All that."

Bowling Green was in flames, burning to the ground, torched by rebel troops who would see it in ashes before they'd let the Union army find anything of use when it broke through.

The sound of cannon-fire all Friday was fearsome. From Baker Hill north of Bowling Green the Union troops hurled shells a mile and a half to the town, striving not to hit the engine house ("the Round House," as it was affectionately known locally, by simple reason of its shape), the government warehouse or the depot, all of them down by the station on Adams Street. Whatever was still stored in them was likely to be worth having, and with enough cannon shot the Federals might keep the rebels and their infernal matches a safe distance away. This they achieved, while at the same time scaring the living daylights out of the citizenry, who fled over the hills in the best interests of their lives. With the panicking townfolk in the chaotic streets were the tatters of the Confederate occupying force and numerous horses, with and without riders. Eventually word was sent out to the Union commanders, advising them that other than civilians there was no one left to kill in Bowling Green, and in the early afternoon the roar of the cannons stopped. An instant after the firing ceased, a squad of Texas Rangers barrelled through to Adams Street and set fire to the buildings by the station. An instant of calm was all they'd needed.

With the shelling's end at Bowling Green, the Shakers could hear from the west the low, distant sound that told them Fort Donelson was under attack and for all they knew had been all day. On the fourteenth of February what the newspapers would call "iron valentines" were being exchanged by the North and South, a constant display of deadly affection that went on and on and on.

By the following morning Union troops had managed to enter the ruins of Bowling Green, in the absence of the bridges wading across the swollen Big Barren.

Down in South Union, white again with fresh snowfall, they could still see smoke, this time rising from Auburn, just a mile or so past Jacob Yost's tavern on the Russellville road. There was nothing of military value there, and thus the Shakers determined the rebels had decided to leave nothing between Nashville and the invading Union troops but ash and scorched ground.

"We could pray they're running too fast to do a thorough job," said Brother John McLean.

"We could do that, and I reckon we will," agreed Brother Jefferson Shannon. "Meantime we'd best keep our eyes open tonight."

It was not, to be sure, the way they normally spent the evening before Sabbath, when by habit they finished up their chores and tidied up in preparation for a day on which no work was to be done except what could not go undone. But if they did not prepare for this Sabbath in unShakerly fashion next week might bring a Sabbath saddened by that neglect, and perforce they made ready for the nightwatch. With the Federal troops in Bowling Green they were once again part of the Union, and on the wings of that thought the tiredness flew.

Next day, just as the dinner things were being cleared away, there came again the thudding sound of horses on the road, and inside the Center every muscle tensed. The long nightmare was perhaps not yet over, and they were not ready. But looking out the windows, they could see – in blue uniforms instead of butternut, with eagles embroidered on their caps – a squad of thirty-two Union troops gathered at the bottom of the Center house steps.

The brethren were out the front door like small boys, tempted to touch the soldiers to assure themselves that these men of the Ohio Volunteer Cavalry were no dream come of too much wishful thinking.

"Are you the leader of this place, sir?" said the tall captain to Brother Urban.

"Nay, but I can speak for all of us," said Urban. "You're kindly welcome here, I tell you. It's been a long winter without you."

"Well, sir, we heard you'd had a little trouble hereabouts, and up to Auburn, and you might be expecting worse yet, so we've been sent out to see nothing happens that you'd just as soon didn't. We'll stay in the area awhile, if it's all the same to you. Maybe you've got a little patch of ground where we could camp."

Brother Urban ran his hand through his thinning hair, surprised by the depth of his own emotion and almost unable to believe that after so many weeks suspended above the war-time candle flame the burn could be salved so simply. The brethren looked at each other, and at the clear-eyed officer, and laughed. "Forgive us, captain," he said finally, and grasped the young man's hand, "but you can't know how good it is to see you."

Eldress Nancy appeared at the door, drying her hands on her apron, her face all joy. "Are you boys hungry?" she asked the soldiers circled around the brethren.

"Well, ma'am," said the captain, "we wouldn't say no, and that's a fact."

The sisters who had pressed up close behind Eldress Nancy retreated to the kitchen to fetch up what was left from dinner, and anything else they could find. They rushed the platters and boxes back up the stairs and watched as the brethren passed it to their guardian angels, never so glad that there was more than enough to go around.

The soldiers had seen the wreckage of Bowling Green firsthand, and it seemed to them some million and a half dollars' damage might have been done, if not more. The rebels had been as thorough as possible in their methods of destruction, given the time they'd had to work with. As much of value as could be sensibly carried or otherwise conveyed had been taken by the evacuating forces. What had to be left behind was piled in the streets and set alight. One burning building approached by the troops was flickering slow, and entering it to see what might be rescued they found shelves filled with explosive shells. Had the abandoned ordnance not been found before the conflagration came, the men would certainly have died in the explosion that followed and that whole end of town been reduced to rubble.

"They can't be travelling too light," Elder Solomon said. "They've stolen just about everything that wasn't tied down, including what was in the beehives and near every decent horse we had. Wasn't just us, either. They went after coming on for everyone we know – took some folks' last mule, even."

One dour sergeant waved his hand at this, almost offended. "Shoot," he said, "time of war that's only sensible, you ask me. If I was in need of a horse and couldn't find one no fair way I'd be quick enough to steal one."

Solomon and Urban found each other's eyes, and in them saw the same alarm at this. Suddenly they were suspicious, each man understanding it in the other's mind without asking.

There was the sound of a wagon: Jefferson Shannon and Lorenzo Pearcifield on horseback riding alongside, with sundry of the brethren on the seat. They were just on their way back from Russellville, having picked up a load of sugar that had been shipped up from Paris, Tennessee – slowly and with unimaginable difficulty. Its arrival within fetching distance after only a month of delays and who-struck-john was little short of miraculous.

"What in tarnation's that?" said the sergeant.

"Some of our brethren..." began Solomon, but the troops had already gone to investigate the arriving wagon. They were back in short order, and – pulling their horses up toward the East – they said they had some matters to attend to but would be back by nightfall.

As the brethren watched them go, some of the shine had already worn off.

"You think they're not Union troops, don't you, brother?" Solomon asked Urban quietly.

"The uniforms are right enough," Urban said as the two men walked back over to the trustees' office. "The words, most of 'em, make tolerable sense. But there's something about it has a scratchy feel – maybe what that sergeant said about the rightness of stealing civilian horses. That tripped you up, too, seemed to me."

They settled in their office chairs and looked at each other. So many things they had been told by so many soldiers of so many ranks of both armies in the last so many weeks, and so many of them had been outright lies.

"If you were looking to take advantage of folks, now would be the time," Solomon said, wrapping his arms over his chest and tapping his feet, as often he did when he was thinking. "There's Unionists a-plenty around here, and after what's happened they'd trust a blue uniform quick as lightning."

"We did," Urban said, nodding.

"We did indeed."

"Better get on over and get the brethren back together," Urban said, tired almost beyond the idea of standing up again. "We'll just have to keep us an eye on those boys."

Then at the sound of raised voices they were on their feet and out the door, and there was Brother Austin – his red hair flying, his hat long gone – running up the road.

"Brother Austin!" Solomon called to him. "What ails you?"

Shouting over his shoulder Austin replied: "Fire!"

Urban and Solomon looked up toward the East, over Austin Innes' head, and saw smoke rising from the culverts just below the Gathering Order. Others of the brethren and sisters, smelling the smoke so near on the winter air, came in a rush to the road.

"Dear Heaven," whispered Solomon. "It's them rebel soldiers, and we thought they were Union boys. They're back to burn us out."

A picture of themselves tomorrow came into the Shakers' minds – burned out, homeless, scattered to the four winds like floating ashes, their community gone and their cause here lost. As one man and woman they sank to their knees in the crossroads and prayed.

Brother Jefferson, still sitting his horse beside the wagon-load of sugar, took off after Brother Austin, and Elder John Rankin and Brother Urban followed, leaving old Solomon to spark the stricken brethren and sisters into action against the spread of flames.

Below the East house Jefferson Shannon found the Union soldiers busily setting fire to the cowpits along the railroad tracks, workmanlike in their efficiency.

"You there, captain!" he said loudly and testily. "This seems passing strange behavior for men sent to protect civilian property, putting a torch to the railroad."

The captain looked up pleasantly, brushed his hands together and walked down the slope to Jefferson's horse.

"Just orders, sir," the captain said, pulling down the yellow uniform scarf that held the smoke back from his throat and stroking the nose of Jefferson's horse. He kept one eye always on the progress of his men as he spoke. "Just orders."

"What orders, then?" Jefferson asked him. "How does it benefit the good people of Logan County to destroy the railway?"

Finally realizing he was being interrogated by an honest man whose trust he had somehow lost, the captain straightened up and assumed a more soldierly posture.

"We don't know what's happening up at Fort Donelson, sir," he explained as Austin Innes, perspiring in the cold, came up alongside. "There's 21,000 Confederate troops up there as far as we can tell, and to the moment of my dispatch the outcome was unsure. There's also some fighting going on in Clarksville. Many of our men are still coming across the river – not having the bridges has slowed things down some – and if the secesh are managing to rout us at Donelson or Clarksville we don't want 'em rushing through here on the cars before we're ready to push 'em back. My orders were to disable the railway line in such a fashion as to make it easily reparable in the event of Union victory – "

"For which we pray," offered Jefferson.

"Yes sir, I'm sure," the captain agreed.

"Well, if you take a notion to burn down anything else we'd be grateful if you could just let us know before you get your matches out. You scared us near out of our wits."

"That was never our intention," the young officer said, red-faced. "You have my apology, sir. The balance of our expressed orders do not involve any further firing."

"That's a blessing," said Jefferson, "for which we're duly grateful."

"Now, if you'll excuse me, I'll see to the job at hand." The captain touched his finger to his hatbrim and pulled his neckerchief back up over his mouth as he walked back to the firing party.

"You believe that?" Jefferson asked down to Austin. The schoolmaster's constant perusal of the news-sheets gave him a greater understanding of military mind and movement than anyone else in the community, and his opinion in such matters was therefore worth having.

Still catching his breath, Austin nodded. "Seems a sensible course if they don't know what's happening west," he said.

"Well, then, get up here and let me take you back before you catch your death," he said. Jefferson put a hand down and Austin jumped up behind him on the horse.

Halfway back to the Center they met up with John Rankin and Urban Johns, and dutifully recounted the conversation as they had heard it. They found amongst themselves a shared inclination to believe, and thus when they arrived at the Center the facts as they knew them were reassuringly conveyed as gospel.

The Ohio boys were as good as their word. When the burning was done (and they did no more, although Urban would learn it had been in their discretion to burn the Auburn bridge) they came back into the village and kept as keen an eye on Shakertown as the Believers themselves had done before. And when word of the Union victory at Fort Donelson came through they went back to the railway line, their instructions to rebuild being clear, likewise the need. Before long the line, which the Shakers had missed for the jovial sound of normalcy it provided, came back to life.

May

I t was spring, and a general time of coming back, for people and for things.

In March two riders arrived at Shakertown, Reuben Wise and Jackson McGowan. Both brethren had gone north rather than be pressed into the service of the Confederacy, and both had come after some days to the Shaker community of Union Village in Ohio. They sent word to South Union, saying they were safe and well amongst Believers, and for their friends now distant this news was a source of relief and distress: that they were protected from conscription was a godsend, but they were needed at home and they were missed there. In Ohio Reuben and Jackson were troubled only by their absence from where they felt they belonged, and when the army of the United States took Bowling Green back from the rebels the two were on their way south and home as soon as was considered prudent.

Reuben and Jackson rejoined the brethren at South Union just as they were returning to the fields, stretching their legs to the land after the long winter behind them, breathing deep the sweet, moderate air and the scent of the peaceful farm country over which it passed. Spring of any year at Shakertown was a time of breaking ground, of preparing the soil for the good things of the earth. The boys were released from their school year – so chaotic that Brother Austin feared he had accomplished little – to help put in peas and clover seed, sweet potatoes and summer corn. In the herb gardens the young plants began to show through the good land of Logan County, and the young boys bent their heads to weeding around them. The elders were glad for this return to a semblance of the normal life they had lived before the occupation: a child should give his life to healthy pursuits, they felt, in the clean and open air, untroubled by matters beyond his understanding. The Shakertown children had seen too much that they did not comprehend over the dreadful winter that was mercifully, finally, gone. They were young and resilient and seemed unchanged, but there had been night terrors and tantrums such as were seldom known before at South Union. With the recapture of Bowling Green by the forces of the Union, the Shakers were glad to hope peace would find the children, too. Better always that a child should see plants growing, than soldiers marching.

In mid-April mail sacks were carried up by wagon from the depot to the post office, the first the Believers had seen for seven months. They could, at last, communicate freely again with the Societies north and east, after depending for so long on the occasional arrival of letters hand-carried by those pilgrims hardy and ingenious enough to move from one community to another, to be answered by similar means. They knew little enough of what was happening with the people for whom they cared most, and – of the eighteen communities the one most sorely tried by the turmoil of the severed nation – little enough was known of they themselves. That, too, was over now. Or so they felt free to hope.

The five hundred and more Shaker sheep were brought to shearing, and as always the children were allowed to observe the proceedings if they had no chores to occupy them. It took eight full days to separate the sheep from their wool, and during those days the children would drape themselves like so much wet laundry over the fences at the sheep house, giggling at the bewildered looks on the animals' faces as the brethren held them for the shears. There was nothing so funny, it would have seemed to anyone who heard the children laugh, as the scrawny, slippery, pink figure of a once-wooly sheep after the brethren had cut his sweater away.

And then the strawberries came.

But the Lord, who so freely gave with one bountiful hand, also took with the other.

Wise, kind, whimsical Brother John McLean died at the age of sixty-seven, suddenly and without warning one early morning in mid-March while the Center family slept. Ten weeks later the ministry sat down to write Brother Harvey Eades – still in his peculiar exile at Union Village – to say his father, Elder Samuel Guy Eades, one of the founding brethren of the South Union Society, had died four months shy of his eighty-fifth year. They thought he would want to know.

The graveyard behind the ministry shop was thus over three months furnished with two new citizens, and the Center house was thereby deprived of the same. The brethren and sisters who could be spared from their work on the two funeral days were present for the buryings, and the children – Shaker children did not attend funerals – spent the morning grouped all together elsewhere in the village. This so seldom occurred that, when it did, they knew without being told that the occasion that brought them all to one place called for quiet rather than noisy tomfoolery. When their caretakers came to reclaim them to their families there would be a somberness about the dwelling houses, and somewhere in the retiring rooms a bed would stand newly empty. Such was their intimacy with death.

The soldiers still came in their hundreds for food and lodging, competing now with the refugees, but they were somehow different from the rebels of winter. It was not uncommon for the Federal troops to ask the sisters not to go to any trouble: whatever happened to be cold in the larder would do just fine, thank you, and they did not wish to make a nuisance of themselves. This to the sisters, after so many nights they had been awakened in the small hours to demands for fresh bread by the hundredweight, was a wonder. So hectic had the months of the rebel occupation been, and so much less frantic did the needs of those first Union forces seem to be, that the sisters almost felt they had free time on their hands. They needed something to fill it.

By April a replacement claim on their idler hours presented itself. The fighting southwest of them at Pittsburg Landing, near Shiloh in Tennessee, filled Bowling Green's four military hospitals, already tasked past endurance, to overflowing – and the graveyards sadly similar. The news from Pittsburg Landing was like a pall draped over the county: with 23,000 dead and wounded from both sides there was no one who knew no one who was there.

When they were not about provisioning the hospitals, as they felt bound to do, the sisters rolled up their sleeves and undertook to repaint the inside of the meeting house. Working from a recipe that, from its sound, was better suited to the kitchen of Beelzebub than the workshop of a Christian, they mixed from blueberries, buttermilk and arsenic buckets and buckets of the hard-wearing blue paint common to the wood fittings in Shaker meeting houses across the country. They brushed the fresh new color across beams in sore need of attention and timed their strokes to the songs they sang as they worked.

"Your hand is dancing," Amos told Sister Elizabeth as he held a bucket high enough to meet her dipping brush.

Brother Reuben Wise, a carpenter of considerable gifts, was meanwhile given a team of brethren and set to building a lumber shed and carriage house east of North Lane, a structure to be handsomely constructed of vertical timber covered with clapboards. Others of the hand-minded brethren were busy taking down the old log kitchen north of the brick shed, carefully – in keeping with the thrift of Shaker habit – saving the remnants in case they should be useful for some other purpose.

The village thus renewed itself as it renewed the crops and, despite the desperate conflict of the Rebellion, every hand seemed blessed with as much as it could hold.

Brother Harry Littlebourne did not much mind winter – as seasons went it was not much better or worse than any other for farming, and it had its uses – but he was always glad when the warmer weather came and he could get out amongst the tall rows of crops he had planted himself, shoots and leaves and vines he had coaxed up from the earth through careful work and attention that bordered on affection. In fact, he loved the expectant look of the fallow fields when the weather broke, knowing as he did that he had it in his gift to make something happen there. It was less a feeling of power than of complicity; the bare earth could use him, and he knew best how to be of service.

The hills of sweet potatoes were being laid in, and he and Amos had been intent after it all day. The seed-sprout bag lay limp and empty over Harry's shoulder, and with the sound of the bell they had been summoned in for supper. Their efforts of the hours past were co-operative: the man's large hands fashioned the hill into which the boy's small fingers laid the sprouts. In all, Harry thought the process might be faster without Amos, but in truth he enjoyed the child's company. He was a sensible, sturdy little individual, with a merry laugh and a growing respect for the soil he was learning to tend. Harry Littlebourne was better pleased to be with him than without him.

They walked back toward the Center, giving thought to whether they were hungry, and it seemed to them as though they most probably were. They wondered as they neared the brick shed whether the sisters might give them strawberries for supper (certainly it was possible and devoutly to be wished) and before this subject was exhausted they stopped for a moment to admire the industry of the brethren who had dismantled the log kitchen. There was a sad, scraggly bare patch where the building had stood, and Amos walked gingerly along its edges, toe to heel, balancing himself so as not to totter either side.

Brother Harry took notice of a nail by the boy's foot, a good nail pulled out straight from a salvaged board. It had evidently been overlooked, hidden as it was in the grass where it dropped, by the brethren when they cleared away. "See that nail?" he said to Amos, pointing with his chin and nose. "Just there, by thy foot."

Amos stopped where he stood, his arms still held out straight from his shoulders, and looked either side of his feet.

"Put it in thy pocket," Harry said. "We'll give it to Brother Reuben when we get back to the house."

"Why?" the boy asked, scrabbling around in the grass with his fingers in the direction suggested, then pocketing the nail when he found it. "Is it good for anything?"

Brother Harry beckoned to him – they had tarried long enough and should be getting on home – and they continued on down North Lane.

"Why, I'd have to think," he said, and let his hand ride the crown of Amos' hat as they walked. Harry seemed to be giving the matter due consideration. "But while I think, here's a puzzle for thee: say thee fell grievous ill and died, and when it came time for our dear Mother to gather thee into Heaven She said, 'But he's only small. Is he good for anything?' What would thee say then?"

"I would say that I could be of use to Mother in Heaven, if She would only let me in," Amos replied earnestly after a moment's deliberation.

"Then let's take that nail back to Brother Reuben, who may find use for it in the shop, lest God think we are not either worth the trouble of picking up when we fall," Brother Harry said.

It was Brother Reuben's turn to notice that something was wrong, and to listen. Something about Austin Innes had seemed off-center since Reuben Wise rode back from Union Village: the little schoolmaster was less willing to smile, more often gone down to the depot to read the newspapers and too interested in what he found there, sharper with the children when they asked him for a story of an evening. Sometimes he could not be found by those who sought him in the tannery, and his absences were not explained. It was not easy to tell at the best of times whether Brother Austin was happy or unhappy, but his eyes since the fighting at Pittsburg Landing and Chickahominy had been a stubborn china-blue, repelling even those whose concern was most earnest. He seemed unapproachable.

Reuben woke himself suddenly one night rolling over in his bed, and across the room he saw Austin sitting up in the moonlight, his knees drawn tight to his chest.

"Austin," he whispered. "What is it?"

His brother's face turned to him, but Reuben could not see it for the moon behind him. "I wish I heard something," he said.

"Don't talk crazy," Wise said, sliding down to sit on the end of his bed nearest the window. "What do you want to hear?"

"Something else," Austin told him. "Some*body* else."

"Are you afraid?"

"I am."

"They won't take us, Austin," Brother Reuben said reassuringly. He had heard it all in Ohio and considered himself something of an authority. "They can't. They couldn't in 1812 and they can't now. There's no reason to fear to go."

"That's not what I'm afraid of."

"Then what?"

Austin Innes turned his face to the window again. Reuben Wise could see the dark copper of his hair and the shadow of his fingers as they rose and fell, like doors opening and closing.

"Then what?"

There was no answer, and Reuben fell silent too, content to sit in the dark with his brother if that was what was being asked of him. William Rice was asleep in the far bed, but there was little chance of waking him with mere conversation. They often joked that the Second Coming would not wake William Rice (to which he replied that, that event being in the past, the assumption must be that he was sleeping off the excitement) and Reuben sat listening to the heavy sound of old Brother William's heavy, sleeping breath. He could not tell how quickly time was passing, and he was interested to know. He affixed a reasonable length to William's breaths and began to count them, then lost count and began again, and tried to multiply, but he could not count the breaths and multiply in his head at the same time.

"Reuben?"

"Hmmm?"

"Why should men quarrel like wolves and hyenas about property?" Austin said abruptly.

Reuben Wise knew by the sound of Austin's voice that he was not really addressing anyone, just speaking his thoughts aloud, that he knew Reuben was listening but did not care.

"What is there in this world's goods that should so sharpen our spirits, and make so many kindhearted men of us fall out with each other as cruelly as we do? When man is at peace with man, how much lighter than a feather is the heaviest of metals in his hand. He pulls out his purse, and looks around himself, as if he sought for another soul to share with..."

"Austin, listen – "

By the window his brother shook his head. "There," he said finally. "If that was what you were thinking, wouldn't you sooner hear something else?"

The Shakers had it in common with the Society of Friends, from whom they had in some several ways descended, this unwillingness to take up arms. It had been with them since the beginning, and had caused them trouble just as long, but they had never abandoned it and would never compromise it. "The servant of the Lord must not strive, but be gentle, peaceable, easy to be entreated," was the way they learned it and the way they lived it.

In this matter of noncompliance, consistency was all: to a man the veterans of the Revolution and the War of 1812 who came to live among the Shakers foreswore the pensions and bounties due them by law – "the price of blood," they called it.

But there was a world of difference between those wars fought against a foreign enemy and this present conflict. The emotions now were of a completely different intensity, and in the winning or losing there were different principles at stake. The Shakers were a constant reminder to everyone who disagreed with their beliefs that there was room to disagree, and since virtually everyone did on some level or other there were few who did not challenge them. They were thus assailed from all sides.

Slave and slaveholder alike received kind attention at Shaker hands, and it was chiefly this that the secessionists found intolerable. Blacks lived in dwellings of their own on Shaker land, were treated as equals, and a Shaker man who needed help around the place – especially with so few brethren to do the heavy work – was as likely to get it from a black brother or hireling as a white man. Neighbors of the South Union Society had watched free colored men and women live and grow old amongst the Shakers, David Barnett and Archie Rhea for two, and the very intimation of equality maddened some of them.

What they did not know was how very seriously the Believers took their commitment to the notion that a black man was every bit as valuable in God's eyes as a white one.

Daily the brethren, who most often were out amongst the world's people – not that the sisters lived in isolation – felt the sharp animosity of their neighbors. The sight of a Shaker man old enough and fit enough for war was like a red flag waved at a family with boys away in the service of either American nation. Understanding did not make life any easier, but this cross too they would have to bear.

There was, after all, no escaping it. For miles around most plantations made use of the capable work done at the Shaker grist and fulling mills; disagree with a man you might, but business was business. Fire-eaters like the planter Shaw Mason Hannon regularly called in to check the progress of their goods, and the brethren knew the opinion, like the man, would come through the door even with the bar down. Hannon was more abusive than most in his pronouncements, but the brethren tried to give him the benefit of their compassion: his boy Teddy had joined up at Camp Boone, and Teddy was his only son. They counted as uncharitable their relief when Hannon took his leave of them. He did go on.

Some said there were as many as 50,000 Union troops now massed in Bowling Green. The brethren came from delivering provisions to the hospitals and told of seeing them flow across the Big Barren on a bridge of steamboats, in the absence of new-built bridges to replace the ones burned by the rebels. More troops came by road from all directions. However many there were, the demand for more persisted like an unslakeable thirst.

Expecting any day to see the enrollment officer come to register those few brethren of an age to serve the Union, Brother Urban Johns began to respond in an ever more anxious voice when the shoulder-straps – those lieutenants, captains and colonels who quartered in the trustees' office while their men camped in the Shaker meadows – engaged him in debate over the Believers' unshakeable refusal to participate in the taking of human lives.

A day or two after the burning of the cowpits on the railroad and the fright that that misunderstanding had put into them all, Urban was engaged in the usual debate by an overnighting Union colonel who brought his curiosity to the ministry office.

"You cannot say your sympathies lie elsewhere than with the Union cause," the colonel said. "I see the Negroes who move as freely about this village as do the white men and there is no question in my mind but that the heart of every man and woman here is with the Union."

Urban smiled at this. "Just because your heart is in a cause," he said with cautiously careful good humor, "it doesn't follow that you should put your foot in it."

God-fearing himself, a praying man by nature, the colonel said however he might feel about killing he could not find it in himself to hang back after the outrage at Fort Sumter. Without the goodness of this nation he would not be here at all, he told Johns, and he could not see it destroyed – if only for the gratitude he felt.

"Then there is where we differ," Brother Urban told him.

"Differ how?" the colonel asked. "My people came to this country because they could not at any price have anywhere else what they were freely given here. For that I believe I owe the strength of my arm to this country's defense. For you it must surely be the same."

"Never more different," Urban said, shaking his head. "Never more."

"Then your logic is faulty, sir," the colonel said, respectful but adamant.

"The first step towards being instructed in any good thing is to become thoroughly interested," Urban said testily, mistaking the colonel's words for dismissal. "Jesus said: 'All men are not able to live as I do; but, whosoever is able, let him live that life.'"

"Would your founders have come here, had they been permitted at home the privilege of their worship undisturbed?" the colonel asked, unwilling to surrender so quickly. "Your right to speak to God in the manner of your own choosing could be achieved only through the tolerance born on these shores. Can you now deny the necessity of fighting to preserve this Union, without which this community of yours would so likely not now exist?"

Worn down by exhaustion, by the long tense nights and the relentless demands placed on the brethren and sisters by those who took no pains to consider the consequences, Brother Urban Johns was nearing the end of his rope. He sounded it.

"It grieves my heart to know how greatly the fervency of my belief that we cannot fight this war, indeed can fight no war at all, may exceed even your belief that we must," he said. He spread his fingers out flat on the desk before him and pressed down, as if the smooth wood represented a reality that would rise up and fly away if he did not hold it safe. "Our union is here. *Here*. And if these brethren take up arms to defend your Union, then they will surely destroy their own."

August

rother Urban Johns was in the ministry shop. He had been waiting for some time. In fact there was some reason to believe George Joiner's errand might go unfinished, the desired end not being attainable, but he assumed that were this to be so the boy would come back and let him know.

He did not like to send for Brother Austin. He had never done so before, not in this way, but the situation in recent days had become something akin to intolerable. Too many times Austin could not be found at the tannery, or in the brethren's shop, or indeed anywhere that he was supposed to be. He seemed to have lost interest in his work, and this in itself was not like him: Austin Innes above many other things could not abide idleness in himself. He was irritable and sometimes rude, and on this past Sabbath Urban had looked around the meeting house and found him not in it. This absenting of himself from meeting Austin Innes had never done before. What even Urban Johns did not know was that Brother Reuben Wise had on two different occasions known without saying as much that Brother Austin was not in his bed the whole night, and on those occasions Reuben knew that Austin had not either been with the brethren at watch over the stock.

Brother Austin was a hardy fellow, never ill in Urban's memory, but it was always possible that he was ailing. The stream of soldiers who passed along the Great Road carried all manner of diseases with them, and it was not unheard of for this one or that in the community to be stricken with some malady kindly provided by the troops. Twiddling his fingers on the desk, Brother Urban hoped that whatever was ailing Austin Innes was mere illness. In such case he could be turned over for doctoring by Sister Lucy or Sister Olive and then returned to the brethren in restored spirits. That would do nicely.

He hoped it was that simple as he swivelled in his office chair. Then out the window he saw floating over the crossroads toward the ministry shop from the Center a straw hat, under which fluttered wisps of that remarkable red hair, and for a second Brother Urban rejoiced in George Joiner's resourcefulness. Certainly the boy had achieved what no one else had been able to accomplish in recent days.

A knock sounded at the door and Brother Austin came through without waiting for response. He was perspiring, and when he took off his hat and ran his fingers through his thick hair the dampness held it where he had pushed it back across his forehead until he shook it loose.

Brother Urban beckoned him to a waiting chair, but Austin preferred to stand. And when Urban opened his mouth Austin spoke first.

"I've meant to come talk to you, Urban," he said. "I should have come weeks ago."

"There's been concern about you for just about that long," Urban said.

"I know that, and I'm sorry. Couldn't be helped," he said breathlessly. "I've fallen behind and I had no right. I'll try to square it before I go."

Brother Urban sat forward, the wind gone from him. "Before you go? Go where? To the world? Austin — "

The schoolmaster was accustomed to putting a stop to interruptions that vexed his purposes. He put one hand to his pocket and another in the air.

"To the world, yes," he said flatly, as if it were something he had often said. "To the army."

"Oh, God," Urban said, and slumped back in his chair now as if pushed there. His face stung with disbelief. "Sit down, brother. Let's talk."

Austin put his fingers to his forehead. "It's no good talking, Urban. You can't say a thing to me that I haven't said to myself a thousand times."

"Bullets may sing and whistle, but they're not pleasant musicians. Have you told yourself that?" Urban asked as Austin moved to the open window and leaned on the casement, unwilling even to look at his slackjawed host. Urban's thoughts and objections hovered around his head like the clouds of road steam that rose around the wagons outside. "What the army is, is all the madness of the world gathered in one terrible place, to accomplish one task you believe to be wrong. You can't possibly walk away without giving me your reason for actually going to that place. That much you owe me, Austin. An explanation, at least."

"What can I say to you?" Austin asked, pounding softly on the window sill with one curled fist. Across the way, at the Center's east well, Union soldiers were fetching water for their horses. "Look at it, Urban. Look what's happening out there. You go out in the world as often as anyone. We needn't go to the war. We're already in it."

"We are in it," Urban agreed. "But it is not in us."

"Then I fear that it is in me."

"It isn't, Austin, and you know that as well as I do. Look at the life you've lived here. Look at why you came, and why you never left. 'Inasmuch as ye have done it unto the least of these my brethren, ye have done it unto me,' said the Son of God. You know that's true; your life depends on it. Can you go with the army and still be a Believer?"

Austin Innes still lacked the courage it took to turn his back to the window. "Brother," he whispered, "in all other things you know me to be a Believer. But in this one thing I am of the world. If this one thing makes me no Believer, I cannot stay. I can be no man other than who I am."

Urban stopped the tears in his eyes by looking to the ceiling, speaking as he did so. " 'As a man feels, so he thinks; as he thinks, so he is,' " he said. They were ministry words, and he had recited them many times before, but never in all his days had they meant so much to him. " 'Therefore, watch your heart and your emotions with all diligence, for out of your emotions are the issues of good and evil to yourself and others.' " He was not sure whether his brother was listening. "Austin, my dear friend, I know you to be no evil man."

They were quiet for many long seconds, Austin at the window and Urban at his desk. Then Urban spoke. "I have to go to Louisville 'fore too long. Might be gone a few days. The one thing needful's to be gotten, but there's... an errand for me to look after before I come back," he said, knowing he was telling only half of what there was but honor-bound not to tell the rest. "I need another man for the wagon. If it's a change of place you need, you could go with me. Must be years since you saw Louisville."

Austin was suddenly unable to contain the rage that hissed like live steam through his veins, and he turned on his pins from the window, the fisted hand tight now and trembling outstretched at shoulder height. He would not be patronized in this, but he could see now what he had tried so hard to avoid: Brother Urban's kind eyes, which had been among the first to see him at this place, and from which he could hide nothing. It was not in him to be angry at Urban Johns for long.

"This is not about what I need," he said, his fury still clear and cold in his voice. Urban had never heard him thus before, and the sound chilled him to the bone. The blue of Austin's eyes flashed from ice to ocean, cornflower to bluejay's wings, in seconds.

His entire soul was a threatening storm finally burst. "It is about what I cannot do, and I cannot not go."

"And what about your boys, brother?"

"What about them? Day after day I know that the greatest thing I can teach them is the duty a man has to listen to his own heart," he said. "What can I say to them, if I know my own heart has a deaf man for a master?"

"And God?"

"Where do they look first for God, if not there? Where do I?"

"Listen to me," Urban said, cut off at this avenue but with others still to try. "What quarrel could you have with any man that would be worth the taking of his life?"

The door beyond which lay the steps that led to the upper rooms stood ajar, and Austin indicated it with his eyes. "It is not for me to say whether the door is half-opened or half-closed. I only know that it is for me to go through it. I cannot stay on this side with you."

"To which army will you go?" Urban asked, and knew the instant the words sounded that they had had no business being voiced at all.

Austin leaned up against the wall and drummed his spread fingers against the cool plaster. "Did you know I once owned a slave?" he asked, knowing that this about him no one at South Union knew. "It's true, you know. This matter of slavery is more to me than just conversation. It was one night in Baton Rouge, and never in my life was I more brilliant at cards. Not ever. My winnings were considerable, just under seven hundred dollars as I recollect, all from a man I knew I'd never see again. He had come to the table without money, as it happened, but I was not easily taken advantage of and he didn't try. This man, Travers his name was, said to me, 'Take Phineas. He's worth more than I owe you.' And he took from his pocket a piece of white paper and signed away to me a black man's life, having told me what it was worth." There was the sound of a horse from the road, and

Austin glanced out the window. "As a gambler, I had been paid what I was owed. A darky is reasonable tender and there was no cause for me to say him nay. So he settled the debt with a black man. This Phineas, with his lifeless eyes, was crouched down in a corner of the room; he had been there all along and I hadn't even known he was there. When I took that note from Travers' hand into my hand, when Phineas passed to me like so much horseflesh, just the feel of that paper against my skin made me feel less a man. Seems to me I was stoking *Buckeye Belle* back then, upriver, and I took Phineas with me. You can do that, did you know? There was always use for a darky, and Phineas had his uses. But I hated the very look of him, and it was knowing he was mine that made me hate him, nothing else. The night before we made Cairo I found him up on deck and said, 'Look here. Tomorrow when we put in we'll be in Illinois. That's a free state. Don't be anywhere I might find you.' And I gave him that piece of paper and went my own way."

Urban Johns could only look at him. The subject had opened and shut of its own accord. "How many years are you?"

"Forty-four," Austin replied. The maximum service age was forty-five, but in the world it was no sin to lie at the enrollment office if the truth would turn you out. "They're short of men and may not ask." Truly he did not look his years: his hair had not dimmed, and despite the collection of lines, creases, dents and dimples that made of his face an ever-changing landscape his look was that of a younger man.

"Lies are like wandering ghosts," Urban said as if to no one, mustering a wry look to accompany the admonition. How many times had he told the children that? Where had he learned it?

"I'll remember that," Austin said. It was the first time in recent weeks that Urban Johns had seen him smile.

Brother Urban understood that there was no dissuading him. His mind, rightly or wrongly, was set on going. Strangely he could no longer sit while Austin stood, and he got himself to his feet.

"I won't know South Union without you in it," he said sadly. "These boys will be lesser men without you, as will I, as will we all."

"And what would I be, if I stayed?"

"A Believer who had made of himself a Daniel."

Austin Innes shook his head. "I fear I am not that man."

"I fear you may learn too late that you are."

Austin reached for his hat and walked to the door.

"When will you go?" Brother Urban asked, following.

"When it's no longer in me to stay," Austin told him.

Urban stood on the steps as this friend beyond price left him for the last time. "Thy hair will make of thee a fearful target," he said.

"Then I will keep it to myself, brother," Austin said, and resettled his hat on his head. He turned his back and crossed the Great Road, making for the tannery. Urban had heard him say he would catch his work up, and his word was as good as his bond.

Shaker mealtimes were businesslike affairs, silent, with the transaction between plate, fork and gullet to be concluded in fifteen minutes so that the hand could return to its work. It was not the easiest of times for the children, the little boys especially. Yet each boy did strive to behave himself at the dining table, if only because – should he fail to do so – before the next meal a copy of *The Table Monitor* would be set beside his plate. Bad enough that the child would have to read this interminable list of rules regarding the manner of comportment at mealtimes, but worse still that every one of the brethren and sisters would see the dreaded reproof by his plate and know that he had, in some way, disgraced himself or otherwise failed to do what was expected of him.

Thursday morning, seeking to occupy their hare-like attention once they had Shakered their breakfast plates, the boys were scrutinizing the brethren. Especially in these weeks when it was not much less hot upstairs at night than it was outside in daylight, it was always reasonably easy to tell which ones of them had not slept well the night before. The boys would ape this haggard condition by pulling down the lower lids of their eyes, which their fellows would find screamingly funny; on the other hand the first boy to laugh aloud was likely to be the first to draw the disapproving glance of one of the brethren. This morning, however, they also noticed the empty place next to Brother Reuben Wise. Amos sat up in his chair: one did not look for Brother Austin, necessarily, one looked for his red hair, and neither it nor its owner was in evidence. Scanning the hats on the peg-rails he did not either see Brother's hat there; he knew it easily by its singular leather band, which Brother Austin had made one day from a slender scrap. The elders did not pronounce it a vanity when it appeared: Austin Innes was prone to use his hatband for the temporary storage of small tools and stray nails, and it thus took something of a beating. None of this mattered now. The hat was not there.

That morning John Perryman wanted the boys up by the wheat threshing, but when he came to collect them together Amos hung back. Amongst the legs that jostled around him on their way to the work of the day he found Sister Elizabeth's.

"Where's Brother Austin?" he asked, taking hold of her apron. Sister's eyes were red, as if she had not herself had much sleep. Her mouth set tensely and she turned her face from him, but Amos knew she was crying and he wondered what he had done to upset her so.

"Come here, child," she said, and took his hand, and led him to a corner of the room. She sat by one of the tables and pulled Amos onto her lap. "Brother Austin's gone away. He went early-burly this morning, so he wouldn't disturb anybody when he left. So that's where he is. Does that answer thy question?" She was fussing with his collar, and when she had finished that small chore and turned the nervousness in her hands to straightening his suspenders he hooked his finger into his collar and put it back the way he liked it.

"Will he be back for supper?"

Sister Elizabeth took her handkerchief from the pocket of her apron, the tears having come again in profusion. "Bless thee, child, nay, he won't."

"Will he be back tomorrow?"

She shook her head. Her hands were pressed to her eyes and she could not speak.

"When is he coming back?" In his limited experience Amos had always known the brethren to come back when they went away. Even if they went far away – to Union Village or Pleasant Hill or even faraway Mount Lebanon – they might be gone awhile, and they were missed, but they always came back.

"Sugar," she said when she had regained herself, "Brother has gone to the army. It's not for us to judge. God will look after him for us, and if we pray very hard that he stays safe then perhaps God will keep him so."

She had strayed too far from his question, and he had lost her.

"*When is he coming back?*" he demanded, then panicked, and slid down from her lap.

"Thee must listen to me, Amos, and try to understand," she said softly as the boy was pulling away from her. "Brother Austin isn't coming back."

Amos turned, and even as Sister Elizabeth reached out to grab at his suspenders to keep him with her he was gone, up the east stairs, down the broad hallway to the front door and out into the early heat of morning. He stopped in the middle of the Great Road and did not know which way to go. He had never been outside the fence without advice, and he did not know where the roads that lay on all sides of him led. But he was looking east and so he went east, running with everything in him, screaming Austin's name. By the time his legs went out from under him and he fell in the road he was well past the blacksmith's shop, farther away from the Center than he had ever been alone. There was nobody in the road ahead of him as far as the eye could see. He sat up in the dirt, hugged at his knees and wept. When at last he saw a carriage coming toward him he stood up, wiped his eyes, and walked back home.

*   *   *

John Barnett came by the ministry shop looking for Urban Johns, and on his way into the village passed alongside a dusty Shaker child walking in the road. It was a strange sight, to be sure – the Believers were uncommon particular about their children – but their youngest were shy of the world's people, and as the boy seemed to be steady on his feet Barnett continued on without stopping.

Barnett had known the Believers all his life, and was that rarity: a world's man who came and went at Shakertown pretty much as he pleased. He had been frequently inside the Center, most sadly perhaps when he helped carry old Elder Samuel to the bed in which he died, the only time he had been upstairs. He transacted business and friendship with the Shakers, and they valued his counsel on the affairs of the world, in which they at times participated almost in the manner of foreigners.

He put his head in the door of the ministry shop and found Elder John Rankin sitting alone.

"Hey, John," he said. "Urban not here?"

"Gone to Louisville," Elder John said. "You just missed him. We're needful of fruit cans and he's trying to get some down here. Not easy to move things from one place to another these days. Not to tell you anything you don't know." He looked at Barnett, standing with his hand on the doorknob, half in and half out. "You coming in or you figure to stand out there forever?"

John Barnett smiled at this backhanded invitation and let himself in. There was cold tea in the jug and, after an inquiring glance at Rankin, he poured a cup and sat down in Urban's swivel chair to drink it.

John Rankin was absorbed in some paperwork or other, and Barnett sipped at his tea, glancing around the spartan room rather than disturb him.

"Something on your mind, John?" Rankin asked, without looking up.

Barnett had hoped to find Urban Johns here, and would have preferred to talk to him on so delicate a subject, but by now his curiosity was almost past penning up. He plucked at a worn patch on the knee of his trousers. Not so easy to get new, and the old was showing the strain.

"I'd swear I saw Austin Innes in the town early, fixing to be on his way up to Eminence," he said.

"Well, then, perhaps you shouldn't swear," said Elder John absently.

"Seems to me something was said about him mustering into the cavalry up there, is where he was headed."

"Is that a fact, now?" mumbled Rankin.

"Something about the Ninth Kentucky. Not that I spoke to him, of course, but that's what I hear."

"Nice to have a thing to hear now and again. Keeps a man's mind active."

Barnett was not exactly surprised by the level of Rankin's ambivalence; he knew it for what it was. There had been many defections from the ranks of the Believers from the very beginning, and increasingly since the war began. The life of a Believer could not be lived by the uncommitted, and many a man and woman had "gone back to the world" to a life that seemed more agreeable. There was a practical side to concern over this problem, in that there were now so many more women and children than able-bodied men on the place that, increasingly, hirelings had to be taken on to help with the field work and other heavy labor. From a standpoint of belief, the ministry at South Union was entirely unsentimental: the choice between Paradise and Perdition was clearer to some than to others, and they who chose the latter earned the prayers of those they left behind but little else. On the other hand, if a departed Believer found his adventures with the world to be less satisfying than he expected and came looking for readmittance, the ministry was usually quick to relent. A brief spell back in the Gathering Order for the prodigal, a few weeks on the outer benches at meeting, and whatever acrimony had resulted from the parting was mutually forgotten. But this matter of Austin Innes was not the same.

John Barnett looked at Rankin's face, intent over his writing. He was hearing every blessed word. Barnett was not content to be ignored by someone so keen that he should keep talking.

"John," he said. "You're not listening to me."

"I'm listening," he replied, and looked up for the first time since Barnett had sat down. "But this is not my business."

It could not have been put more coldly. "Not your business?" Barnett asked. "For God's sake, John, I'm talking about Austin Innes, on his way up to Eminence to join the Ninth Kentucky Cavalry."

"That's the world's business, not mine," Rankin said, raising both hands in the air as if to say the conversation had gone as far as it was going.

"The world's business? Austin's business!" Barnett said, and stood, now pacing like a vexed cat. "What's that, if not your business?"

Rankin slapped his pen down on the desk, a kind of fire in his eyes. "What is it you think, John? Do you think I sent him? Nay, friend, the way it is is that Austin Innes went back to the world of his own accord at the behest of his own conscience, and his business is therefore with the world and not with me."

Barnett's tone softened. John Rankin was more troubled by Austin's decision than he had imagined. "You don't believe that, John," he said. "Don't expect me to believe it."

"Believe what you will," said Rankin. "But there are some two hundred souls and more who are still here and faithful, and the responsibility of my energy and my time and my concern is with them. Austin Innes has chosen the world, and the world can worry for him. I have all I can do to look after what goes on amongst Believers."

Barnett shook his head and extended his hand. "For God's sake, John..."

"Yea, for God's sake, John," said Rankin, nodding, "for you have been a friend to the Society on days when it had none other. But this is the way it must be."

"Fine," said Barnett, turning his hat in his hands. The awkward moment passed at its own poor speed. "Tell Urban I was by, then, will you?"

"He wants to take a look at that new bull of yours," offered Rankin.

"Any time he feels the notion," Barnett said. "Jefferson told me he was interested." Fences were being mended, and the effort was well worth the making for what would come of it. "Rebs've taken Clarksville. Just heard down the town."

"That's a sadness." Rankin put the end of his pen to his lip. "Come back by in a day or two if you can, John. Might be someone here you'd like to see."

Barnett looked at him, curious, but did not ask.

"How you keeping, allright?"

"I could do with a little less of this heat," Barnett said as he backed toward the door. "Can't sleep when it's like this. You?"

"Seems like we never get any younger," said Rankin.

Barnett smiled and waved his farewell as he went out to his carriage.

Brother John looked down at the paper beneath his chin, at the corner where he had written "Eminence, Ninth Kentucky Cavalry." As soon as Urban got back from Louisville, he would tell them both.

Yellow Jenny came by the Center after Saturday dinner was cleared away to spin Eldress Jency Dillon a tale, as she often did. Aunt Jenny, as the mulatto woman was called at Shakertown, cooked for the hired hands and was friend to many of the colored folk in the town. As such she heard much silliness and an occasional fact, all of which she dispensed with equal gravity.

"Y'all sure are unpopular these days," she told Jency. "Folks say what with all the niggers and trash you got here, if you got any money hid around they'll sure come find it."

"Who said this, Jenny?" Eldress Jency asked.

"Looked familiar to me, some folks I seen," she replied. "Some no 'counts, I guess, to come here and eat your supper and then go 'round the county talkin' like that."

"But who, Jenny?"

To be half white was no protection, as Jenny knew, and she did not want more trouble with the local secesh population than she earned by the simple color of her skin. "Don't do to call names," she said with a dramatic display of caution. "But it seemed to me like y'all ought to know what the talk is."

There was a hubbub toward the front of the house, and Eldress Jency took herself upstairs to see what uproar which army was creating for them on this hot Sabbath eve.

Looking through the open door she saw the wagon that Brother Urban had taken to Louisville, but while Urban Johns' return was an event for which to be truly grateful it was not usually cause for such congregation or comment. Then suddenly she saw enveloped in a noisy cluster of the brethren a small man, with angular features and fine, white hair. Her hands flew to her cheeks, her eyes alight. It was Brother Harvey Eades, and the mere sight of him explained everything. It would not do to say one man of South Union had ever been best beloved of Shakertown's inhabitants, but if it could be fairly said of anyone it could be said of Harvey Eades.

Jefferson Shannon came up the steps from the road in a hurry of sorts, but such was Jency's surprise that she stopped him anyway. "Brother Shannon, whatever is Brother Harvey doing here?" she asked. "We didn't know to be expecting his visit, and there's nothing ready..."

"Not a visit, Eldress," Brother Jefferson said. "Mount Lebanon's let him come back. He's staying here with us." He excused himself and went on.

That night in the Center's first-floor meeting room Elder John Rankin read a letter from the lead ministry back in New York.

Harvey Eades, it said, had been sent back to South Union to fill a gap in its ministerial order, as he had done more than eighteen years before. In that time his chores had been tended by Urban Johns, who would by the same appointment be allowed to return to his position as first trustee in the office. The church family was happy to consent to the changes suggested.

As it happened, Brother Urban had also managed to arrange a shipment of fruit cans.

After supper Brother John Perryman came to the door of the retiring room Harry Littlebourne shared with Jefferson Shannon and William Ware. So early in the evening, he was still alone. There was a mischievous smile on John's face as he leaned himself on the jamb, and Brother Harry gave the young man his attention.

"Think maybe I'd better send Amos to see you before he goes off to bed," Perryman told him.

Harry looked at him with curiosity, but said nothing.

Young Perryman raised a restraining hand. "Nay, nay," he said. "If you've got some time for him, I'll just send him down."

Within a few minutes the nightshirted little figure appeared sideways at the door, shyly, ear-first and slowly, until he could stand no other way than to show his full face. At the crest of his cheekbone rode the broad and angry smear of a purple bruise that curled up toward his eyebrow: unmistakeably, a black eye.

"How came thee to have that?" Brother Harry asked with some alarm, leaning forward in the room's solitary rocking chair.

Amos seemed reluctant to venture beyond the short passage that lay just inside the door. He put one bare foot on top of the other, twined his toes, and looked away. "I slept on my fist," he said.

"Since this morning?" Harry's voice was full of dubiousness, his eyes narrow. He extended his hand. "Come here now, thee needn't stop so far off."

Amos edged into the room and leaned on Brother Jefferson's bed. "Maybe Isham Jenkins hit me. A little."

"Isham Jenkins?" Harry asked, angling himself to survey the extent of the injury. "He's twice thy size. Why did he hit thee? Thee boys know how wicked fighting is. How did thee vex Isham Jenkins?"

"I didn't," the boy replied.

"Oh, I see," Harry said, nodding and biting thoughtfully at his lower lip. "One minute thee was clearing brush with the other boys, the next minute thee was taking Isham's fist. Is that the way it went?"

"There was maybe a little more."

"How much little more?"

"It was maybe that I pushed him, and he fell."

"And why did thee push him?"

Amos was chewing on his thumb, and Brother reached over with his long arm to pull the child's hand away from his mouth.

"Tell me, Amos, why did thee push Isham Jenkins?"

The boy crossed his arms behind his back and examined the never-ending circles of the rag rug under his feet. "He called Brother Austin a sinner," he whispered.

"What?"

"Isham said that Brother Austin was a sinner, and that's why he went away, and I pushed him, and he hit me," Amos said, raising his head for the first time.

"Well," Harry said. "That was an unkind thing for Isham to say, and he had no right to say it, nor reason. But thee can't go around pushing people when they say things that make thee unhappy. Life is very long, and thee may have to push a lot of people. It could make a difficult life for thy eyes, Amos."

He climbed onto Brother Harry's bed and sat Indian-style. Looking at the bed by the window he said, "Is it a sin if I don't like Brother William?"

Harry had been idly rocking, but so stark was this question that he stopped, realizing his footsteps here must be cautious, lest they be misguided. "Perhaps it's not a sin if Brother William is in thy bad books," he said. "The question is, how came his name to be written there, and is it thy writing or is it his?"

The little boy was exhausted, and Brother Harry's questions were never simple. The heat of the day had been withering, and the boys had been out tidying up the Knob through most of it. But perhaps most tiring of all was the work of separation, which was still far from over.

"It's mine," he said, fighting to steady his quivering lip.

"And will thee tell me why?" Harry had been waiting for this. It was a credit to the boy's heart that so nearly a week had passed before his misery bubbled into rage. He turned his ear to Amos, looking to be led by the boy's own words. There was no need to tell him more than he asked to know.

"When is Brother Austin coming back?"

With the question loose in the air Harry Littlebourne knew he was no more ready now to give Amos an answer than he would have been with another year to consider his reply. He wished he were a wiser man. He wished children were not quite so vulnerable, not quite so sure there was no knot ever tied that could not be untangled by the grown folks in their lives. And here was a child who had no concept of state or nation, who had never in barely eight years been beyond the accumulated fences owned by the Society in which he had been raised. All Amos knew of the world was that he was not part of it. He did not know that little boys come of mothers and fathers, just as lambs and calves do. How would anyone explain to such a child the ugliest of truths, that he might well never see Austin Innes again, that one of the people closest to his heart might die in defense of a nation he did not know existed, to oppose an injustice he had never seen?

"If I tell thee Brother may not come back, it will be true, and it will hurt thee, but – " Harry saw the boy's neck stiffen, his soft green eyes glisten and fill, " – but, remember that we are still here, and we have each other, and with Holy Mother's help that will always be so. And if thee remembers Brother Austin with love, and so thee surely will, he can never be very far away."

Amos palmed at his damp eyes, and in so doing sparked the bruise. "It's not the same," he said through his tears. "Sister Elizabeth said Brother William would teach us this year when school comes, but it isn't the same. He doesn't talk like Brother Austin at all."

Harry smiled. If there was one thing to be remembered about Austin Innes, it would no doubt be the music of his voice, if not the color of his hair. "No one does, little brother," he said. "It was God's gift to him, and it wasn't like anyone else's. That Brother William's gifts lie elsewhere is a sign of God's diversity, not of Brother William's shortcomings."

"Granderson Carey said he went away because we misbehaved."

A child will always consider himself the point on which the top spins, Harry thought. "It's nothing to do with thee, or the other boys, or me, or any one of us," he said. "The world is having problems of its own, and when Brother turned his mind to those troubles he decided they were his troubles, too. He thought it might be he could help put things right."

"But Elder John always says the world looks after its problems and we look after our own."

"And Elder John is a wise man," Harry said, and nodded. "But sometimes it's hard to keep the world out of thy heart and mind – like when the soldiers are making noise out by the pond at night, when thee might sooner to be asleep – and one morning Brother Austin couldn't see the two for separate."

"But why?"

Brother Harry rubbed at his chin. If a nation of grown people was still puzzling that particular riddle, his chances of explaining to this child the connection between states' rights and the loss of a beloved schoolmaster were slim to none.

"Does thee notice how the soldiers wear two colors, some blue and some grey...?"

"Bedford was a grey one," Amos offered, remembering the splendid suit of clothes Forrest had worn that night. It seemed a very long time ago, a year almost to the day. And he had not come back.

"So he was," Harry said. "The greys and the blues have an itch on one another, and since they can't get close enough to scratch it without scrapping they're scrapping to settle up."

"Like when I pushed Isham and he hit me," Amos offered, his logic clear.

"Something like that," Harry said. "It was wrong of thee and Isham, and it's wrong of the blues and the greys, but it's the only way they know to do."

"If scrapping makes God so unhappy, why do they do it?"

"The grey men say there's some folks in this world who aren't quite so good as other folks, and the blue men reckon that's wrong."

"And that's why they're pushing each other?"

"That's what it comes down to."

"Who is it they don't like?"

Harry pointed to Amos' hand. "See how fair thy fingers are? Notice sometimes how other people aren't so fair? Like old Brother Archie was? Or Aunt Jenny down the road?"

"Or you?"

Brother Harry had never thought of it quite that way, but now he did he reckoned it was so. "And like me," he said, and smiled. "Brother Austin thought that wasn't the way things ought to be, and that's why he went off with the blue soldiers. It seemed to him that folks are just folks and ought to be treated similar."

"Then why do the brethren look after the grey ones like they were friends to us?"

"Because *they are not our enemies*," Harry said, too aware of the urgency of his words to temper them before he spoke, too late to soften their sound on his tongue. "Those grey men are children of God, just as thee and me, and what we have we'll share with them until it's all gone and then just like them we'll do without." He looked Amos in the eye, anxious that if he heard nothing else he should hear this. "Hold no anger for them in thy heart, Amos, ever. None of these things are easy to understand, for thee or for me, but it matters that thee makes good sense of them."

He noticed that Amos' nose had begun to drip, and he held out his handkerchief. "Now in this matter of Brother William, I think I know what Brother Austin would tell thee."

"What would he say?"

"He would say that, when school time comes, thee should give Brother William thy best ear and all thy mind, just as thee did him. If thee fails at that, thee will have made Brother Austin unhappy."

Understanding and forgetting would be two different things, and Harry could see doubts in the boy's face. They would have this conversation more than once.

He pointed at Amos' wounded eye. "Does it hurt?"

"Nay, but it pesters me."

"I'll ask Sister to bring thee a camomile bag. Now best thee go on up," Harry said.

Amos pushed himself off the bed and would have been gone, but at the last instant he turned.

"Something else?" Brother Harry prodded, but gently.

The boy had wound the handkerchief around one hand, and he picked at the folds with the fingers of the other.

"What else?"

"Is it a sin if I still miss him?" Amos asked.

September

For those who wished to know which way the wind was blowing, it was no longer enough to lick a finger and hold it aloft.

A body now had to be a good listener and a keen observer. A good memory was also useful, likewise oak-solid nerves. The Confederate winds had begun to blow up from the South, meeting near-parallel Union gales, and both would kick up the dust of the Great Road between Bowling Green and Russellville while they picked up speed on their way to the Bluegrass.

On the last Sabbath Eve of August Brother Urban Johns had himself started up toward Frankfort, at the behest of the ministry at Pleasant Hill. There was, it seemed, yet to be reckoned with the matter of the drafting of able-bodied Shaker brethren, and at Pleasant Hill they thought it best that representatives of both Kentucky communities attend the meeting of the legislature, carrying petitions signed in their support by friendly neighbors. With Brother Rufus Bryant and others of the brethren Urban Johns therefore dutifully set out. Given the ebb and flow of troops around the state he left without optimism, and as it turned out he was right: long before the brethren could reach the capital the governor and the legislature boarded up the windows and adjourned, decamping with whatever valuables were at Frankfort and Lexington to ride out the weather in Louisville. There was good reason for this.

The Confederate forces had been flitting around the Tennessee-Kentucky border for weeks, like flies drawn to molasses, just asking for the swatter. Colonel John Hunt Morgan and Brigadier General Nathan Bedford Forrest had been bedevilling the Louisville & Nashville Railroad, fouling the lines that provisioned General Don Carlos Buell's forces south of Murfreesboro. Riding north of the line to Lexington from Knoxville were 21,000 troops led by Major General Edmund Kirby Smith (who with Major General Braxton Bragg formed the double-barrelled shotgun aimed at the Union's hold on Kentucky, an arrangement that suited neither the men nor the purpose). In this enterprise Smith manifested his envy of Morgan's thousand miles of rebel-rousing, will-o'-the-wisp exploits across Kentucky by rushing off in search of similar – veering east a little as he looked first to loosen Union General George Morgan's death grip on the Cumberland Gap. Stricken with a sudden and serious case of common sense, Smith realized the job could not be done with any speed if it could be done at all. He therefore left behind him a force of 9,000 men, assigned the tedious chore of wearing down the 8,000 Union troops and their stubborn general Morgan, then turned his ragged, underfed soldiers toward Lexington again as August waned. Rejoining John Hunt Morgan at Barbourville he hopscotched his way north, and by the first of September Smith had chewed through the untried recruits run by General William Nelson at Richmond – just seventy-five miles from Cincinnati – to put Lexington under Confederate occupation. Frankfort followed suit two days later and, absent anything else more appropriate, Smith's men struck Old Glory from the capitol building's flagpole and ran up the flag of the 1st Louisiana Cavalry instead. By then the Kentucky Legislature had made tracks up to Louisville and Brother Urban Johns was back in

Shakertown, having presented the Shaker case for draft exemption to absolutely no one.

Brother Urban would not have chosen to leave the village on the Sabbath that followed, either, but on September's first Sunday he had no choice. Two letters fetched up at Bowling Green the day before – for some weeks previous the mails had come no closer than that to Shakertown – had alerted the brethren that Brother David Parker from the New Hampshire society at Canterbury was nearing Cincinnati and was wishful to visit the Believers at South Union if there was a chance he could get through the lines. That Sabbath morning then, in hopes of catching Brother David with a wire to Cincinnati, he arrived in Bowling Green to find the telegraph office in a state of flux: there was trouble on the lines, no messages to be sent or received until the afternoon. Unable to wait, Urban sat himself down and penned a letter instead, listening to the idle chatter as he wrote.

It seemed that Buell and several of his divisions were expected to come up the road from Nashville at any time. General Lovell Harrison Rousseau with his brigade had already crossed into Kentucky, the story went, and there seemed to be growing in the Union army a will to slam into the Confederate forces head-on, on commonwealth soil.

This seemed to Urban Johns a natural reaction, given recent events.

The excitement in the telegraph office seemed to multiply with every new general whose name was mentioned. By the time words were exchanged concerning the imminent arrival of Major General William Starke Rosecrans and heaven could only guess how many troops, Urban had decided the talk had degenerated into full-fledged rumor. Rumors he could get aplenty in South Union, so he mailed his letter to Brother David, suggesting he confine his travels to lands north of the Ohio, and went on home.

By Tuesday, matters were beginning to establish themselves and rumors were beginning to dissolve into the occasional fact.

Clarksville had been retaken by the Union army and Rousseau was marching as many as 15,000 men into Bowling Green, which would make 22,000 in and around the town when they arrived. The perimeter was closed off, no one able to get in or out absent a military permit, and thus the Believers were made to do without their mail. Even the cars as they neared the South Union depot neither slowed nor stopped.

Braxton Bragg meanwhile had finally set off on his way north from Chattanooga with 30,000 men, mulling over the logistics of an attack on the accumulated forces of Don Carlos Buell and expecting his wandering counterpart Edmund Kirby Smith to rejoin him for it. He was still laboring under the delusion that of the two men, he was the one in charge, although Smith had a well-known problem with authority.

A furloughed Federal soldier on his way west from Buell's encampment to see relatives at Hopkinsville stopped at the trustees' office, and as he wolfed down the supper brought him by the sisters he spun the tale to Brother Jess Rankin: Bragg was intent on bringing his 60,000 men down from Glasgow to drive the Federals out, planning as he did to winter there and wishful to resolve all enemy objections before settling in. Brother Jess listened with good-natured skepticism. Depending on who was talking, and from which army or persuasion he came, the Shakers had learned to divide the tarradiddle by factors that ranged anywhere between two and fifty in pursuit of accuracy. The truth lay somewhere in the middle, but with people's minds more readily influenced by mixtures of fear, loyalty, dread and pure desperate desire than by common sense, reality was as hard to grasp as the halo 'round the moon.

Despite the deterioration of the Bragg-Smith offensive into a strategy best described as catch-as-catch-can, the Union line had been pushed back to the Ohio and the citizens of the river's major ports were painfully aware of the precariousness of their position. It was clear that if Bragg and Smith ever actually clapped eyes on each other again and thrashed out a means of working in harness the result might teach the Union forces a lesson they'd wish they hadn't learned.

It was no wonder, then, that with Smith eating lightning in the Bluegrass Buell could be lured up from Tennessee with half the 40,000 men at his disposal. Even taken as independent from anything else the rebels might achieve, possession of the Bluegrass opened the gate to Ohio and Indiana. For the Confederates it was well worth trying; for the Federals it was well worth discouraging.

Sabbath Eve of the thirteenth arrived, and with it a pair of ailing, furloughed Federal soldiers from Brigadier General James M. Shackelford's army – hoping for dinner at the trustees' office as they made their way home – who offered the unsettling news that the Union troops had gone north to deal with Bragg, leaving Russellville to fend for itself. The game was up as far as the town's abolitionists were concerned; life had been precarious enough with the Federal army always visible in the streets. Without that security a Union man's neck was only as good as the rope hung around it failed to be, and anyone with the means to do so packed his carpetbag and left.

In no time flat Braxton Bragg was issuing a fire-eating proclamation to the people of the commonwealth from his camp at Glasgow, where he was snug with his men. He hoped throngs of Kentuckians would read his words and rally to the defense of the Confederacy, but he was wrong. Meanwhile Buell and his men arrived to join the troops already manning the extensive rebel-built fortifications at Bowling Green some thirty-five miles from Glasgow. Reports came that the townfolk were exhausted and sick at heart. Everything that man or horse could even attempt to digest was gone – along with every turkey, chicken or egg that military hands could locate – appropriated without perceptible courtesy or reimbursement by the troops who ultimately numbered some 55,000. When the citizens heard that the rebel Bragg and his men had seized the railroad and thus cut them off from Louisville, their desolation was as complete as their isolation.

* * *

Newspapers remained hard to come by, even when the pickets allowed civilians to pass into Bowling Green. And when they could be got at all the price was no longer a dime, as it had been, but a dollar. On the other hand, with Bragg and his thousands hovering around Glasgow, and with Buell and his forces at Bowling Green, what a man didn't need a newspaper to know was that the powder was bound to blow somewhere.

Munfordville was as logical a place as any, and so it blew.

Over a hundred and fifty Union officers and nearly 4,000 of their men were disarmed as a result of the Confederates' success in that pursuit, were issued rations, paroled and pointed back toward Bowling Green. Bragg hoped their presence would throw into a tailspin whatever provisioning strategies Buell had managed to rig, given the hobbled condition of the railroad lines. What Bragg did not dispatch south to trouble Buell was himself, or any of his forces, and this was nothing if not a mistake.

One sad old man, a refugee, wept as he sopped his cornbread in beef gravy and told young Logan Johns of being taken captive by the Confederate army during the occupation of Bowling Green. When a consortium of Confederate forces led by Johnson, Hardee, Buckner and Hindman had been forced south by the approaching Federal forces back in February they had taken him with them, and it was only now – with the rebels gathered up at Glasgow and Cave City – that he had been able to get away during the confusion at Munfordville.

"Criminy," said Logan, who was unfortunately now almost completely possessed of the soldiers' less appropriate colloquialisms. "Why'd they take you in the first place? What did you do?"

The old man burst into fresh tears and wiped his face with a filthy sleeve. "My boy's in Buell's army," he said. "That's all there was to it. And for all I know by now he ain't in Buell's army no more."

By Sabbath morning the news from the Great Road bordered on the Homeric. Major-General Grant and General Curtis had moved up to Louisville to co-operate with Buell in the retaking of the Green River bridges. The number of Confederates camped around Glasgow had grown to a staggering 100,000, commanded by almost as many generals.

Having achieved nothing but a handful of bridges he hadn't wanted in the first place and now didn't much need, Bragg began to think of centering his men at one spot – Danville, say. He could then draw Buell in, defend, defeat and go after the prizes: Cincinnati and Louisville. Certainly it was no longer worth believing that Smith intended to join him for a joint campaign. Smith, he finally learned, had gone back down to pester George Morgan and his men at Cumberland Gap, but had let them slip through to the Ohio. Confederate uniforms were strewn, warm willing bodies and all, from one end of the Bluegrass to the other, and it was up to Bragg to collect them all together, store them in safe places, and bring them back again when the trap was ready to spring.

The brethren and sisters had only just gone to their beds when, through the open windows, they heard shouting and commotion from the East.

Brother Jefferson put his feet to the floor and motioned to Brother Harry to get his clothes back on. "I don't know that there's a grain of sense in getting out of day clothes anymore, and that's a fact," he said as he shoved the tail of his nightshirt into his trousers and thumbed his suspenders up over his shoulders. He plucked his hat from the peg, and with Brother Harry behind him took to the stairs and was out the door.

Some of the black hirelings were running toward them, clearly terrified. They were babbling as they neared, and Jefferson slowed his pace.

"Shush, now," he said. "I can't understand a thing when you go on so..."

"There's Confederates down there," said Shem Watkins. "They got young Fred, whuppin' on him, something about some gal I never heard of they're looking for."

Jefferson's eyes narrowed, and there was no humor in him. "Where are they?"

"Nigger house, down the East farm," Shem said.

"You all get up the Center and stay there til I say," Jefferson told them. "We won't have this."

Through the open door of the hirelings' house he and Harry saw a handful of armed rebel troops holding the petrified Fred Griggs by his hair, his broad nostrils blocked by the business end of a Smith & Wesson revolver held cocked and ready by one of the soldiers.

"Brother Jefferson, please!" Fred shrieked when, from the corner of his eye, he saw the two Shaker men walk in.

"What is this?" Jefferson asked, and the rebel party turned as they heard the sound of his voice. "You have no call to be here."

The pistol came down from Fred's nose, and he straightened his neck gratefully.

"There's a brown girl run away from Hannon's, and this nigger here knows where she is," one of the soldiers said, keeping his gun upright by his shoulder.

"I don't know her, I swear, she don't mean nothin' to me," Fred said. One of the rebel party kicked at his legs and he put his head down, fearing that blows to his face would come next.

"Whatever you may think he knows, you have no call to be here," Brother Jefferson said. "We'd be much obliged if you'd leave. Now."

"Ain't finished yet," said another of the soldiers, scraping the blade of his Bowie knife softly against his stubbled cheek. The look on his face was menacing, and Harry and Jefferson knew they were being threatened. "He ain't told us where Hannon's girl is."

Brother Jefferson put his hands on his hips, exasperated. "Perhaps he doesn't know," he said and, with a look to the man's shoulder added, "corporal."

"He b'long to you?"

"Nay, he belongs to himself and he works for us," Jefferson said, knowing the possibility that Fred was a runaway would be raised next. "I have copies of the papers. You could come have a look at them, or you could just go on."

Behind Jefferson the corporal could see the dark and towering figure of Harry Littlebourne, stooped to avoid the low ceiling, and as he surveyed Brother Harry's face his lip curled. "It ain't just niggers with y'all, is it?" he asked. "You keep injuns, too?"

Nearly out of patience, Brother Jefferson aimed his finger at the door.

"Ain't goin' nowheres 'thout we find where Hannon's girl is."

Jefferson leaned over, taking his weight on the arms of Fred's chair. Looking at him square, watching the perspiration leak down the man's face, Jefferson asked: "Fred, you tell me now, in the fear of God, do you know the whereabouts of this girl of Hannon's?"

Fred swallowed hard and shook his head. "I don't know who they mean, sir. I swear 'fore God I don't."

"There, now," Jefferson told the rebel party. "Seems enough for a man to see he doesn't know." His eyes were cold and uncompromising.

The corporal relaxed his pistol and reholstered it. "Guess that's so," he said. "Come on, y'all," he said to his men, and went on out with them into the night.

The tension released from Jefferson's shoulders and he pushed his hat back on his head. "Fred," he said when he was sure the soldiers were gone, "you know where that girl is?"

Fred shook his head. "You been good to me, Brother Jeff. I wouldn't lie." He was desperate to be believed.

"Allright," Jefferson said softly, touching him on the shoulder, sorry to have had to ask again but needing to make it clear he had had to ask. "Let's all just try to forget this and go on to whatever's next. If there's any more trouble tonight, there's Elder Jess over the East if you need help. Coming down the Center takes too long."

With a beckoning hand to Brother Harry he made for the door, then had one last thought. Shannon held one finger up, unsure whether he would say what he had to say or not. Then, having made his decision, he spoke. "Tell you what, Fred," he said. "If you'd stop cattin' around Shaw Hannon's place we might all get a little more sleep."

"I swear, sir – "

"Don't swear," Brother Jefferson said. "Just think about it. Goodnight."

Outside the door they found four shadowy forms, the mere sight of which made them flinch, lest they be four of the Confederates come back to finish the job. Then, readjusting to the darkness, they saw instead several familiar faces from the East. "Elder Jess thought you might need a little help," said Ambrose McKee.

Jefferson raised his eyes. "A little help," he said, "and one night of peace."

October 8

Night, and the days that followed

Amos had turned often in his sleep, and his nightshirt was so wound round his legs that he could not move them.

But in his dream his legs were free. They dangled down through the octopuslike arms of the biggest lamp he had ever seen. It was strung thick with translucent marbles and other bits of glass, amongst which flickered a thousand lights. He was high up off the ground, higher than ever he had been on Old Sorrow's back, or even standing on Brother Harry's shoulders picking apples. Still, he had no fear of falling.

The room over which the glittering lamp hung was vast, much bigger than the meeting house, and it seemed to Amos that all the Believers everywhere could come from where they were to this room and dance on the floor below him without ever coming to grief or injury. Near to his eye level a railed gallery went all the way round the room, overlooking the floor from high above. Tables and chairs were stacked along it, like a haymow kept specially for the fine and fancy goods that would not do to be left to the weather. But they looked all anyhow, as if they had been put there in haste.

Amos spun on his perch a little and craned his neck to see the business being transacted below him. Now that he turned his attention to it, he found his eyes and ears, nose and throat were choked by what he saw. That anyone could take notice of the manner in which this glorious room was tricked out was a wonder, so awful were its contents.

There were a hundred pallets and more down there, and on each one lay the twisted remnants of a man. Amos had thought before that he could see the wooden floor shiny between them, but now he could not. There was blood everywhere – on the men, on the linens, on the walls, on the upright souls who moved betwixt and between. He felt his own thoughts vanishing beneath the screams and he could not hear himself think. Arms waved in the air, heads tossed back and forth on whatever had been placed beneath them instead of pillows. He heard over and over again the shrieks for water, but there was none. There had been no rain for weeks. The stink of the room lodged high in his throat, reminding him a little of the days when the brethren butchered the hogs, but it was different here, worse. The smell hung like green wood smoke in his nostrils and made him turn his head in hopes of finding sweeter air.

And turning his head Amos saw below and behind a small man, a redheaded man, moving from one pallet to another, holding brief but fast to whatever hand was thrust at him, pausing now and again to do some fiddling kindness. Amos watched him with fascination. Even from so high above the room he sensed a familiarity in the way this little man stood, and the white apron – surely it had once been white, smeared though it now was – only drew further the boy's curiosity. He leaned forward, balancing carefully on the stout arm of the lamp.

He followed the red hair, the peculiar dark blue shirt with its blurred yellow markings, the white apron, as they moved through the wreckage, but he lost them in the corona of the lamplight. Then the little man was there again, this time struggling to hold down the leg of one of the broken inmates of this awful sickroom. Others in white aprons had joined him and together they held fast to this flailing limb or that as a grey-haired carpenter of a fellow labored to saw away the leg to which the redhead now applied the full of his restraining weight. He tossed like a poor rider on that tortured horse, and as his red hair dipped and bobbed Amos looked with all his might to see his face.

Instead he saw the little man step back as the body on the pallet went limp. He was holding the severed leg in his hands. The ghastly gift lay across his arm then like death's own dearest child, and Amos stared long at it. He watched as its nurserymaid threaded his way across the room and threw it high onto a tapering pile of legs and arms, hands and feet, that stretched up to the overlook on which the things Amos had just a few minutes ago counted as precious were stored out of harm's way.

There was a sound, like whistling up a tunnel, and a voice was calling his name. He could hear it clearly, despite the horrible confusion that rose up toward him like a wind. He knew the voice, but could not place it, and as he struggled to find below him a face he knew he found instead that he could not see through the flickering lights that tickled his toes.

"Amos!" the voice demanded sharply. "Why aren't you in bed?"

"I thought I was," he called back, shielding his eyes with his hand, still trying to see.

"You shouldn't be here. Go home."

"Will you come with me?" he asked.

"Nay, nay, I can't. Now go home."

The voice seemed to be moving now, in circular fashion, but no matter how Amos turned on the lamp he could not see its face.

"Let me stay just a little while, please," the boy pleaded. "I only want to see you."

The voice now rolled like comfort above the despair beneath it, found the child's cool cheek, and spoke.

"Tell them, when you see them, that I'm alive," it said.

Amos touched his hand to his face. It was as if he had been kissed, but he was still alone in the arms of the lamp. From above him now the voice said again, "Tell them, I'm alive."

He looked down at the many lights and saw that they had become a thousand stars. The room was gone and it was night, and Amos was falling. His nightshirt billowed around him like a sail and still he was not afraid. The crested sea of pallets was gone, swallowed up in the darkness, but the farther he fell the more clearly he could see below him a single small bed that looked remarkably like his own. He fell on and now saw that it was not his bed – or was it? – but that of a little redheaded boy who slept fitfully, his fingers twined in the curls that hung at his ears.

He did not feel himself fall from the sky into his bed; he simply knew he was there. And when he opened his eyes he saw the night was still with him, but the little boy in his bed was gone. He felt first one side, then the other, but he was alone.

Suddenly Amos was frightened. He sat up and looked at the other boys, fast asleep in their own beds. Slipping down to the floor he padded quietly down the stairs and along the hall to the retiring room where Brother Harry slept. He crept in through the door which stood slightly ajar in the heat, and dropping down slid under Harry's bed. There, with the soft sound of breath and safety above him, he fell asleep.

In the morning the bell sounded at half-past-six and the brethren put their feet quickly to the floor. Day, only just announced, was already wasting.

Moving about the room, closing the door so that they might make themselves presentable, Jefferson Shannon noticed the little hand which had worked its way out from under the bed.

"Seems to me you've got a bedbug, Brother Harry," he said to the tall man pulling up his suspenders.

Harry looked up, curious but silent. Jefferson jerked a thumb towards the small fingers resting, still in sleep, by the headpost.

Kneeling by the bed, Harry reached gently underneath the rails and pulled the boy out. Amos had been on the verge of wakefulness and now opened his eyes. Instinctively he put his arms around

Brother Harry's neck, as if to anchor himself in this reality having delivered himself from – he could not remember.

"What brings thee here, little brother?" Harry asked softly.

"I don't know," Amos said, rubbing his eyes with the heels of his hands. "I just woke up and you were here."

"Did thee have a bad dream?" Harry did not know Amos for a dreamer, but with the nightmare of the world banging at the front door it made sense that it should someday find a home somewhere inside.

"I don't remember."

"Well, then, it couldn't have been so bad," Harry said, setting the child on his feet. "Better go back upstairs and get into thy clothes. Have thy breakfast. Brother John may have a thing or two for thee and the boys to do today."

"Couldn't I stay with you?" Amos asked.

With those words something suddenly jumped out of the fog in the boy's mind, a memory or thought Harry could sense but not read in his eyes.

"What is it?" Harry asked, his voice touched by a sudden concern that made Brother Jefferson turn to see what had alarmed this placid, quiet man.

Amos reached up and closed his hands around Brother Harry's wrists. "He's alive," he said, not really sure what he was saying but driven to say it. "I was to tell you when I saw you, he's alive."

Brother Jefferson bent down and looked Amos in the eye. "Who's alive, boy?"

"I don't know," Amos said, drawing back into the safety of Harry Littlebourne's legs. Frightened by his own confusion, he was anxious to deliver the message entrusted to him and be finished with the errand. "I tried to see his face. There were lights. I couldn't see. He told me to tell you he's alive. And then I fell through a hole in the sky."

"My dear Father," Jefferson whispered under his breath. "We'd better tell Elder Harvey."

*   *   *

Perhaps more than anyone else at South Union, Elder Harvey Eades believed in the wisdom that lay behind dreams, and in the power of the spirit to make itself known to those who still had their being on the earthly plane. This did not make him unique among Believers – far from it, in fact, the Shakers as far back as Mother Ann Lee having been devoted mystics – but perhaps Elder Harvey was more fervently convinced than most that those things which lack logical explanations are sometimes themselves attempts to explain, instruct and guide.

Less than twenty years ago had ended seven years of profound mystical experience in the Shaker communities – felt most intensely in the eastern societies, possibly, but the west was not unaffected. It might even have been argued that the spirit visitations began there.

Typically the spirits visited Shaker young people, as they did little Emily Pearcifield at South Union in December of 1835. Emily was twelve years old when the vision appeared to her, and after her earthly sight was restored she described for the astonished ministry the things she had seen in her absence, on her travels in the kind care and keeping of Jesus, Mother Ann, and the first fathers and mothers of the Believers. It seemed to some at the time that the spirit of a recently-departed eldress had come from the nether shore to show the child the wonders of the world to which all the deserving would someday travel. Emily's journey was a source of inspiration and joy to the faithful, a gift for which they hoped they too might one day prove worthy.

Two years later in New York, at the Niskayuna Society, a group of adolescent girls took to inspired, involuntary whirling and singing, and young Ann Maria Goff was blessed with a vision. Not long after, another group of young girls at Ohio's Union Village seemed almost to have been gripped by the unseen hands of unearthly forces: their frantic, animated exercises, their lengthy and unpartnered conversations in unknown tongues, were all recognized as gifts bestowed by spirit guides – perhaps even angels. In time the old as well as the young were being adopted by a multitude of spirits apparently anxious to set the Shakers square on the godly course, and anyone who received messages or songs as the result of such discourse was expected to share resultant revelations with the rest. Some 2,000 of the songs the Shakers sang were said to have been played by spirits through the listening "instruments" among the brethren and sisters. So it went from community to community.

But at South Union the seven years of mystical manifestation visited upon Believers were felt as keenly as at any of the eighteen societies. Their young people especially were beset by the physical effects of spirit contact, and trances were common. Harvey Eades himself was often visited by the heavenly travellers who sought to influence and strengthen Shaker lives. Spirits invaded his thoughts and his dreams, and as was expected of all visionary Believers he recounted to the elders his experiences, as exactly and dispassionately as he could recall them. They gleaned from those messages what good they could derive and shared the resulting wisdom with the community.

When, in 1844, the spirits told the Shakers they were embarking on new travels, keen as they were to explore the rest of the peoples of the world, there was among Believers a kind of sadness, an awareness that an important source of inspiration and guidance would henceforth be denied them. But surely it was the very nature of such beings not to be bound. Before taking their leave, the spirits said manifestations such as had blessed the Shakers' lives would someday occur elsewhere, and when in 1848 they read in their newspapers of the "rappings" heard in New York by the Fox sisters of Hydesville, the Believers knew their family of spirit guides had at last come upon others receptive to their messages. Spiritualism had found the world's people, but perhaps as a reward for their sacrifices the Believers had been allowed first glimpse of "the mansions of the blessed."

Thus, when Brother Jefferson Shannon called in at the ministry office that Thursday morning with little Amos Anger in tow, saying the boy had had a most peculiar dream, Elder Harvey was more than anxious to listen. If young Amos had been visited perhaps it was the long-awaited signal of the spirits' return.

Amos flinched a little bit when Brother Jefferson loosed his hand, sat him down and left him alone with this stranger. He had once sat on Elder Harvey's knee. Brother Harry had told him so. But that was back in 1858, the last time Elder Harvey visited South Union, and Amos was then only three years old. His memory of Harvey Eades was as vague as his memory of the man in his dream.

"Brother Jefferson tells me you got a message in your sleep last night," Elder Harvey said, bringing his chair up close to Amos. "Supposing you tell me about it."

"I don't remember anything much," the boy said, looking to get the thing over with as quickly as might be.

"Well, sure you do, if you just think about it a little," Eades said hopefully. Most often, in his recollection, the spirits selected older children to impart their messages, but their ways were most assuredly their own and Harvey Eades would not dispute the wisdom of them. Perhaps the choice of so young an instrument was their challenge to his wit.

"There was just a man, and I couldn't see his face," Amos said, kicking the heels of his boots against the legs of his chair.

"Tell me where you were, when you saw him," Harvey said.

"I was asleep."

"Of course you were, but where were you in your dream?"

Amos understood where Elder Harvey was headed now. "In a big room. A big beautiful room, like no room I ever saw," he said enthusiastically.

"Ah, I see," Eades said. "And this man whose face you couldn't see, what did he sound like?"

"He sounded like he was singing, only he was just talking," Amos said. There was as he said this a nag at him, just nipping around the edges of his mind, light enough to feel but hard enough to pester.

Elder Harvey began to smile. "And tell me what he said..."

"He said, when I saw you, I was to tell you he's alive. He said it twice, to tell you he's alive, so he was most particular that I shouldn't forget," Amos told him. "But that's all I remember."

Elder Harvey sat back in his chair. It was a very simple dream, to be sure, the Son of God looking to assure His chosen children through one of their own lambs that they were following the path that would through their diligence lead them to Him. If it was a beginning, the precursor of new visions yet to come, it was a clear and logical one. "Jesus wants you to know how much He loves you," he explained to the boy. "He came all the way from Heaven to tell you that. Now isn't that fine?"

Amos shifted in his seat. "Eldress Nancy told us that," he said. "I already knew."

"Well, now you know from Jesus Himself, and that's a lovely gift for you to have," Harvey said. Someday Amos would learn to appreciate what he'd been given, but for now it was understandable, given his age, that the spiritual value of his dream should elude him.

"Brother John wants me, I think," Amos said, restless and anxious to get outside, where the drought-dry grass was the color of winter wheat in the autumn sun. "They're all picking apples."

"Then you'd better get yourself out to him, I'd say," Harvey said kindly. "But let me see you get over the road in one piece. Folks out there in their carriages are like maniacs. And that doesn't begin to think about the saddlemen..." He walked the boy out to the steps and watched until he was sure Amos had safely reached the Center gate. Sad: used to be a child could go out in the road alone, but those days were surely gone.

Harvey Eades went back inside the ministry shop as Amos, happy to be finished finally with the chore his dream had set him, broke into a free-legged run toward the apple orchard. His limbs sang as he went, and his mind hummed along with them. Elder Harvey surely had kicked up a fuss about Jesus, and it was a puzzle to Amos that he should have done so. Amos had not said a word about seeing Jesus in his dream.

Shakertown at South Union was desperate to hear word from Pleasant Hill. What little they knew was that all the forces of Buell and Bragg were gathered in the central region of the Bluegrass, and with Pleasant Hill so close to Lexington their sister society to the west was frantic with worry. For over a year the Shakers at South Union had lived in the maelstrom and survived it as best they could, doing what they could. But their travails had been born with the war and grown along with it; much of what they daily endured now without complaint would have been considered intolerable had Nathan Bedford Forrest and his men inflicted it upon them that summer night fourteen months ago. For Pleasant Hill there would be no such period of adjustment, and the brethren and sisters were therefore fretful on their behalf.

It was not until Friday afternoon that they learned how desperate the effect of so much firepower might be on their friends at Pleasant Hill, and again it was John Barnett who brought the news. He came banging through the trustees' office door, absent a knock so rattled by the tidings was he.

Urban Johns was there, and Jesse Rankin, and John Rankin, all of whom turned and looked at him as if he had two heads – as well he might have, for all he knew, given the thunderous pounding at his temples.

"I just heard down to Russellville," he said.

"Heard what?" asked Jess Rankin. "Sit down, John, 'fore you fall down."

"No, thanks," he said. "I came straight here. Knew you'd want to know: there was the most godawful battle up at Chaplin Hill two days ago..."

"Don't swear, John," Rankin said without thinking. "Chaplin

Hill? I don't know it..."

"I do," Urban Johns said. "It's almost to Perryville, isn't it? North of Lebanon, before you get to Harrodsburg?"

"That's the one," Barnett nodded. "It was all of 'em – Buell and Bragg, everybody – fifty-odd thousand men, North and South, can you imagine?"

"That's right around Pleasant Hill, Urban," John Rankin said.

"I don't know," Urban replied, searching the map of his mind. "Far off enough. They might be allright there. What else, John?"

"Who took the worst of it?" asked Jess Rankin.

"Hard to tell, way I heard. Bragg's boys were there, and Buell came up on him. It started on Tuesday, somebody said. I heard they were fighting over water: the secesh had it and the Federals wanted it. There's been no rain up the Bluegrass for weeks, any more than we've had down here. The corn's shocked up, so they got their crops in right enough, but Chaplin's Creek is dry as a bone. Anyway, the sparks didn't really fly for fair til Wednesday afternoon. It only lasted about four hours, but there was plenty of damage done: bodies so cheek-by-jowl on the hills you couldn't walk without stepping on 'em. They were using wagons for ambulances, all they could find, but even so there weren't conveyances enough to carry all the dead and down. General Jackson got hisself the long sleep – Jim Jackson from Elkton, you know him? – and nobody knew he was dead out there. Starling from over Hopkinsville, he was in it. Only joined up a couple of weeks ago, as a captain. He came through just fine, but he saw Jackson fall, and he went back next day and picked him up. They got him washed and salted til the army can ship him home..." The messenger drew breath.

"Lord in Heaven," Jess Rankin said. "What a sight for a Christian."

"Federals took over a passel of the houses in Perryville as field hospitals, but it was worse than that," Barnett went on. "They started taking the hotels for the wounded, too. Don't know which all, but there was the ballroom at the Harrodsburg Springs for one.

All the tables and chairs got shoved up on the balcony to free up the dance floor so the doctors could work clear. Way I heard it, the blood was splattered up as far as the chandelier, and there 's so many arms and legs for the surgeon to take off that by ten o'clock there was a pile of 'em stretched as far up as the balcony..."

"That's enough, John, please," said Elder Jess, wincing.

"And that was just the Union dead," he persevered, having either not heard Jess Rankin or being too full of the tale he was telling to stop. "Doesn't sound like anybody much got the best of it, but at least it was Bragg left first. He shot off south toward Camp Dick Robinson, through Crab Orchard, on his way down to Cumberland Gap I reckon, and just left the bodies where they fell. Still out there, I suppose."

"Buell went after him?" John Rankin asked.

"I don't rightly know."

"Where'd you get all this?"

"Somebody come through on the cars had a New York paper," he said, obviously impressed at the opportunity to repeat the dispatches of so august a journal. "And Starling got a letter to his daughter somehow. Seemed the soldiers over the depot know a little bit to tell. Ought to be pretty reliable."

Suddenly all four men had the urge to sit, and they sat quietly, just looking at each other.

"What do you reckon it means?" John Barnett asked.

"I reckon it means there's mothers looking for their boys to come home, and they'll be disappointed," the grim-faced Brother Urban said.

"Urban?"

"Hmm?"

"The Ninth Kentucky Cavalry was there," Barnett said carefully. He was treading fragile ground and knew it. "Fellow in Russellville wrote down some of the list before the train pulled out, and they were on it."

"There was no list of the dead?" Urban asked.

"Too soon, I reckon," Barnett replied quietly. The name was suspended like a feather in the air between the four of them, kept at eye level but no one spoke it. "If there was, I'd have looked." He felt uncomfortable, as if he had saddled this group of friends with a worry they hadn't expected and in such troubled times didn't need, and he looked for a way to sugar the temper of the moment. "Did you know Bragg and Buell are related?" he asked suddenly. "Bragg's married to Buell's sister. Now, don't that beat all?"

Within days the hospitals in Bowling Green were full up again, and paroled rebels from the battle at Chaplin Hill near Perryville began to wander through South Union on their way home – the war now being behind them in more ways than one. They were mostly tired of soldiering, and they were only too happy to say so.

The first frost came a week after the battle, and the sweet potatoes were dug, and the first snow fell a week later. The ground gave up nearly 7,000 cabbages – Amos and the other boys wore themselves out collecting them up for storage – and despite the drought that dragged on even after the frost Brother Harry Littlebourne and the other farmers went ahead with putting in the winter wheat.

One evening, as Harry was coming in from the fields for supper, with Old Sorrow behind him, he crossed the path of a little band of rebel parolees, scrawny and ragged and fed up, on their way south. He stopped to let them pass, and was looking at their faces when suddenly he waded into their midst, searching for just the right man.

"A word with thee," he stuttered when he found the pair of eyes that emboldened him to speak. "A word with thee..."

The soldier did not break his stride, but looked up at tall Harry. "I'm listenin'."

"Did thee kill a red-haired man?"

"Did I what?"

"There was a red-haired man at Chaplin Hill," Harry said,

slowing his long legs to match the soldier stride for stride. "Did thee kill him? Did thee see him there?"

The soldier put his head back and laughed. "Mister," he said, "when you aim to blow a man's head off you don't necessarily notice what color hair's on it."

Brother Harry had not thought of it that way, the etiquette of killing being far beyond his ken. He stopped mid-stride and the soldiers flowed around him, leaving him alone with his unanswered question in the middle of the Great Road as the light faded.

When he turned back toward the Center he saw that Old Sorrow was still following along behind, and together he and Harry carried on toward the stable.

On October's final Sabbath Eve Elder Harvey looked out the window of the ministry shop and saw something he had never in his life thought to see. He stood up and put his hands against the cold glass panes, defying the vision to be real. Three bulky colored men were being driven down the road like a team of oxen: hands tied behind them, lashed together shoulder to shoulder, pushed along at gunpoint by the white man riding behind them on his horse.

"No wonder God has a bone to pick with this nation," he thought. He would have much on his mind at meeting tomorrow, and as always he would speak it.

November

J ohn Hunt Morgan and his men had occupied Russellville. So it was said; so the Shakers heard. He had put his pickets out all around the town. If this was so, the company of Union cavalry they saw riding through the village on the first night of the month was unlikely to strike fear in a rebel raider's heart: an unimpressive group in general, one rider among the two hundred and fifty in Captain Waltham's command was so drunk he had been tied onto his horse to stop him falling off. His head lay on the horse's neck and his nose bounced up and down in the animal's mane as it went. Brother Jefferson pointed out this spectacular disgrace to Waltham as he and the officer stood watching the men pass by, and the captain shrugged helplessly.

"You downright hate to make a start when they're like that," Waltham said. He and Brother Jefferson had come to know one another in recent months, so often had the cavalry passed this way, and he spoke with honest exasperation. "With that kind of start the finish is barely worth thinking about."

They might have liked a bit more notice, but there was nothing to be gained by mentioning it. The two couriers arrived on Tuesday afternoon to advise the Shakers that five cavalry regiments from the army of Major General William Starke Rosecrans – after the grim draw at Perryville Don Carlos Buell had been compelled to stand down, and Rosecrans was his replacement – would be on their way to South Union, expecting to camp on suitable premises for the night.

"If Morgan and his varmints are around here or anywheres south of the line the gen'ral reckons to run him out once't and for all," declared one of the couriers with admirable conviction. "We'll git Morgan or git got tryin', is my bet."

"That's certainly a noble aspiration," Brother Jefferson told him. "I just hope five regiments of cavalry's enough."

As the clock neared six the first cavalry company pulled up by the meeting house and Jefferson met them at the crossroads.

"You'll have to show us the best place to camp," the captain said.

"Figured I might," said Brother Jefferson, clambering up on the horse he'd kept waiting outside the trustees' office for just such an eventuality. He rode beside the captain at the head of the column, leading them up to the meadow west of the sheep house.

"I'm afraid we'll need wood for camp fires," he told Jefferson as they passed the North. "And corn for the horses." The young officer looked around as they reached the sheep house meadow. "Seems like the easiest thing is we can burn your fence rails."

Jefferson winced. Easiest only for the army.

"We'll try to do as little damage as we can," the young man said. "Such a nice place you've got here, it's a shame to muss it."

"We'd be much obliged, captain, if your men could be careful with themselves and their matches," Jefferson told him. "It's been a good three months since we saw any rain."

For the first of many times that evening Brother Shannon pointed out an open meadow on Shaker land and watched as troops and horses pulled off the road to fill it. Then he reined in and hastened himself back to the trustees' office. By seven o'clock the Great Road was jammed with troops coming down from Bowling Green, mounted men as far as the eye could see, and behind them was the swirling dust that meant there were still more beyond. Six hundred wagons were intermingled with the thousands of blue-coated soldiers and their horses: artillery carriages, ambulances, ammunition wagons, provision and forage wagons.

Alonzo Chaddock had managed to wangle himself two days' leave from the camp at Bowling Green to come visit his sister Lydia, who lived at the North. Eldress Nancy had a definite soft spot for Alonzo, and as he leaned up against the Center fence she watched with him, listening with interest while he explained the functions of the different wagons that clattered by.

"They'll be lucky to get 'em all here by two in the morning," Alonzo told her. "Them brethren of yours won't be gettin' to sleep any time soon."

Until tonight the brethren from all the families had generally gathered together only for Sabbath meeting, but with the chaos in the road every man was needed to work with the army, hauling provender and assisting at the camps in the interest of minimizing the inevitable damage. As evening came on the campfires became visible in the fading light, thousands of them, lit from the sheep house to the depot on every available plot of ground. Amos was watching with the other children from the Center windows as the soldiers arrived. The dull greenish glow from the fires seemed to keep the darkness from reaching the ground, and the children were captivated by the sight of it.

Below them, the kitchen was in near-panic. In all three dwelling houses the sisters had been alerted, and they were hard at the ovens. They could not feed all the soldiers, had not been asked to, but they had been advised of some hundred officers who might or might not be taking meals in the office as they chose, and in the absence of a good breakfast the sisters reckoned the enlisted men would likely welcome as much bread as might be baked in a long night. On this last Brother Jefferson and Eldress Nancy agreed despite the sorry state of the ovens: in nearly fifteen months they had never once had a proper cool-down, and the cracks were beginning to show at an alarming rate.

Drawn by the noisy flutter that wafted up from downstairs, Amos went down to investigate. The sisters in their numbers had with time and practice learned to move about the kitchen as in a dance. He remembered watching from under the stairs that first evening, when Bedford and his men came to call, how the sisters had bumped into each other and dropped things in the confusion of so many trying to tend the ovens at once. It was all different now. The pace in the warm, fragrant kitchen was furious but smooth; a new routine had established itself amid the shards of the peaceful life order shattered by the pressure of war.

Sister Elizabeth spotted him inching around the worktable. "Amos, if thee've come around looking for raw pastry thee can go straight back upstairs," she said sharply. "We're making bread, not pies. Now, shoo."

The boy knew this tone of voice. She wasn't angry, just busy. He could safely stall his departure without fear of reproach.

"That's the blue soldiers out there, isn't it?" he asked, resting his chin on the cool, flour-dusted table top.

"The blue – why, bless thee, yea, it's the Union army," she told him, smiling. "And thee never did see so many soldiers as there are out there tonight. Everywhere we have grass to sleep on friend Lincoln has put soldiers. That's where all the brethren are, out helping to settle them in."

"Looks like a lot," Amos said, reaching up and snatching a peach from the basket. Sister Elizabeth raised her hand from the dough she was working to swat at his wrist, but he knew she wasn't serious. He rubbed the fuzzy skin against his cheek. It was worth playing with a peach before you ate it. "They're still coming down the road."

"Alonzo Chaddock told Eldress Nancy they'd be hours yet getting here," she said. She was sprinkling flour on the table and it blew up Amos' nose. "Like as not we'll have the whole Union army camped out on our doorstep, there's so many of 'em coming."

"The whole army?" he asked, putting his finger to his nose to stop the sneeze that itched him.

"Wouldn't surprise me one little bit," she said.

Amos scooted himself under the worktable and sank his bottom teeth up through the tart skin of the peach. The juice dribbled down onto his collar and tickled his neck. From where he sat there was nothing in life but skirts and feet and flying flour. He watched for a minute or two, thinking about having every blue soldier there was out in the meadows, even if it was only for one night. They almost always left in the morning. All the blue soldiers... Turning over on all fours he crawled to the bucket and dropped in his peach pit, then made for the archway that led to the dining hall. With all the kerfuffle in the kitchen Sister did not see him go. Up the east staircase to the first floor, to the low peg-rails where the children's hats and coats were hung, and he was astonished by the quiet in the house. With the brethren all gone to tend the soldiers, the sisters all at work around the kitchen and in the near lots, the children upstairs at the windows, he felt almost alone. Holding his hat and coat to his chest he crept back to the doors by the meeting room and let himself out. Alone in the house and alone outside were two different things, and of the two he preferred the latter.

He was not, of course, alone. The lawn around the Center was abubble with soldiers busy about their business. With night falling they took no notice of him, and he started up in the direction of the North. He was mindful that there might be some of the brethren amongst the troops, but he saw none: forty Shaker men moving in the company of thousands of soldiers would most likely be swallowed up like minnows.

As Amos walked he was examining faces. These blue soldiers all looked alike, except for the ones with hair beneath their noses or sprouted on their chins or both, and he could not see enough to tell what they looked like. The army men's hair was shorter than that of the brethren, harder to see under their hats. But he could not afford not to look: if they would only be here for a night he would have to be sharp about it. The hundreds of campfires in his line of vision were lovely, a kind of rebellion of light against sunset, and then he saw that the soldiers were tearing down the fences to stoke the flames.

He ran and caught the arm of one wood-gatherer. "Nay, nay, don't do that!" he said. "The chickens'll all run off if you take those away!"

"Don't worry about that, young fella," said the soldier, rapping him gently on the head with his grimy knuckles. "We'll take care of the chickens." He laughed, and his companions laughed, and one of them reached out and pushed the boy along.

Farther up, near the meadow, he saw how the tents formed long lines that ran like arrows west toward the Gasper's Clear Fork. He stopped where he was and saw how the campfires seemed to stack one on top of the other in the distance, making a torch flame that jumped toward the sky. The soldiers had anchored the tents in place with their bayoneted muskets, and firelight bounced off the blades. Smoke billowed around the fires, gusting with ash, and as Amos brushed a flitting ember that had flown across his nose he felt a hand close on his shoulder.

"Whoa, whoa, whoa, little soldier," said the voice above him, and he looked up at it. "What brings you up here so late in the evening?"

"I'm looking for someone," he replied.

"Well, I might could help you look," the soldier said, bringing himself down to the child's eye level. "I got a boy back home, just about your age, you know. Where's your man from?"

Amos considered this. "Not from around here," he said, remembering something Sister Elizabeth had once told him.

"Most o' these boys here's from Ohio or Illinois," said the soldier. "Your man from Ohio or Illinois?"

"I don't know," Amos said. "Maybe he's from here."

"Seems like if he's from here he'd be looking for you, not t'other way around. Is it your father you're looking for?"

"My Father's in Heaven," he said. Soldiers didn't seem to know much about the Bible, if the ones Amos had met were any indication.

"That's a shame. What's the name of the fella you're huntin'?"

"Brother Austin," Amos said. "He has red hair."

"Brother Austin?" The soldier drew his head back, a little puzzled until he cottoned on. "You from Uncle Tom's Cabin back yonder?"

Amos turned himself and pointed to the Center. "Nay," he said. "I live there."

"All the same thing to me, son," he said. "What's your name?"

"Amos."

"Well, Amos, you just call me Jack and we'll see if we can find your brother for you. Maybe ain't the best idea you go wanderin' around here by yourself."

Sister Elizabeth was all of a state when she came down to the kitchen after getting the little ones into their beds. She had come up one nose short when she counted the smalls in her care, and this news she confided to Eldress Betsy when she found her out by the well.

"Amos isn't in the house," she said, well nigh overwrought. "I've looked for him everywhere. He was down in the kitchen for a little while, and it seemed to me like he might have fallen asleep somewhere thereabouts, but now I've looked and he isn't anywhere."

"Now don't fret, sister," Eldress Betsy said reassuringly, although truth to tell the boy's absence at such an hour and with so many strangers wandering the village unsettled her. "He'll turn up. Boys do get the urge to have a look-see at the most inconvenient times. He may be out looking for Brother Harry – those two are thick as flies. You ask the sisters to keep a sharp eye for him and I'll see if I can find Brother Jefferson."

Urban Johns and Jefferson Shannon had divided the complicated business of overseeing the brethren's chores on this extraordinary evening, and while Brother Urban was out on some expedition or other with the officers Jefferson remained in the trustees' office, keeping careful track of each new calamity as it arose. The disappearance of one of the children on any other evening would have brought out every spare hand for a search party, but tonight Eldress Betsy's concern for a lost child was that much more fat thrown in the fire.

"You'll just have to look after it," he said, not completely drained of patience but near to. "Every one of the brethren's got more than he can handle as it is, and there's not one of 'em I can bring in to look for a wandering child."

"I just thought you'd want to know," Eldress Betsy told him. "Perhaps any of the brethren you see, you could just ask 'em to keep an eye to the ground, 'case they might notice him."

"That much I can do," Brother Jefferson said, and his eyebrows went up when one of the hired boys banged through the door. "It's not –"

"They're breakin' into the beehives, Brother Jeff," the boy interrupted. "I'm half-expectin' Elder Harvey to come after 'em with a broom..."

"I'll see to it, Ly," he said. One hand on the boy's shoulder, one extended toward Eldress Betsy, it was clear that both might as well be tied behind his back for all that he could do the bidding of his conscience with them. "It's not that he doesn't worry me, it's –"

"You go with Lysander," Eldress Betsy said quietly. "If the boy's to be found, we'll find him."

Harry Littlebourne and Joseph Averett were hauling provender from the cow barn by the Negroes' house to the soldiers by the depot, and even in the evening chill they were perspiring. Harry had lost count of the jaggs they had already taken, and men in need of more were still arriving. Out of the corner of his eye as he boosted a bundle of oats toward the wagon bed he saw Jefferson Shannon, following Lysander Ruley, coming out the office door. Just at that instant, Shannon was looking at him.

"Brother Harry!" he shouted, hurrying himself along the south side of the road until he thought Littlebourne could hear him on the north side. "You seen Amos?"

He stopped still, with the load balanced against his chest.

"Boy's missing from the house," came Jefferson's voice on the night air. "You see him, you send him home, allright? The sisters are worried sick..."

Lysander Ruley was pulling at him, and Shannon's form faded in the darkness, moving toward the dry house.

Over the noise of the soldiers then came a shout from young Brother Joe by the barn door. "There's no time now, Harry," he said. "We can't stop now. Harry... Come *on*."

There was an ugly thud at the side door and Sister Lucy jumped. Her struggle to stay awake through the night was not made any easier by the number of hours she had already done without sleep. With the brethren all away in the meadows and thousands of Federal soldiers camped around the place the sisters felt very much alone in the dwelling houses. Those who could be spared for a spell were upstairs dozing on pallets next to the children. The rest were working in the kitchen, and Sister Lucy was drowsing on a chair when she heard the noise. She looked up at Sister Hannah Freehart with terror in her eyes.

Sister Hannah clasped her hands at waist height, her determination that no harm should befall them as strong as any weapon she could wield at an intruder. "Open the door, sister," she said firmly.

Lucy Shackelford took the latch in her hand as if it might be hot as the oven behind her, and as she opened the door saw on the paving stone outside a barefoot Union soldier with Amos asleep in his arms. He had kicked at the door with his foot rather than disturb the child.

"Lord save us," Sister Hannah cried, running toward the door, "there he is!"

"Hope you wasn't fussed after him," said Jack. "We was all havin' such a time with him, and he fell asleep by the fire, and we didn't like to roust him, but the corporal said he couldn't stay, and the boy said he come from here, so..."

"Let me take him," Sister Hannah said, and Amos was slipped lightly from Jack's shoulder to hers. There was a grumbling, humming sound as his head tumbled but he was soon sound asleep again. The soldier handed Sister Lucy the boy's hat.

"My boy's same age as him," he said, enjoying the warm kitchen, the smell of fresh bread, the look of home around him. He was in no particular hurry to leave.

"Mighty cold to be out with no shoes," said Sister Sally McComb, glancing at his filthy feet.

He tried to hide one behind the other, but nature being what it is he could not make both disappear at the same time. "My gunboats went to tatters a long time back," he said, smiling shyly. "Long walk down from Perryville."

"And the army hasn't given you new ones?" Sister Sally asked. Sister Hannah had taken Amos upstairs and Sister Lucy was too young to appreciate the depth of her consternation.

"Ma'am, they can't give you what they ain't got."

"Well, we'll just see about that," Sister Sally said.

"No'm, please," said the earnest Jack, raising his hands to halt her mid-cluck, "don't make no fuss to the shoulder-straps."

"Never mind the officers," she told him, having long ago become conversant in the language spoken by enlisted men. "We must have something you can wear, if we take a look. Sister Lucy, you see if you can't find this young man something to eat and I'll just see whether there's shoes he can get himself down the road in." She was still muttering to herself as she went up the stairs. "Barefoot in November. However can they..."

"There's some ham left from supper," Sister Lucy told Jack, indicating a chair by the stove, "and cornbread, and plenty of pie, if you think that would be nice."

A muscle jumped in Jack's skinny jaw. "Miss Lucy, you ever ate salt horse?"

Lucy Shackelford's giggle told him she hadn't.

"Then I reckon ham and cornbread would be real nice."

Robert Johns caught up with Harry Littlebourne by the smoke house and told him Amos was back in the fold.

"Seems like he wandered off to the camp," Brother Robert said. "One of the soldiers brought him back. No telling what he was doing out there. Eldress Nancy said he was sleeping like Moses in the basket when the fella brought him back in."

Harry knew why he'd gone, without being told, without having to ask. But he was unwilling simply to accept that all was well, and took himself back to the Center to have his own look. Upstairs in the little boys' room he leaned over the prodigal's low bed, and touched his dusty finger to the small open palm that lay on the bed linen beneath Amos' nose.

The boy stirred slightly and rolled his head back on the pillow. "I looked everywhere," Amos said, almost talking in his sleep. "The whole army's here but him."

"Not now," Harry said, pulling the blanket up around his chin. "We'll talk tomorrow."

"They surely do like birds," he said before he drifted off again. "Funny how partial they are to birds..."

Colonel Henry Kennett had set pickets all around the village, on every lane that gave access and at the crossroads, and they sat their horses patiently through the night, safeguarding the houses and alert to any rebel mischief that might be worked against the sleeping troops. And while none such threatened from outside the pickets' line, with daylight came the first grim sight of the troops' own destructive handiwork.

It was as if the meadowlands had been burned off under cover of darkness. In the dim light of morning, as the men were moving out and after they had gone, the smoke from half-doused campfires drifted over the chewed-up grass, trampled ground, and wagon ruts that scarred the land. Mad fieldhands might have got in with ploughs and harrows and worked the ground all anyhow, so dreadful was the state of the soil and grass. These men of Brigadier General Joshua Woodrow Sill's division had, despite the brethren's best efforts, broken down all the fences and set themselves up even where they had been asked most particularly not to go, and from the depot to the Woodland pasture south of the Great Road, up to the mill pond and the stone shop and beef stables to the north, the devastation was much the same or worse. The dry white oak fence rails had been pulled out and burned, and as the Shaker men walked through the ruins the troops had left behind they mourned the mindless destruction but they were also peculiarly grateful: in these drought-dried meadows, it might have been so much worse. The soldiers had set their fires right up close to the stables and barns, and they being so stacked up with hay one single ambitious spark from a soldier's fire could easily have found the mows.

From the debris that covered the scarred ground it was clear that the troops, hungry from days and days on half rations, were resourceful if less than honorable in supplementing what little they were given to eat. Not only had they robbed the beehives, the potato hole had been uncovered and the seed potatoes taken as well. The pilfering of the hen houses stopped when the brethren set guards to keep the thieving soldiers out, but the corn cribs had all been raided and three barns emptied of provender.

It was left to Brother Urban to fashion an account of the damage done, based on the reports of the brethren. When the list was finished, even he was slow to believe the extent of it:

12 tons of hay
245 bushels of corn
4800 bushels of fodder
5000 bushels of oats
2500 fence rails

For all but the fence rails the quartermaster was willing to pay the Shakers three hundred and seventy-eight dollars. The officer refused to discuss the price the army would offer by way of reimbursement for the use of fine fence timbers as firewood; he was not, he said, authorized to value such things. Brother Urban would have to take the matter up with the post quartermaster in Bowling Green, the very idea of which would have driven him to despair had he had sufficient energy.

"How many were there out there last night, Colonel Kennett?" Urban Johns finally asked before the officers took their leave of the trustees' office Wednesday morning.

Kennett had met Brother Urban for the first time only the night previous, and he eyed him with some suspicion before answering – perhaps for some reason thinking word of Union strength might be passed along for the edification of the Confederates. He soon thought better of it, however, and gave begrudging answer. "You might put the number at 6,000 troops and 7,000 horses," he said.

The damage was well equal to those numbers, but the chore of clearing up after them and putting the place to rights would be left to a number considerably smaller. The brethren, still awake after their long night, set to work first thing, hauling water out to drown the fires still burning.

Out in the meadows the sisters and children were bent to the task of setting the meadows straight while the brethren began the tedious business of rebuilding the fences. By the abandoned fires coffee rations drawn by the enlisted men still lay in uncooked heaps, alongside useable hardtack and pieces of smoked and fresh beef that would make good soap. All these were collected up in baskets and put by. The soldiers' palates had obviously been more sorely tempted by the proceeds of their raids on the hen house: remains of the stolen chickens were strewn everywhere. If ever the Shakers had thought the Federal soldiers easier to put up with than the Confederates, that thought was now departed.

With so many at work in the meadows there was in this one or the other a feeling that perhaps the time would pass more quickly if they sang, or made games of the collecting and clearing, as so often they did with the seasonal chore days and bees that came now and again. But there was among them no great heart for such a thing. Even the children looked at the destruction done by the soldiers to this home ground of theirs, and there was no joy – only a desire to put it back the way God liked it.

Amos didn't see Brother Harry, not to speak to, for another day or two. Brother John Perryman had the boys busy around the meadows with baskets, collecting and clearing, and the brethren were doing the heavy work. The sisters carried dinner and supper out to them in boxes, so not to slow the fence-mending down by calling the families in for mealtimes.

But by Friday things were quieter, after a fashion. One Michigan soldier, Zenais Clark Cheney, had been reckoned too ill to travel with his unit when Kennett's men left, and was being looked after in a room over the post office by Sister Lucy and Sister Olive. Brother Jefferson was away down past Franklin to Mitchellville in pursuit of the seventy-five dollars allotted by the army to pay for the burned fence rails. Every night now a different squad of soldiers camped up by the mill pond.

Thus Harry was splitting rails that afternoon, working fit to keep the supply sufficient to meet the demand, and Amos was lending his hands to the effort, putting the pegs in place and sitting astride the log set for sundering while Harry swung the axe. With each strike the boy would bounce to the jolt, and as the peg drove farther into the wood he pushed down against the drifting sides with his hands. Then, when the log fell in two he would be left sitting across the two hornless half-moons of timber, dropped flat and laughing on the ground.

Over and over again the axe rose high up above Harry Littlebourne's head and came down with a crack on the peg, and with the rhythm of the axe-fall Amos began to sing:

> *Union forever – hurrah, boys, hurrah!*
> *Down with the traitor!*
> *Up with the star!*
> *While we rally round the flag, boys,*
> *Rally once again,*
> *Shouting the battle cry of freedom...*

Through the noise of his own motion and the crash of the axe on the pegs Brother Harry could barely hear the boy's thin voice, but he was aware that Amos was singing and thus he strained his ears to hear:

> *Yes, we'll rally round the flag, boys,*
> *We'll rally once again,*
> *Shouting the battle cry of freedom.*
> *We will rally from the hillside,*
> *We'll gather from the plain,*
> *Shouting the battle cry of freedom.*
> *Union, forever – hurrah, boys, hurrah!*
> *Down with the traitor, up...*

Harry sank the axe down deep in the wood beside the peg and let go the helve.

"Amos," he said, "what's that I hear thee singing?"

"It's a hymn," he said as he fiddled with a piece of flown bark.

"Where did thee learn this hymn?"

"In the soldier camp," Amos told him. "They taught it to me. Magee said it was about here, and I should know it."

Harry Littlebourne passed his handkerchief across his face. Better for the soldiers to destroy the land than confuse a child for mischief's sake alone, and a rare scrap of anger seeped up through his words. "That is no song of South Union," he said, sharp as the axe. "It's an army song, pure and simple. Don't sing it again. Those words have no place in thee. Hear me?"

Amos ducked his head, ashamed and unclear on the reason why.

"Now, now," said Harry, swinging one long leg over the half-split log and sitting himself just knee-to-knee of the boy. "There's nothing to be sorry for. The soldiers taught thee a song thee has no business to know. If there's anyone to be sorry it's for them to be, unless thee go on singing a world's song knowing thee shouldn't."

The boy's mind jumped like a flea to the things Jack had shown him that night among the Federals. "It seems they like birds more than anything," Amos said, seeking the peace offered by a change of subject.

This he had mentioned in his sleep that night; Harry remembered it. "What makes thee say so?"

"They have them on their arms, little birds flying, like this," he said, and reached out to draw a widespread "v" on the drop of Brother Harry's shoulder. "Some of 'em have one, some don't have any, but most of 'em have yellow flying birds like that stitched to their coats. I don't know why, but it's pretty." Amos crossed his hands and laced his thumbs between a span of flapping fingers, as in the evenings the children sometimes did to cast bird-shaped shadows on the wall. "And you know what else?"

"Tell me."

"I saw a man who could make a box sing."

Harry poked the boy's knee. "Could make what?"

"Jack took me to see him, Sam his name is. He had this shiny little wooden box with holes in it like esses, and it stuck out one side so – " he extended his left arm " – and there were wires and he sawed on them with a stick and it all sang." He could see Harry eyeing him oddly and in the midst of this most unlikely memory Amos worried that he might be suspected of storying. "It's true," he said with great seriousness. "I heard him myself. It sang. And sometimes he sang. It was a nice sound, like Brother Austin telling Jonah and the whale."

"That's a wonder, isn't it?" Harry asked, leaning forward close enough to feel the boy's exhilaration on his face. Amos had not since that sad morning been able to speak of Austin Innes without the accompaniment of tears, and Harry was pleased to see him dry-eyed now. "Truly? A singing box?"

"That's what it was."

"Then here's a question for thee, little brother," Harry said, resting his arms across his knees. "Which pleased thee more, the sound of the soldier's magic box at the camp or Brother Austin when he would tell thee the story of Jonah?"

Amos could not discount entirely the possibility that he'd been scolded. On the other hand, Brother Harry could see the point had been taken, and he therefore sought to ease the boy's confusion.

"I'll tell thee a thing," he said in his friendliest fashion. "It wasn't a singing box thee saw the soldier play. That was what the world will call a violin. In the world violins and similars are used to make the sound of singing." Amos eyed him with pure wonder, that all this too should come as no surprise to Harry. "World's people think the Lord likes their singing better when they have such engines as that to sing with. But Believers say the Lord likes it best when His children sing on their own, so we let the world have its violins and we'll just listen to Brother Austin tell about Jonah and the whale. Which would thee sooner?"

Amos laughed at the thought of trading Brother Austin for anything the world had to offer, laughed so hard his hat fell off.

Elder Lorenzo showed the lieutenant and his company to the head of the mill pond, but when he pointed out the best place for fetching firewood and said it was no bother to get it for them the soldiers were up and boisterous about the gathering even without their lieutenant's bidding.

"No, sir," said one fresh-faced young soldier, as if he knew it was Sabbath and Lorenzo ought not to be doing such things. "That wouldn't be fittin'. We're all of us plenty young enough, sir, and we can look after it for ourselves."

Lorenzo had admitted to a few unchristian thoughts about the troops of the Union army in recent days, but the boys camped out by the mill pond had touched him. For the first time in many days he said he hated to think where those children of God would be in a week.

This story Lorenzo told to Eldress Nancy, and as he did so his eyes brimmed. "It doesn't do to have uncharitable thoughts," he said quietly. "The Lord will always come along and show you how wrong you've been."

Far behind the Federals as they chased Bragg's army south came news from Pleasant Hill, the first since the rebel invasion of the Bluegrass: the Believers there had survived their ordeal, and mercifully well. Some 20,000 grey-coats had passed through that village, and during those difficult days the sisters were kept up cooking and baking round the clock for nearly a week, but with the last of the army they saw the last of the demands for food. A few horses and a wagon or two had been pressed by the Confederates, but otherwise Pleasant Hill had overcome the indignity of invasion without serious injury to property or beliefs. The Lord, Elder Harvey reckoned, was generous in His protection.

The turnips meanwhile were selling well, and on the evening of the seventeenth the farmers looked at the clouds and saw there the blessed threat of rain. The day before they had noticed the cattle seeking the shelter of the trees, an omen they regarded with cautious optimism. A train of cars passed on its way south, and as it stopped at South Union the stationmaster heard delivery of the mails was about to be regularized, sacks to arrive at the depot once a day. And in the evening the rain began to fall. Brother Cyrus said it seemed to him a soak sufficient to do the winter wheat. Brother Urban said it was a soak sufficient to fill the trustees' office with refugees and soldiers. As it happened, both men were right.

1863

There was some unpleasantness between the government back East and the Louisville & Nashville Railroad, the upshot of it all being that Logan County's mail delivery was discontinued. Seemed the Postmaster General at Washington City had been sending the mail on the cars without paying the railroad for its trouble; when the L&N finally realized the mail was riding free, the arrangement was studied on and pronounced unacceptable. Until the dispute was settled, then, the Shakers received their letters in occasional bundles by a circuitous route. Meanwhile they hoped at least one set of the warring parties disrupting their lives would be able to thrash out its differences. Certainly the Federals and the Confederates were making no headway in that direction.

There had been little of the Christmas spirit in evidence around the county in a season to which the brotherly disposition of mind should have come naturally. A few armed men had, for instance, lately appointed themselves "patrols" and roamed the roads as unauthorized keepers of the peace. This peacekeeping largely consisted of terrorizing whatever darkies they happened to come across in their travels around the countryside. The wrath of the patrols was strong, and one of the Hopkins house slaves got himself shot through the head when he tried to defend himself against a beating at the hands of a peacekeeper. Violence against Negroes was in a peculiar ascendance: in Woodburn a score of the town blacks were whipped and beaten by vigilantes who feared a slaves' uprising. It seemed unlikely that such was in the offing, of course; certainly the Shakers had heard no rumors of any such, and matters of that type were exactly the sort of thing of which the yellow woman, Aunt Jenny, kept them well informed.

On the Christmas Day just gone, when all the families gathered together in the meeting house, Elder Harvey spoke with grace and feeling of the importance of setting out in earnest on the road of true gospel travel.

"What is this life but a series of little, mean actions?" he told them. "We lie down and rise again, dress and undress, feed and wax hungry, work and sometimes play and are weary, and then we lie down again. And then the circle turns. We spend the day in trifles, and when the night comes we throw ourselves into the bed of folly amongst dreams and broken thoughts and wild imaginations. Our reason lies asleep with us, and we are for the time arrant brutes, as those that sleep in the stalls or in the field.

"Are not the capacities of man and woman higher than these?" he asked. "And ought not our ambitions and expectations to be greater? Then let us be adventurers for another world. It is at least a fair and noble chance, and is there nothing in this that is worth our thoughts and our passions? If we should be disappointed, we are still no worse off than the rest of our fellow mortals. And if we succeed, we are eternally happy..."

By year's end the gospel road was no easy thoroughfare, and some Believers who had started out the year in the travelling of it had abandoned the attempt and decided on some other path. Carter Shackelford was gone back to the world, likewise John Buchanan, Sarah Stephens, Jonathan Cornwall, Austin Innes, crazy old James Richards – the loss of any soul to the world was a sorrow, but how the Believers did mourn the loss of the young ones! They had buried Anna Fisher, John McLean, Samuel Guy Eades, and Archie Rhea, and looking at the many aged faces amongst the families there was no question that there would be more buryings before the New Year became a newer year yet. The world was a temptation, the grave beckoned, and the patience of those who remained in the earthly Heaven was sorely tried. Thus as the Believers considered the birth of the Christ Child they listened to Elder Harvey with concentrated spirits and a stillness of purpose.

February

The troubles between the Postmaster General and the Louisville & Nashville were resolved to apparently mutual satisfaction and mail was once again arriving at the depot. The Shakers were therefore restored in not one but two means of communication, there having been a revival of portending dreams in the community of late.

Elder Harvey had a strange dream in which two steerlike beasts – the one sleek and reddy-brown (surely a symbol of the North) the other motley pied and of crooked horns (mayhap Confederate) – battled each other in ferocious, bloody fashion. Only when the reddish steer gored the pied animal to death did Harvey Eades awaken, not so much frightened as uplifted. A week later, Lucetta Buchanan told of a dream in which she walked through a magnificent garden tended by the departed Elder John McLean. In her dream she hoped he would offer her some of the abundant fruit that grew there, but while he bade her look and remember he made not the slightest move to gift her with a share. Neither did Sister Lucetta ask. All this she took as a sure sign that for the labors of his life Elder John had found his reward – and so would she if, as he had, she persevered in treading the godly path. In troubled times like these such reassurances of the rewards of righteousness were gratefully received.

Angeline Perryman was frightened. She had seen all forms of children's mischief, but such as this she had never witnessed in her life and the terror was clear on her face.

It was Sabbath night, nearing nine o'clock, and as she always did at this hour Angeline had one last look-in at the ten little girls of the North family before taking herself to her retiring room. Holding the latch in her fingers she sensed nothing untoward, but when she opened the door nothing inside the children's room was right. There was a second room full of North girls, and – hoping her eyes had deceived her at the first – she pushed open the door to the next chamber and found the same incredible scene inside.

There was the sound of mad hammering on the tables and bedsteads, which furniture seemed to tremble against the floorboards, and even as this noise filled the room the girls' pillows and bed linens, books, stockings, shoes, a broom, indeed anything not stuck fast to the spot it generally occupied was dashing wildly around the rooms. Some of the little ones lay fast asleep and miraculously unperturbed in their jittering beds, but others seemed wracked by spasms while still others stood stark and rigid in the whirlwind, gazing through sightless eyes at something Sister Angeline was powerless to see.

She fainted dead away.

At intervals for fully seven hours the mayhem gripped the rooms of the little girls, while across the passage the boys slept soundly, oblivious to the phenomena. When Sister Angeline returned to herself she fetched Eldress Susan Smith, who woke Elder Robert Johns, and the three stood stymied in the doorway for several minutes before words came.

"Just leave it be," said Elder Robert. "I've seen this before. When it's ready, it'll go of its own accord. Til that happens, we can't persuade it to move on. Just leave them." The manifestations of the '30s and '40s were as vivid in his mind on this cold evening as they had been in those winter months when they began more than twenty years ago. Once again the spirits had chosen to visit the children, and it was not for the grown folks to interfere.

Eldress Susan had her arm tight around the shoulder of the near-hysterical Sister Angeline. "What if they hurt themselves, brother?" she asked. It seemed to her that they could not simply stand by and watch the girls – the youngest barely seven years old – behave so, and with such a maelstrom swirling around them.

"There's no intention to harm them, sister," Elder Robert said. "Whatever's got them's just wanting to speak its piece, and when it's done that it'll go on. Best we just let it be."

Down the road at the Center Robert Johns' younger brother Urban sat up suddenly in his bed, propped on his hands, perspiring despite the sharp winter air that blew through the half-opened window. He looked around himself and saw the brethren with whom he shared this retiring room still quiet and soundly asleep, but someone was calling his name. He recognized the voice and struggled in his waking fog to place it.

"Urban, listen to me," the voice said from the ceiling by the door, "there's trouble coming. Listen to me, now. Are you awake?"

Urban looked up and saw the face of Samuel Shannon. Shannon was long in his grave, but his son, Sam Jr., was a contentious secessionist rascal who had caused his share of aggravation round and about since the war began. "Sam Shannon?" Urban asked aloud.

"There's robbers about, Urban," the voice told him. "Robbers everywhere. Mind what you've got, and be careful you don't lose it. They're coming to get it all, so mind they don't. Hear me?"

"When, Sam? Now?" Urban was looking, but the face was gone and the voice gone with it. "Sam?" He got out of bed and stood in his nightshirt under the spot where he had seen the apparition.

Behind him the brethren slept on. Urban dressed quietly in the darkness and went outside, but he could hear nothing, no sound of horses or bandits. There was a sudden inexplicable itch at him, a nudge to go back and check the children, and as he opened the door to each of their retiring rooms he found, as he expected, the little ones quiet in their low-slung beds. Then in the middle of one of the boys' rooms he noticed a broom lying sprawled across the floor, its handle pointing to Zecheriah Miles and its flat straw brush to Amos Anger. This seemed peculiar to Urban: Sister Elizabeth would have looked in on them before retiring to bed herself, and if the boys had left it there she would certainly have hung it where it belonged on the wall before closing the door. He crept into the room and put the broom back on its peg, lest one of the boys trip over it in the waking clamor of their morning. When he went back to his room the wayward broom was still pestering his mind, sweeping him clear of sleep.

He couldn't stop thinking about the broom.

"Sister," Johns said when he saw Elizabeth Barrie in the morning, "did you notice the broom on the floor of the boys' room last night?"

"Why, Brother Urban," teased Sister Elizabeth, "I thought thee had too much sense to go up to the children's rooms."

Urban smiled a smile that belied his restless night. "To tell the truth, I don't know what got into me. Just thought I'd look in, and there was a broom on the floor between Zecheriah and Amos."

She looked at him with a peculiar concern. "There's no broom in that room, Brother Urban," she said. "I've spent too long chasing after little boys to trust them with a long-handled broom when they're out of sight."

"There was one in there last night. Could have taken it from the girls' room, I suppose."

"Wouldn't be very like them, brother."

"I don't know. I suppose I could have dreamed it." His head was beginning to bother him and he hadn't put himself between breakfast and the day as yet.

Brother Urban and Sister Elizabeth looked at each other, and with one thought they made for the stairs: he up the east, she up the west, and they met again at the top floor.

"Just there's where I – " Urban was pointing through the open door to an empty peg. George Joiner blundered past in search of his boots, and Urban caught him by the suspenders. "George," he said, "where's the broom that was here this morning?"

George gave him that stare, that blend of equal parts curiosity and stupefaction, common to most boys his age. "Broom, Brother?" He looked sheepishly at Sister Elizabeth from the corner of his eye. "Sister doesn't trust us with a broom."

"So there wasn't one here this morning?"

"Nay, none's I saw." He scooped his boots from the floor and was gone.

Eldress Betsy was on her way up the stairs and was nearing the landing when she took sight of Urban and Elizabeth. "Eldress Susan was just by here," she said. "It was all of a madness up the North last night in the little girls' rooms. Two of the youngest ones were in a right state, Susan says, and there was furniture banging itself, brooms and such flying everywhere..." It was a second or two before she understood that it was this last that brought the peculiar look into her listeners' eyes.

As Monday got some age on it the brethren discovered that uninvited guests had prowled the lots the night before. There were signs of tampering at the horse stables, but the iron bars put up by the brethren had proved so inhospitable the would-be thieves had given up. Instead they made their way to the ox barn, and there fed their horses rather than go away with nothing. The brethren guessed there were five bandits and their horses, judging from what was left behind: ten cobs here, eight there, about right to see to five horses.

Before suppertime Aunt Jenny descended on the kitchen sisters, a wandering newsmonger harboring a near-uncontrollable urge to edify. Up in Auburn, she said, she'd come upon "two of the Hannon house niggers and talk from them was Sunday all y'alls' horses was set to git stole by the secesh trash." What became of this plan Hannon's slaves didn't know and Aunt Jenny hadn't heard elsewhere, but she reckoned what she knew was worth the Shakers' hearing.

After the upset at the North the ministry deemed it best that their eldresses, Nancy Moore and Betsy Smith, should spend the night up close to the little girls, lest the previous night's happenings recur.

This the two women did, but in the morning their reports were inconclusive.

"Saw the tables move a few times," Eldress Nancy said dismissively when Elder Harvey asked her how the night progressed, "but that was all."

May

Brother Urban Johns was sitting in the trustees' office with a copy of the Louisville *Journal* across his knees. He had read through the letter, written by a Tennessee minister named Franklin to the religious leaders of the nations North and South, several times. His eyes stung and he rubbed at his nose, as if that would solve the problem either side.

"You allright, Urban?" asked John Rankin, sitting across from him.

"Look at this," said Johns, holding out the paper and indicating with his finger the spot to which he had so carefully folded it.

Elder John adjusted his spectacles and read from the point Urban had indicated:

> Now that the rebellion has been raging for two years, I beg you to pause and see the awful whirlpool into which our people are drifting. Behold the shattered limbs and mangled bodies of those men whom you have urged onto the battlefield. Look over our desolate and mourning country. Our country is wasted, and more than half of all our boys who entered the old regiments have died in camps, or are in their bloody graves. Call to mind vividly the recent battles of Fredericksburg, Port Gibson, Baker's

Creek, Raymond, Jackson, Big Black Bridge, Haynes' Bluff and Vicksburg. Count if you can the thousands of our young men who have been slaughtered in these battles. Then ask yourself honestly, Have I caused any of this? Did I use my holy influence to lead my flock to these fields of blood and slaughter?

He looked over the top of the paper to catch Urban's eye. "You think this has something to do with you?" he asked. "Is that what you think?"

"Don't you?"

"I most certainly don't." Rankin set the paper on his desk. "And you shouldn't either."

"It's difficult for a man not to notice when his name's been called," Brother Urban said.

"Horsefeathers," said Rankin. "Anybody'd think you shoved him out the door."

"I didn't stop him."

"You tried."

"Not hard enough."

"What difference does that make?"

"Quite a bit, if he dies. Perhaps that much more if anyone dies because of him." He reached over to take the newspaper back, but Rankin put his hand down flat across it. "Haven't finished reading it yet," Urban said and, rising from his chair, he slid it out from under Rankin's fingers. Raising the lid of his desk to put the troublesome *Journal* inside he saw amid his other papers a copy of the public notice issued and posted at the South Union post office some weeks before.

Headquarters, U.S. Forces
Russellville, Ky.
February 24th, 1863

All the male citizens above the age of 18 years, loyal or disloyal
– Union or Southern Rights – within six miles of South Union,

are required to report themselves here, without fail, on Thursday March 5th, 1863, at 11 o'clock a.m. A prompt compliance with this order will save trouble to those concerned.

> *C. Maxwell, Colonel*
> *26th Regiment, Kentucky Volunteers*
> *Commanding Post*

The calendar told Urban Johns fully two months had come and gone since the day of Maxwell's ultimatum, and no Shaker brother of fighting age had yet presented himself. His head told him the brethren could not with impunity defy the order indefinitely. He put his copy of the *Journal* on top of the army's order and lowered the lid.

A light rain was coming down that afternoon, and the eldresses of the ministry, Nancy Moore and Betsy Smith, had been up at the East most of the day. There was a let-up about half-past-four and, hoping to get home to the Center before the next shower came, they set off down the road. The air was damp but not unpleasant, and they heard the cars coming down from Bowling Green to the depot. Of this they thought nothing; except when the guerrillas were loose in the world the sound of the cars had been part of life since the railway line went through. Then they heard Ambrose McKee shout, and they knew all was not as it should be.

The brethren were in the fields south of the Great Road with the work animals, furrowing, getting the soil ready to put the Irish potatoes in. They first heard and then saw a party of perhaps fifty Confederate guerrillas on horseback, coming across the rails that ran below the East and continuing up the road into the woods by the Shakertown fence.

Cyrus Blakey unhitched the traces that held his horse to the whippletree of the plough, and was on him and over to the section Brother Harry was working in a fast hurry.

"You see 'em, brother?" he asked, already flushed and out of breath. "Must be after that train. We've got to get the animals under cover. You get after the train and warn 'em, fast as you can. They got to stop before they get here. Now, go!"

He jerked his horse back and was off to sound the alarm, clinging precariously to the animal's mane. Within minutes every wagon, every cart in the village, would stand abandoned where it had been when the man who had charge of it got the order to shelter his horse. There was a ghostly look about the place, as if by magic every animal worth the trouble of stealing had been made to disappear. By now the brethren knew the price of sloth, and the economy of their actions was sure.

Harry Littlebourne unbuckled Old Sorrow's tugs, jumped up on the animal's broad, harnessed back, and wound his fingers in the coarse hair above the withers. Hunkered down low over the piebald's neck, the brim of his hat touching at the jumping grey mane, he lit off in a wide arc along the railroad tracks, out of rebel range. He quickly saw what he needed to see: most of the soldiers were still mounted and had hidden themselves and their ragged firing line in the brush just inside the woods north of the tracks. From that vantage point they watched protectively as three of their number hooked one of the stout Shaker fence timbers across the line, anchoring its low end under an iron rail, resting the other end on the parallel rail. One of the soldiers put his ear to the line, and when he stood he raised his hat high and ran like hell back toward the cover of the trees.

The big horse was surprisingly comfortable and swiftly sure with this unfamiliar gait, and Brother Harry raced along with his knees pressed tight against Old Sorrow's sides until he could see the approaching train and the smoke billowing black from its stack. Then he pulled up and stood on the animal's back, waving his hat in the air. There was no slowing of the locomotive's speed, and Brother Harry dropped back down, turned the horse toward the village, and made back west, letting the train catch him up. Up ahead he saw young Brother Logan Johns running toward the tracks, and over the sound of the jangling harness he could hear the rain beginning to fall again. With Old Sorrow at his best lumbering speed and the train bearing down, Harry hooked his boots in the harness, raised up as best he could and tried to shout the engineer down.

"Ambush!" he yelled. "Line's blocked! Rebels with guns!"

He saw the engineer narrow his eyes and tilt his window ear down – as if he were trying his best to hear something besides the roar of machinery and couldn't – and the train left the rider in the trail of its smoke.

Farther on up the track the engineer saw what the shouting rider's fuss was about: a formation of rifles was pointed at the train from the north-lying woods, and ahead of him he could see an obstruction on the line. He pulled hard on the brakes, pitching every passenger on board into the lap of his neighbor, but with so much steam the train was running too fast and too close to the timber to stop short. He let up.

What the three soldiers who placed the fence rail on the tracks had not noticed in their hurry was how the stout oak was held high by an uneven ridge of earth between the sleepers. They soon learned the lesson: as the locomotive screeched through in front of the rebel firing line the pointed edge of its cowcatcher caught the fence rail and tossed it skyward. But while they had not stopped the train, the guerrillas had at least achieved the purpose of slowing it, the better to take aim at it, and at its snail's pace they opened fire. Inside the cars – as no doubt the guerrillas had known full well – was a squad of Union soldiers, and leaning out the windows they returned fire on the rebel snipers.

The sound of the gunfire echoed in the village end to end. Amos was up at the Knob, picking strawberries, when he and the other boys heard the noise.

"What's that?" asked Zecheriah Miles.

Brother John Perryman had posed the same question to himself before Zecheriah thought to ask it. His nose turned south, as if sound found the nostrils before the ears, and he held up a hand to quiet his berriers. "It's gunfire," he said. "A lot of gunfire, coming from down by the East."

The boys erupted into nervous clamor, and he shushed them. "It's nothing to worry about," he told them. "The brethren are all over there getting ready to put the potatoes in. If there's anything to be done, they'll do it."

Amos dropped his berrying basket, spilling strawberries in the damp grass, and ran. John Perryman's voice echoed after him, but the boy wasn't listening. He knew where Brother Harry was.

Harry pulled Logan Johns up behind him as he passed him near the tracks, then made as quickly as he could for the cover of the barn. Lying flat on the ground they watched from the corner as the Confederates moved in from the woods, buzzing around the train from the caboose end to surround it, and when a bullet caught one young rider clean through the heart they saw his horse carry him on another forty strides before the life left him and he fell to the ground. Three others of the Confederates were wounded, perhaps four, but they kept their saddles, and when one horse was shot from under its rider the thrown soldier clambered up quickly onto the riderless horse of the fallen rebel and carried on. The Federals, from the safe cover of the cars, had too great an advantage for the wide-open rebels, and when the guerrillas had had enough they spurred their horses and fled.

One Confederate minie ball had put a clean hole through the locomotive's water tank, and a steady stream spurted from the puncture. The engineer leaned himself out the window for a better look at the damage, then sounded the whistle and pressed on toward the safe haven of the depot.

Even with the train grinding on the line, the rain now falling in earnest, a kind of quiet settled over the meadow. Brother Logan rolled over on his back – unworried by the damp grass and glad still to be in a condition to listen – and Brother Harry pushed himself up onto his feet, then put his hand down to Logan. Old Sorrow stood cropping at the grass, foaming from the run but unbothered by the shooting. The rebel horse was not dead, only wounded at the neck, and it had got to its feet again. Some yards away lay the dead soldier, his arms splayed out wide from his shoulders, one leg twisted crazily under the other. Harry had not seen the shot that severed the boy's hand almost completely at the wrist, but he saw the result clearly now. The young face was turned south, and his eyes were wide open. There was something there, a question of sorts, but Harry was not sure what it was.

He leaned around the edge of the barn and saw some of the brethren nearing the tracks, but no rebel riders. Stepping out carefully into the open ground he heard Logan's fearful voice behind him.

"Don't go out there, Harry," he said, trying without success to catch hold of his brother's departing arm. "They could be anywhere."

On his long legs, all of him damper by the step as he walked through the rain, Harry was already halfway to the spot where the soldier lay. There might be life in him, and waning life would not wait on those who lacked the spit to look for it. But stooping down to the boy's body he knew that whatever it was that had made him his mother's child was gone. He put down a large, dark hand and gently closed the brown eyes, and remembered doing the same for his father when he was not much younger than the fearless young man who today had looked his last while Harry watched. He stayed where he was, crouched in the rain, with his hand over his own face, offering words that might hold the dead boy in good stead wherever he was going.

"Not very old, is he? Anything to be done for him?" Urban Johns had come up behind Harry, with Eli McLean and John Rankin, and they stood with their hands in their pockets and rain dripping off the wide brims of their straw hats, looking on helplessly. "God help us all, to have a man die this way on our own land," he said, his fuse short. "God help this boy." His fingers twitched, and a trace of anger creased his face. "God forgive the men who sent him here."

"Anything on him, to say who he might be?" Brother Eli asked. His pockets were empty; only the letters "GCT" on his hat were left behind to say who he might have been in this life, and they meant nothing to the brethren. "Nice looking boy. Not twenty yet, I'd say."

"Looks a bit familiar to me," John Rankin ventured. "To you, Urban?"

They heard a high-pitched shout behind them, and Elder John turned to see Amos, soaked to the skin, running down the slope toward the tracks. Logan Johns was still standing by the barn and Rankin called to him to stop the boy, but it was already too late. Amos was with them quick as a rabbit, breaking through the wall of legs, and when he saw the buckled, bloody body in the grass he screamed and couldn't stop screaming.

"Take him, Harry," Brother Urban said. "He shouldn't be here."

Brother Harry rose up off his knees and took Amos with him as he went, hoisting the boy onto his hip. Amos was hysterical, still screaming, and Harry hurried him out of sight of the dead soldier, whispering to him in hopes of calming him. Old Sorrow fell into step behind them, but Harry took no notice. When they reached the road he set Amos back on his feet, pinned the small, shaking shoulders with his strong hands to steady the rest of him and tried to talk through the sound of the child's terrified, wracking tears.

"What did John say?" Harry asked him, loudly, almost shouting.

The boy could not look at him.

"Eldress Nancy has told thee this, so now tell me: what did John say?" Harry shook him, hard, and suddenly he could see the boy's face.

"John said Jesus said."

"John said Jesus said what?"

"About the wheat."

"The wheat what?" There was no reasoning with Amos through the image that had frightened him so. " 'Except a corn of wheat fall into the ground and die, it abideth alone; but if it die, it bringeth forth much fruit.' That's right, isn't it? And then what? 'He that loveth his life shall lose it; and he that hateth his life in this world shall keep it unto life eternal.' That's what John said Jesus said." The rain was slowing up, and the tears now stood alone on Amos' face. "Thee'll never help that boy this way, Amos. He already knows more than we'll know til we follow him where he's going." Amos was quieter; he was looking for every breath, but at last he was listening. "Pray for him, then," Harry told him, "but don't grieve him this way."

The Federals came soon after, swinging their hats in the air and full of victorious shouts of sending three Confederates to their Maker. Brother Urban told their captain, Johnson, of the dead boy down by the tracks, and gave him the story to the extent that he had got it from Logan Johns. Johnson said he knew that band of guerrillas well: he and his men had been chasing them for a day or two, had in fact run into them at Hogs Hill that very day and dispatched three of their number.

Urban Johns and John Rankin took to horse and led the captain and his men down to the tracks, where a sodden Ambrose McKee stood sentry over the blanket-covered body.

"We'd be much obliged if you'd take charge of him. We don't know who he is," Brother Urban said. "We'll make up a coffin for him, but after that – "

"Make him a coffin?" The captain's snort was full of derision and he punctuated it with a spit of chaw that struck perilously close to Brother Ambrose's boot. "Damn him to Hell, and that's more'n he's worth. String him up and let the crows eat him, if there's rope to spare, but don't waste good wood on a coffin for no rebel bastard."

Urban accepted this instruction without comment, having no intention of taking it up in any fashion, and was glad when the captain took his men back down toward Russellville, still in pursuit of the depleted guerrilla band.

Brother Ambrose looked up at him. "What now?"

"I'll ask John Merrifield to hammer a coffin together for him right quick," Brother Urban said. "Shouldn't take too long, if you wouldn't mind staying out here with him just a little while longer. Eldress Fanny'll have someone run you out some supper 'fore you perish, and something to keep the weather off."

Brother Ambrose had no objection to this arrangement, and Johns and Rankin turned their horses back toward the trustees' office.

"We can take him up to Bowling Green," said Elder John, knowing they would be able to find at the post there an agreeable face, someone willing to take charge of the coffin and its contents – somebody's boy now apparently an orphan in death.

"We needn't go to the war. We're already in it," Urban muttered under his breath.

"How's that?" asked Elder John.

"Nothing," said Urban. "Just remembering something I was fool enough to take no notice of first time I heard it."

General Order Number 18 was nailed to the door of the post office the following day, an hour or so after a party of Federals came to take the coffined body – now believed to be what remained of George Crittenden Townsend, cousin of Livonia Roberts of the East family – to Russellville as a warning to whatever secesh might still be open to sensible persuasion.

Headquarters, U.S. Forces
Russellville, Ky.
May 14th, 1863

All male citizens of Logan County who have not taken the Oath are required to report at the Provost Marshal's Office in the town of Russellville, on or before the first day of June next and take the Oath of Allegiance to the United States government. Anyone failing to comply with this order will be at once arrested and sent south of the Federal lines, not to return again during the rebellion under penalty of death.

Brig. General J. Shackelford

Within a few days an enrollment officer was on Shakertown's doorstep, looking to take the names of all the brethren who might be of fighting age. This list Elder Harvey firmly refused to provide, and he offered what he thought was good cause: back East, the Mount Lebanon ministry had in a letter already advised the brethren and sisters of Union Village "to give freely to the Sanitary Committee for the benefit of the soldiers," but added sternly that they were "not to take hold of a gun or do anything as a soldier, not pay a fine, hire a substitute, or pay instead, that the government may hire one in the room of a Shaker." A list of service-aged Shaker men would be the first step on the road to wicked disobedience of this edict, and Elder Harvey would not see it taken.

The enrollment officer was unpersuaded of the brethren's right to disregard the army's summons, and Harvey Eades was rapidly coming to an understanding that Shackelford's order would be more difficult to ignore than had been Maxwell's. Eades and the enrollment officer would neither of them budge and, on the morning of the twenty-ninth, in the interests of resolving the impasse before it came to unpleasantness, Eades asked for a horse and carriage. He set off toward Bowling Green with Brother Solomon Rankin (by his own request released from his duties as an elder after many years' good service), declaring he would see James Shackelford before he got back to Shakertown or know the reason why. He was back by evening, having not seen Shackelford, but as good as his word he knew the reason for this: the general was not at the post to be seen. Among his aides there, however, had been a lieutenant who heard the Shakers' argument out and, having done so, suggested they might best go home and await the general's decision on this matter – which would be put to him directly he returned. It was not easy to say no to Elder Harvey, and the general did not try. Within a day or so came a letter from Shackelford, saying the brethren at South Union would not be asked to take the oath of allegiance, nor would they be sent south for declining to do so. Harvey Eades suspected the matter would not end there, but at least for the moment it was possible to hope the army would leave them be.

August

T

he rain was coming down in torrents and had been so doing for days, with attendant thunder and cracks of bright lightning that struck at the trees and killed a steer over by the East. The water was fully three feet over the dam, and the mills were all but drowned. The brethren despaired of saving in full the nearly fifteen hundred bushels of wheat threshed – stacked in shocks it took the rainfall badly – and contented themselves with rescuing what they thought possible to save. Down at Canaan there was need of someone to oversee harvesting of the Shakers' orchard of fine Binford peach trees, and Brother Jefferson Shannon was released from his chores in the trustees' office for the time it would take to dispose of that responsibility. There were dwellings for those who worked the crops at Canaan, and the change was thus of domicile as well as duty, albeit temporary. Even so, for days after Brother Jefferson moved his few belongings from the Center to Canaan the retiring room they shared seemed very large and hollow to William Ware and Harry Littlebourne.

Most of the war was these days well into Tennessee and beyond, but outside the Center windows soldiers from North

and South nonetheless passed in numbers great and small, some
of them parolees, all of them in need of something to eat (Thus
it seemed at least to the sisters, who after two long years at a
crossroads of the war would have been weary of the endless cooking
chores were they not so sorely aware of the greater suffering they
had so far been spared). It was, in fact, a paroled Confederate
infantryman who first advised his Shaker hosts that John Hunt
Morgan and all but thirty or forty of his raiders had managed to
get themselves captured near some godforsaken town in Ohio and
were now inmates of the state penitentiary there.

And with a letter that arrived from Mount Lebanon on the
fifteenth day came news to shiver the soul: the committee sent
down from New York to Washington City to secure for all Shaker
brethren exemption from the army had failed in its mission. Worse,
a dozen young Shaker men had already been taken from the
northern societies through the intransigence of the draft.

The committee of two elders, Benjamin Gates and Frederick
Evans, made their journey south from Mount Lebanon in hopes of
putting the tall authority of the White House behind the pacifist
instructions given to the Shaker societies. They waited upon the
President and were at length granted an interview with Abraham
Lincoln and his Secretary of War, Edward M. Stanton, which
exchange they considered most cordial and helpful, even enjoyable.
The arguments they put to Lincoln – of individual conscience and
of the religious nature of the Constitution, among others – were,
they felt and took great pains to explain, were borne up by a simple
and undeniable fact of bookkeeping: Shaker veterans who had in
the interests of their beliefs declined to draw their military pensions
or take up the bounty lands due them had over the years granted the
U.S. government a windfall that, with interest, totalled the thick
end of half a million dollars. If three hundred dollars would buy a
man his commutation from a draft lottery or even the services of a
substitute to take his place altogether, then, the Union had been

well paid by the United Society of Believers in Christ's Second Appearing for the exemption of its few score of draftable brethren.

However jolly his conversation, Abraham Lincoln was either not convinced by the elders' arguments against the drafting of their brethren or was persuaded to unconvince himself – perhaps by Stanton, who was prone to such things. Of this Gates and Evans would never be sure, but the technicalities mattered little when the result was the same: Shaker brethren were expected to present themselves for military service if summoned, to do that which violated the dearest of their beliefs.

At meeting on the warm Sabbath that followed, Elder Harvey Eades read the whole of the Mount Lebanon ministry's letter aloud to the brethren and sisters. As the morning clouds cleared away he told them that he and Elder John Rankin had put pen to paper themselves in their own communication to the President. Perhaps friend Lincoln had not completely understood the heart of the matter.

The letter ran to several pages in Elder Harvey's large, no-nonsense hand, and friend Lincoln's answer was a long time coming.

The Binford peaches were sent up from Canaan by Brother Jefferson Shannon in abundance, and the sisters had a job to do getting all the putting-up and preserve-making done while at the same time looking after the increasing number of visitors who came down from town. These day-travellers were the greatest tax on the efforts of the Believers as August passed its halfway mark: for a spell they saw mostly straggling soldiers and occasional parolees rather than the whole companies and divisions that had for so long vexed them. The sometimes sizeable parties of townfolk would be out enjoying the clear weather now that the rain had let up and the roads were tolerably safe to travel. Before long, while the weather was good, the ministry opened the Sabbath laboring meetings to them, so that they could see for themselves the fabled proceedings. Now and again these gawkers, for such they certainly were, had the foresight to bring their boxed dinners along with them, and on those occasions the Shakers rejoiced in their generally unexpected good fortune. But more often it happened that the sisters were expected to abandon whatever their occupation of the moment to fetch up a meal for the callers, and – although they did this with grace and good heart – they far preferred those rare birds who did not expect to be done for.

On that last Sabbath Eve of August Brother Harry took a wagon down to the farm to fetch up more fruit, and Amos went with him. The harvest was well finished, the last of the oats had been hauled up, and the boys had been at work coring and cutting fruit for the preserve-making and canning for days. Amos was relentless in his pursuit: he whined and nagged at him until Harry could no longer say the boy nay.

But by late afternoon the day's hauling was pronounced a sufficiency, time to wash for supper was very nearly upon them, and Brother Harry and Amos were lolling a spell under the trees by the Center's east well. Amos was without his boots and stockings and was poking in the cool grass with his bare toes. Above his head Eldress Nancy was talking to Sister Jane Wing about a strayed house slave.

His master's wife, a lady called Hawkins, had come up from her home south of Russellville on the cars a day or two before on the scout for him. Her concern was being put about Shakertown not only by Eldress Nancy but also by Aunt Jenny to everyone else in Logan County who would sit still for gossip, which was pretty much anybody. Their diligence aside, no one either woman had spoken to had seen the Hawkins' runaway, dead or alive. This was not the first time Shakertown was hearing of a Negro vanished without a trace. Many a black man was beginning to believe his freedom might not after all be the outcome of the conflict at hand and was therefore taking matters up on his own behalf. There was not much chance of Mrs. Hawkins finding her man, but Eldress Nancy was slow to be so blunt.

Amos had made himself a shaving brush out of pulled grass and was rubbing it against his cheek, looking through the fence pickets at the dust rising up off the road. There were a few horsemen coming to the crossroads – none of the brethren, no man or horse he knew – and behind them a few straggling blue-coated soldiers. He lathered at his nose with the tuft of grass and shifted to his knees. The soldiers were clearer now through the swirl of road steam. Amos pointed a tentative finger and turned back over his shoulder. "Look!" he said in a strangled tone, unable to find but the smallest part of his voice.

Brother Harry leaned lazily to one side but could not see past him, and when Eldress Nancy turned away from Sister Jane it was just long enough to notice one of the Federals coming away from his companions, heading for the door of the ministry shop.

"Bless you, child," she said, looking back from the road now and down at the wide-eyed boy, "he's not the first soldier to try the wrong door before he finds the right one. Elder Harvey will send him on."

Amos bent quickly and tugged at Harry's arm. "Nay, nay," he said, his voice rising. "Look!" He was still pointing with his other hand. "It's Brother Austin..."

Harry Littlebourne might have been half-dozing in the summer sunlight, but he now got to his feet and followed the trace of the boy's finger to the road. The small man coming hatless over the crossroads was unmistakeable; it was as if he were bringing the autumn maples with him. For the rest of his life Amos would remember the colors of Brother Austin's hair that afternoon: pearwood and cinnamon, honey and cornbread, cherry and apple and matchlight. He heard October stories in his head and tasted strawberries, and he planted his feet to run.

"Nay," Harry said sharply, catching him by the collar. "Stay here with me. His business here is between himself and God and Elder Harvey. Until they make it ours, best we leave it to them. We have other things to do."

Amos was wriggling against the hold Brother Harry had shifted to his shoulder, and he wrenched away and ran to the fence, the white soles of his feet showing as he ran like the white tails of deer in flight. Harry could not catch him and did not try.

Just as the boy reached the fenceline Austin Innes was putting one boot to the stoop of the ministry shop. He turned from the door in time to catch quick sight of little Amos Anger, looking much as his schoolmaster had left him, stepped up on the low rail of the fence – his straw hat raised high over his head by way of greeting.

There was no harm in Amos standing where he was so long as he went no farther, Brother Harry thought, but when the door opened and Austin Innes emerged with Elder Harvey behind him Harry Littlebourne wasn't watching. The boy was down off the fence rail and through the gate quick as cat's paws, forgetting even to shut it behind him. With the rare energy of heart fueled by pure childish joy Amos jumped up into the arms of the startled little man, his own embrace as tight as he could make it – as if by holding on with all his might he could keep his universe from splintering again, now it had so unexpectedly come back together.

He rubbed his cheek against Austin's face and felt the unaccustomed bristle of untended whiskers – palest red they were and almost invisible – against his own soft skin. As he did so Amos felt a dampness as Austin's eyelashes brushed him, then a salty sting where the whiskers had scratched him. He rested his ear on the nearest shoulder, saw the frayed blue collar, and twitched with a finger at the raggedly cropped red hair that brushed around it.

The boy played his fingers along the rough cloth. " The birdmen took some of your hair." He had not noticed the three birds flying on the little man's arm, with a diamond resting on the nest of their wings.

"The birdmen took some of my hair," Austin repeated, unsure of Amos' meaning but glad of his sound, and rubbed the boy's back with one hand as if to be sure this was none of it a dream.

"What did they do with it?"

Austin tilted his head back, looking at the sky. Quietly, so quietly only Amos could hear, he replied: "We sent it to friend Lincoln, and he fed it to the eagles."

Smiling, Amos touched a finger to the temple nearest him, where the hair that had been red now grew white. "It's white here," he said.

"Is it?" Austin asked, genuinely surprised. Where he had been there were no mirrors. "White as an angel's wings?"

On this, Amos had no opinion. "It makes you look like a flag," he said instead.

"Whyever a flag?"

The boy touched a finger to the hair lapping at Austin's collar, to that by his ear, and to the crow's-footed corner of one of his eyes. "Red, white and blue," Amos said, and felt the powerful arms close tight around him.

Austin Innes looked to the man still standing on the steps of the ministry shop. "Harvey," he said, rocking slightly, "don't let them take my boys."

"I'm doing what I can, Austin," Harvey Eades told him.

Elder Harvey was taken up discussing the proprieties with Eldress Nancy, who had followed Amos across the Great Road, but now he said the boy's name and the sound alone was rebuke sufficient to bring his bare feet back to the dusty, hard ground by the steps.

Amos stood shamefaced, absently picking at the worn yellow stripe that ran down the length of Austin Innes' trouser leg and disappeared into the top of his tall, heavy cavalry boot. His fingers found in their travels a small, round hole by the mule-eared pocket, around which the weave was unravelling. Austin's hand came down quickly and closed around the boy's to move it away as Elder Harvey spoke.

"Have you business here?" Eades asked sternly.

"Nay," said the boy, his eyes down.

"Then you have no business here," he said. "Go along now. Get yourself washed up for supper."

Just inside the fence opposite Amos saw Brother Harry waiting, holding out his hand. He looked up at Austin Innes.

"Stay," he said, with damp fear in his eyes.

"Scat yourself," Elder Harvey told him.

Reluctantly, Amos let go of the little man's hand and walked obediently, if slowly, across the road to Brother Harry. Looking always over his shoulder as he went, and even as he stooped to rescue his hat from the dust where it had fallen, he kept Austin Innes in sight as long as he could.

September

Eight of the aged brethren and sisters of Union Village were expected at Shakertown for a visit, and it was Brother Urban Johns who went up to meet them on the Louisville platform, to see to their safe arrival at South Union.

An industrious band of rebel guerrillas was at work disrupting the railroad line above Bowling Green that day, and their main mischief consisted of setting fire to the bridge over Nolin Creek in two places. Although there were fully thirty of them to get the job done they commandeered the less-than-enthusiastic assistance of some local Irishmen, but even so the job was ultimately left undone; these rebels clearly feared the arrival of Federal troops more keenly than they did the wrath of a disappointed commander. The Irishmen departed before their hurried hosts, spurred by their lack of interest in the intended arson; a Negro passed with his horse and wagon and they jumped him, having to their way of thinking a better use for his conveyance.

What small headway the rebels managed toward the destruction of the bridge was telegraphed to the oncoming train, and well in advance of Nolin Creek Urban Johns looked up to see one of several Federal officers on his way to Louisville squeezing along the crowded aisle of the car he was riding. By straining to hear Urban could just make out the lieutenant's explanation of the situation up ahead. Now the officer was looking to see the civilian men aboard the car in his care were armed – just in case.

"Anybody hasn't got his gun on him, don't worry," said the lieutenant to the crowd of faces now turned to him. "There's seventy of us from the army on the train and we got plenty enough rifles aboard for every man hasn't got a weapon of his own. But if there's reb raiders at Nolin Creek what we'll need more'n rifles is men to fire 'em, so you'll have to stand to if it comes to that." This car was as crowded as the rest; there were people standing wherever there was room to put a pair of feet down and their excitement was warm to the touch. "Can't be any man aboard wouldn't help protect these women and children we got here."

A minute or so later a sergeant appeared behind the officer with an armload of Maynard carbines. Seeing the crush of passengers between the benches he boosted the rifles nimbly to shoulder height while he worked his way along the rapidly disappearing path that had been cleared for the lieutenant by the jostling civilians.

The lieutenant was checking the readiness of every man as he came along the car. Now and again he turned to the sergeant and with a word a rifle was dispensed. They came closer, and Urban's throat tightened. Two weeks earlier the Federal army's enrollment officer had come to the trustees' office from Bowling Green to obtain the long-denied list of the Shaker brethren who were eligible for the draft. While Urban Johns' was not among the names sought, Elder Harvey Eades had been compelled to give up the particulars of those who did make up that number. The Believers might not vote, but they paid their taxes and they obeyed the law, and however earnestly Elder Harvey believed the exemption would come in time he did not yet have it in his hand. The enrollment officer thus left South Union that day with what he had looked for months to get. And now here was Urban Johns sitting three benches away from a pleasant-looking sergeant who showed every sign of handing him a rifle in full expectation that he would use it.

Across from him a dusty-looking gentleman showed a long-nosed pistol to the inquiring officer, and as he listened to the words exchanged between the two men concerning the nature of the danger Brother Urban sat up in his seat, the better to be ready when his time came. The Lord would not send him more trouble than he could bear, this Urban Johns firmly believed, and he would not therefore shrink from whatever it was that was coming.

Suddenly the lieutenant's face found him with its fine grey eyes, and Urban was filled with the peculiar realization that he had nothing to fear.

"Good, fine day, isn't it?" the officer said pleasantly.

"It is indeed, lieutenant," Urban replied.

"Thank you for your help, sir," he said, and moved on down the aisle.

"What about him?" asked the sergeant roughly. "He got a pistol or what?"

"He doesn't need one," the lieutenant said sharply, without looking around. "Hand me one of those things, now, over here."

Brother Urban's shoulders fell. The man sitting across from him played his fingers along the barrel of the pistol and eyed Johns with curiosity that might have strayed into disgust. Urban's relief was in his face and his seatmate wasn't blind.

The train slowed as it neared Nolin Creek, but there was no sign of guerrillas. Still the progress along the tracks was cautious, and the Federals aboard stayed close by the windows lest firing from the treeline sound. South of the bridge the engineer brought the locomotive to a halt and a military party spilled out to check the area and the condition of the span.

Some of the spar timbers were in fact burned away and would need replacing, and Urban Johns among others of the civilian men aboard climbed down from the cars to help replace them while the soldiers kept lookout over the area. When the engineer inspected the fruits of the makeshift work crew's labors he pronounced the bridge trainworthy, and the perspiring men made back for the cars. As they went, Brother Urban passed the lieutenant who had organized the defense of the car he was riding.

He caught Urban's eye and smiled.

"Good, fine day, isn't it?" the officer said pleasantly.

"It is indeed, lieutenant," Urban replied.

"Thank you for your help, sir," he said, and a few minutes later the train continued on its way to Louisville.

October

The boys were busy at raking mown grass near the smokehouse when Amos saw Brother Austin walking down from the East. There was something under his arm as he approached the Center's east door, and as soon as seemed proper Amos laid down his rake and followed quietly after.

Through the retiring room door he saw Brother's back, and in some ways it was as if he had never been away. His dark blue cavalry blouse and trousers were gone, and the clean white linen of his shirt made him appear broader and stronger than Amos remembered. Innes shifted back and forth from his bed to the cupboard, gradually putting straight his things, and Amos began to see that something had changed: he was less graceful, not clumsy but uncomfortable on his feet. One leg seemed less willing than the other.

With so few men about the house there had been no question that when his time at the East was deemed sufficient he would come back to his old retiring room at the Center, and indeed to the bed in which no other brother had slept in his absence. Sister Elizabeth had been unable to bring herself to give his clothes away, and she had thus produced from the box rooms in the Center's attic a bundle of his clothes, the summer proceeds of which were now strewn across the unmussed surface of his bed. On a peg nearby hung his hat, with its peculiar and familiar leather band. Even that token of the life he thought to abandon had been left behind, and he could not have imagined it would be kept safe for his return. Amos saw it, recalled that first day when it had not been where it belonged, and listened to the uneven sound of Austin's cavalry boots as he shuffled back and forth on the sleek floorboards.

Unable to linger a second longer in the doorway Amos went in quietly, and simply stood next to Austin Innes. The little schoolmaster regarded the boy but said nothing, merely moved around him, content that he should be there but with nothing yet to say.

Amos poked at the bedroll Austin had used to carry his possessions from wherever he had been all this time, and down from the East today. He had seen them on the shoulders of so many soldiers, but had never considered that someone he knew might have need of one.

"Did you use this?" he asked, and the sound of his voice made Austin jump.

"Sometimes," Austin told him as he folded one of his Sabbath shirts.

"Did you like it?"

"Some nights were better than others."

Browsing gently on, the boy found Innes' uniform and pulled at it slightly.

"What happens to this now?"

"We'll give it to one of the parolees," Austin said. "I need to mend it a bit, but there's use in it yet."

Amos relocated the tattered hole his fingers in their anxious travels had found those several weeks ago.

"Did they hurt you?" he asked.

"No more than I hurt myself," Austin said.

Folded inside the trousers, as if to make as little of an unpleasant matter as possible, was the heavy blouse, and Amos rubbed its yellow stripes between his thumb and forefinger.

"Do we have to give your birds away?"

Austin looked down at him, suddenly mindful of what the boy had meant that day, and realized just how far inside the fences of Shakertown the war had reached.

"Those aren't birds, son, and never have been," he said. "They're nothing that sings or flies or does good for anybody."

"What are they?"

Austin looked him in the eye, slow to answer, but when he spoke again there was a passion in his voice. "They're the false measure of a man," he said. "Nothing more."

"I don't understand," Amos told him.

"I didn't mean you to," Austin replied, and went on about his business.

Amongst a jumble of shaving things the boy suddenly saw the glint of glass, and he reached for it. He found a shiny little leatherbound square, and as he turned it in his hand he suddenly saw a woman's face returning his own curiosity. Freezing where he stood he yelped and the glass slipped from his fingers to the hardwood floor. Instinctively Austin caught the boy as he fell back, and both heard the gentle crack of glass breaking.

"What's the matter?" Innes asked him when the boy regained his wits.

Amos pointed a shaking finger at the glass Austin now held cradled in his hand.

"There's somebody in there," he said, fearing the worst.

Austin smiled the smile his boys knew so well, the smile that came over him when they had no idea what he was thinking. "Look here," he said, and bent down with the glass in his hand. "It's not a ghost, it's a *photograph*."

Amos examined the shimmering image, of a woman not much unlike Sister Elizabeth now he saw her from a position of safety –

but wearing world's clothes and with a look on her face that said much about mischief.

"A man with a magic box can make sunlight paint on glass like that, but it's surer than any artist could ever hope to paint," he said.

"It's broken," Amos said, his voice a mixture of apology and wonder, and Austin traced with his finger the fresh crack that ran below the woman's throat like a necklace.

"Not your fault," said Austin, and he slid the little photograph beneath his shirts and closed the cupboard door.

"Will she come and see you?" Amos asked.

"I don't think so," Austin replied, rolling his uniform inside the bedroll and tying it.

"Will you go and see her?"

The look came over him again, only this time without the smile, and he shook his head. "I don't think so," he said.

December

S ouls take flight in all kinds of ways, and evidences of this they had many at Shakertown in the weeks that preceded Christmas.

On the second Thursday Brother Patterson Johns came down with a bilious fever and took leave of the earthly life three days later, not yet sixty years in age. Seventeen days on from his passing Sister Julia Powell would follow him from the East family to the graveyard, three years younger, although – correct as it was within a year or two – her exact age had always been a matter of some conjecture. There were deaths too amongst those they loved more out of Christian obligation than a natural disposition to do so, one of these being George Milligan, who August before last had been inspired by the exploits of John Hunt Morgan to raise up his own company of rebel raiders. The Federals had finally caught up to Milligan with the bullets that took his life – just twenty-four hours, it was said, before the raid he meant to lead against Shakertown.

Late in November sixteen cars full of soldiers had been shipped south to Tennessee through Russellville to reinforce General Ambrose Burnside's efforts there. And the feast of Thanksgiving brought with it to South Union word of a Federal victory at

Chattanooga by the troops of Major General Ulysses S. Grant over the beleaguered rebel General Braxton Bragg. The Confederate cause might be said to be dying of losses such as that suffered by its men at Chattanooga, but its soul could yet be said to remain very much alive. On the same Thanksgiving Day that soul, too, in a manner of speaking, took flight: the nation counted whatever blessings it could credit, and as it did so John Hunt Morgan made good an escape from the Ohio State Penitentiary at Columbus.

Brother Austin did not often let the boys out early, but the first few school-bound afternoons of winter always seemed uncommonly long, while the cold outside beckoned mightily to restless young men warmed to doziness by the heat of the stove. And now and again there just came a day when it seemed to him that a few hours in broad daylight with nothing to do but what they chose was as instructive as any lesson he could devise for his restless scholars. With this in mind he opened the door and shooed the boys out as he let the cold air in.

Austin Innes checked the sky for signs of lowering weather. It must be threatening snow: his leg was bothering him. He liked to think the sawbones who worked on him after the fighting at Buffington Island got all of what he went in after, but sometimes he thought maybe not. The Federals had certainly got what they wanted, if at considerable cost, but it seemed to Brother Austin that there had not been much point in the taking of John Hunt Morgan on that occasion if Ohio couldn't keep him. The air smelled of snow, and he shut the door.

Outside the boys had scattered to play baseball back behind the wash house. Brother Austin had come upon the game in his year away from them, and – once the elders gave him leave to move back to the Center from the East – he taught it to the boys, betraying to them as he demonstrated the art of base-running the uncomfortable truth that he no longer ran with ease. The new endeavor suited them, and although he was still too small to hit the ball with strength, it suited Amos. But on this particular afternoon Amos was tempted less by the bat than by the presence of a world's boy a bit older than himself, playing alone next to the heavy-laden wagon braked up in front of the trustees' office. The boy had a small wooden ball connected by a string to the little wooden cup he held in his hand, and he would jerk the ball into the air and sometimes catch it in the cup as it fell. Amos wandered along the fence until he was opposite the trustees' office, and stood dreamily watching the ball fly and fall. In his mind's eye that agile hand was his own, and he willed it to do his bidding, rejoicing when it did. After a few minutes at this, Amos realized the boy was watching him far more carefully than he was the tethered ball, and he flicked his fingers in greeting.

"Hey," he called across the fence.

"Hello back," the young stranger replied. He peered over the rumps of the horses hitched to the wagon, saw the office door still tight shut, and stole across the road to the fence. "Can't you come out?"

Amos shook his head. "Not supposed to. You can come in if you want."

"Naw," the boy said. "Ma'll be out in a tick, wantin' to get on." He and his mother had come down from Michigan, he told Amos, looking for his father. There had been some thought that he was in one of the military hospitals at Bowling Green, but they had found no sign of him there. Now his mother thought to try at Nashville, if they could get through. When they found him they would take him back to Michigan. The boy's sister had recently taken sick and died, and his mother had had enough of death and mourning and of her man being in the war. The boy didn't mind the wander: this arrangement kept him out of school, of which he was not much fond.

"Brother Austin let us out early," Amos said. Far behind him sounded the crack of the bat.

"Mr. Parsons don't never let us out," offered the boy, gripping a post with his hands and bouncing himself against the fence.

"I'm gonna be a soldier, so I got no use for lessons. You?"

"I like 'em fine," Amos said. "Geography's nice."

The little Michigan wayfarer knew a thing or two of geography and the wonders of the world. Back in the summer of '61, he said, before his father went away, they had taken themselves into Ann Arbor to see J.J. Nathan's American Circus, just the two of them, and there he had seen Mr. Craven and his performing elephants. Despite the damp and cold Amos stood motionless on the opposite side of the fence, mesmerized by visions of dancing creatures whose size put the very wash house to shame, until the boy's mother emerged from the trustees' office. At first alarmed to find her child gone from the place she had bid him stay, she sighted him across the road and her shrill call made Amos wince.

"Got to go," said the boy, and so he ran, tossing the tethered ball from the cup as he went, back to his mother and the waiting wagon.

Amos stayed where he was, scratching at an itchy ear with the fence post nearest. The Michigan boy had said things that left him with a queasy feel about the gut, and he was troubled by the thoughts that chased around his head like summer flies. The rest of his schoolmates were still playing baseball, but he had no heart to join them. A runny snow had begun to fall, and as he wandered toward the stable he pulled his winter hat down snug to his ears and put his hands in his pockets.

Brother Harry was not long coming back to the barn with Old Sorrow, both of them wet and tired, and they found Amos lying in the haymow, looking more wretched by the minute.

"Did thee vex Brother in school today?" Harry asked as he began drying the plough horse down.

"Nay," Amos replied, and climbed up on the gate of Old Sorrow's stall. "But supposing I did something wrong, what would you say?"

"It would depend what it was," Harry said, drawing the coarse brush along the horse's flank, working the stiff bristles deep. Old Sorrow was delighted; his muscles rippled. "Am I supposing thee did some harm?"

"Not exactly," Amos said, kicking his toes against the slats. "Say I was talking to a world's boy, and say I thought maybe I wished I was him instead of me. Would that be wrong?"

Harry's hands were still in motion, moving back and forth, one over the other, and Amos did not have his eye. "Is that for me to say, or thee?"

"That's why I'm asking you."

Stopped mid-stroke, Harry propped his arms on the piebald's back and gave the matter the first signs of his full attention. Amos was looking at him, as always with it in mind that Brother Harry could solve the riddles of the universe if approached to do so. Out the windows of the stable the ground was going greyish-white under the mushy snow, and it was easier to look there than into the expectant green eyes of the child. "What is it thee needs, little brother, that is not somewhere here in this place?" he asked.

"I don't know," Amos told him. "I don't know what all there is."

"Then thee'd better go and have a talk to Elder Harvey," Harry Littlebourne said, and carried on with the brush.

"Why?" Amos asked, less frightened than unsettled by this development, the finality with which the subject had been closed. "Is just not knowing wrong?"

"It isn't a matter of right and wrong," Harry said, and the brim of his hat bounced against Old Sorrow's broad back as the stroke line of his brush descended along the nether reaches of the animal's side. "If there's a trouble to thy heart in this regard it's a matter best tended by the ministry's counsel, not mine."

Amos considered this in silence. Never once before had Harry referred his troubles to a third party, and the boy sensed instantly that the nature of their relationship had changed – barely perceptibly, but it had changed.

It was as if Brother Harry could hear his mind churn. "Thee has thy ninth year with comfort," he said. "An older boy has an

older boy's thoughts. Some of those it's best thee give to Elder
Harvey."

"Now?"

"He'll be there."

There was an odd, sweet terror to such moments, he knew.
Strangely – for it might as easily be the opposite – the occasional
confessions of the children lightened Elder Harvey's days, so
thoroughly did they remind him of life as it is lived, of the trueness
of human nature and the native purity of the soul's endeavors.
As little Amos fidgeted in the chair, turning his hat in his hands,
unsure how to proceed in this which he had never done before,
Harvey Eades recalled the gravity with which a boy had once
confessed his struggles against the desire to ambush then-Sister
Nancy Moore from behind with a slingshot. Mere possession of the
slingshot was transgression sufficient; intent to use it in the pursuit
of mischief was surely worse. While the young man in question
ultimately won the war of his conscience he nonetheless found
the internal skirmish a matter for confessing, no less so than if the
potentially deadly peach pit had found its generous mark. Elder
Harvey's smile was one of remembrance: he had more than once
done similar battle and lost, without confessing thought or deed.

Eades was not ignoring the boy, but Amos was struggling to find
his own feet in this affair of the heart and – to give him ground to
do so in a kind of privacy – Elder Harvey went back to his reading
and waited for the boy's spirit to move him.

Amos looked beyond the silent little man's head to the
glass-doored cupboard of his desk, and saw behind the light
reflected there the leather spines of books. Some had names
stamped with gold letters (he could tell they were not Bibles); on
others the titles were more difficult to see. Not that by any of these
indications could he imagine what stories they told.

"I know a boy who's seen an elephant!" he blurted out suddenly,
surprising even himself with the sound.

Elder Harvey's white eyebrows went up, but he kept his eyes to the page. "I'm listening, Amos," he said quietly.

"Truly, an elephant," Amos insisted.

"I believe you. Did you believe him?"

"I did."

"Then, is this his confession or yours?"

"Mine," said the boy. "I've never seen an elephant."

This Eades knew without being told, and while he worked at not smiling he looked kindly at the troubled little soul squirming on the swivel chair. The squeak told him the chair needed oiling, and he took note of the need to see to it. "Not that I know of, you haven't," he said, "but if that's what you've come to confess, my boy, believe me it's no sin never to have seen an elephant. Nor have I."

Amos found difficulty in returning Eades's gaze eye to eye. "But I'm sorry I never have," he told his attentive knee. "It pesters me. I wish it was me had seen an elephant."

"Well," said Elder Harvey, "I suppose that's the difference. But if it was you'd seen this elephant, Amos, what would you be?" The boy was lost; Eades began again. "Would the seeing of an elephant bring you closer to God, or closer to the world?" he asked. "And where would you rather be?"

"Elephants aren't close to God?"

"I have no eye to see into the soul of an elephant, Amos, nor really to see into yours," Elder Harvey told him. "But I know the elephant in his innocence finds his place in the world God makes available to him, as does any man, unless that man comes away to be a Believer. An elephant has no such choice, that I know of, but all men do. And before you become a man it's for you to decide whether your place is here, with us, in pursuit of Heaven, or in the world."

"Sometimes I think I know what Heaven is, but mostly I guess I don't," the boy said. Not knowing that, he seemed to think, was ample reason not to know the importance of arriving there.

"Heaven is within you," the old man told him. "It is a condition or state of the mind, devoid of error or remorse."

Harvey Eades obviously had no remarkable gift in speaking to children, and Amos rather wished he would ask a different kind of question, not a schoolhouse question but a question that was more like an answer, as Brother Harry did. Brother Harry's questions always made a thing more clear to Amos than if the thing had been told him outright. Clearly Elder Harvey pursued a rabbit in his own way.

"How am I supposed to know?" he asked finally.

"That's something you'll have to tell me," said Eades. "The course of your own heart is for you to discover, with God's help. When you want to show me where it's going, you let me know."

"But how am I supposed to know?"

Grown men and small boys, the question was always the same, and the answer defied men wiser than Harvey Lauderdale Eades. "Remember your dream?" he asked. "The lovely voice that gave you the message?" The boy nodded. "Listen very hard, whenever you can, and perhaps that voice will come again."

"Maybe in Sabbath meeting?" Today was Thursday. He might not have long to worry.

"Maybe not this Sabbath, but some Sabbath, or some other day, if you're quiet and still and listen, Amos."

Amos chewed at his lip. He could think of nothing else to say. "Is it allright if I go now?" he asked.

"Let me see you safe across the road," Elder Harvey said, and watched nervously from the ministry steps as the little fellow trotted the width of the rutted wagonway, headed back toward the Center.

The other boys had been called in from their baseball game, and other than a few brethren on their way back from the fields and shops there was no one about. The road was curiously empty of wagons, of soldiers, of noise and horses and grinding earth.

Inside the fence smoke billowed from the chimneys above Amos' head, and in the moist air were the home-smells of new bread and lit firewood. But as he closed the gate behind him he saw Brother Austin sitting by himself on the schoolhouse steps, and more than he wanted to go in and be amongst them he wanted to drift down the road along the fence, to be in Brother Austin's company and to have it.

The schoolmaster heard the boy's solitary footsteps and watched him as he neared. "You look like a man with something on his mind," he said, and moved over on the step.

Amos sank down in front of the door and felt the cold of the stone rise up along his spine to rattle his teeth. Brother Austin had taken off his coat, as he always seemed to do when he was alone. He did not feel the weather, and Amos admired the steadiness of the older man's arm as his own trembled in the evening chill.

"Did Mother Ann truly hear voices?" Amos asked him.

"I believe she did." The questions of the boys seldom surprised him.

"Do you ever hear voices?"

"I hope I do."

Amos inched nearer to Austin Innes. "Brother," he asked, "have you ever seen an elephant?"

"The honest truth," he said, "is nay, not an elephant. Not ever in my life. Why?"

"Would you like to?"

"I reckon so," he said, shrugging. "If somebody rode one down toward Russellville, I'd come right out and watch til it was gone," he said, looking out at the Great Road as if there was a pachyderm to be seen there even as he spoke. "But I'll tell you a secret..."

The boy looked up at him.

"Sometimes in my life I thought I'd give my soul, gloves and all, to see a whale."

The lamps were suddenly lit in the windows of Amos' mind, and a hundred retellings of the story of Jonah echoed off its walls.

"Could you see one, if you wanted?"

"Indeed I could."

"Then why don't you?"

Brother Austin scratched behind his ear with his forefinger, as often he did when he was stuck for an answer. Still he did not look back from the road, and his voice was with what he saw there. "I suppose, not too long back, I was that way bound," he said. "Maybe a whale is just a kind of dream, Amos, when you go to look for one. What I found was just as blue, or just as grey, and when it died the blood was just as red."

"Brother?"

The ghost pachyderm was still parading the Great Road and, as promised, Austin Innes had not taken his eyes off it. Then, suddenly, he looked down at his little listener and said: "I'll bet, if you tried, you could fit three elephants in a whale and still have room to lay the table for supper." His eyes were clear and mischievous. "What would you say to that?"

Amos giggled, and lowered his voice, and straightened himself up as he tried to mimic the schoolmaster: "Well, by sugar, *that's* news!"

Now Austin laughed, and said, "How many mice do you suppose an elephant would hold?"

"A thousand thousand, maybe?"

"And a thousand more?" asked Austin, and put his arm around the boy's shivering shoulders. "Have we got that many mice here, you reckon?"

"Nay, not so I know of," Amos replied, leaning into the warmth of the schoolmaster's chest.

"Then count the mice, boy, every mouse you see and every one you think you see," said Austin. "And when you think you have enough, maybe go find your elephant and see if it's as big as you dreamt it. Home will still be here when you find you're still a thousand mice shy." The pair of them erupted into fresh paroxysms of laughter. They were still sitting there on the schoolhouse steps, conjuring the image of an elephant stuffed to the flop of its ears with squeaking mice, when Sister Elizabeth, bundled in her shawl, came along the path to tell them they'd catch their death and scold them in to supper.

Amos thereafter seemed increasingly slow and quiet, unusually so for all that he made no further mention to anyone of elephants and in general seemed less troubled by his exchange with the young visitor from Michigan. Still he was less boisterous with the other boys, less interested in his plate at table. Except that he had never been truly ill, having resisted even the bygone invasion of measles, Sister Elizabeth Barrie might have thought him to be ailing. She asked after him of Brother Harry, who in as few words as possible told the tale of the boy's temptation insofar as he knew it, and between the two Amos' withdrawal was assumed to be no more than the struggle of a conscience to find the light again.

And indeed at meeting, come that final Sabbath afternoon before Christmas – a traditional day of sacrifice and fasting – he seemed most peculiarly intent. The children's benches stood behind those occupied by the older brethren and sisters, and now and again Brother Harry turned for an instant to see the boy quiet with his head down, serious in whatever his thoughts. Sometimes his eyes did not even rise with those of the other boys to watch the faces of the speakers, so focused was Amos on his private vision. When finally the benches were moved back to the walls to make room for the marching and dancing, Amos was slow to rise and help with the shifting. There seemed to be something else in possession of the child's arms and legs, and his skin seemed white, although the meeting house was warm from the stove and the breath of the worshipers.

They formed what they called the endless circle, which was in fact two circles: one composed of the brethren within a second made up of the sisterhood. Several brethren and sisters more formed at its center the core of singers around which the dancers moved, their feet sounding against the floorboards and their hands in constant movement to shake off the worst of the world that might have caught hold of them. The step and line of the dance was simple, as was its aim: to bring the community face to face again in the labors of Heaven after a week apart in the labors of the present life, and the words they sang as they moved – "Oh, I feel it's good to be here, good to be here, good to be here" – sounded their joy at the result.

Their pleasure, in fact, made off with them on this particular wintry morning, and the twin swirling circles moved faster and faster around the singers until soon the words assumed the sound of laughter. Some in the swift-moving lines broke away into dances of their own, and Brother Harry saw from the corner of his eye that one of these was little Amos, with his arms stretched out to the blue walls either side of him, his feet moving more rapidly than the rest of him could follow, his brown hair clinging to his forehead in damp clumps. Harry realized he was not the only one to notice the boy's rapture. On all sides the dancers had stepped back, and around Amos Anger had formed an altogether different kind of circle with the child whirling crazily at its center. First admiring of the boy's involvement, Harry Littlebourne was suddenly afraid, and he held out his hand, calling the child's name. At once he felt his arm being pulled back, out of harm's way, and he turned to see Elder Harvey, come down from the ministry's vantage point at the railing above to witness at close range the extraordinary event that might be unfolding below.

"Leave him, Harry," Eades said, his voice brittle with excitement. Suddenly the boy tottered, and finally fell, and still Harvey Eades held Brother Harry's arm. "Nay. Let him speak to us, if he will. You don't know who it might be."

On the other side of the room Brother Austin watched the boy fall and broke through the concentration of awestruck bodies around him. In an instant he was on his knees with Amos gathered in his arms. The boy's head fell to the man's chest and blood ran from his nose, spreading on the clean white cloth of the schoolmaster's shirt like breath spent on a cold windowpane.

"Leave him, brother," Elder Harvey said, still hopeful of new manifestations to come. "Leave him be."

Brother Austin came uneasily back to his feet with the boy in his arms, shaking his head, and was fast on his way. "*This is not a miracle*," he muttered through his teeth as he ran, and banged through the front door, back across the Great Road to the Center.

The door fell shut again behind him, and with that sound there was an awakening in them all, as if from a shared dream. The brethren and sisters spoke fearfully to one another, and at once came a gift that it was time for prayer. Elder Harvey still stood with his hand on Brother Harry's arm, a look of astonishment on his face which was suddenly gone, replaced by an understanding of what had happened and what should happen next. He looked around him, searching for someone, and then he saw the Shannon sisters.

"Sister Lucy, Sister Olive," he said quietly, "go with them. They will have need of you." As the two women found their shawls on the peg-rails Eades addressed those who remained. "Meanwhile there is that which we can do here, and let us lose no time in doing it."

Across the road Brother Austin had taken Amos up to the sickroom, at the end of the second floor passage, and was mopping the child's face with his own handkerchief, soaked in the jug-water from a retiring room two doors down. Fast behind him arrived the Shannon sisters, and while Sister Olive stripped Amos' clothes from him Sister Lucy opened his shuttered eyes, then peered inside his mouth.

"Brother," said Sister Olive, looking over her shoulder at Austin Innes, "fetch me his nightdress."

His footsteps were loud and rapid on the passage planks toward the staircase, and the emptiness of the house was eerie. He did not know which of the cupboard drawers held Amos' things; thus he pulled a likely garment from the first drawer he opened and went back downstairs to the sickroom.

"What is it, sister?" he asked from the door. The window had been opened and cold air filled the room which had been warm when he left it. Sister Lucy took the little gown from him and put it on the sideboard. Sister Olive had brought cool water up the back stairs from the kitchen and was sponging the boy's bare body down. "Do you know what it is?" he asked again.

Lucy Shannon beckoned him into the room with her eyes. She took one of Amos' hands in her own and lifted it, working the fingers. They were swollen, the skin of them drawn tight and unnatural-looking. She looked from the child's hand to the schoolmaster's eyes.

"Scarlatina," she said.

The house that afternoon was in mayhem. The sisters were busy burning Amos' bedding and his clothes, even his hat, washing down the walls and floors of the boys' retiring room, their playthings and furniture, anything he might have touched. The women East, North and Center were on tenterhooks, lest symptoms show in the other children, and even the younger adults were eyed for indications of poorliness. In the sickroom the sisters Lucy and Olive worked in shifts, washing their little patient, dosing him with tincture of belladonna, soaking his feet and hands in hot water mixed with mustard and pulverized cayenne. The rash came first to the boy's legs and arms, then erupted over his chest. He had not opened his eyes since he had closed them in the meeting house and begun to spin.

Until the pieces came to one whole, it seemed a marvel that Amos should be stricken with scarlet fever. But hidden in confidences to this one or that of the brethren lay the sense of the matter. Elder Harvey knew the boy had spent a quarter of an hour, possibly more, nose to nose with a world's boy; Elder John Rankin recalled the woman from Michigan who called at the office on her way to Nashville with her young son, a boy who chose to stay outside while his mother sought advice on passing through the southerly lines. Tired to tears, the woman wept as she told of losing her youngest child, her girl, to scarlet fever. Her boy had passed through a mild case of the same eruption years before, and thus the elders remained confused that Amos should contract it so, but here Sister Lucy tied the tatters with expert string: in the Michigan boy's clothes, she said, the miasm of his sister's infection could live for months without surrendering any of its deadly properties.

"Seems to stretch things a bit," said Elder John.

"In the absence of facts we must occasionally make use of conjecture," said Elder Harvey, in rendering his decision on the subject. "But if, as in this case, a known cause is sufficient, we must not postulate an unknown."

To Harry Littlebourne, a simpler man, it mattered less how it had come to pass than that it had, and he took scant notice of the inquiry. All through the Sabbath the nursing sisters, clucking and concerned, denied him entry to the sickroom, forbid him to come closer than the doorway, and by nightfall even that concession was withdrawn. But by Monday morning, when Amos had not opened his eyes and neither Lucy nor Olive had closed hers, they relented. The doctor was summoned up from Russellville to administer belladonna and yarrow tea to the other children – and those of the brethren and sisters who might still be vulnerable – in hopes of heading off a full-scale outbreak. All able hands were needed to maintain order around Amos. Asked for his help once the doctor had confirmed the sisters' preliminary diagnosis, the tall, silent brother brought in a rocker from the hallway and sat by the bedside, rocking and watching and reading his Bible. The boy's body was by now covered with the darkening red rash, the few unaffected patches showing white as winter alongside, and his jowls were swollen up twice their size.

The temperature outside had plummeted, with the mercury no more than a degree or two above the freezing mark, and thus –

with little of purpose to occupy him in the fields – Brother Harry stayed all day in the infirmary, interrupted only by the return of one sister or the other to soak Amos' hands and feet again. They tried to dose him with spirits of nitre, then with diluted nitrate of potash, but without the boy's own assistance to work the medicine down his constricted throat there was little success.

Late in the afternoon, the business of his visit behind him, the doctor stopped in again, with Sister Lucy close behind.

"The worry," Lucy Shannon said, "is that he hasn't waked up nor spoken."

"It's rare," the doctor told them, "but I've seen it before. The alternative being delirium, it's not time to worry. See the purpling here, Sister? It's a severe bout, no sense not to say it. But what's important now is to keep it from the other children. And, for God's sake, shut that window."

They were doing what could be done, he said. Should the other children develop symptoms, he could offer no further thoughts for treatment but he'd like to know. Meanwhile he had no advice other than to wait.

He was an infrequent visitor to the house but he knew the way, and Sister Lucy stayed behind in the sickroom when the doctor left. She went about her business with no word to Harry Littlebourne, and he sat firm in his rocker, fearful but silent. If even the doctor was concerned, there was cause to believe the child might die. Opening his Bible again he found himself reading the same line over and over, and as it was not one that gave him comfort he abandoned the effort. Sister Lucy started as the pages slapped shut, and Brother Harry looked at her apologetically. In seeing that she also saw the rest.

"If his place is with the Lord, brother, it is not for us to disagree," she said, not unkindly, only the voice of common sense.

She had not suggested that Amos might die, but she did not need to. And she kept looking at Brother Harry, as if waiting for him to speak, finally, no matter what he might say. He felt, for the first time, less a man for saying nothing in the face of this awesome expectation. But in examining all the things he might tell her, he found that more than anything else he wanted to say, "He's all I have." This, he knew, he could not say, and thus he said nothing at all.

As evening came the lamps were lit and the purple rash seemed still darker, more ominous. The lamplight wavered around him, and Brother Harry heard footsteps nearing in the still passage. A shadow appeared suddenly, thrown by a visitor Harry recognized by the stature of his dark double, cast wavering by the candlelight to the fireplace wall.

"I brought thee some supper," said the shadow's singular voice, and there followed the sound of a plate being set on the sideboard.

Brother Harry, with his back to the door, could not look. He shook his head.

Silence. Then: "Does this make of thee a Daniel, brother?" came the question.

"What lion I would not face for this boy, I cannot tell thee," said Harry, his voice husky from lack of use. "Nor can I tell thee how many he has faced for me."

The shadow by the fireplace lowered and then disappeared altogether as the small man who cast it settled to the floor, propping himself against the skirting board.

"Where will thy faith be, Harry, if he's taken?"

"In truth?" replied Harry Littlebourne. "I don't know."

There were fish everywhere, fish such as he and the boys had never pulled from the Gasper. Neither eels nor trout, they changed shapes as he watched them. He knew that if he could raise his arms he could catch them with his hands, but however sternly he spoke to his muscles they would not take his commands. Instead, the fish seemed to close in around him, flying around his eyes, like silver-feathered birds. The warm, still water that ran between them was first blue, then green, finally red, and he felt himself squeezing up into the space left him by the fish. Then he was very small, moving between this one and that, and he was swimming, not among fish now, but between the seconds of the ticking clock, even as the fish moved between the rocks and sawyers of the Gasper. It maddened him, not to be able to put his hands out, to catch a fish for supper. He swam higher, and the ticking was louder, the seconds farther apart. The red faded to a warm pink, and he could see the ripples of the surface above, the fish now swimming below. High above the moving ceiling of water he could see, almost transparent, two people – a man, a woman. There was a baby in the man's arms. He swam up higher, wanting to see better. The brethren did not tend the smallest children, and he had never seen a man hold a baby so. The man was not familiar, but there was a look to the woman, a look of himself, and he swam still higher. There was a word in his mind, and as he reached higher with a hand that had at long last taken his meaning, pulling the water down from above and pushing it below, the word came up farther into him. His throat hurt, and as the word came up in his gullet he swallowed hard, not meaning to send it back from whence it came but anxious that it should not hurt him further. It tickled behind his tongue and suddenly pushed at the back of his lips and he could not stop himself saying it. The light now was no longer pink but faint yellowish, and it broke into his head like dawn as the single word found its way out into the air that felt chilly on his skin.

"Papa," he said slowly, and felt – for the first time in all the seconds he had swum between – the weight of his own head. The light separated, and into it came a dark face, eyes he knew, a voice he would recognize when it spoke to him.

"Papa's gone a-hunting," it whispered, "but Harry's here."

Saturday had found them again, the day after Christmas, and Amos had terrified them all, having remained in that intractable sleeping state while the fever took its course. As those days passed the sisters also nursed Sister Julia Powell, stricken with the winter fever, then lost her and buried her, fearing at all times that the fast-wasting boy would follow. No amount of conversation had reached him, no method known to the sisters or the doctor served to lift the spell that kept him beyond the sound of their voices. All that week Brother Harry had remained in the sickroom, taking his meals and (with Elder Harvey's unhesitating permission) even his Sabbathday worship there, and perhaps it was only the prayer of that devotion that had convinced little Amos he was not, in being where he was, where he belonged.

In truth the sisters Lucy and Olive were puzzled as to why he had lived at all. The scarlatina had ravaged him, inside and out, until he was now just the skin that kept himself inside himself. Even that skin was being shed as the weakened body cast off the mottled old and fashioned new. Amos was like a small and bony lizard remaking its hide, and the sisters brought thin soup which Brother Harry coaxed into the changeling. He would take it from no other hand.

But he did love to hear Brother Austin spin a story, and in this special circumstance the schoolmaster was willing to bend his own reluctance to spin winter tales. While the boy was in the sickroom he came every night for a little while, and every minute he was there the rest of the children clustered themselves as near to the door as Lucy and Olive Shannon would permit, threatened with banishment if they made the slightest sound.

On the night before the new year came they found Brother Austin rocking in the chair while Brother Harry leaned against the window. He was just talking, and Amos, lying thin and quiet and barely visible in the bed, was curled on his side, listening.

"He was the biggest liar I ever heard of, was Joe Mulhatton," said Austin. "He was a drummer, and I forget what he sold, but there never was the like for a liar. Once I remember he put it in the paper that on such-and-such a date he'd be in such-and-such a town – I forget exactly, south Kentucky somewhere – to buy a carload of cats. Just think of that, would you, a carload of cats! Sure as you're born he was miles away from that town come the day, but the cats weren't, come from all over they were, or leastways brought. Some come along in sacks over the shoulders of young'ns who walked up or come on muleback. There were some cats come along in buggies and wagons, but never you mind how, there was never such a lot of cats of all sorts and kinds and colors as there was that day. Folks stood there for hours on end, with their cats just spittin' and scratchin', and the poor freight agent just didn't know what to do, and..."

From amongst the nest of pillows and blankets came the thinnest sound of merriment, a weak wisp of a laugh that grew and at last became nearly audible against the strength of the storyteller's own resonant voice.

Brother Austin, rocking by the bed, saw the grin that preceded it but he kept on talking. When the laughter came he stopped mid-rock and looked to his brother.

"There, Harry," he said, and put his hand on the boy's. "If he can laugh, he'll live."

1864

No one could remember a time when Logan County had had more snow. During the first two weeks of the new year the snow came almost daily, and in the bitterest cold the old did not melt away before the new commenced to fall. Most of the peach blossoms died in the early freeze, and the few that survived seemed likely to go in the March frosts. Firewood ran short and the sisters did their finework in the dwelling houses, not in their shops – the better to make best use of what wood there was left. For the same purpose each of the families was directed to have its Sabbath meeting in its own home, rather than in community at the meeting house.

And there was more time now to think of things like firewood, firewood as something of which the community did not have enough to keep itself warm rather than firewood as something that would have to be located for overnighting soldiers if the fence rails were not be used as a substitute. The sad battle at Perryville fifteen months earlier had successfully erased from the Confederate military mind almost all thoughts of retaking Kentucky, and the fighting was in largest measure south or east of the commonwealth. The sisters were thus called upon far less often to put up supper or breakfast for migrating soldiers, the brethren less often needed to look after the camp needs of the same. Confederate troops came into the Bluegrass and the western counties only on what amounted to day trips.

This discounted, of course, the frequent presence of Nathan Bedford Forrest, whose forays into Western Kentucky in search of fresh horses for the mount-shy rebel cavalry were many. Likewise John Hunt Morgan who – after his escape from Ohio – lost no time resuming his agenda of raids on the state's railroads and bridges in the interest of disrupting lines that carried Union troops to the south and fed them once they got there. The absence of sustained and active offensive effort on the part of the Confederacy depressed the spirits of Kentucky secessionists, but did not dampen their personal resolve that the South should prevail in spite of its leaders' occasional shortcomings.

Their resentment centered itself on Braxton Bragg, who had achieved in the public eye the reputation of a lallygagger or worse if there could be such. Having vacated Perryville prematurely, as near as the populace could determine, Bragg had put himself in the undignified position of being chased south and on into Tennessee by Don Carlos Buell – when he might have come about and attacked, sending Buell packing in his stead. That Buell had not by his actions in that engagement earned the admiration of his superiors did not appease the disillusioned: Bragg had not done the South proud.

But if the ferocious fighting over control of Kentucky was, for all intents and purposes, a thing of the past, the resulting bitterness and resentment of secessionists lay that much more sourly on the tongue and prompted that much more reprisal against those who sided with the Federal cause. Abolitionists, and those lumped in with them, suffered renewed devilment at the hands of guerrillas who seemed to be everywhere and at all hours of the day and night. These bandits and raiders threatened violence and often acted upon it, taking what little might be left in the coffers of Northern sympathizers already drained nearly bone dry by the war that was well into its third year.

*   *   *

Elder Lorenzo Pearcifield had spent much of the late winter fulling and dressing the cloth woven by the sisterhood, and had therefore volunteered to deliver bedding to the clothiers' shop in the interest of protecting it from the attentions of light-fingered wayfarers. The trustees accepted this offer unanimously and with gratitude.

Late one evening, as Lorenzo kept watch, a band of disreputables was seen by him as they skulked around the mill. Not least of the group was a trio of rebels known to the watchful brother by sight. Fearing they might come back, but more afraid to leave the shop in search of reinforcements lest they not in fact be gone but only lying low in hopes the cloth stores might be left unguarded, he stayed well inside the shop. A bull dog, the property of a doctor who lived nearby, wandered past, as occasionally he did in his nocturnal travels, and Lorenzo – thinking any ally was better than none – shared his supper with the animal in an attempt to gain his companionship until such time as the crisis anticipated should pass. The dog allowed himself to be lured into the shop, tail wagging and generally of good heart, but on being shut in he commenced to whine and object. Lorenzo gave him the rest of what there was to eat, and the animal ate but was not thereby convinced to persevere in the arrangement. To make his point he snapped at Lorenzo, bit him on the leg and arm, and barked sufficient to wake the dead. His mouth was open and his teeth showed fierce, but by now the dog was between Lorenzo and the door, preventing by his own unpleasantness the granting of his canine heart's desire. Hoisting a chair over his head, Lorenzo brought it down hard on his doubtful guest, but while the chair would hold a man it would not fell a dog.

Looking around for another means of driving the animal from the path to the door he finally spied the heavy hickory plank he used to tighten down the cloth press and, by judicious application of that device, he was at last able to reach the door and drive the bull dog through it. He charged out behind the yowling animal, waving the plank above his head for emphasis, and as the dog ran barking toward home the Shaker saw two riders on the bridge – two of those he had seen before. At the frenzied sound of man and dog they took off in a fast hurry. Elder Lorenzo went back to the clothier's shop and spent the night alone, but resolved that he should never again wonder why it was that Believers did not keep dogs – if indeed he had ever wondered before, which he didn't think he had.

On New Year's Eve Jackson McGowan rode back from Bowling Green agitated and fearful, having overheard (Brother Jackson's talent for overhearing was a thing of sheer amazement) that the Provost Marshal was in receipt of some communication from Washington City, concerning the drafting of Shaker brethren. This news he took straight to Elder Harvey, along with some letters he'd been given at the post office.

"What else, brother?" asked Eades, alarmed from the first instant that there should be news on this front. There was no more to tell, Jackson told him, only the hearing of it.

Eades and Elder John Rankin had so far received no response at all to their letter to President Lincoln, dispatched August last, but neither had the village been troubled by the enrollment officer since, and this they took as an answer with which they could be content. Response of an official nature might well come down against them, and it was this that Elder Harvey feared when he heard Brother Jackson's news.

The gospel truth of the matter did not reach them for yet another week, and the tenth day of January – when the mercury stood at a degree below zero – came before the telegram that had raised such anxiety at Shakertown could be read out in Sabbath meeting to the community assembled.

TO THE PROVOST MARSHAL, BOWLING GREEN
Sir: If there is any religious community within your district
whose conscientious scruples abjure war, or the payment of the
commutation fee, you will parole them indefinitely, still holding
them subject to any demand from the authority here.

E.M. STANTON
SECRETARY OF WAR
Washington, D.C.
December 30, 1863

This last was worthy of further consideration, but in their zeal to derive the very best that might be had from this long-awaited communication the elders were prone to give greatest emphasis to the words that came before. As he stood reading Stanton's telegram, Elder Harvey could not help but look to the rows of the brethren, to the face of Austin Innes, but there was no reaction to be found there. The man's eyes were closed, whether to keep intruders out or his thoughts in Harvey Eades could not begin to say.

In the Center Amos Anger was still mending in the sickroom, uneasy on his feet as yet and with insufficient beef on his bones for the nursing sisters to let him loose again despite his noisy protests against the prolonged incarceration. The other children had escaped the scourge, and for this the sisters and the rest of the community gave copious thanks: another bout as severe as that which had befallen Amos would have felled the grown-ups if no one else.

For Amos himself it was enough that there should have been one child taken with scarlatina, and after two weeks he was fed up and ornery, ready to be out and about. A few weeks more and the brethren would begin breaking up the north field for sowing in clover, oats and timothy, the south field for corn. As he lay captive in his sickbed he was missing the ice-cutting, a winter ritual not to be ailing through, and – perhaps even worse than this – he was lonesome for the schoolroom.

As regarded the former there was no appeal against the will of the Shannon sisters, and no obvious substitute presented itself. But for the latter deprivation Brother Austin continued to offer what consolation he could. On that Sabbath night, after Stanton's telegram was read, Austin went to the sickroom (as he usually did of an evening so that Harry Littlebourne might be persuaded to take himself some supper) and for once he shut the door behind him.

"Found something in the paper," he said as he took his seat by the bed. "Thought I'd read it to the boys tomorrow, but then I thought maybe you'd like to have an earful of it first. Just between you and me."

From the pocket of his waistcoat he brought an oft-folded page torn from the Bowling Green *Gazette* and, laying it open with a rustling flutter, he began to read aloud the following item of note:

> A famous fish factor found himself the father of five flirting females: Fernanda, Fanny, Florence, Francesca and Fennella. The four first were flat-featured, ill-favored, flippant, fretful, forbidding-faced, freckled, frumpy, foolish and flaunting. Fennella was a fine-featured, fresh, fleet-footed fairy, frank, free and full of fun. The fisher failed, and was forced by fickle fortune to forego footmen, forfeit his forefathers' fine field, for a forlorn farmhouse in a forsaken forest...

On and on the story went, relentless in its consonance, following the dismal fortunes of the hapless fish factor and his five daughters, and with each sound of an "f" that blew softly off the schoolmaster's lip Amos began to laugh again, until the shrieks of the boy were nearly sufficient to render the man speechless.

The tale finally brought itself to a close, with Fennella the only one of the factor's daughters to stand by her father in his hour of need, and Brother Austin rocked back in his chair until it braced itself against the wall.

"I declare," said Sister Olive, who had been fussing around the next-door dispensary while Austin Innes read, "I don't know how this boy's supposed to get himself to sleep after all that ruckus. Honestly, Brother..."

Fearing she might be on the verge of ejecting the schoolmaster for a nuisance, Amos sat up against his pillows and mustered his most winning smile. "I can sleep, Sister, honest I can. Please don't make him go."

Austin Innes rocked forward on his chair again and the front legs rejoined the floorboards with a dull clomping sound. "Nay, son, I've got to go as it is." He slipped his pocket watch from the niche it had shared until recently with a page from the *Gazette*, and showed the boy the time. "Work for me and the pillow for you, now, hear?"

He stood and opened the door again, with Sister Olive behind him to see it shut until Brother Harry came to say goodnight.

"Seems to me you might have saved that child's life just a little," she told Innes as he left.

"Just returning the favor," he said, and walked back down the hall to his room.

April

"**M**ay, honey," said Shaw Mason Hannon down the length of the dining table, "don't you think I'd have this war over and done with, quicker'n you can say jack robinson, if I could – just to make you happy? Don't you think I'd sooner your brother was home?" This last came before he thought about the discomfort that came of saying it. "I don't even know where he is." One of the house slaves ladled some soup into his bowl, but he took no notice, of soup nor hand. "I know you're bored, but it isn't up to me." He was exasperated, having had this argument from his daughter without benefit of sugar for days on end.

May Howard Hannon was unconvinced. She was seventeen and knew better about most everything. In this she was like her mother, dead these many years, but so like the woman was the child that there was little to tell between them. On those certain days when this likeness was its most vivid it assumed for her father a kind of exquisite pain, like a mosquito's bite, and on such occasions Shaw Hannon passed his nights in the quarters. But most often he delighted in the mere sight of his youngest, and in peacetime he had spoiled her shamefully.

Now, with Teddy so long gone with his Tennessee regiment, May Howard was his chief source of joy. His dismissals of her complaints that – with all the boys of her acquaintance away and soldiering – there were few ways for a girl to while away the hours bore the earmarks of annoyance to him, but in truth they were more helpless than brisk. This she knew, and he knew that she knew it. She also knew her Papa would buy her a basketful of boys if they would make her smile, but there were precious few to buy and those there were were old or black or both.

May sat sulking down the table, her bottom lip set for maximum effect. "Papa..." The sound was a reproach; her mother had on many occasions wrung the same tone from her husband's Christian name. Perhaps it was a talent passed down, mother to daughter, since Eve.

Hannon had had as much of this conversation as he was inclined to bear on this occasion. He jerked his napkin from his lap, drew it in cursory fashion across his chin and slapped it on the table by his plate. "Darlin'," he said as he stood, "there's not one word more to say now. I've got places to be and no time to be arguing here with you about things there's not a particle of sense to argue about."

"Where are you going?" she asked.

"I've got to go down to South Union and see to the flour accounts," he said. "Depending how contentious they want to be it shouldn't take too long."

She looked up at him and smiled. "Let me come with you, Papa."

He put his hands on his hips and scowled. "There's nothing down there but a lot of dried-up, nigger-loving old men, May," he told her. "There's nothing down there for you, that's for sure. Sooner for me you stayed put."

"Just let me go with you, for the airing," she said. "It's such a pretty day, not near so cold as it was, and I never get out to see the country anymore. *Please.*"

There was not much he could refuse May Howard at the worst of times, and – however maddening the who-struck-john she gave him about the sorry plight of a homebound girl in war-time – they had not yet approached those. She could see her father begin to crumble and she leaned forward and smiled at him, just as her mother used to do when she felt close to getting her own way and wished to push her husband over the edge of his own stubbornness.

It was Shaw Mason Hannon who blinked. "Tell Bolt I want the carriage, then," he said, "and have Jupie put your coat on you." His daughter's face was all victory but he did not feel vanquished. "Catch your death of cold and I'll have Jimmy Sweet and hell to pay when he and Teddy get home."

May

I t was the little blue mittens on Old Sorrow's ears. That was what he liked best about mowing. Not mittens, exactly, because they had no thumbs, but close enough, and they kept the clouds of little insects that wheeled up from the fresh-cut grass away from the horse's ears. Amos was not sure what the attraction was: the thousands of flies awakened by the mower blades never seemed to bother him, or Brother Harry, but they were powerfully keen to get into Old Sorrow's twitching ears, and Amos turned on the rump of his piebald conveyance and watched the little winged invaders bumping into the woolen ear-mittens. He shifted again until he was facing Harry Littlebourne, riding the mower's seat with a rein in each hand, clucking instructions to the horse. Behind him the Center lawn lay in cropped stripes that marked where the mower had been. Clouds of angry flies hovered above the neat mown avenues, indignant at the destruction of their deep, warm domiciles. Amos put his hands flat on Sorrow's backside to steady himself and hooked his toes in the harness.

The weather had been most peculiar for the past little while, with the mercury dancing a jig from eighty degrees two weeks ago, while Elder Harvey and a hireling were laying a new stone path outside the meeting house, to the freezing mark on the third of May. As Amos bounced along ahead of the mower there were ninety degrees of temperature. Up and down the thermometer the weather had gone, so many times that (although yesterday they had put on their light, striped Sabbath gowns for the first time this year) the sisters did not know whether to keep the community's winter clothes out or put them by for the season.

As uncertain as the weather was the steadiness of the local Negroes. Many had disappeared in recent days (and nearly as many horses as slaves), gone to the army now they were actually allowed to fire a musket at the enemy in the interest of their own emancipation. Union enrollment officers had been up and down Logan County in recent months looking to join them up, and by all accounts with results that pleased the army while heartily dismaying local slaveowners. Two of the Shakers' own colored hirelings left, and of the near neighbors James Copeland lost five men, while on the other side of Black Lick by the Coon Range road Winfield Hall lost the last three men he owned. Four of Shaw Mason Hannon's Negroes – including James, one of his house slaves – went in a single night, and on the morning that followed Hannon came thundering to the trustees' office, ready to believe before anything else that the Shakers had somehow conspired in this.

Daily it seemed Kentucky would be rid of the peculiar institution one way or the other; abolition would become the law of the land or the last of the slaves would skedaddle, and either way the result would be the same. The woods were meanwhile populated by a race of guerrilla bandits, and the village was tensed up, agitated, vigilant, yet making all motions toward normalcy despite the contradictions of the times. The brethren found one of the milk cows dead one morning, a bellyful of nails and scrap iron the cause of her demise, and as they hauled her away they thought the sound they heard from the treeline was laughter, not that they could be sure.

* * *

Harvey Eades had last year begun laying stone walkways in the village, and he was at work in May on the walk that would connect the meeting house to the East, an ambitious distance of some third of a mile. A few days ago – with all the sheep sheared and the wool washed, the flour milled and conveyed to the depot – two dozen of the brethren turned their hands to hauling dirt for grading, over a hundred wagon loads in all, and now Elder Harvey was often to be seen about the Great Road, measuring and thinking. John Barnett came by often to cast a critical eye on the work in progress, but today he had arrived with a newspaper in his pocket. Harvey saw it and their attention was forthwith distracted from the task at hand; there was considerable fighting in Virginia, at Rapidan, and while the mower tamed the lawn across the Great Road the two men stood with their heads together, studying the reports offered by the Louisville *Courier*.

As Old Sorrow turned ahead of the mower Amos found himself facing the road again. He spotted Elder Jess Rankin by the trustees' office and waved, but his greeting went unnoticed. Amos wasn't bothered. He was thinking of other things.

"Do you believe in angels, Brother?" he asked.

"Angels?" Most recently they had been discussing the asparagus crop, and the route from asparagus to angels was clearer to the boy than to the man. "What makes thee think of angels?"

"I think about angels sometimes," Amos said. "Don't you?"

"Sometimes."

"But do you believe in angels?"

"I do indeed." Harry leaned right with the reins and clicked loudly to the horse as they rounded the well and turned up toward the wash house. The rank of the mow was uneven and he sought to correct it.

"Have you ever seen one?"

"Not to know it. And thee?"

"Has Elder John?"

"I don't know," said Brother Harry, licking at the sweat that beaded above his lip. "He's old enough. I suppose he might have. Thee might do better to ask him."

"Sometimes I wonder what angels look like. Do you?"

Harry considered this for a second and remembered something, dimly, so many years gone that the halo was as much a matter of the dimness of memory as holiness. "I saw a picture once, in a book, a long time ago. She had the most beautiful face thee ever could think to see, and yellow hair that was all around her shoulders like a shawl and eyes so blue thee might imagine all the sky lived there at night. Thee never saw such a face, Amos. Only God could make such a one."

"Wonder what you have to do, to see an angel." The boy's hat bounced up on his head and came down over his eyes. He straightened it, but despite the dampness of his hair it would not stay put. It was last year's and he had grown. He needed a new one, and the sisters had him in mind.

"There's some say it's enough to be young, to see an angel. There was some young'ns here, before my time, who saw some angels. Ask Elder Harvey. He remembers."

"But wouldn't you like to, if you could?"

"If I had anything to give I reckon I'd give it to see an angel, Amos. But I'm guessing by now I'm too old for seeing angels – til I'm gone from this Heaven and looking to the next, leastways." Brother Harry's face did not often register dismay, or regret, or disappointment, but on this occasion it was clear that Harry Littlebourne considered denial of an acquaintanceship with angels a reflection of something lacking in himself, although it was hard to imagine what that might be. "That grieves me. I'd like to have a chance at that, the better to tell thee. But thee can tell me, little brother, if ever thee should chance to see an angel."

*   *   *

On Sabbath Eve, the fourteenth, the brethren rode out to the Knob and found there a length of fence broken down. Five score adventurous, fresh-shorn sheep had already found their way through to the sumptuous and forbidden grazing land. The strawberry patch, in full fragrant bloom, was nearly destroyed, a calamity which affected the children sorely: to the younger citizens of Shakertown Maytime was a hubbub of sheep-shearing and expectations of strawberries to come, and to see their beloved and blossoming vines in such ruinous state unsettled them as would little else.

"First the milk cow, now the Knob," said Brother Cyrus Blakey, slow to boil but simmering sure as he looked at the footprints around the downed fence. "You tell me what's gained by this and I'll tell you another."

Decision was swiftly made to post guards on the surviving strawberries to keep them from night thieves and, as the brethren turned their attention to rebuilding the damaged fence and sorting out the sorry condition of the Knob, Gracy Roberts arrived from the loom house with a message. Sister Polly Rankin was after her to fetch Amos if he could be spared. The boys had been busied at clearing the broken vines – listening and watching while Brother Cyrus explained how best to tell what might yet grow from what needed to be yanked up to encourage new – but if Sister needed Amos at the looms that was fine, too, and Brother Cyrus waved him on.

Amos ran down to the shop with Gracy, seeing as he went a pair of army forage wagons in the Great Road. The shop door stood open in the heat, and Sister Polly was just inside, waiting for him, full of amiable mischief.

"Well, Amos, what would you you say to this?" she said, and brought from behind her long skirt a new straw hat.

His eyes were wide at the sight of it, and she took his old hat from him as he took the new one in his hands. He tried it on: a perfect fit, stiff and bright and his own. He took it off again (manners were manners, whatever the occasion), examined it and looked to Sister.

"Why, what ails you, child?" Polly Rankin said, her eyes still playful beneath the brow of her linen cap.

"Doesn't it need a band, here?" he asked, anxious not to be perceived as ungrateful, yet tracing with his forefinger the bare circumference where there was clearly something missing.

At their looms, as the shuttles ran back and forth, the sisters were laughing as quietly as they could.

"Why, so it does, Amos, so it does." She pursed her lips and looked thoughtfully to the stores of thread. "What color calls to you?"

He blushed. Never, ever in his life had he been invited to voice an opinion concerning the clothes he wore, which always appeared, correct to their season, correct for size, as and when needed. The brethren's hat bands were uniformly black, except for Brother Austin's leather one, but he was equal to the task of choosing and when he saw what he wanted he raised a finger and pointed. "That'n there, please," he said. "That green."

"Then green it will be," said Polly Rankin, and took the spools of green thread down as Amos peered into the boxes where ambitious silkworms were making the best of fresh mulberry leaves. She put a hand on his shoulder, taking in her eye how much bigger he was this spring, and how well he'd come on since the fever. They'd been so fearful of losing him, and it was therefore difficult to resist a chance to spoil him when one arose. "Would you like to help me weave it?"

Amos nodded, and she led him to the tape loom they used for finework. Sister Polly showed him how to set the warp threads in place, then took her seat and while she worked the little shuttle watched his face as he tried to see it all. Now and again she took his hands and made as if to let him handle the mechanism on his own, but he was fearful and perforce she never quite let go. Instead he stood like a little statue by her, watching her hands fly back and forth, listening to the hum of the woof strings as they sounded against the warp. Slowly the slender band of green appeared by her long-skirted knees.

When it was finished she sewed it in place and watched how tall Amos stood when he put his hat back on, how he waited to be admired in it before running back up to the Knob. When he arrived, with afternoon waning, the rest of the boys were still bent over the wreckage of the strawberry patch, and the brethren had nearly restored the fence. No one mentioned Amos' new and singular finery, if anyone had even noticed it, and he did not point it out. It was his secret, his and Sister Polly Rankin's, and to keep it to himself would make the new last that much longer.

July

May Howard Hannon waited in the carriage while her father transacted his business. There was no requirement that she remain where she was: at all times she was invited to seek refuge from the heat in the trustees' office, but she did not do so. She never did. Since that first visit here, begged from her father as an alternative to the tedious company of the house slaves at home, she had come here with him many times. In fact, whenever Shaw Mason Hannon had accounts to discuss at Shakertown May Howard nagged at him until he agreed to take her with him. She did not tell him why she was so touched to go, or why she stayed with the carriage rather than come inside, however oppressive the heat. To her father she was young and silly and bored, three factors that answered many questions without elaboration.

May Hannon knew better. She was waiting for someone. She had only seen him twice, but now it seemed she lived to see him, and would sit in the glare of Hell's fire itself for the chance to see him again. There was no one to tell her his name; she knew no one at Shakertown to speak to and she could never ask her father. That first time she drove down with her Papa, those several weeks ago, it was then that she had caught sight of him, and with the certainty that comes only in youth she knew she would never in her life love anyone so much as she would love him if only he would let her. But until such time as he should do so, she could only sit in the carriage and wait, hoping as the minutes ticked by that the orbit of his life would bring him close to her carriage before her father emerged from the trustees' office and took her home. If he passed near, perhaps, with a little courage, she might speak to him. He might, perhaps, have noticed her, and himself lacked the bone to speak. Of such cross-purposes of the heart she had read often in novels.

She waited.

Patience being, as May Howard Hannon knew, a virtue, she was in due course rewarded. It was the first time she had seen him with his little boy, if the boy was his, although now that she looked carefully there was no reason to believe that he was. The child was small and fair; the man who had caught her breath was tall, tall almost beyond imagining, and very dark – the most beautiful man she had ever seen, not like any of the boys she had grown up with. His fair little friend was riding the bare back of a big horse that walked along behind her heart's desire, like a bashful but devoted friend. She liked to think of him that way: fond of animals, fonder still of children.

She watched the three from the corner of her eye, shielding herself with her parasol, loving him ever more with every second she watched him, anxious not to be seen to watch, and was disappointed when her tall and beautiful man left the boy and the horse in the road and went inside the fence, toward the looming brick house at the crossroads. Immediately the door closed behind him May Howard was missing him, almost as if she had been walking along beside him and he had gone for good without her knowing.

The little boy leaned forward on the horse's back. His fingers were wound in its pale grey mane and he touched his nose to its neck. Sensing this nuzzle the animal suddenly shook its great head, as if it had been tickled, and the boy put his head back and laughed.

The boy...

It would be so easy, she thought, and so young a child would not understand the impropriety. It would not do to stand in the carriage, of course, but she straightened herself and sat as high as she might, and mustered as much strength to her voice as she could. "*Little boy!*" she called to him, tentatively at first. Then again, more certainly: "*Little boy!*"

Amos turned on Old Sorrow's back and blinked with disbelief at what he saw, and was then unsure whether to be fearful or prayerful. There she sat, all in white ruffles, with a bright halo of yellow hair that curled like the magic of Heaven around her head, and great blue eyes, and never in his few years had he seen a face with so much to speak for it. He looked back toward the house, his left arm outstretched to pinpoint the vision, but Brother Harry was not there.

"*Little boy!*"

He was awake again. It would not do, not to extend what kindly welcome he could, or at least to be polite. He swatted Old Sorrow's wide sides with his bare feet and moved toward the carriage. Now he could not take his eyes off her. Did they have wings, when they spoke to mortals? Or, like Jesus, did they appear to folks as folks? He craned his neck but could not see behind her to tell. It did not take gentle Sorrow long to lumber up beside the buggy that carried her like the sweet chariots of the Bible stories, and while Sorrow and the buggy horse conversed amiably Amos sought to catch his breath from the sight of her, to return the hinges of his jaw to working order.

"Ma'am?" he said, and finally remembered to take off his straw hat. The beauty of its fine green band paled before the glory of this angel; he was not ashamed but he had learned a lesson in the nature of appreciation.

"That man, that very tall man..." It was a voice that rang with small bells, and Amos concentrated very hard to hear the words rather than the music.

"Brother Harry?"

"His name is Harry?"

"Brother Harry."

"He's your brother?"

Amos nodded.

The door of the trustees' office opened and Shaw Mason Hannon came through it, squinting at the sunlight after so long inside. He saw by his daughter in the carriage an unknown boy on a common field horse and made as if to wave both away, like irksome flies. "What are you doing, boy?" he said. "Get on, now. You're no business of ours."

"It's allright, Papa," said May Howard Hannon, and put her hand out to Amos, squeezing his fingers tight. "We were just talking."

"No mind, but shoo," said Hannon, and Amos backed Old Sorrow from their path as the carriage pulled away.

He stared after them, still stunned, and held to his face the hand she had touched as if to bless him – his transformed hand. There was about it now the smell of June roses, and he breathed deep. When the sisters gathered the roses in to harvest the hips the head of each red flower was clipped stemless, lest the gatherers be tempted to the vanity of wearing the gathered. Only an angel, then, would dare carry the scent of roses.

"Oh, my," he said aloud as the carriage passed out of sight. "Oh, my."

August

"Lord's sake, boy, what would make me go out that time of night?" Harry asked. Amos had come to his retiring room with the message and found him with his shirtsleeves rolled high and his face a haze of soap lather. So tall as he was, and bending as he did to meet the washbasin halfway, he looked to the boy as if he might just topple on in.

"She asked," said the shrugging messenger, hard pressed to see the necessity for further explanation. Having once been assigned a similar errand by a mere voice in a dream, he felt doubly responsible for doing the personal bidding of an angel. "She asked me to ask you."

"Some days are too long for silliness," Harry told him, straightening up and reaching for a cloth to dry his face. "Did the boys put thee up to this?"

"I told you before when I saw her, and today she came back. She wants to talk to you."

Harry Littlebourne sat himself in the rocking chair and leaned back as far as gravity would allow. All day long the brethren had been threshing the wheat and rye, picking next season's seed, in the heat that showed no sign of let-up, and the day's-end pranks of the little boys were of minor interest to him at this one moment. "I'll tell thee again what I told thee then..."

"No, truly," Amos said, trying to wring from his voice all the earnestness he possessed. "An angel as ever was, she is. And she come again today and told me: she's wishful to see you by the mill bridge tonight and she'll wait. Truly." His hands were deep in his pockets and suddenly he looked very grown-up to Brother Harry, sober and serious. "Tell me you'll go," Amos said.

Harry laughed and shook his head. "I'll tell thee no such thing. Now give me a minute's peace from pestering and go wash up for supper."

"Not until you say you'll go."

"Now."

Amos was inclined to stand his ground, but the look on Brother Harry's face told him he had pushed as hard as he could hope to push and he acted accordingly. Even so, at the door to Harry's room he paused an instant, with one last try on his mind. "You told me I was to tell you if ever I did see one, and I did."

"*Now.*"

There was a heavy rain that came on Friday night, August's last, which made the travelling that much worse for the army. The Federals were moving in their numbers on Sabbath Eve toward Russellville, on the way down to Nashville: there might be 2,000 of them passing over the next few days, more than South Union had seen for quite some several months. The troops were Union, but there was less comfort in this than there might have been. First four hundred came, followed a day later by hundreds more driving two hundred head of cattle pressed from sundry rebel civilians, and the rest of the men were said to follow. It was not that the Shaker community had so quickly forgotten how to manage on behalf of so many; more it was that they had come to hope such demands as the troops would surely make were behind them. That hope faded quickly under the crunch of so many soldiers' boots on the sun-dried village lawns.

Brother Urban's task was in the trustees' office, taking note of the needs of over two hundred cavalrymen set to stay the night by the East house. He was in considerable haste to have matters well in hand before supper on this night before Sabbath, and – with so much noise and confusion about the place – the sudden imposing presence of Sheriff George Blakey did not instantly come to the fore of his attention.

"Urban?" said Blakey, reaching through the tangle of officers to make himself known.

"Why, George," replied Urban, looking up from his desk, surprised to see the sheriff there. "Just a little minute, if you wouldn't mind..."

"Tell you the truth, I would mind," he said, his impatience self-conscious in its officiousness. "Could I see you in the hall?"

Urban Johns waved away the objections of the army with what politeness he could and followed the sheriff through the door.

George Blakey was already by the bottom stair, leaning on the newel post. The leather of his gunbelt creaked as he shifted his weight from one leg to the other and Urban knew without asking that his business here was official.

"You got a man Harry here, Urban?" he asked.

"We do," the Shaker said, nodding. "He works on the farms."

"Know him well?"

"Most all of his life."

"How long's that?"

"Oh," said Urban, raising his eyes as he did the mental calculations, "nigh on fifteen years I reckon."

"Well," said Blakey, "he killed a little girl last night. I got to take him with me."

Urban Johns' knees gave way on him. Blakey caught him as he buckled and eased him down onto the stairs.

"You don't know what you're saying, George," he stammered when he found his voice. "He's not your man."

" 'Fraid he is," the sheriff said, long accustomed to such protests, and sat down next to him. "Shaw Hannon's child, May. She left their place last evening, wrote her daddy a note to say where she's going and she wouldn't be back. Said she's in love with the Shakerman Harry and they were going off together." Urban Johns was still shaking his head. "Seventeen years old, Urban. Seventeen."

"It isn't possible," Johns insisted.

"Soldiers coming down to Russellville this morning found her in the road, all crumpled up, halfway between here'n Yost's. Neck snapped clean as a whistle," Blakey told him.

"Harry simply would do no such thing."

George Blakey spread his hands and shrugged his shoulders, helpless to say more than he knew and paid to keep the peace, no small task in time of war. "Shaw's brought me the note," he said. "It's her hand, he says, and she was found right close to your place. No way else to see it."

"You can't take him." It was pure bluff and Urban Johns was fooling nobody with it. He had conviction but no authority, however no-nonsense his tone: Believers paid their taxes and obeyed the law.

"You hide him if you like," said Blakey with good nature, knowing the Shaker would see reason and relent in a minute or so. "But take this in mind: if Shaw Hannon doesn't see me down the jail with your man in an hour or two he'll come up here and kill him his own self. Your choice, but I know what I'd do if I was you." He had only to wait.

Urban rubbed his face with his hands. "I can't," he said, his despair greater than his face or hands could hold. "See Harvey Eades with me, George, will you?"

Sheriff Blakey helped Urban, still shaking, to his feet, and they crushed by the noisy, demanding officers, out the front door and up the road to the ministry. The path might have been filled to mayhem with dancing donkeys for all Urban Johns could see of what was happening around him; his thoughts were taken by dead May Hannon, and by Harry Littlebourne somewhere in the apple orchards, gentle and happy in his ignorance.

Elder Harvey listened politely to the sheriff's tale and denied it without an instant's consideration.

"You ever met Harry Littlebourne?" Eades asked.

Blakey considered this and shook his head. "Not so's I know of, Harvey, no."

"If you had, George, you'd know what an absurdity you're making here," he said.

All of this Blakey had expected, in some form or other. "Tell you what I told Urban," he said. "You give me this fellow and we'll let the law take its course, or you let Shaw Hannon come down here with the demon in his eye and see where that gets you. I was you, I'd turn him over."

Blakey was right, of course: Brother Harry should go on down to the jail with the sheriff and when this lunacy was all cleared up he could come along home and there would be no lasting harm done. Eades knew this full well, and he sent Urban Johns down to the orchard to fetch Harry back.

He was quick about it.

"Brother," said Eades as the two men came through the ministry door, "you don't know George Blakey, do you?" Harry looked to the stranger, pleasant-eyed but silent. "He's the sheriff down to Russellville."

Blakey moved to speak, but Eades was already mid-breath.

"The soldiers found a young girl dead near down to Yost's tavern this early morning," he said. "You know anything about that?"

Harry was grieved by the news, but his eyes revealed no more than sympathy.

"Sheriff Blakey seems to think you do," said Eades.

Brother Harry shook his head.

"He doesn't talk?" whispered Blakey to Urban behind his hand.

"Not enough to annoy anybody," replied Johns.

"You know Shaw Hannon's daughter, May?" asked Blakey loudly, taking Harry for deaf and trying without noticeable success to catch his eye.

Harry shook his head again.

"She knew you."

There was no response.

"You had no cause to kill her." If Blakey was looking for a rise he was disappointed.

Harry's eyes narrowed with a question he did not ask. Harvey Eades was his lead, and he looked to him.

"I'll have to take him, Harvey," the sheriff said.

"Will we be able to bring him home for Sabbath?"

Blakey dug his handkerchief from his pocket and mopped his forehead before realizing he was damp all over: his neck, his jowls, his chin. Christ Almighty, he thought, how many ways can a summer heat up? "This is murder, Harvey," he said testily. "This is Hannon's girl-child dead as she can be and one of y'all's men to blame. I'll tell you when you can take him, and it won't be til it's safe for you, me, him and the town, if he isn't guilty, and who's to say he isn't?"

"I say he isn't," said Eades flatly.

"You can come visit him if you like, maybe do you sensible to send a lawyer, too," the sheriff told him. "And by the time you get down to the jail maybe we'll see. Meanwhile nose yourself around and, if you can, make out where he was last night."

"He was here," Brother Urban said, fearing that, things being what they were, once Harry Littlebourne was out the door in Blakey's custody he would not be back. "He hasn't left this village since the winter of '49."

"You and I both know you folks got plenty of here to be at," said Blakey without sarcasm. "If he was here, then find out where, and when, hear?"

The sheriff's tone defined the borders of his authority, and Urban Johns ventured no further. In the silence that ensued Blakey fingered his newfangled handcuffs, dangling from his gunbelt, but Eades stopped him.

"Nay, George, please," he said. That Harry should suffer this indignity was more than he could bear. "He won't give you any trouble." Eades looked to Harry Littlebourne. "Go along with George Blakey, now," he said kindly, desperate for a way out of this but clean out of ideas. "We'll see you tonight, and we'll bring you home the minute we can. You'll find us moving around as when you left us."

There was obedience in Brother Harry's dark eyes as George Blakey turned him by the shoulder and walked him back down to the trustees' office. The sight of them climbing onto the sheriff's waiting wagon, of the wagon then fading into the distance down the Russellville road, was worse than a dream. The soldiers were milling around the crossroads and their movement blotted out all signs of the sheriff's visit as soon as he was gone. Urban and Harvey looked at each other. Their thoughts were similar, and perforce they did not share them.

Jefferson Shannon was at Canaan overseeing what fruit had survived the early frosts, and since March William Ware was eldering at the Junior Order, which secondings left their beds empty at the Center. His retiring room thus being deserted except for himself, there was no one who could allow for a fact whether Brother Harry Littlebourne was where he should have been the night before. He had arisen from his own bed this morning, to be sure, but when he had put himself into it was difficult to say for certain. Urban set himself the task of asking around the Center, trying hard as he might not to let slip the grim tiding that Brother Harry had been taken by the sheriff, or why. It might be that this dreadful matter could be swiftly dealt with and Harry fetched home – the misunderstanding cleared up, the entirety forgotten – before the community need be troubled by it in the first place. But the more he asked the less he seemed to know, the less he would be able to tell George Blakey.

Finally he had spoken to all of the Center's brethren save Austin Innes and he walked out to the tannery, glad to be outside. On this still and windless afternoon there was not much relief from the heat there, but the weight of his anguish threatened to crush him, and for some reason he felt safer with nothing but God and His cloudless domain overhead.

Austin was alone so late in the day, bent over a hide with his clicking awl, when Urban arrived. Perspiration dripped from his nose onto the leather, and every minute or so he felt called upon to pass the back of his hand across his face to discourage the flow. The legs of his trousers were a damp, dark blue where he had so often wiped his hands on them. The door of the shop stood open, like the windows, and Urban balanced himself on the sill.

"You see Brother Harry last night?" he asked abruptly.

"Peculiar sort of question," Austin said as he looked up for an instant at this infrequent visitor. " 'Course I did. Didn't you?"

"When did you see him?"

"Supper," said Austin. " 'Fore I went to bed, too, he was in the passage. After that I reckon nobody much saw him."

"That's my problem."

"I don't follow you," Austin told him. Urban stood silently, propped in the doorway, staring at the task sheets on the wall. "You could tell me why you're asking, I suppose."

Urban Johns had gone as far as he could go in this without friendship, and Austin Innes was his friend. He unfolded the story, and as he told it Austin abandoned his work on the bench. When it was all out, cockeyed and deadly, the little schoolmaster too seemed lost for words.

"Say something, Austin," Urban said, unnerved by the silence. "Nobody knows where he was. I don't have anything to save him." He raised his hands, unsure how to use them.

"You're asking the wrong people," Austin Innes told him. "Have you talked to the boy?"

*   *   *

George Blakey braked up his wagon on Fourth Street, beside the stone fortress of the Logan County Jail. His passenger had sat the whole way like a bug-eyed wayfarer, captivated by the flat and unremarkable landscape that lay between this dusty town and South Union. Russellville to Harry Littlebourne must appear like Bombay or Cape Town to another man, and from his passenger's placid and extraordinary silence George Blakey began to get a feeling that made him most uneasy. By the jailhouse Blakey jumped down and quickly took the arm of his prisoner; trouble was already there, most likely had been waiting for them all the time the sheriff was on his Shakertown errand.

Shaw Mason Hannon came toward them, his face streaked with the grimy traces of tears. Blakey looked away, insofar as he could reasonably do so – it embarrassed him to see a grown man in that undignified state – and held his arm out in front of him, as if to show Hannon that vigilante justice might do for a black man but in this case the proprieties would be observed.

Hannon's face suddenly seemed to glow red, and the words came from him like spit at Brother Harry Littlebourne.

"Mr. Shaker," he howled, restrained only by the sheriff's protective hand, "you may be God's friend, but by God you are my enemy."

"That's enough, Shaw," said Blakey as he walked Harry by. "You'd better just go on home."

"Take care now, you, just take care," Hannon ranted, his voice gravelly with grief, as the lawman and his prisoner took to the steps and disappeared inside. "If you give me a chance, you redskinned bastard, I'll blow your goddamned head off!"

They went for a walk together, Austin and Amos, before supper. If the errand were left until later Amos would learn in the cruellest of fashions that Brother Harry was missing, and there was no wisdom in pretending there would not be grief in that arrangement. As it was, with no fact presently in hand that would be sufficient to convince George Blakey of Harry Littlebourne's blamelessness, the brethren and sisters would have to know of his predicament. Of the little ones, Amos was to anyone's eye the most vulnerable. Harry spoke to no one else; even to the other children he was something of a benevolent cipher.

They walked together up North Lane, toward the gardens. The brethren were heading home for the evening, walking next to rumbling wagons and with tools slung over their shoulders. Austin was aware that Amos was absent-mindedly looking for Brother Harry, and his chest tightened.

"Seen him since breakfast?" asked Austin.

The boy shook his head; he and the others had been up by the wheat threshing.

"I'm going to ask you a question," Austin said slowly, "and it might seem a peculiar thing to ask."

Amos looked up at him.

"Did you see Brother Harry last night, before you went up to bed?"

"For a bit," said Amos, cautious of Austin's obvious caution. "There was just something."

"Just something what?"

"To tell him."

"To tell him what?"

Brother Austin's gait was uneven, something like a limp. Amos was used to walking next to Harry, with those long legs, and he found keeping pace with Austin Innes disconcerting, like singing with someone who couldn't. "A message."

"What message?"

Amos seemed more interested in the evening scents of the gardens than in the matter at hand, unwilling to answer, and Austin's blood raced.

"Answer me, son," he said, not harsh but firm.

"I wasn't meant to," the boy replied. "I was told not to."

"Told not to?" Brother Austin left the road and cut in toward the patch west of the lane. It was cooler around the plants, calmer. "Who told you not to?"

"Is it a sin to go against an angel?" Amos asked suddenly.

"Depends which angel," said Austin, who had learned long ago the adventure that sometimes lay in following the thought processes of a child.

"The most beautiful one that ever was," he said, the wonder of her so clear in his eyes that, on another day, his listener might have seen her reflected in them.

"It was a girl angel gave you the message?" asked Austin, dropping down and spreading himself out on the grass. He took his hat off and set it down beside his knee. Even at this hour the evening sounds of treefrogs and homebound birds had begun in earnest overhead, and he wished for time and peace enough just to listen.

"You should've seen," said the boy, unimpressed by the treefrogs, anxious to share his vision with someone else, excited that his secret should be vouchsafed to such a one. "You never saw the like of her, Brother. She was every last scrap of what Brother Harry told me she'd be."

Austin Innes rolled over and propped himself on his elbow, feigning an easiness he did not feel. "And she gave you a message for him." Amos nodded. "What did she want you to tell him?"

"To meet her." He saw the schoolmaster go white, even beneath the brown brought on him by the sun, and was confused. "By the mill bridge, she wanted him to be, and she said she'd wait."

Austin seemed to be catching his breath. "Who was she, Amos?" he asked.

"An angel, like I told you," the boy told him, unshakeable in his conviction and desperate to be believed. "In a big fine buggy, like a chariot almost."

"Where did you see her?" He sat up again, and there were blades of mown grass in his red hair.

"Front of the trustees'." Amos reached out and pulled a few of the strays away.

"And she told you she was an angel?"

"Nay, Brother," he said quietly, beginning to shrink a little under the weight of Austin's questions, "but I just thought so. When I saw her I just naturally thought so."

Austin ran his fingers through his hair, and Amos watched him, not sure exactly how he had done wrong but convinced by the schoolmaster's strange, sharp manner that he had. "Listen to me, Amos, and think carefully," Innes said, taking the boy by his shoulder and looking him square in the eye. "What did Brother say to you, when you told him what she said?"

The child was poking in the grass with his fingers. "He said I was to go wash for supper," he said without looking up.

"But did he tell you he'd go?"

"He sent me to wash."

"*But did he say thee nay?*" Austin demanded, pushed short of patience by his own disquiet.

"He didn't say yea or nay," whispered Amos.

Sabbath meeting was not joyless, by its very nature it could not be, but there was a grief to be shared by them all and it was not for the public eye. Perforce Elder Harvey closed the doors to the gawkers and cityfolk who regularly came to investigate the mysteries of Shaker worship in warm weather. Even with the doors closed the world would not be excluded altogether; they gathered close at the windows, noses pressed against the clean glass lest there be something to miss, and the sisters knew it would all need wiping down again come Monday. By then, they hoped, Harry Littlebourne would be home again. Until such time as that should happen there would be a gap to be felt in all of them, an empty space in the heart into which the spirit tripped and fell as it moved about in them. On that sweltering Sabbath, then, it was the task of each brother, each sister, to reach down as far as might be, to rescue that which was most precious. Elder Harvey spoke and each soul gathered on the benches was glad to have his voice to listen to.

Sitting amongst the little boys, Amos could sense the trouble that crowded all along the walls, glowered from the strangely empty benches usually taken up by world's folk, and threatened to burst the meeting house at the seams. Brother Austin had explained it all to him, as best he could, and Amos thought he understood: it was all a mistake and it would be settled soon. He was older now – ten years old in just a few weeks – and his own fears were not the same as when Brother Austin went away. He wondered how Brother Harry must be feeling, so far from home and surrounded by people he didn't know. Amos himself felt a little lost, as if he had been sent again to stay at the North, the way it was the time the boys came out in measles. Perhaps Brother Harry felt the same where he was now. Amos looked around at the sisters and brethren, at Brother Urban and Elder John.

Urban saw the boy's reflection in the window glass and realized he was being watched. He looked up and smiled, but there was not a great deal to fuel him in this endeavor; he and Elder Harvey had had little joy from their ride into Russellville the night before. George Blakey showed them the letter, and true enough she mentioned Harry by name. Urban Johns saw in that girlish handwriting the face of May Howard Hannon, a sweet but strong-willed child he knew, not much like her father. Such a woman had Joanna Hannon been before she died.

Silent in meeting now Urban studied his hands folded in his lap and hoped his prayers would find Harry Littlebourne in that sad and bare little cell. Would George tell him the hour? How did it happen that they had not asked him to? They had fetched up James Littlebourne's Bible from Harry's retiring room and taken it to his son, along with a clean shirt, knowing he would not like to be without it, even for a night. And George Blakey showed no inclination to let him go, the reverse in fact: there was more reason to keep him than to free him, he said.

Urban Johns leaned forward and put his face in his hands. On this Sabbath of all those he could remember he wished the light would find him, set him spinning, but there was nothing in the eye of his spirit but darkness.

There was a lamp there, brought by the deputy, and in this stone-walled cell its hiss was louder than he was accustomed to. He was alone, and it was peaceful. Except that he missed getting out and about, working through the day, he did not mind it so very much, but it would please him no end to go home again. He did not know when that would be. These men's minds were strange to him.

Harry Littlebourne opened his Bible, simply let it fall open. Whatever should be found on his behalf he would read, and when he looked down he could not keep his laughter back: the Book of Jonah.

"*Hey!*" growled an angry voice a few cells down. "Shut that fool racket."

This noisy objection masked the sound of a rider, quiet, moving outside the windows, along the outer walls of the jail, looking. There were not many cells, and of those few only one was lit. He pulled up at that barred opening, through which was visible a single halo of light, and leaning into it the form of a man. The rider bent forward over the mane of his horse, stroked its neck to steady and quiet it, then looked back toward the window. Standing in the stirrups to see clearly over the casement, open in the heat, he hated what he saw: a red man, reading, alive while a white child lay in the grim care of the undertaker.

He steadied himself, pressing the fingers of one hand against the handsome handcut stone, quarried long before he was born. With his other hand he reached into the flap of his jacket for the gun. It was a peculiar weapon, new to him, and he did not know it well. Standing with one foot in the stirrup, one knee on the saddle, he held the cool gun with its angular, brass-plated body against his cheek, idly working the ring-bottomed lever ever-so-slightly with his fingers. In the cell the quiet man turned the pages of the book that lay open across his knees, and the sudden realization that this miserable son of a bitch was reading the Bible tore through his unannounced companion like winter wind. Leaning briefly away from the bars, looking into Fourth Street, he took care no one was watching and – working the lever forward in earnest now – he pumped a bullet to the chamber.

Harry Littlebourne heard a noise and turned to the sound. There was a face visible through the bars, just a pale shadow. He narrowed his eyes and would have stood had there been time.

"You, redskin!" came the muted, furious voice, and Harry was lifting his hand to his chin – what made him think of Marcy Burke after all these years? – as the first shot hit him above his left eye.

He looked down, and with the last of his life Harry Littlebourne turned his face back to the book in his lap, thereby offering the right side of his head to the second bullet when it struck. The third, final shot did not find him at all.

"You had it coming!" came the voice through the bars as the long body folded and fell. "You had it coming!" He looked at what he'd done: the blood that ran toward the cell gate, downhill on the uneven floor, the Bible that had fallen still open by the cot. The smell of the shots was strong in his nose; however often he had fired a gun he could not recall the acrid smell of metal so sharp as this. It was not the sight but the smell he fled, and when he dropped back into the saddle with the blue butt of the gun still snug in his hand he rode low and fast as he had ever ridden before.

He did not hear behind him the shouts of the other prisoners, meant to summon Blakey from his bed.

"Sheriff!" yelled the same fractious inmate who seconds ago had sought to silence the sound of late-night laughter, never intending the arrangement to be a permanent one. He banged against the bars with some implement, whatever came to hand,

and in the next cell down a drunk regained consciousness and attempted similar. "Goddamn, Blakey, get in here!"

George Blakey appeared in his house slippers, the tails of his nightshirt jammed in rumpled fashion into his trousers, his suspenders still dangling below his pockets. The shots, not the profanity, had stirred him. "Allright, allright," he said as the bright of his lamp filled the corridor. "What's happenin' here? Sounded like shooting..."

The prisoner stopped his clanging and thrust a pointing finger through the bars. "That injun fella's dead as they come," he said.

Blakey looked and realized it was true as spoken. "Jesus Christ," he whispered. In the spitting lamplight Harry Littlebourne lay in a heap with two clean shots to the head.

"Don't touch anything!" he shouted, and went running for his deputy.

Pulling his hand back in, awake sufficient to see the humor even in this, the fellow sat back down on his rumpled, sweaty cot. "What in hell could I touch?" he asked the drunk in the next cell.

The deputies were out in the street with torches, looking for shells – anything, really – and fast losing hope of success. Their man was certainly long gone; the hoofprints were clearly visible in the rain-softened earth below the cell window. Else from runaway Negroes and guerrillas of all persuasions nobody in his right mind was out this time of night, and the deputies would surely ask but they would find no witnesses.

Inside the cell the doctor examined the body and told George Blakey what any fool would have known without being told, that Harry Littlebourne was as dead as he was ever likely to get.

"Just take him, Doc," said Blakey. "I'll see you in the morning."

"You going out there?"

"Not tonight. No sense wakin' 'em up. They won't sleep tomorrow; might as well leave 'em be tonight."

*   *   *

George Blakey was heartsick. He'd gone to sleep with a lump of lead in his stomach and waked up to hear bullets flying. Settling on the dead man's cot he looked at the ruby-colored slick on the floor, then reached down and rescued the Bible from the spot where it had fallen. A piece of folded paper fell away; he caught it and closed the pages over it.

"Want me to go out and get Shaw?" said his deputy from the cell door.

"What?" said Blakey, as if waking himself, perhaps hoping to begin again and try for better. "No. Well, I don't know. I'm thinking." He saw a small lump of metal lying by the wall. "What's that?" he asked, pointing.

The deputy bent down and handed it to him. "Looks like a bullet. Sort of."

The misshapen scrap lay in his palm. A third shot had been mentioned. "So it is."

George Blakey regarded the bullet but said nothing, and the deputy shifted from foot to foot, bored. "Whatcha think?" he asked, looking to break the deadlock. "Want me to go on out to Hannon's?"

"What for?"

"You don't think he did it?" This to the deputy was a wonder. Shaw Mason Hannon had told everybody in Russellville the Shaker wouldn't live long enough to hang.

"I know he didn't." He pushed the bullet around his palm with the forefinger of his other hand. It suddenly occurred to him that he needed a drink. "Tell you something else."

"What's that?"

"Harry Littlebourne didn't do it, either."

The sheriff rode out to Hannon's place before he took himself up to Shakertown, not because he thought there was anything there to find but because he reckoned he'd have to explain himself if he didn't at least look. He felt foolish: nothing like having to tell a man there'd been a killing before asking him if he was the one responsible. There was no joy in Shaw's red-rimmed eyes when he heard, and if he had expected there would be satisfaction to be gained from thinking the man who killed his daughter was dead he learned in a quick minute that there was no such thing.

"Let me take a look at your guns?" Blakey said, and there was no objection. Hannon had nice guns, rifles mostly: sporting rifles and a couple of double-barrelled shotguns. His only revolvers were a Smith & Wesson .22 caliber rim-fire and a Colt pocket: nothing wrong with either gun but neither one had killed Harry Littlebourne.

"What is it you're looking for, George?" asked Shaw Hannon. Blakey had never known him so docile.

"A Volcanic," said Blakey. "Out of New Haven. Know it?"

"Never seen one."

"Neither have I." He dug in his pocket for the bullet he had found in the cell, willing to show it if only to distract the man from thoughts of his daughter. "See this?" He rolled the bullet over in his hand. "No cartridge. Doesn't need one. They call it 'Hunt's Rocket Ball'. Powder's all inside." He opened and closed the fingers of his hand. "Doesn't even have a cylinder like this'n," he said, indicating the Colt lying on Hannon's desk. "There's this hinge kinda pushes the ball up into the barrel. Damnedest thing."

"Doesn't make much sense."

"Guess not," said Blakey, nodding. "None made anymore, not for a long time. Couldn't be many out there."

"I don't know anybody's got one," Hannon told him.

"Not surprising," said the sheriff. "I'd take a sizeable bet there isn't one in Kentucky. Whoever shot that poor Shaker bastard sure knew how to keep himself to himself." He put the peculiar bullet back in his pocket. There was no point saying he did not believe it was Harry Littlebourne who killed May Howard Hannon.

What mattered was that Shaw believed it, and with Littlebourne
shot down by a man who would be found only through divine
intervention there was a natural end to things. "You bringing
Teddy back?"

Shaw Hannon's breath caught in his throat at the mention of
his boy, his only surviving child. "I wrote to him," he said. "God
only knows where he is."

Blakey put his hand on the planter's shaking shoulder. "You
think of anything I can do, Shaw, you let me know, hear?"

Harvey Eades wasn't strong enough to hold Amos. The boy
wrenched away and ran, and Harvey looked at Urban Johns.

"I could go after him," Urban said.

"You don't need to," Eades replied. "He knows where he's going,
and when he gets there he'll have what he needs."

When he stopped running he was at the brethren's shop, and
he dropped himself down in the corner, pulled up small. It would
be a long time before he stopped crying.

"So you know," said Austin. There was a cobbler's stirrup
gripped between his knees; Sister Pru was next on his list of the
sisters in need of new shoes before winter. With his free hand he
pulled his handkerchief from his pocket and threw it to the boy.

"He told me, that time down the East, what John said Jesus
said," Amos whispered, "about the wheat?" Austin knew from
the tremor of his voice that he was shaking. In Amos' mind's
eye he saw the rebel boy, George Crittenden Townsend, shot
full of holes, crazy-legged as a discarded ragdoll in the grass
by the tracks that rainy day. His was the only dead body Amos
had ever seen. Whatever Jesus had said about wheat was no
longer so easy to accept, now that the rebel boy had Brother
Harry's face.

"He was right," Austin said, waiting to be asked but slow to
intrude.

"When you went away, he told me you might die," Amos said, and his face emerged from his folded arms. "He told me to remember you. But you came back."

Austin Innes put his hammer down, loosed the stirrup from his knees and set it on the bench. He could not keep working now. "He was right," Austin said, "but this isn't like that. I wish it could be, but it isn't."

Amos looked at him, and the depth of sorrow in his swollen young face was more than Austin could bear. What a child he was, and how like grown folks he was trying to be.

"He would tell me not to grieve," Amos said.

"And he'd be right."

"But is it a sin if I still miss him?"

Austin touched his fist briefly to his lips, then opened his arms. "Come here," he said.

Amos was not in his chair come suppertime, but the alarm was not raised to find him. Brother Urban Johns was wise enough to know there were things he needed to think about – away even from the eyes of those who loved him – and while Sister Elizabeth Barrie was inclined to fret he asked her to keep a plate by for him and wait. Eventually he would come home.

He walked a long time, stopping at all the places they liked best to go, still child enough to harbor hopes of finding Brother Harry whole and alive at one of them. There was always a chance. Jesus was dead, so the disciples said, but it turned out they were wrong. The gardens that lay either side of North Lane were deserted, silent, and it was then that Amos realized there was no mistake this time. He walked over to the stables and sat on the gate of Old Sorrow's stall. The animal looked at him with its enormous round eyes and the boy reached out to give the proffered nose a scratch.

Dark was closing in, and Amos took his hat off. Holding it in his hand he felt foolish, ashamed to have been so proud of it, with its fine green band. He threw it down and Sorrow lowered his nose to investigate, pushing it slowly along on the floor of his stall. His bedding was usually provided in simpler form.

"You think I should keep it?" Amos asked.

The horse cropped gently at the crown and the boy was suddenly protective. He jumped down and pulled the hat away.

"This is yours," he said playfully, and offered Old Sorrow a handful of loose straw. "This is mine." In fact, he thought – not so much a thought as a revelation – it truly was his. "It's mine," he repeated. The words sounded peculiar to him, different.

He lifted the latch of the gate and let himself out. The ladder rose up into the haymow, and he climbed it, and beyond that he crept along the beams into the eaves. Farther and farther back he went, until he could barely see in the darkness, but in the narrow shaft of light that came through a crack in the roof there was visible a crotched brace. Holding on with one hand he reached out as far as he could, with his magnificent hat held fast in the fingers of the other. His arm was just long enough, and the ledge was just wide enough, as if the space had been purpose-built.

He left his hat safe there and went home bareheaded.

September

How long ago was it they had been witness to that dreadful sight, of three black men driven up the Great Road in harness like yoke stock? A year ago, perhaps? Maybe two? Jesse Rankin was willing to stop a minute to think, just to be sure. That day – a Sabbath Eve, now he remembered, because Elder Harvey addressed them on the subject at meeting the very next morning – was chillier than this one, so it might have been October. October it was; just after the fighting at Perryville. Not even a year ago. How time did refuse to fly.

But if it would not fly, at least it would change, and evidence of this there was ample just in front of him in the Great Road this Tuesday afternoon.

The Corps d'Afrique, they were called, the black forces, a regiment all their own and armed as thoroughly as were the white troops. He never really thought he'd see the day; now here it was, and there were they, some fifty soldiers black as the ace of spades and with supply wagons rolling on behind them.

There was a funeral just over, the Center's Sister Keturah Harrison having gone to the better life after sixty-five years of making do in this one, and while the colored troops headed south the children – who had been up with their caretakers gathering pawpaws during the burying – were reappearing and the village was coming back to itself. The two ministry elders, Harvey Eades and John Rankin, were several days gone, having taken themselves up to Union Village on a ministerial visit. It was not their gift to see this sight after so many months watching the war go by, and that to Jesse was a sadness. Having seen their dark brothers in the worst imaginable state of degradation it was only fair they should see such men as now walked by, wearing uniforms rather than chains. Maybe not today, then, but someday surely.

The dust of the soldiers' passing began to settle back, and on the other side of the crossroads Brother Jess could see Cyrus Blakey, walking up toward the East. In his hand was a rope whose nether reach fastened to a halter buckled around the great head of the piebald, Old Sorrow. The horse did not strain against this arrangement; he had never been less than a willing worker. Even so, Jesse Rankin would never accustom himself to the sight of Old Sorrow, haltered and led that way. The loss was surely to them all.

When Harvey and John arrived home from Ohio they listened with admiration to descriptions of the Corps d'Afrique, and allowed as how they'd have given, well, something, they weren't sure what, to see that jubilant sight.

And while of an act to give Elder Harvey did what he had meant to do for some time now. He sent for Amos Anger and gave him a little parcel tied with brown paper and string. George Blakey had given it to Harvey, and after keeping it safe in his desk these past few weeks Harvey now gave it to Amos. The boy was old enough to cherish it, and Eades was certain Harry Littlebourne would have had him do no differently.

Amos did not open it right away, but stood with it flat in his hands. He took himself back across the road and up to the brick shed, and sat on the steps for what seemed a long time with the little parcel balanced on his knees. It was not that he feared anything about it would bite him, not at all; more it was that, with the string still knotted around it, the ghosts could not get out.

He drew a long breath, and with one hand pulled the string away. Loosed, the brown paper fell open and Amos saw what he had expected to find: James Littlebourne's Bible. He opened the soft leather cover and saw on the flyleaf Harry's father's signature, and beneath it Harry's own. Amos riffled the pages to hear the breathlike sound they made, and found a folded sheet of foolscap poked into the Book of Daniel.

There was writing on the paper, in Brother Harry's hand, and when Amos looked again he saw the ink was the same as that he used to sign his name below his father's.

Sabbath

Little Amos,

How this letter will come to find thee I cannot say. It is impossible even to know what will happen to me now. The men who speak to me here say little, and that with bitterness. Their minds are not much known to me. But let no one tell thee these are bad men, and give me thy promise thee will not think it of thy own accord. They are as good as they know how to be, and the rest is only fear and confusion and lost way. It is not for me to place blame, nor should it be for thee, my dear little brother.

Whatever may happen to me in this place, believe I am not gone from thee. For truly, if I have but one confession left to me in this life, then it must be to thee: to say that I have loved thee best of all. For every one time in thy short life that I spoke with pride to thee of crops brought in or meadows mown, twice again and more have I thought what I did not tell thee, that no seedling I could have fetched up from the earth brought me greater joy than did thee. Was thee my own I could not love thee more.

My hope for thee is that thee never come to see the world as I have done. It is no place for thee, and as thee trusted me in all things then trust me in this last. If thee remains among Believers, in the home that is truly thy own in this Heaven of ours, then my life will have been truly well spent. If thee grows pure and straight and true at God's pleasure and in fear of Him, all my seedlings will have finished well.

Of angels, be it said that I did see one, and may see more, but the first of those was thine, and for that vision I bless thee kindly.

Then trust to Brother Austin, whose care for thee is deep, and mind thee watch thy fingers around Old Sorrow's teeth. Take care in this as in all things and thee needn't fear to be bit again.

Harry Littlebourne

Black Jupie did not have to ask whether her master would see Jimmy Sweet. Jimmy was as much a part of this household as was Teddy Hannon himself. The boys had known each other since they were babies together and, once he had mastered independent navigation, Jimmy had had the run of the house and lands with as much right of way as the master's son. In recent years he and May Howard had taken particular notice of one another, and some things had been said, but that was sadly over now.

"Mister Shaw's in the liberry, honey," said Jupie as she saw him come through the kitchen door. That boy never would learn to use the front porch like folks. He did not stop at the pantry on his way through to check for cornbread, as was his habit – how that boy did love her cornbread! – and this in itself was unusual. But there was as well a curious hesitation in his step, a kind of apprehensive hitch, that made her turn from her potatoes, the better to check him for damage. "Sure good to see y'all back with all y' parts to you," she said, finally satisfied that he was sound, but he had gone on to the library without taking much notice of her. There was something in his hand.

*   *   *

Shaw Mason Hannon told Jimmy Sweet he was sorry, he could not ask him to stay. At this instant he hated no soul alive with the energy he devoted to hating Jimmy. He could not see this tall, handsome boy, proud in his uniform of Tuscaloosa grey, without seeing his own charming, maddening, magnificent Teddy standing close by. He hardly recognized one without the other beside him.

"Forgive me," he said, taking the haversack Jimmy had been given leave to deliver, setting it gently on the desk, "but you might better go."

Jimmy surveyed his boots, dusty from the long ride, and cleared his throat, believing a man would protest and he had been sent on a man's errand.

"He just ran at it, sir," said Jimmy, his voice failing him, "like he wanted it. He hadn't been the same, and it was like he was looking for it." But Shaw Mason Hannon, nearly as much a part of Jimmy Sweet's life as his own father, could not hear more.

"No, son, I can't," said Hannon quietly. His hands were nervous. He could not think what to do with them. "You go on, now. We'll talk another time. But you just go on."

Jimmy had said only half of what he had come to say, farther to be sure than he had expected to get without breaking down himself, but now he found it even harder not to finish. "I'm so sorry, Mr. Hannon," he said. "I wasn't near enough. I couldn't have stopped him."

"Just go," Hannon said through his teeth, and eased himself into the nearest chair.

The slender young man half-ran back down the hallway, past Jupie, through the kitchen. He could not separate the sounds in his ears into the words she called after him, and kept running, past the quarters and on through the fields. His breath came in loud gasps as he took ever-lengthening strides, but even over the sound of his pounding footsteps he was sure he could hear Shaw Mason Hannon loosening the straps that bound Teddy's haversack.

The letter lay neatly across the top, as if none of this had been unexpected. Shaw Hannon slit the seal with a silver knife and unfolded the many sheets.

> *Sulphur Branch,*
> *Tennessee*
> *September 24, 1864*
>
> *Dear Papa,*
>
> *By the time you read this I figure to be in Hell, and the way I see it what the Devil has in store for me is to wonder what will be harder for you, to hear that I'm gone or to know what I can't leave this earth without telling you. All these times me and Jimmy and the boys have set off to the fighting with Old Bedford and not been sure whether we'd come back from wherever we got to, but it seems we always knew, us ones that came back in one piece. Who knows why we know? But sometimes sitting around at night we spare a thought for such things and it seems there's more than one man in this army who reckons he'll know when it's time.*
>
> *Today it's for me to say. Federals after us with every man they can find, and it seems like things can't last long in this war, and there may not be many chances left for me to put things right. I'm not sorry, except for how it leaves you without me or May. But believe me, Papa, when I tell you it's easier to put my eye to the barrel of a Yankee gun than it is to tell you it wasn't that Shakerman killed my sister. It was me.*
>
> *Must've been the foreman needed everybody in the fields til late because nobody was in the house when I come home that night, not so much as the house niggers, even dark as it was getting. I was looking to surprise you, being back so sudden after so long. But there was that letter May left you to say where she'd be, and I was anxious not to waste my leave and I read it. There was all*

that molasses she had to spill about wanting to be with some no-account Shakerman and I knew you'd see blood only I saw it first. No sister of mine was going to run off with some coward no better than a black man, maybe not even as good, and it was like I couldn't stop myself. I got back on Linnet and rode down to where she said she'd meet him, and she was there but all alone and crying, and I asked did he hurt her, I'd kill him if he hurt her, and she said no, she reckoned he didn't want anything of her. I said good riddance to him and she wouldn't stop crying, just wanted me to hold her like a good brother and make like I was sorry he didn't want her, only I wasn't. She cried as if her heart would break and I slapped her hard until she shushed and I put her up on Linnet to ride her on home. Then she started to fight on me and when she fell I heard the crack. I never meant to hurt her, only to teach her she was better than any good-for-nothing Shakerman. I near went blind inside when I saw how out of kilter her head was and I knew straight off there was nothing left of her. It scared me back onto my horse and gone from there, and I hid out in the woods that night for want of better plans. I thought I'd find a way to tell you, but I didn't. What kind of words that would take I wouldn't know, for I am not so brave a man.

Next night I figured I'd better get back on my way to camp, and going through Russellville there was some folks talking, I don't know who, and they allowed as how that redskin bastard would get it through the neck killing poor May that way, and then I knew how it was and how it ought to go. Who knows how people decide to do an evil thing to hide an evil thing, Papa? I thought, well, if that worthless skunk had acted like a man he might have saved a life or two out here with me and the rest, and if he lost his now to save mine then maybe that was just the way it was meant to be. And I rode around back behind the jail and saw him there, and Papa in my life I never hated all the Federals that ever lived bad as I hated that redskin for making my sister cry. I had a little pistol I'd took off a Yankee lieutenant dead at Tupelo back in July and it was in my hand and he was as easy to shoot as any nigger-loving scum I ever killed in this war. I got out of there before anyone could clap an eye on me and thought I was well out of it.

A time or two in my dreams I've seen the look on that man's face when he turned to me and fell, and I've wanted to tell you how it all happened, Papa, and how I never meant for any of it to happen. But you were always so proud of me. I kept thinking God would square it, there'd come a bullet or a bayonet and no one would be the wiser, but maybe He was waiting for me to set it right with you so I could set it right for myself.

Today we're sitting here at Sulphur Branch and the blow we get from farther on is that the Yankee trash by the trestles know we're after their blockhouses and have all they need to give us holy how. I can't come home, but the price of drawing a last breath is telling it all to you. So I'm writing this letter to say I'm sorry, to tell you it was wrong from start to finish. Now you'll curse my memory and that's one more thing I'll have to think about in Hell. But I'll always love you, Papa, and May. Might be if people knew how killing could get to be such a fearsome habit they'd spare a thought for that very first time.

*Try to forgive
Your loving boy,
Edmund Shaw Hannon*

The stiff papers loosed from Hannon's fingers and fluttered to the carpet between his feet. Deeper in the haversack Jimmy Sweet had brought home for him were a razor, a looking glass, a pair of socks, and a small bundle bound with a ragged Confederate flag. He unwound it slowly and found at its core a peculiar, lever-actioned pistol. He turned it over in his hand and saw etched on the barrel THE VOLCANIC/REPEATING ARMS CO., then his eyes failed him. The tears came and his shoulders shook with an emotion long past grief. He could not breathe and went to the window. He shook his head, and shook it, and shook it, then stood stock still where he was, with the gun cradled in his hands. The widower was now childless. He had not realized, as he grieved for his sweet May Howard, how grateful he should be that he would only have to grieve her once. How many times could Teddy die to him?

Stiff-legged, unsure on his feet, Hannon went back to the far corner of the room and put his handkerchief to his face. He did not want his Negroes to hear him. It would not do for his Negroes to hear him.

1865

T he backsliding of those sisters and brethren who returned to the world routinely earned more notice from Harvey Eades in his journal than did the end of the Rebellion:

April 12. Gen. Lee. The rebel leader surrendered to Gen. Grant himself & 22,000 men.

Perhaps after four years of war, almost to the day, he was unable to persuade himself that it was over. Nothing, after all, could set itself to rights as quickly as that. On the same day he recorded unpleasant tidings of an attack by guerrillas on the home of Old Nick, a hired contraband whose belongings the night previous had amounted to no more than twenty dollars and some sugar. That claim he could no longer make the following morning, after the bandits departed the cabin provided him by the Shakers.

The following day Eades dutifully noted the presence of Abraham Lincoln in the captured Confederate capital city of Richmond; the day after that the firing of the big guns at Nashville to celebrate the Union victory; and the day after that the assassination

of President Lincoln. "The best living Man on the Natural plane
is gone," wrote Elder Harvey in his journal.

Perhaps he knew even then that any change in their lives at
Shakertown would be a long time coming.

That month of April the Binford peaches were in blossom at
Canaan, the first promise of a decent harvest in a few years. The
apples were likewise in flower, and perhaps it was the scent of the
orchards that tempted so many of South Union's citizens back to
the world: defections were many, mostly among the young people.
So few able-bodied brethren were in Society now, and so few
dollars were available in the village purse to spare for hirelings,
that the younger boys were put to work at tasks usually reserved
for the grown brethren, even shearing sheep now that the season
for it was upon them. The boys learned in a fast hurry that it was
easier to lean over the fences and laugh at the process than to
provide the entertainment.

A child struggling at a man's chore was deviation sufficient
from established Shaker practice, but there was more. With
guerrilla interest in Shaker horseflesh and dry goods continuing
unabated, the Believers had no choice but to make nocturnal
vigils the rule rather than the exception. Lights were kept burning
in the houses all night, every night, to put raiders on notice that
someone suspected there might be mischief made. And, despite
the United Society's general prohibition against the keeping of
mules, the village at South Union bought several and traded a
few of their horses for others. Having lost nearly a score in horses
to bandits and troops – if difference could be told between the
two – they decided it was preferable to keep mules than to be in
constant dread of horse thieves. In surrendering to this necessity
they did what they could to quiet their own consciences and soothe
the offended sensitivities of the Lord: they resolved that, insofar
as was possible, they would inflict reason and persuasion on the
fractious beasts before resorting to the whip, and meanwhile they

would hope the generous Heavens would forgive an act of sheerest desperation.

Harvey Eades made mention of his own fifty-eighth birthday on the twenty-eighth of April, and a few weeks later – with a spate of magnificent spring weather settling in – he was glad to record an expedition by Sister Melissa Minter and some of the girls to the Knob, for the purpose of picking strawberries.

But if Elder Harvey thought the worst had all come, outstayed its welcome, and gone, the celestial dominions had another lesson to impart: on the twentieth of May the floodgates overhead opened, and for awhile it seemed they would never close again.

There had been at Groveland, New York, the year before, a rain to end all rains, or so it was thought – thirteen inches that fell in a single day. Elder Harvey joked that there had surely never been such a storm, that whoever imparted the story must have suffered from water on the brain, although in this he was wrong and the tale was true as told. But on that Sabbath Eve at Shakertown, as the rain began to fall, the trustees put out a bucket nearly a foot deep. Six hours later it was overflowing, and with two more hours' unslacked rainfall yet to follow.

The deluge brought with it a steady display of lightning and cracks of thunder to shake the soul, all of which frightened the youngest children. By the time the sky wore itself out, the trustees felt safe in assuming that in eight hours the tempest had sent down fifteen inches of weather. They looked at one another, wondering who would be the first to accuse the others of water on the brain. No one did.

The proof, however, was not only in the bucket but in the fields. What the soldiers had not destroyed over the years the floodwaters now sought to drown.

Harvey Eades rode out with John Rankin, once there was reason to believe the storm had well and truly passed, to assess the damage. They came back in the fading light thunderstruck by the sight of all that nature's fury could achieve when compared with man's own relentlessly mindless perniciousness. Fully a hundred acres of the farm were underwater; some sheep and cattle had drowned. In two places by the East several rods of the railroad line were washed away, and in the cellar of the East dwelling house stood four feet of water. The cooking stove was completely submerged, and the family would thus need supplies and provisions from the North and Center until the situation righted itself.

Considerable amounts of fencing were gone, along with the covered bridge at the mill. Inside the mill itself the factory's loom and spinning jenny were underwater, and across the meadows west of the sheep barn between the Center and the depot extended a rainwater lake. Folks who had been in Logan County all their lives had no memory of such a thing before.

Elder Harvey was shaken by the scope of the calamity, having contented himself over the years that South Union was safe from flood. But as was like him he sought and quickly located reason to rejoice in the knowledge that they might have fared worse. The year 1865 had, in fact, already been a year notorious for its floods: the Smithsonian Institute in Washington City recorded five inches of rain that fell there in a single hour. Had they suffered the same fate at South Union over the eight hours – and Eades was at pains to complete the computations lest their significance be lost – the forty inches of rain resulting would naturally have done considerably more damage.

"And instead of rebuilding the mill bridge we'd have built ourselves an ark," said Eli McLean with good humor.

In the morning, as the floodwaters receded, the hand of every brother, sister and child was turned, even on the Sabbath, to do what could be done. That it might have been worse was less than comforting. Machinery needed cleaning and fences mending, but the plight of the East family was seen to first: the cellar was emptied, the mud that lay some half-inch deep scrubbed away, the pantry restored and restocked.

Harvey Eades put the loss at three thousand dollars, and the village smelled of damp for weeks.

But as the weather warmed, reminders of the inundation faded – to be replaced by the onset of another deluge: refugees, desperate to get back to wherever they'd fled from, and once again the sisters stood long hours by the ovens to keep pace with the renewed demands for food. Soldiers too were migrating south to north, west to east, hundreds of them on their way home, all hungry and ornery with tiredness. The war was shaking itself out. Beyond this last burst of chaos calm could be dimly seen, but that merest of glimpses was enough.

With peace at least on the creep, the brethren and sisters saw the toll the war had taken on the village: the battered and peeling buildings, the trampled lawns and fields, the depleted coffers which could not possibly cope with the cost of fixing it all up and making spruce. But what could be done would indeed be done. Elder Harvey organized the sisters and the abler children into painting parties, himself supervising the little boys in whitewashing the picket fence outside the meeting house, and carefully located funds to build new roofs for dwellings and factories whose state of delapidation could no longer be ignored.

In June the buildings at the depot were looted and torched by guerrillas, and despite the alarm raised to rescue what could be saved the cost to the Society came to some three thousand dollars – just as had the flood – when the tally was complete. At the Shaker village at Hancock, Masschusetts, there were similar fire problems: a letter to South Union in July said the great stone barn had burned. But there they believed the cause to be accidental. That was different.

Months passed, and autumn became winter, and the soldiers were mostly gone, the refugees mostly resettled, the quiet in many ways restored. In October an early frost nipped at the leaves of the sweet potatoes, then came sufficient rain to permit ploughing for the winter wheat, and then a partial eclipse of the sun.

Late in November a paroled colored soldier stopped in at Black Lick for lodging, and two strangers who called him away from his bed that night shot him dead, then ran. Brother Jefferson Shannon notified the authorities and a squad of Negro soldiers came in due course to collect the corpse. When they left Black Lick that Friday, the first day of December – perhaps to search out the culprit, perhaps not – Jefferson watched them go, not realizing the war was leaving Shaker land for the last time.

On the mild, rainy Sabbath that was the final day of the year Elder Harvey sat down to tend to his journal. He made mention of the fact that meetings were held in the families rather than at the meeting house, and might have ended his entry there had 1865 been inclined to let him go so easily. From his pen came this:

> *Thus ends one of the most important years of the last hundred. A long and bloody war closed & at last, by the Action of the States, Kentucky thank God has been compelled to abolish slavery. I long ago said she who might & should have been head in this movement would, as has proved true, be the tail. Poor Kentucky lost both honor and dollars for a few months' dominance over the Negro. But nearly all slaveholders have been insane for the last quarter of a century – especially the last 4 years.*
>
> *H.L. Eades*

1868

South Union, Ky.
Febuary 9, 1868

My dea mother and father

I resieved your very kind letter which gave me and howell much pleasure to hear of you all being well I am happy to in form you that me and howell are in good helth gitting along rigght well we go to scool I am now in the third realder and howell is in the second I hope soon to be able to read and right well we should like very much to see you all when you right let us know how you all are getting along let us know how Silas Boyd is getting along give our love to sitter emma tell her we should like to see her howell wants to know the exact date of his age when you write I hope you will write to us soon for we want to hear from you you must please excuse my bad writing and spelling for this is my first attempt at letter righting in conclusion except the kind love of myself and belive us to remain your

Afectionate
howell and john edmonds

The boy had copied the letter from one sheet to another, to eliminate the blots and repair some of his spelling. Even so, the letter said little for the education of a fifteen-year-old, and less for his nearly illiterate brother, whose voice John had to be under the circumstances.

Their parents had sent John and Howell up from their home in Dresden, Tennessee, for an upbringing and education the boys could not otherwise expect to have, and it was Austin Innes who was set the task of determining what they might know and what they might not. John was a bright young fellow, eager and responsive, but unlettered and lacking in much of anything to do with booklearning. Howell was less easy to place in this regard: he was quiet and shy, difficult to draw out.

He stood next to Brother Austin's desk, laboring hard to answer the questions put to him, embarrassed by his lack of schooling and anxious to thwart charting of the exact depths of this deficiency. Tall for his age, slender, with dark hair and dark eyes to match his summery complexion, he was somehow familiar. Austin was touched by his predicament and sought to soften the edge of his evident discomfort.

"Never mind this, now, son," he said over the rims of his spectacles, willing to abandon the inquiry and allow the boy to reveal himself in other ways. "Let's talk about something else. When was your birthday?"

"Don't know, sir," said Howell.

"How old are you?"

"Don't know, sir."

"Your birthday or your age, Howell?"

"Neither," the boy said.

Austin rocked back in his chair. He knew now why the face was so familiar. His own face grew hot with memory, and he shook his head. "Nay," he said, "we can't have this." He took a sheet of paper from his desk and held it out to Howell Edmonds. "Write your mother, young'n, right now. A man has to know how old he is."

"Can't, sir," said Howell, distancing himself from the foolscap as from a snake. "Don't know how."

Austin looked around the room and beckoned to John Edmonds. "Take this," he told the older brother. "Write your mother, John. Tell her you're well if you think you are and make sure before you're done you tell her Howell needs to know how old he is. Finish it before the day's out and I'll send it off for you."

Even John seemed overwhelmed by the enormity of the task set to him. "I never wrote a letter before," he told Brother Austin. The paper was stiff and foreign in his hand.

"Nothing like being able to communicate with folks," said Austin, smiling now. But he would not be swayed by John Edmonds' helpless, vulnerable look. "A gentleman needs to know how to express himself on paper and your family'll take it best if you make your mistakes to them first. So hop to it. Amos!" He looked to the far side of the room "Give John and Howell the benefit of your learned advice, will you?"

The two new boys sat themselves next to Amos, and Austin Innes watched for a minute as they confided the full scope of their chore to him. Sitting next to John, less than two years his senior, Amos did not look quite so small as he might have. He had grown and was filling out, on his way to being an admirable young man. He sorted through his things and found his spare pen, which he dealt to John. A few hours later Amos had guided John's hand through an exploratory effort, which his pupil then painstakingly transferred to a tidier sheet begged from Brother Austin's supply. The resulting second effort was not much better than the first, but John seemed pleased and Austin had not the heart to insist on a third.

Eleven days had come and gone since then. Today John Edmonds was dead: a lovely child, respectful to his elders and kind of disposition insofar as Austin Innes could judge, dead of spotted fever. His soul had left this life behind at two o'clock in the morning, and while the dead boy's cheek was still warm to the touch Eldress Betsy had clipped a lock of his light brown hair to send to his mother, then another for the family at South Union to remember him by.

Howell Edmonds seemed all at sea without his brother to anchor him, and Austin at first considered it might be best to suggest Elder Harvey send the boy straight back home to Tennessee.

What changed his mind was what should not have been a curiosity to him: Amos took Howell Edmonds under his wing.

"Is it that Howell may be what Amos knows he's lost, and he wants what he hopes Howell can give?" Austin asked Elder Harvey, finding an opportunity to call in at the ministry shop and taking it for the sake of his own conscience. "Or is it that Amos knows Howell's loss, and has that much of his own to give to Howell?"

Harvey Eades looked at the little schoolmaster, his eyes strangely full of admiration.

"Dear brother," he said finally, "I have sometimes had cause to wonder who among us here knows better the complications of the human heart than you do. Perhaps if the Lord that lies in each of us recognized Himself in us all as quickly as He that lies in those two boys has done, the world would be a kinder place in which to live." He folded his arms over his watch chain and smiled. "Who in this community should see that more clearly than you I really couldn't say, Austin, but if you needed to hear it from somebody else you're kindly welcome for the favor."

Some days later came the reply from Howell Edmonds' mother, and its receipt was duly noted in the trustees' office before it was given to Brother Austin to read to the addressee. Such, however, had never been his intention. On that same night Amos Anger was summoned to Brother's retiring room to take charge of the letter: Howell would not be able to decipher his mother's joined-up writing, and the schoolmaster thought it best to let the matter rest between the two boys.

The following morning, when Howell and Amos reported for their lessons, Howell pushed through the cluster of bodies and with unusual confidence propped himself on Brother Austin's desk.

"It seems I'm eleven years old, sir," he said, smiling and showing the space where he was missing a tooth. "That's if you wanted to write it down."

Austin saw Amos behind him, leaning against the wall with his hands in his pockets, watching. In his life he had learned to give away gladly that which he had been given, the better to be given it again.

1922

Sister Mary Bently Wann sang as she came up the staircase with an armload of linens.

In my father's house there are many mansions,
Prepared for those who truly follow me.
They will shine like stars in the firmament of glory:
Yea, they shall forever abide with me.

The words were no trouble to remember, especially today, and the soft and comfortable sound of her own creaky voice in the empty hallway chased away for a minute or two the disquiet she felt at the prospect of leaving this dear place. To her own mind only so many tears were seemly, and she had already cried them: her Scottish pragmatism had not left her in all these many years. After the auction she meant to make a home together with Sister Alice Bass. It would not be the same (nothing would ever be the same again) but she could not bear to think of living alone and she could not go to strangers.

Then, be comforted, my chosen people!
Though dark seems the day seems the day,
And the vision tarry long –

Her footsteps slowed ever-so-slightly as she walked down the passage from the sisters' staircase. She would not walk with haste, not now that the steps left to her here were so carefully numbered, and she savored the feel of the polished white oak under her feet. Every inch of the smooth timber was familiar to her; she had lived in this house nearly all of her seventy-five years.

For, lo, in the East, a golden light is beaming,
Then with songs of rejoicing sweet praise prolong.

Walking so softly now Sister Mary heard a tiny thud, and she stopped still across the hall from the open door of Brother Amos' retiring room. A small straw hat, no bigger than one made for a boy, had dropped brim-up to the floor and was gently spinning itself to a stop.

She could see from the door sill that the little hat had fallen from Brother Amos' fingers. One arm hung outstretched over the wing of the rocking chair in which he sat peacefully asleep, and his hand was extended, palm up, as if waiting for the return of something recently lost. Sister Mary tiptoed into the room and, with her linens shifted to one arm to free up the other, she stooped and picked the hat up by its brim.

Turning it this way and that she puzzled over its faded green band, the slight smell of dust and age that clung to it. Where had Brother Amos managed to find such a thing? She glanced at his own straw hat, solitary on the wall, battered and chinked although the sisters had offered to make him a new one. How very small this hat in her hand looked in comparison, and how very sadly long it had been since there was a boy at South Union the size to do it justice.

But once, she thought, looking to Amos and remembering the

rosy, lovely child he had grown from.

Once...

Sister Mary Wann shook her head. The floor was no place for a hat, however it had come to be there. Reaching up, she hooked it on the peg-rail next to Amos Anger's.

With a quick look over her shoulder she made sure there was nothing more to be done before she went about her work, but it was finished. All was in order.

Acknowledgements

I n Vienna, Maryland, maybe forty years ago, I paid two dollars for an 1856 *Webster's Dictionary*, unable to leave it sit but clueless as to what use it might serve. Little does one ever know. There were eventually nearly a hundred kindred volumes clubbed around it on my shelves, just the working collection I needed to get on with writing *Kindly Welcome* day-to-day, and public libraries on two continents furnished a hundred more on loan. One learns very early on in such an endeavor, however, certain home truths: books are not enough, and without the kindness of strangers no amount of research will get the job done. The extent to which institutions and individuals with other things on their minds were willing to advise, counsel and generally shed light during those research years of the early 1990s is believable only because the book reflects their generosity (or so I hope), and I am therefore indebted to: Mac Brown, Assistant Vice President, Southern Deposit Bank, Russellville, KY; Fred Dahlinger Jr., Director, Robert L. Parkinson Library and Research Center, Circus World Museum, Baraboo, WI; Anne Gilbert, Librarian/ Archivist, the Shaker Library, Sabbathday Lake, ME; Tommy Hines, Executive Director, Shakertown at South Union, South

Union, KY; P.R. Geissler, Department of Prosthetic Dentistry, University of Edinburgh, Scotland; Roy J. Jinks, Historian, Smith & Wesson, Springfield, MA; Julia Neal; John Polacsek, Curator, Dossin Great Lakes Museum, Belle Isle, MI; Deborah Coffin Rearick, Education Coordinator, The Museum at Lower Shaker Village, Enfield, NH; Dr. Michael C. Robinson, Historian of the Lower Mississippi River Division, U.S. Army Corps of Engineers, Vicksburg, MS; Harry F. Ryan Jr., Landscape Engineer, Bellingrath Gardens, Theodore, AL; Jessica Travis, Reference Librarian, The Historic New Orleans Collection of the Kemper and Leila Williams Foundation, New Orleans, LA; Field Marshal Sir Richard Vincent, Baron Vincent of Coleshill, GBE, KCB, DSO (then Chairman of the North Atlantic Treaty Organization Military Committee); Deborah W. Walk, Museum Archivist, the John and Mable Ringling Museum of Art, Sarasota, FL; the Whaling Museum Library of the Old Dartmouth Historical Society, New Bedford, MA.; Richard J. Wolfe, Curator of Rare Books and Manuscripts, Joseph Garland Librarian of the Boston Medical Library, Boston, MA; Doug Wicklund, Curator, the National Firearms Museum, Washington, D.C.; Virginia Steele Wood, Reference Librarian, the Library of Congress, Washington, D.C.

It is common, as a researcher working at a scholarly institution, to be asked to sign an agreement to acknowledge the use of its books, papers and other materials. At the Kentucky Library, on the campus of Western Kentucky University in Bowling Green, I signed such agreements daily during the weeks I spent foraging through its extraordinary Department of Special Collections: Folklife Archives, Manuscripts and University Archives. To the Kentucky Library, in the person of those who then staffed it – including but by no means limited to Connie Mills, Sue Lynn McGuire, Riley Handy, Nancy Baird, Betty Yambrek, Jonathan Jeffrey and Stephanie Davenport – for their time, interest, comaraderie, good humor, persistence and support I regret the agreed-upon acknowledgement was never possible. The gratitude offered here to the Kentucky Library for the use of its assets, printed and personal, is enormous (and insufficient even so) but it is offered voluntarily and from the heart. They can whistle for the other.

Any number of folks kept the home fires burning, offered tea and withheld sympathy, and asked mercifully few questions. To some whose nobility may not have been its own reward then or later go special thanks: Anna and Willie Burnside gave up the banqueting hall of their home in the Maryhill section of Glasgow, Scotland, for what was probably the longest two months they can recall. Barbara James and Larry Dillner told me to get on with it at a time when anyone else would have counseled the opposite. Jane Riggin and John Cardinal O'Connor read the manuscript (repeatedly). Sam Graff kept talking. Mel Padbury, my captive audience on Salisbury Plain, gave more wise counsel than he knows. Page Ashley said the magic words. Her late, great husband, Warner Brothers' Ted Ashley, said: "I love it, but it's not a movie." Tom Smothers pointed out the positives when I couldn't see them. David Rigby somehow dragged a floppy disk document stuck in twentieth-century computer technology forward to the present. Tom Hanks, unwittingly and armed only with a manual typewriter, reminded me of the value of memories. Kind, generous, inestimable Shelby Foote looked deep into the heart of Nathan Bedford Forrest, just because I asked him to. That's the sort of man he was.

Go thou, and do likewise.

Linda Stevens

Norfolk, England
July 2017